monsoonbooks

EMPORIUM

British by birth, Rose Gan first arrived in Kuala Lumpur in 1978 and has been living and working between both UK and South East Asia ever since. Married to a Malaysian, and formerly a teacher of History and Latin in UK and Malaysia, Rose was also Vice Chair for Museums of the Indonesian Heritage Society, a guide and docent in Museum National Indonesia, Jakarta, and Muzium Negara and the Textile Museum in KL. In addition to lecturing to cultural associations, Rose has been actively involved with museum publications in Malaysia and Indonesia, both as a writer and editor.

Emporium is volume three of Penang Chronicles, a series of historical fiction that delves into the backstory of the British settlement of Penang. It is preceded by *Dragon* and *Pearl* followed by *Legacy*. *Pearl* was shortlisted for the Popular Readers' Choice Awards 2023 in Malaysia. For more information about Rose and her books, visit *roseganauthor.com*.

Praise for Penang Chronicles

'Enthralling ... brings a forgotten hero back to rumbustious life.'
John Keay, author of *The Honourable Company*

'Deeply researched and beautifully written, *Dragon* convincingly evokes the East of the period.'
Nigel Barley, author of *In the Footsteps of Stamford Raffles*

'Takes the reader on a masterfully compelling eighteenth-century birth-to-death journey alongside Francis Light. Vividly imagined scenarios interwoven with the threads of history are guaranteed to keep the reader fully engaged. *Dragon*, *Pearl* and *Emporium* set the benchmark for historical fiction of the region.'
Marcus Langdon, author of *Penang: The Fourth Presidency of India 1805–1830*

‘At last, a novel which engages a crucial and fascinating period of British merchant imperialism and Southeast Asian history. Penang, meeting place of Malays, Bugis and Siamese, here too are freebooting English and a more staid company in Calcutta. Here are mixed marriages, innumerable cross currents with the Dutch in Java and Sumatra, Chinese and Tamil traders, Achenese sultans and a Burma too close for comfort. And in the middle of it all is Francis Light, founder of modern Penang, a man of his times and of history. Britons today are woefully ignorant of the legacy of maritime Southeast Asia in which they played such a key role. This novel is a good start to re-engagement with this region, a meeting place of races, religions and cultures.’

Philip Bowring, author of *Empire of the Winds*

‘Rose Gan, in this fascinating and well-researched novel, skilfully provides the reader with a colourful illustration to the early life and times of Light and those historically connected to him. The author cleverly unveils Light’s rise to the rank of captain and his travels to this part of the world while meeting the people who would set the stage for his lustrous future.’

Dennis De Witt, author of *History of the Dutch in Malaysia*

‘Swashbuckler or swindler, trader or statesman, the mere mention of the name Captain Francis Light in the state of Penang is bound to draw an array of clashing reactions. Gan explores the twists and turns of what Light’s life could have been in this historical fiction narrative.’

Andrea Filmer, *The Star*, Malaysia

‘An engaging and lively tale about the earliest years of the East India Company settlement of Penang. In *Emporium*, Gan weaves her narrative skilfully into the historic backdrop – bringing alive key figures and events and offering an enjoyable way to access the momentous moments and big personalities of those early years.’

Andrew Barber, author of *Colonial Penang 1786-1957*

'As a veteran journalist who read History at university – and one who has remained fascinated with Captain Francis Light ever since – I find *Dragon* truly enjoyable. Ms Gan has carried out extensive research in creating the world of this novel.'

Wong Chun Wai, Star Media Group, Malaysia

'After exploring the intra-Asian country trade in *Dragon* and the rich cultural complexity of the East Indies in *Pearl*, *Emporium* tackles the sensitive subjects of prejudice, the British illusory superiority and even the rarely acknowledged east African slave trade. Whilst it cannot be denied that the British, in the guise of the misnamed Honourable Company, played an important part in the development of such far off corners of the world, their stubborn ignorance of the age-old politics of the region speaks volumes. The attitudes and behaviours of their British-born womenfolk provide a stark contrast to the resourcefulness of those with local roots. Emporium provides a readable lesson in the politics of the Peninsula that remains important for us to understand today.'

Sue Paul, author of *Jeopardy of Every Wind: the biography of Captain Thomas Bowrey*

'A richly imagined yet historically faithful account of the career of Francis Light, the founder of modern Penang. We follow his journey from his clever revenge on a bully during his schooldays in Suffolk to his heroic service with the Royal Navy, from his apprenticeship as country trader with a Madras agency to his delicate negotiations with the Sultan of Queddah, which will set him on the path leading to the founding of Pulau Penang as the first British settlement in the East Indies. Along the way Light has to weather storm and shipwreck, survive betrayal by company officials, balance palace intrigues and interpret the signals of ambitious royal wives and widows – all the while navigating the cross currents of British, Dutch, Malay, Siamese and Bugis interests in the region, with only his wits, moral compass and ambition to guide him. A marvelous cast of characters populates this well-researched work of historical fiction, with just the right blend of the real and the imaginary.'

John D. Greenwood, author of the Singapore Saga series

In the same series

Dragon
Pearl
Emporium
Legacy

EMPORIUM

Penang Chronicles, Vol. III

Rose Gan

monsoonbooks

First published in 2023
by Monsoon Books Ltd
www.monsoonbooks.co.uk

No.1 The Lodge, Burrough Court, Burrough on the Hill,
Melton Mowbray LE14 2QS, UK.

ISBN (paperback): 9781915310088
ISBN (ebook): 9781915310095

First edition.

Cover design by Cover Kitchen.

A Cataloguing-in-Publication data record is available from the British Library.

Map of Tanjong Penaga, Prince of Wales Island, on page XVI by Maganjeet Kaur.

Printed and bound in Great Britain by Clays Ltd, Elcograf S.p.A.
25 24 23 1 2 3

For Zoë, Daniel and Dominic,
my very best creations.

harimau mati meninggalkan belang,
manusia mati meninggalkan nama
('When a tiger dies, he leaves behind his stripes;
but of a man only his name remains.')
Malay proverb

Glossary

Malay unless otherwise stated.

adat	Malay customary laws
amah	a servant who looks after children.
ang moh	(Hokkien) European, lit. 'red-haired'
bapak, *pak*	father
begum	married Muslim woman in Bengal
belukar	scrub land, bush
cangkul	wedged shape hoe with a handle of bamboo
datuk	grandfather (also honorary title)
Fateh	(Arabic) title, Conqueror or Ruler.
feng shui	ancient Chinese geomancy, lit. 'wind-water'
garay	Illanun war vessel
golandaz	Indian auxiliary artillerymen
gudang	warehouse, godown
Ibu, 'bu	mother
istana	(Arabic) palace
juragan	skipper of boat
kampong	village
kampilan	Illanun sword
kowtow	(Chinese) act of subservience
laksamana	admiral, minister of Malay court
lanong	Illanun two-decked warships
lascar	sailor from the East
lebuh	street
madrasah	(Arabic) Islamic religious school

mandor	(Portuguese) foreman, supervisor
maund	Asian unit of measure, equivalent to about 37 kg
nakhoda	captain or leader
nenek	grandmother
nona	(Portuguese) polite address for married woman
orang putih	white man
orang selat	a person of the Straits
padewakang	early Bugis schooner
padi	rice fields (paddy)
pasar	market, bazaar
perahu	Malay boat (prow)
pendatang	immigrant
penghulu	community leader, chief
pontianak	female vampire
rajah muda	crown prince, heir to throne
rani	(Hindi) queen
rumah kebun	garden house
sablay	woven belt/shoulder cloth of Mindanao
salisipan	Illanun war canoes
songket	rich silk brocade fabric
tanjong	cape, headland
tindal	(Indian) petty officer amongst lascar crews
tsap tsing	(Hokkien) mixed race (derogatory)
tuanku	address for sultan, highness
VOC	(Dutch) Dutch East India Company
zenana	(Hindi) place of seclusion for women

Place Names and Peoples of the Archipelago

Batta	from Batticaloa, Dutch Ceylon, a source for Indian and African slaves
Belanda	the Dutch *(orang Belanda)*
The Boontings	islands west of Langkawi (Buntings)
Caffree	African slaves, lit. *kaffir* (Arabic) non-Muslims
Cina	Chinese, pronounced 'Cheena'
China Street	as shown on The Popham Map (1791)
Chulia	An India Muslim from the Coromandel coast
Illanun	pirate raiders from Mindanao, the Phillippines
Île de France	Mauritius
the Laddas	European name for the Langkawi Island chain
Minangkabau	an indigenous people of West Sumatra, known for their matrilineal culture
Rembau	Minangkabau territory north of Melaka
Siak	sultanate of East Sumatra and nearby islands
Sinhala	language of Ceylon, Sinhalese
Terengganu	sultanate of East Malay Peninsula

List of Characters

The Light family	
Francis Light	Superintendent of Prince of Wales Island
Martinha Rozells	Francis Light's Eurasian wife
Sarah, Lucy Ann, Mary	Francis and Martinha's daughters
William and Francis	Francis and Martinha's sons
Soliman	Francis Light's Malay adopted son
Lady Thong Di Rozells	Martinha's Siamese mother
Felipe Rozells	Martinha's brother

Pinang	
James Scott	influential merchant, Light's friend
Thomas Pigou	Light's assistant
John Glass	captain and commander of the fort
James Gray	lieutenant of marines
William Lindesay	a country captain
James Hutton	doctor
Nakhoda Kecil	Ismail, penghulu of the Malays
Robert Hamilton	captain, later commander of fort
Norman Macalister	young Scottish lieutenant
Lydia Hardwick	a governess from Calcutta
Khoh Lay Huan	kapitan cina of Pinang
Hussain Sayyid Aidid	rich merchant from Aceh
Nathaniel Bacon	junior writer
Marlbro	orderly at the hospital

Queddah

Sultan Abdullah	sultan of Queddah
Tunku Ya	laksamana of Queddah

East India Company

Alexander Kyd	major and surveyor
Eliza Kyd	Alexander Kyd's wife
William Fairlie	Calcutta merchant and friend of Light
Earl Charles Cornwallis	Governor-General of India
William Cornwallis	Commodore of East Indies Fleet
Diana Hill	miniaturist
William Hickey	lawyer
Peter Rainier	later Commodore of East Indies Fleet
John Ogilvy	senior merchant
Margaret Ogilvy	daughter of John Ogilvy

Suffolk

Mary Light	adoptive mother of Light
James Light	adoptive brother of Light
George Doughty	childhood friend of Light

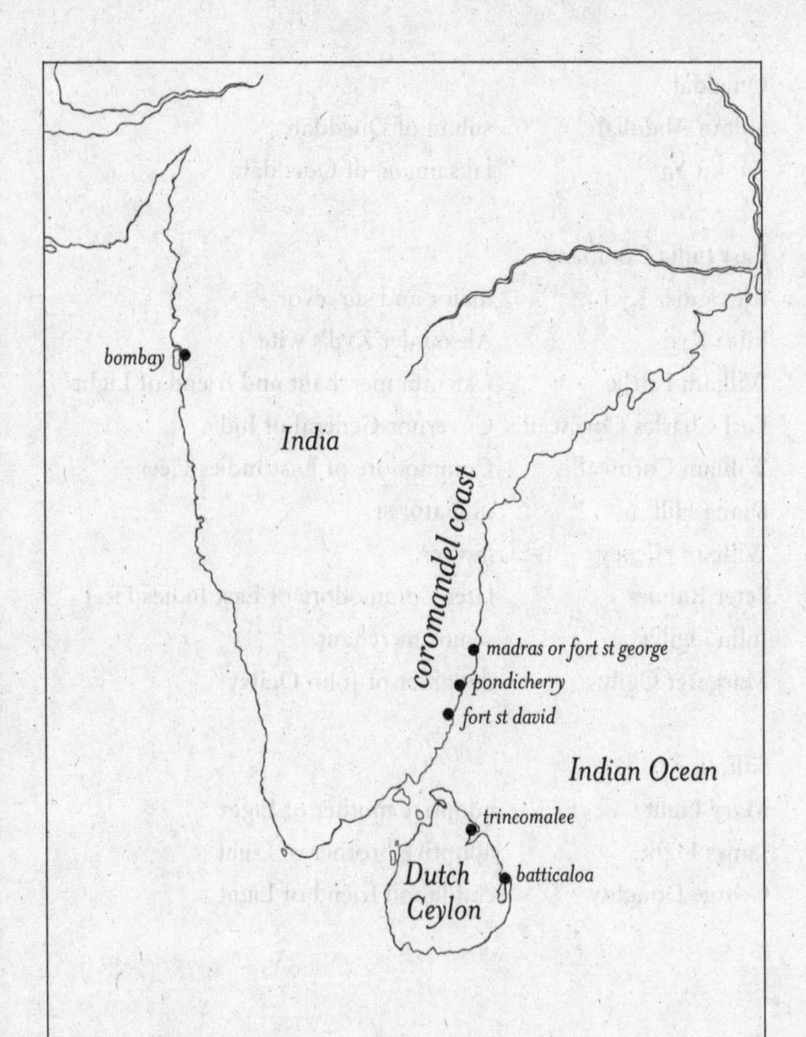

India and the Malay Peninsula

adapted from "A Map of the East-Indies", produced for the East India Company by Herman Moll, Geographer, 1736.

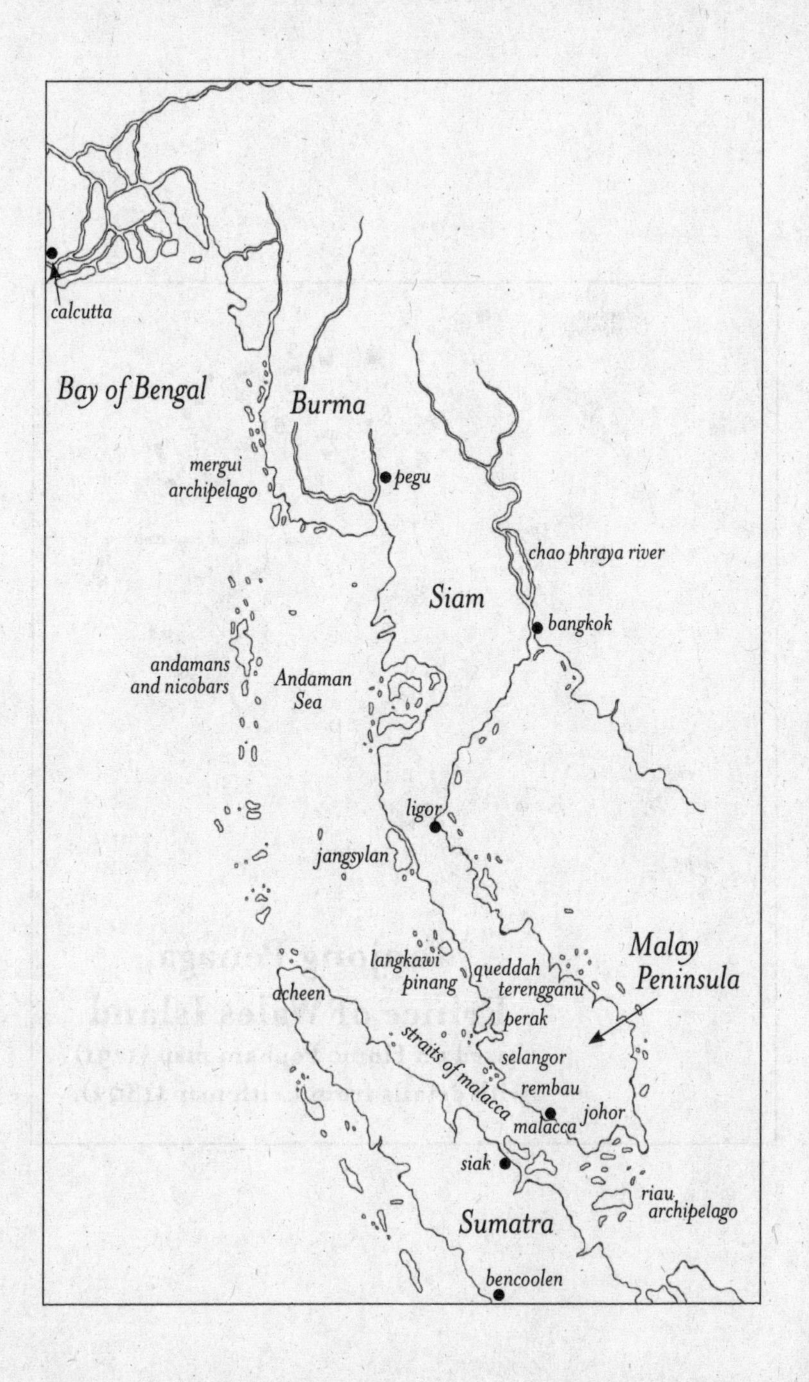
calcutta
Bay of Bengal
Burma
mergui
archipelago
pegu
chao phraya river
Siam
bangkok
andamans
and nicobars
Andaman
Sea
ligor
jangsylan
Malay
Peninsula
langkawi
pinang
queddah
terengganu
acheen
perak
straits of malacca
selangor
rembau
johor
malacca
siak
riau
archipelago
Sumatra
bencoolen

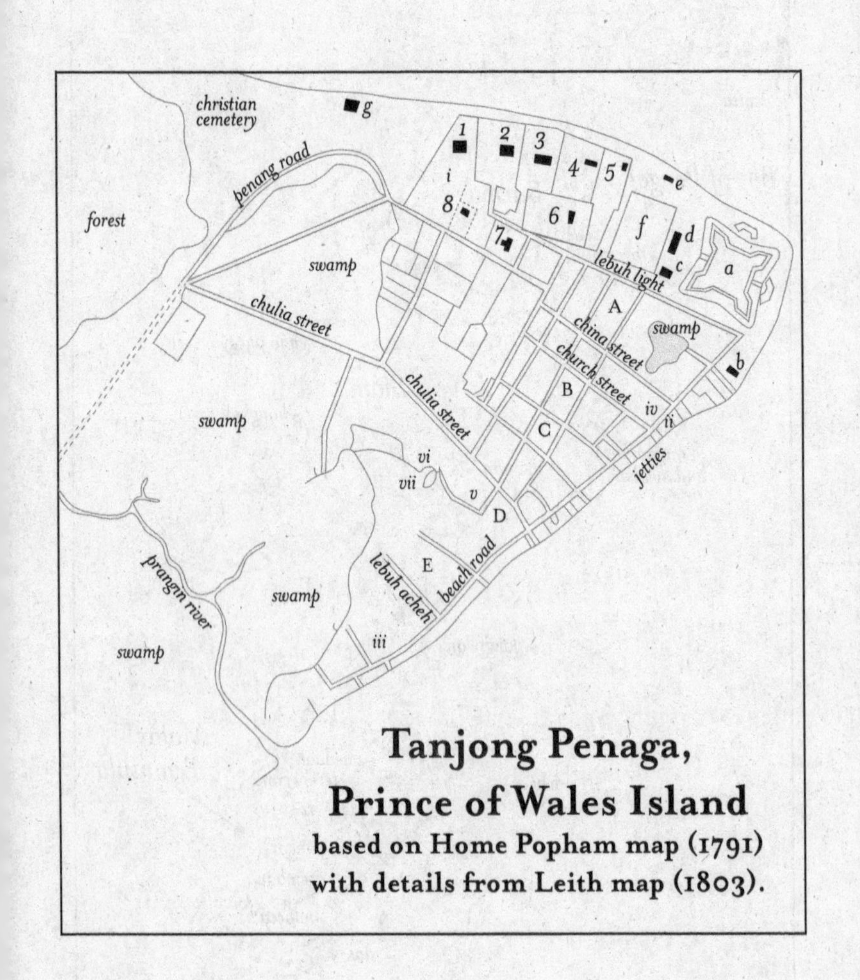

Tanjong Penaga, Prince of Wales Island
based on Home Popham map (1791) with details from Leith map (1803).

Key

Residences

1	*Martinha*
2	*Government House*
3	*Mr and Mrs Gray*
4	*Captain Glass*
5	*Officer quarters*
6	*James Scott*
7	*Dr Hutton*
8	*Mr Pigou*

The Fort

a	*Fort Cornwallis*
b	*Custom houses / stores*
c	*Guardhouse*
d	*Hospital*
e	*Guesthouse*
f	*Barracks*
g	*General hospital*

The Settlement

A	*Chinatown*
B	*Eurasians*
C	*Chulias*
D	*Malay Town*
E	*Acheh quarter*

Amenities

i	*Well*
ii	*Warehouse*
iii	*Kilns*
iv	*Catholic church*
v	*Chulia mosque*
vi	*Malay mosque*
vii	*Muslim cemetery*

Contents

Prologue

Shalimar Point, Calcutta. 8th April 1788

Early morning, the sun barely risen, a line of pleasure boats queued at the jetty on a verdant promontory. Eager guests disembarked in gales of laughter, excitement in the air, already a merry gathering. Gentlemen gallantly assisted their ladies, sweeping them up and setting them down where no mud or dust might soil their satin slippers; they giggled or feigned fear, swatting at their menfolk for their bravado and audacity. Children were passed hand-to-hand to be reunited with their servants whose task – to keep them out of mischief – was an onerous one indeed on such an occasion. Once ashore, each party ambled up the slight incline to the handsome property ahead, whose resplendent gardens reached down to the river from a well-appointed pukka house atop the hill. This was Shalimar, home of Lieutenant Colonel Kyd, Surveyor-General of Bengal.

Today was Easter Sunday, deemed the perfect occasion by the reclusive Robert Kyd to throw open his house and gardens to 'the right people', whose support he required at Council. Everyone was eager to view the estate, particularly its gardens, for Robert Kyd was a keen horticulturalist whose personal mission was to collect and collate every known species of tree, plant, and flower in the East. It was both a private obsession and a public service, for who knew what benefit to mankind and the Treasury might be found in the wondrous natural world of the Indies?

Breakfast was served in marquees with excellent views of the river, yet at sufficient distance to avoid the worst of its ripe stench. Punkah-wallahs kept insects at bay and provided a welcome breeze as the heat of the morning rose. Little woven baskets were handed out to the children to search for painted Easter eggs hidden amongst the foliage, although they were directed not to root around themselves; even boys and girls were sensible to the dangers in the undergrowth of a lurking cobra. The servants would retrieve the eggs once they were sighted by the children.

An inexperienced observer might have wondered at the shortage of females for, although a few men had brought their wives, most had not – yet children were in abundance. It was a mark of every such gathering in India, one never spoken of but understood by all, that most Company ladies were not acceptable in society. They were local women, and the times were changing. The new wave of Company employees, petty quill drivers with their narrowminded wives, or supercilious aristocrats and their socially fastidious miladies, had imported to Bengal the prudish sensibilities of home. Where once there had been tolerance for such liaisons, those days were at an end. Now one must 'prove' one's Britishness at every turn – or hide away the embarrassing reality.

Major Alexander Kyd – cousin to the host – arrived on one of the later launches with his beautiful wife, Eliza. Somewhat of a flamboyant character, the major of the flaxen locks and sculpted features little resembled his serious-minded cousin in either appearance or personality. Where Colonel Kyd was solitary,

Alexander revelled in the social gaze, particularly delighting in a good entrance. Excepting his famous cousin, Alexander Kyd had arrived in Calcutta with little else to recommend him other than his wits and good looks. But, unlike other such dandies, he had proved to be as talented as he was charming, with the ambition and work ethic to accompany it.

Kyd circulated, conversing with the men and courting the glances of the ladies. His wife, Eliza, also drew attention on this her first social outing since the birth of their son, James; the society favourite had been sorely missed. The couple gradually gravitated to their close friends, who were already tucking into their repast. They were welcomed with genuine pleasure. Alexander and Eliza settled down to a hearty breakfast of kedgeree and eggs and mutton curry with paratha, accompanied by spicy fried potatoes, washed down with copious cups of sweet milky tea.

'So, Sandy, what's this I hear about your new appointment?' There was no such thing as a secret in Bengal.

'Pigou, have you been listening at keyholes again?' Alexander grinned back. Thomas Pigou, at the age of twenty-one, was already a Company writer on the make, keen as mustard to climb the ladder. As well as his natural abilities as an accountant and administrator, he also made it his business to know everyone else's business – a guaranteed method of advancement. Pigou blushed but did not gainsay his friend.

'For those amongst you who are not aware, I have been appointed by the GG to survey our newly acquired Prince of Wales Island,' Kyd continued with a flourish. 'The Council has furnished me with a ship, the *Viper*, under good old Archie Blair. Wish me luck, gentlemen!'

His friends were suitably impressed, nodding their heads in approval, and clapping him upon the back. 'An excellent choice, dear Major,' commented John Ogilvy, senior merchant. 'Reports on the new settlement are propitious. Everyone's eager for more information. The captains that have already made landing are most complimentary. This could make your name, you know?'

Ogilvy raised his bushy eyebrows expressively. 'Don't forget to share your good fortune, man. Keep an eye out for investment opportunities. We must snap up prime land before the hoi polloi arrive. There's much profit to be made in the coming years.'

Kyd admonished him with a mock frown. 'Good God, John, are you suggesting profiteering?' Ogilvy chuckled whilst Kyd feigned horror at the suggestion. 'No loot this trip, I'm afraid, good sirs,' he added. 'I must behave myself for the time being. I'm there merely to survey. It does not, however, preclude me from returning at a later date for my own benefit. You may be assured I intend to keep my eyes open to opportunity. I promise you will be the "second" to know!'

A burly man, his red face damp with perspiration, smiled wryly. 'I take it none of you are familiar with Francis Light, the new Superintendent? Or his good pal, James Scott? I wouldn't underestimate either fellow. Those two men have seen it all. Do not think for one moment you can pull the wool over their eyes, my lad!'

'You know Light?' Kyd inquired.

'For years,' replied William Fairlie. 'Good man. Honourable. Decent. Charming. But he's remarkably shrewd and ruthless by the same token. Get on his good side, Kyd. That's my advice to you. You'll gain nothing on the island without his leave.'

Thomas Pigou agreed entirely with Fairlie's assessment. 'My dear departed father was his friend since their Madras days. I've known Uncle Francis all my life. In fact, I may be joining him there before too long. Superintendent Light has *personally* asked for my services as his assistant –'

The group applauded this unexpected nugget of news. 'You were saving that to steal my thunder, you wretch!' Kyd laughed. 'Good man, though. Quite the opportunity for a young 'un. Richly deserved, Tommy. Light is clearly no fool.'

Pigou received the congratulations graciously, placing a finger on his lips. 'Keep it to yourselves for now, gentlemen. I have not yet been granted leave. I must complete a few important tasks for Council first. Meantime, some eager chap may steal the opportunity from beneath my nose. You know how it is in the arena here. But, to return to your visit, Sandy. If you want to impress the superintendent, you could do no better than get to know those two little ladies.' Pigou pointed out a group of children sitting on the lawn, showing off their haul of colourful eggs. 'The Misses Sarah and Lucy Ann Light.'

'They attend school with my girl Margaret,' added John Ogilvy. 'Thick as thieves they are. Nice girls. Clever, good-looking little things – although the younger is a little too opinionated for my taste.'

Pigou laughed fondly. 'They're lovely girls. I will admit little Lucy is one to speak her mind, but she is generally obedient and studious, if a little "spirited". Has ambitions to be a famous writer, no less.' At this absurdity, the men of the group sniggered. Eliza Kyd rolled her eyes – but not at the lofty ambition of a little girl. She had spent a lifetime listening to the scorn of men and had little tolerance for it.

'They board with us at holiday times', continued Pigou. 'Mother loves to have children about the house again.' The Pigous were an extended family of many branches scattered about the major port cities, their British womenfolk having settled in India years ago. They were quintessentially English yet fully habituated, of great use as facilitators in every aspect of society, with fingers in every Bengal pie. It was a happy, rather haphazard, household. No wonder Pigou was in good favour with Superintendent Light for offering a genial home to his daughters far away.

'Many thanks for the advice, Mr Pigou. I shall make a point to introduce myself before the morning is out. And now perhaps, before the heat becomes unbearable, how about we walk off this excellent breakfast with a tour around the gardens. Mrs Kyd, let us take the air ...'

***

The gardens were untypical of Calcutta. Where towering trees were usually limited to the perimeter of green spaces and flamboyant tropical plants tamed in carefully curated borders, Robert Kyd had used his acres to plant a horticultural delight of dizzying profusion.

Paved walks were laid through shady paths flanked by the various wonders of the subcontinent. To an unseasoned eye, he had re-established the original forest that had once covered the whole of the city, yet all of this was artifice. Man had taken possession of abundant nature and shaped it to his will. No unwanted plant or weed, grass or fern was allowed to interfere with the grand design. Each tree had its own appointed location and sufficient space in which to thrive without competition, all set out in measured rows. The wild confusion of native forest was wholly absent. At one eye-catching location a waterfall had been fashioned, flowing over uniform moss-free rocks into a luxuriant pond of lotus flowers, the whole effect akin to waterlilies on an English lake. It was the Garden of Eden reimagined, rather than Indian jungle reclaimed.

The pathway led to a central grove, where the tree cover fell away, and a wooden pavilion had been erected. Servants waited with fresh juices served from earthenware jugs; cool cloths were handed out for perspiring brows. The guests thankfully settled on the benches to quench their thirst, whilst the children took their refreshments with their servants on rattan mats in the shade. Lt. Col. Kyd then proceeded to deliver a short talk on his vision for a Botanical Gardens, which he hoped would be sited contiguous to his own garden.

'No doubt it will be a park for the enjoyment of all, where families might roam the wonders of the local flora and fauna, but that is not my only purpose,' concluded Kyd. 'This Botanical Gardens will serve as a living museum for every type of tree and plant in the East. Here we will collect, study and distribute cuttings to add to the scientific knowledge of the world. Medicines will be identified, substances will be discovered, new foodstuffs will be revealed that will bring prodigious improvements in the lives of men–'

'Not to mention prodigious profits!' heckled one member of the crowd. Robert Kyd's brow furrowed; his lip curling in distaste at the uncouth mention of money. His aims were entirely philanthropic, although he well understood that the average Englishman in Calcutta judged only the quantity of coin accrued as proof of any endeavour. On this occasion, however, he chose to ignore the remark and the amused tittering that accompanied it. If future discoveries meant only profits in the bank to most, then so be it. He would have his gardens, cupidity be damned. After all, the purpose of the invasion of his private idyll was to ensure that the subject of the Botanic Gardens was on every lip until it became the fashionable topic of the day, the better to make his case at Council.

Whilst those of a more scholarly inclination gathered round Robert Kyd to ask further questions, Alexander Kyd took the opportunity to slip away, sauntering across to where the children were playing. He espied the Light girls with sketch books on their laps, leaning back against a tree.

'Hullo there, ladies!' Kyd bent over to look at their drawings. 'I say! What talented artists! Such charming views! This is indeed a perfect spot for sketching. But I forget myself – Major Alexander Kyd, cousin of the good lieutenant-colonel, our gracious host. Welcome to Shalimar on this beautiful morning. May I join you on the mat?'

The two girls stared upwards at the tall gentleman, wrinkling their eyes against the sun. 'It would be an honour, sir,' said one, a striking child with auburn ringlets and sea green eyes. The other smiled shyly and lowered her eyes, her pale cheeks flushing red. Her long hair was chestnut brown, held back with a pink ribbon, but the freckly white of her cheeks against the golden glow of her friend's skin told Alexander all he needed to know. Only one of these children belonged to Francis Light.

'I believe I am addressing the Misses Light, daughters of the famous Superintendent of Prince of Wales Island?' ventured Kyd grandly.

The braver one laughed, her friend giggling. 'No, sir, only I have that distinction. I'm Miss Sarah Light, and this is my friend, Miss Margaret Ogilvy!'

Kyd placed his hand on his heart. 'Forgive me, Miss Ogilvy, for I believe we have already met. I have oft times visited your fine home. My sincere apologies for failing to recognise you. You have grown into quite the young lady, so perhaps you will excuse my ignorance?' Kyd knew they must have been introduced before, but she was an unmemorable child, pretty enough, but pasty and prim. Nothing to compare to the deep natural beauty of Eurasian children, who inevitably inherited the best physical qualities of their complex heritages.

Miss Ogilvy continued to make doe eyes as if to further confirm his opinion of her. Miss Light, however, responded confidently. 'Please sit down, sir. My sister Lucy is also here but she's running around with the other children. I fear she is still quite giddy in her head and something of a tomboy.' She pointed out Miss Lucy Ann Light, who was dashing madly here and there, her skirts gathered in her hands as she chased after other children – mostly boys.

'High spirited, I would say! Let her enjoy her childhood while she may. I hear you ladies are all at school in Calcutta. You must miss your family, Miss Light.'

'Please call me Sarah, sir. Yes, we miss home awfully, especially now that father and mother have settled on Pulau Pinang – I mean Prince of Wales Island. We both long to visit! It is tiresome only to receive letters and to miss out on all the excitement!'

'And we have a brother we have never even met!' Lucy Ann plumped herself down unannounced, curious to meet the handsome stranger. 'I'm Lucy Ann. I'm her sister,' she added by way of an introduction and then extended her hand awkwardly as if realising her lack of manners.

Sarah rolled her eyes, Margaret giggled more, while Alexander Kyd held out his right hand. 'Pleased to meet you, Miss Lucy Ann Light. I was curious to meet you both for I am soon to visit the island myself,' he added.

'SO ARE WE!' screeched Lucy until her sister's horrified face restrained her. She continued in more demure fashion. 'I mean, we too are to visit the island. Father is sending a ship for us next month. We return home for six whole months because he is so busy that he is unable to bring mother over to visit us. We shall have a governess in the meantime,' Lucy blurted out all on one breath. Kyd decided he rather liked this little hurricane of a girl. She was already quite a character.

'Then we shall become firm friends, I'm sure,' he replied smartly. 'I look forward to continuing our acquaintance in your new home. Ladies? My thanks for your genteel company.' And with that he bowed again and withdrew, leaving the three girls chortling in delight at having entertained the handsome major. No adult normally noticed their presence.

Alexander Kyd strolled away, already mentally composing his letter to Superintendent Light, requesting passage on one of his ships in May. It would be a perfect opportunity to make a positive impression on Mr Light, who must be nurturing some reservations about the survey on his establishment. A good word from his daughters and Thomas Pigou would ease any awkwardness in their first meetings. Kyd had no wish to find himself on the wrong side of Light. In fact, he intended to present his most amiable and innocuous face. Far more would be revealed about the true situation of the establishment if Light deemed him a harmless Company officer who might easily be taken in.

Now late enough in the day for stronger drink, Kyd accepted a glass of wine, still musing upon his continued good fortune in the matter of Prince of Wales Island. It was typical of Bengal that a chance meeting could so unexpectedly fall into one's lap. There was always someone who knew someone who turned out to be exactly the someone one most needed to meet. Eliza touched his arm fondly, throwing him a quizzical look. He smiled back at her with genuine pleasure, his breath – as always – quite taken away by her shimmering beauty. The elder Light girl would one day be another such as long as she kept her native mother well hidden. 'I shall tell you all about it later, dear Lizzie. What a perfectly lovely Easter Day! Hallelujah indeed!'

PART ONE

The Superintendent

(1787)

Pulau Pinang has a New Town and Captain Light is its King.
Do not recall the days that are gone,
or you will bow down your head,
And the tears will gush forth!

A pantun of the men of Kedah as sung by Raja Haji Hamid
[from *In Court and Kampong* by Hugh Clifford 1898]

1
Expectations

George Town, Prince of Wales Island. 27th May 1787

A gentle sea breeze dappled the smooth green waters, barely rippling the glassy surface that sparkled in the morning sun. Two women were seated in the shade of a tree near the jetty, sheltering beneath parasols held by servants. It was unthinkable to expose the skin to the sun at any time of day.

The eyes of the entire party – two ladies, two children and several servants accompanied by a few house boys – remained fixed upon the channel where the larger vessels lay, watching for signs of activity around a particular ship they all knew well. The *Speedwell* had arrived on the horizon just past dawn and reached the roads an hour or so later. Its passengers were disembarking. After an absence of almost a year and a half, the superintendent's daughters were finally returning to the island.

Francis Light had taken a transport over earlier. His wife, Martinha, and her mother, Lady Thong Di, had chosen to remain ashore. The latter was near breathless with excitement, dabbing at her forehead with a cloth dampened in fragrant water whilst fanning herself vigorously. She could not wait to hold her precious girls again. Their mother, however, was more subdued, riven with apprehension. For days she had slept badly and eaten little in anticipation of this very moment.

At least one anxiety had been allayed by the safe arrival of the *Speedwell.* Martinha had feared that something might befall them on the journey. It was the southwest monsoon. Who knew what storms might bedevil them on their crossing? Her husband had laughed away her concerns. 'May is the ideal time! The winds are behind you all the way. Mark my words, they'll be here in record time!' Of course, he had been right. The journey had taken a mere eleven days. Her fears had been groundless – but then she had never been a lover of the open sea.

Even now with their appearance only minutes away, her heart was not at peace. Insidious voices whispered in her head of her shortcomings as a mother. It was unnatural for her daughters to be raised by strangers in an alien land. They should have stayed with their parents and accepted their allotted station in life. How would it profit them to become English gentlewomen if they turned their backs on family and tradition? Children were highly impressionable, changing moment to moment as they grew apace. Would this protracted separation have changed them? Were they different now? Had she lost them forever? Martinha recalled how English women had once treated her in Calcutta. Would her girls now be ashamed of their own mother, a native woman of lesser status, an embarrassment in their new circles?

Martinha reached out for her little son, William, to dandle on her knee despite his squirming to escape her embrace, more for her own comfort than for his. She needed the reassurance of motherhood in the face of what might be an awkward, even painful, reunion. At least her babies still loved her.

'Little mosquito larva!' William's grandmother laughed, gently pinching at his chubby cheeks. The child grinned back, momentarily distracted, settling down on his mother's lap to suck his thumb. His sister, Mary, slipped between the two women, burrowing shyly against her mother's breast. Although thrilled for the return of the sisters she scarce remembered, she too was overcome with insecurity. Mary would no more be the big sister. What would they think of her? Would her mother love her less now?

'There! I see the little boat! It is the master and the little mistresses!" exclaimed Bun Lek, a house boy with the acute vision of the young, shading his eyes against the glare of the sun. True enough, bobbing along from the direction of the *Speedwell* was a jolly carrying passengers. It would not be long now. Martinha's heart beat faster, her mouth dry. She could barely keep her composure.

Her mother's hand slipped into hers. 'Don't be afraid, *sayang*. You are their mother. Nothing has changed!'

'God willing, *'bu*. It would kill me to see disappointment on their faces!'

Aboard the boat, Major Alexander Kyd lounged back against the bench, his hand idly trailing in the spray washing against the side, eyes fixed on the approaching island. This visit was a great opportunity, his first real chance to prove himself to the Council. He was thirty-three, a significant age in the youthful circles of Company officers. Had it not been for his cousin Robert, Surveyor-General of Bengal, even this venture might not have fallen at his feet. He must make a success of it.

The island was a glorious sight to behold, a verdant jewel rising from the harmonious waters of the narrow strait, soaked in sunlight that frolicked on the wave. The skies overhead were of such a blue that no artist could hope to replicate, scattered with white clouds frothing as lazily as their little boat bobbed through the tranquil sea. Dotted around were islets, some little more than large rocks, that created even calmer channels, sheltering the coastline from the open sea. The island itself – thickly forested in arboreal variety – rose to lofty green peaks that shimmered in the heat. Nothing could be further from the murky stench of the Hooghly on the approach to Calcutta. And yet, there was a smallness to this world that Kyd could not deny. Their landing place on a flat open stretch of littoral was unremarkable: a few low wooden structures and a smattering of local prows clustered around the small jetty, the forlorn flag of St George hanging listlessly in the humid stillness.

This settlement was still a rudimentary outpost, far from the centre of everything that mattered, a controversial new possession not much favoured by Earl Cornwallis, the new governor-general. Yet, despite the ambivalence of the Council, the sea captains who had already visited spoke highly of it; there was much enthusiasm amongst them for its prospects. Kyd himself remained impartial. His first impressions might be favourable, but he had to weigh them against what Cornwallis wished to hear. He must not to be swayed by the superficial delights of this charming spot. Superintendent Light had waxed lyrical long enough about its benefits – and he was known to be a manipulator of the truth. Kyd was here to uncover its disadvantages.

Was the island indeed the treasure-trove that Light believed it to be? Undoubtedly it was well favoured by nature, geography, and the disposition of its people. On the world's busiest sea lane, it lay outside the maw of the Dutch and the Bugis, enjoying peaceful relations with local rulers. This free port already attracted traders from east and west providing easy access to tin, rice, opium and spices. How could it fail?

His deliberations were interrupted by the cries of the girls at the front clinging either side of their father, Francis Light. Kyd had come to know them well as they shared the intimacies of shipboard life and could not deny he was fond of them already. They had certainly helped to pass the time. Furthermore, as Light had greeted him with hearty thanks for his attentions to the girls, he knew his inspired ploy had achieved its aim. The visit was off to the most excellent of starts.

'Major Sandy! Major Sandy! Look at the island! It's so pretty and unspoilt! I told you that you would love the Straits!' shouted the younger girl, lively Lucy Ann, who had won him over from the start. Her sister, the more reserved Sarah, was also unusually animated.

'See how clear the waters are! You can even see the shoals of little fishes!' she exclaimed.

Sarah and Lucy Ann were besides themselves with joy to be finally within sight of their new home after many boring days at sea. Receiving letters whilst confined to school had been a torment. As young and inexperienced as they were in such matters, they had felt the imperceptible change in their social status in Calcutta, which now singled them out as the daughters of a significant father. Where once, as children of mixed heritage whose father was a mere country ship captain, they had been overlooked, suddenly that same father's name was on every tongue.

It had not only been at school that their prestige had risen. Since the settlement of Prince of Wales Island and their father's appointment as its superintendent, they were suddenly favoured by many leading families with children of similar age, now invited to parties and picnics as companions to the daughters of the influential. Already they recognised the value of such connections. One day it would open doors for them. They would meet suitable husbands. Even girls of ten years old knew as much.

Sarah, with her outwardly calm demeanour, contained her excitement, betraying herself only by the tinge of high colour in her cheeks and the constant wringing of her hands. Otherwise, she sat meekly beside her father, listening to his explanations without really hearing him, straining to see who might be waiting at the jetty. Lucy Ann made no such effort, jumping up and down despite the firm hand of her father, screaming out at everything that caught her eye: the sandy beach, the silver streak of a leaping fish, a brightly painted *perahu*, an eagle hovering far above. She named each in Malay as if determined to recall her mother tongue, unspoken for so long: '*Pantai! Ikan! Perahu! Helang kawi*!'

The girls had already embraced their father aboard ship, clinging to him for dear life, exchanging hugs and kisses, and a few tears. He was their hero but now that he had become the famous man and the whole world regarded him with high esteem, their pride was all the greater. As for Francis Light, this moment had been too long in coming. When he had placed his girls in school, he had expected to see them every few months, but events on the island had made it impossible to leave. No more was he the sea captain going back and forth between India and the Straits. He was a landlocked governor with onerous responsibilities and a desk piled high with papers. Today his heart sang out for the joy of reunion – his entire family together in the home he had made for them. For whom was this for if not for those he loved the most?

Behind the girls, a young lady perched beneath a parasol. Miss Lydia Hardwick, teacher at the Calcutta Anglican School for Young Christian Ladies, had eagerly put herself forward as volunteer to accompany the Misses Light in the role of chaperone and governess. Most of the teachers – a most righteous lot of puritanical old spinsters in Miss Hardwick's opinion – had been aghast at the suggestion. Bengal was far enough for their tastes, waging their Christian battle against heathen ignorance for the Lord. But to visit a desert island in the middle of nowhere? It was unthinkable. There was even talk of hostile cannibals and man-eating tigers circulating until the teachers had quite fomented themselves into a state of nervous agitation.

As a result, Lydia Hardwick had been the only teacher to step forward. The scurrilous rumours she had dropped into the ears of colleagues had done their work. Although Mrs Hedges, the principal, had not entirely been convinced that Miss Hardwick was the best choice – a more homely and devout girl would be preferable – she had no option but to agree. Fanning herself as they approached the jetty, Lydia could not help but feel a sense of achievement. She had found a way to exchange her tedious life as a lowly schoolmistress for the pleasing prospect of an island full of officers and gentlemen, with little competition. A girl must take her opportunities where she may!

The business of disembarking children, passengers and luggage began, distracting those on board. Moments passed during which Martinha caught her first glimpses of her daughters before they noticed her, permitting her the chance to observe them in their glory. How they had grown! Sarah, always slender and tall, now seemed almost a woman; she had her father's height. Clad in pale blue muslin, her mother noted the imminent budding of her female body. Tears pricked at her eyes for the time they had lost, the last years of her childhood almost gone. Then Lucy Ann bounded across, her bonnet hanging on for dear life, secured only by its ribbons. She wore pink; it was rumpled and stained already. So, typical of messy Ann! But she had grown as well. The chubby little girl was no more, replaced by a leggy sprite. My little ones! Where are you now?

'MOTHER!' Sarah was the first to shriek.

'No, not mother … IBU! NENEK!" screamed Lucy Ann as both girls hared along the wooden walkway. Martinha was unable to contain herself. The next moment she was almost bowled over by her daughters, jabbering and weeping, kissing and embracing in an unintelligible outpouring of joy. Little William immediately began to cry, soon followed by Mary, neither able to fathom what was happening to their mother and grandmother. They were whisked away by servants while the reunion carried on. Francis stood back, his hands upon his hips, laughing out loud at the hullabaloo.

'Oh mother! Oh mother! You are so beautiful!' gasped Sarah. 'I have missed you every day. The journey was interminable but Major Kyd has been so kind to us, playing card games and walking around the deck. Mother, I love your hair! It is so shiny and sleek. No one else has hair like you. I cannot wait to get out of these tight dresses and wear my lovely sarongs again! Nenek! Nenek! I have longed to embrace you!' The older girl went from one to the other, touching their hair and faces as if she scarce believed they were real.

Her sister danced about, talking nonstop, nineteen to the dozen. 'Mother, they call me Lucy Ann at school, but I won't have it here!' she screeched. 'It's too priggish ... oh, I don't know how to say that in Malay! It means ... it means ... well, it means it's too English or something like that! Never mind, I'm home now and I want to be Lukey Ann again!' It was a garbled comment, such as children often make when excited – but it contained its own indisputable logic. Tears poured down Martinha's cheeks. Her girls hadn't given one pause at the sight of their mother. She was their Ibu. That was all that mattered. Now they were home, all they wanted was to be hers again.

***

As he had hoped, no time was lost before he began his survey. As soon as the children were seen off with their countless servants and adoring family, Superintendent Light approached Major Kyd, politely waiting in the shade for the impassioned reunion to conclude. Light's handshake was firm, accompanied by a gracious manner. He was a man whose first impression was most favourable: a tolerable face with regular features, lit by the same limpid eyes that Kyd had noticed on his daughter Sarah. One warmed to the man immediately. He exuded genuine welcome with little apparent arrogance or guile.

'We meet at last, Major!' Light exclaimed. 'It was such a relief to receive your mail and to know that a Company officer was aboard as escort for the girls. It helped to allay my wife's fears for she worries dreadfully of the dangers of sea travel, a singularly unfortunate circumstance for the wife of a merchant captain!' he added with a hearty laugh.

Kyd acknowledged the gratitude but felt bound to add: 'I cannot pretend it was altruism alone. A mutual friend alerted me to the news that you were sending a ship for your daughters at the very same time when I was arranging transport here. Blair is meeting me here with the *Viper*, my survey ship. All in all, the matter was as useful to me as it was to you, sir!'

The two men sauntered along a track that led from the jetty in the direction of the wooden stockade, now clearly visible ahead. To their left lay the higgledy-piggledy streets of the fledgling shanty town that clustered around the small harbour and its warehouses. It was Beach Street, the superintendent informed him, although 'beach' and 'street' were somewhat grand designations for the sandy track edging a muddy stretch of shoreline.

'This "mutual" friend, you say? Who spoke to you about my daughters?' Light inquired. Kyd recognised that he was being tested for his honesty. The superintendent knew the social tricks and deceits.

'A Mr Thomas Pigou. I believe you knew his father? We move in the same circle,' Kyd replied, unable to remove smugness from his reply.

'Little Tommy! My word, it is a small world indeed! I hope to have him here forthwith as my assistant. He's a clever lad and a fellow I trust implicitly unlike –' Light's voice trailed off.

'Unlike others that the Company might force upon you?' Kyd riposted, a twinkle in his eye. Light grinned, appreciating Kyd's direct and frank approach.

'Indeed, sir. I cannot deny that Company men must generally be taken with a strong pinch of salt. They have little familiarity with the Straits. This is not India, sir. Things work differently here. There is a singular experiment on this island which is not always fully understood by our betters in Calcutta,' Light added wryly.

'Have no fear, Superintendent Light. I am not here to confound you in any way, very much the opposite. My purpose is to apprise the Council all you have achieved. There is no hidden intent to undermine this valuable acquisition.'

Light acknowledged Kyd's comment with a slight nod – and then completely changed the subject. It was too early in their acquaintanceship for an excessive show of commonality. 'This is your first foray into these waters?'

'Indeed, sir. I was most keen to make the journey. Favourable reports reach Bengal daily. East Indiamen captains are not easy to impress. I am most keen to see for myself what has so markedly won their favour.'

His compliment was received with a pursing of Light's lips. 'Prince of Wales Island is more than just a victualling station, Major, as I hope you will come to appreciate. It has the potential to answer every question posed by the limitations of our current situation. It can be a centre, not just for trade, but a much-needed base for our forces. Furthermore, with some investment, the island could become a major producer of those goods that are so valued at home and abroad, which currently lie mainly in the hands of the Dutch.'

This was perhaps not the time for such a debate. They continued awhile in an awkward silence, leaving the shanty settlement behind and heading towards the stockade. Reaching the pathway to the wooden fort itself, Light paused and waved his arm ostentatiously in its general direction. 'Fort Cornwallis, Major Kyd.' There was a hint of challenge.

Before him stood a singularly unremarkable structure. In Kyd's expert eyes, the defensive qualities of this fort were minimal to say the least. Constructed from tall thin palm trunks already whitened and battered by salt, sun and rain, the single line of perimeter fencing was in urgent need of extensive repair. Nor were there any turrets or platforms from which to repulse an attack, nothing but a muddy ditch serving as an embankment. Kyd struggled to keep his appraisal to himself but the engineer in him showed clearly on his face.

'I am wholly aware of its inadequacies, sir.' Light said. 'This was a temporary stockade for the purpose of protection in the initial weeks of our occupation. Since then, I have been peppering the governor-general's desk with requests for funds to erect an adequate structure in its place. We need money to build up this settlement or we may lose it before Calcutta makes its mind up. My apologies, sir, I run ahead of myself. Let us settle you in your lodgings and allow you to spend your first day recovering from the journey. There will be plenty of time for such discussions later.'

They entered the main gate where two sepoys lounged in desultory fashion, although they snapped to attention soon enough at the sight of the superintendent. To be fair, there was little need for security; the environs of the fort were quiet. Light led Kyd across the open parade ground, past wooden buildings that housed the officers, the mess, and storehouses, by way of a recently constructed brick arsenal, towards a small house set at some distance apart from the rest. Its roof was thatched in palm and it was raised on stilts in the local fashion.

'Your quarters, Major Kyd,' Light announced with a flourish. 'Somewhat humble, I'll confess, but they have served me well in the past. It is a somewhat more comfortable berth than a shanty in the town or a bunk in the barracks!'

'I hope I'm not inconveniencing you, sir,' Kyd replied. 'Am I expelling you from your home?'

Light shook his head. 'Not at all, sir. This humble abode was originally fabricated for my family on our arrival but since then we have built a more comfortable property along North Beach. It now serves as my office, sleeping quarters when I'm up half the night working, and a place to entertain significant guests, of which you, dear Major, are by far the most distinguished. You may have the entire use of it whilst you are here – and when Blair arrives, he is also welcome to come ashore and join you. There are two bedrooms. I've arranged for a cook and several servants to be at your disposal. I wouldn't expect too much, though. They are unschooled in service, I'm afraid, but very willing.'

Several natives lined up before them: Ah Wong, a middle-aged Chinese whom Kyd presumed was the cook, and a few Indians, two women and a young male. It was evident they spoke no English. 'Language will be a problem, I fear,' Light admitted, as if reading his thoughts. 'Have you any Malay?'

Kyd shrugged. 'A few words learned aboard ship. But no doubt I shall have more by the time I leave, sir!'

'That's the spirit, Major. I would advise you work at it. In these parts it is the lingua franca. Your life will be immeasurably eased by fluency. I shall leave you alone now. I recommend a bath, some refreshment, and a nap during the heat of the day.

Tomorrow we shall hold a formal dinner to introduce you to the significant residents of the island. The servants have been instructed to prepare something palatable and not overly spicy in the local style until you are more accustomed to our diet. There are wine and spirits, too. Make yourself at home, Major!'

Kyd suspected that Light was less concerned with allowing him rest than spending the day with his own family. Who could blame him? For his own part, he relished some time alone to explore and take in the glorious views that were set before him.

It was already approaching midday by now, the sun burning overhead, inexorably working its way to its zenith. Kyd was parched, his body drenched in sweat. He was hungry, too. Clean water, food and rest seemed most appealing. Mounting the steps to the small veranda, he found his travelling chest awaiting him, being dragged along by the young Indian boy. Inside, a rattan table had been set with simple refreshments under a bamboo dome; ants were already marching up the table leg.

Ripping off his cravat and jacket, Kyd took a deep swig from the water jug and investigated the repast. It was a platter of local fruits: small bananas fashioned like the chubby hand of a small child, hairy rambutans, juicy stars of carambola, and a papaya halved and served with tiny limes. It was a most satisfying and thirst-quenching array, exactly what he needed.

The room itself was small and furnished in utilitarian fashion: desk, chair, bookshelf and cane armchair. Beyond were the two bedrooms, rudimentary affairs with charpoy-like cane frames topped with kapok mattresses. An outside kitchen at the back led to a small vegetable patch and a tiny shack, inside which there was a deep and sufficiently noxious hole, flanked by two slabs of stone. But there was no evidence of a bathhouse.

Returning to the main cottage, Kyd attempted to determine its whereabouts, mimicking washing his face and body, at which performance the servants' smiles grew even wider.

'*Mandi,* sir?' giggled one of the girls.

'Mandi?' Kyd repeated without any idea of her meaning, following her out back again. She directed him to the side of the house. There was indeed a bathroom. Two screens of woven fibre had been strung between upright poles attached to the house wall. The open end was covering by a cloth hanging from a bamboo rail. Within, a huge terracotta jar stood full to the brim with water, on top of which bobbed a large coconut shell.

'Mandi, sir,' repeated the young girl with a grin.

'Ingenious!' replied Kyd. 'Mandi. Yes, exactly. Many thanks. Your name?'

The girl recognised this word. 'Nama Shanti, sir.'

'Thank you, Shanti.' She handed him a cloth, presumably a towel, and withdrew.

The water was deliciously cold if somewhat reddish brown in colour, an oddity he intended to inquire about later. Bathed and clothed in clean cotton shirt and breeches, Kyd stretched out on his cot. It had begun well. Light was a decent fellow. The island was tranquil. His accommodation, whilst basic, was clean and well provided. The next few weeks would be most interesting, Kyd had no doubt.

2
Towkay Cina

China Street, George Town. 28th May 1787

It was fortunate that Kyd was an early riser for the sky was still streaked with purple smudges of night when booted footsteps on the veranda and a polite clearing of the throat announced the arrival of a visitor. He set down his razor, wiped the soap from his face, and opened the door.

'My apologies, Major Kyd, but I suggest an early start before the infernal heat drives us back inside and the opportunity for "surveying" is lost to us.' Francis Light was waiting, dressed in a casual fashion: loose cotton shirt over breeches and a neckcloth. He did, at least, wear a hat. 'Feel free to discard the jacket, Major. It will become fiercely hot as the morning progresses. I plan to take you on a stroll through the native streets where we might break our fast with the local people and you may thus orientate yourself through the settlement in these days before your ship arrives and your survey proper begins.'

Kyd took his cue from Light with some relief. The humidity was brutal in western garb. Tossing his jacket on a rattan chair by the door, he joined the superintendent for the reconnoitre. It was a glorious time of day, still cool and fresh, with the sky lightening to a rose-tinged blue. The tide lapped lazily on the shore, as indolent as the coming morning, the regular pulse of the wave a restorative heartbeat to the soul. It was hard not to be drawn into the soporific allure of the island.

This time their route took the opposite direction along a main thoroughfare already known as Light Street. The superintendent raised his eyes at the mention of its name. 'It was our only track for some long time when we first arrived and, before I knew it, the settlers had nicknamed it for me. Captain Glass has recently insisted that we formally accept the designation, although I would have preferred something a tad more regal, in keeping with the town's name, perhaps King Street or the like. Glass pointed out, however, that I could call it what I will, but the people will always refer to it as Light Street. So, I conceded.' Light finished with a bashful shrug that could not hide a hint of pride.

'No one deserves it more than you, sir!' Kyd responded. 'Your vision made this possible.'

Light bowed graciously but was not inclined to claim all the glory for himself. 'Perhaps, sir. But this settlement is the product of the endeavours of many different people working for a mutual end. I cannot lay claim to all the accolades. Prince of Wales Island is not just a Company acquisition. Without the support and hard work, not to mention the expertise, of many of the settlers – and by that, I mean most particularly the local people – we would not be where we are today. While you are here with us, Major Kyd, you will have plenty of opportunity to hobnob with the island's men of influence, those European fellows who have already arrived from India and elsewhere, but you would do well not to ignore the other communities, each with their own worthy fellows. The future of this establishment rests as much on their endeavours as our own. This morning I shall introduce you to one such,' Light added cryptically.

They passed the barrack houses of the troops and several wooden residences, each set in its own spacious garden. Kyd learned that senior officers stayed in these. Light also indicated a large property in the native style flanking the road itself. 'The home of James Scott, merchant, my good friend and partner. His contribution to this adventure is as great as mine own but he prefers to shun the public gaze.'

'I have heard of Scott. A somewhat eccentric character?' Kyd enquired politely.

Light laughed. 'It would depend upon which side you stand. He is both admired and loathed in equal measure. James Scott cares not a hoot for public opinion, so expect him to be provocative when you meet. Once he has established that he is a surly curmudgeon, he then feels more inclined to reveal his genial side – should he take to you, that is. Should he not, well we can expect a fine old line in repartee.'

'Then I look forward to our first joust,' Kyd grinned back. 'I expect he'll have it in for me most particularly as a Company officer, furthermore one sent here to poke his nose in.'

'Aye, Major, you would be well to anticipate the worst,' Light replied with a chuckle.

By then they had crossed the street, still quiet at the early hour. A few bullock carts plodded along towards the civilian settlement, farmers bringing goods to market; several humble folk were weaving their sleepy way in the direction of the fort, labourers and cleaners on the way to their workplaces. But no one hurried; dawdling seemed to be the accepted pace in this humid climate where the air hung heavy – and one conserved one's efforts.

Leaving the main street, Light and Kyd took a path over the rough, uneven ground that lay at the edge of the dwellings of the local settlers. Light indicated planted fields beyond. 'There's a decent plot of *padi* over there, but it is nowhere near enough for our growing needs. We import the rest from the mainland. Unfortunately, however, there have been problems in supply of late, the implications of which I have recently relayed to Calcutta. We shall discuss more of that anon. Rice farming is not suited to this terrain, sadly, but we do the best we can.'

'I thought there was much expectation of plantations in the future?' Kyd asked astutely. This verdant tropical landscape appeared ripe for growing any type of crop.

'Plantations, yes. But reclaimed forest is not good agricultural land, particularly here on the promontory. You will have observed the red tinge of the water?'

'Indeed,' Kyd responded. 'I noticed it while bathing and intended to ask you about it.'

'This promontory, Tanjong Penaga in the local lingo, is named for the penaga trees that originally covered it. Their roots go deep and discolour the soil, with the result that water drawn here is stained. It is safe to use but has an unpleasant aftertaste. I sank a well just off the tanjong when we first arrived for the purposes of drinking and cooking – and we have plenty of rivers – so pure water is available in abundance. We are constantly clearing forest for agriculture and may eventually meet our needs, but as far as profits are concerned, we aim to devote the new farming grounds to plantations of spices and the like, crops that flourish on this land and are high yield in terms of income.'

Kyd was impressed. 'The Dutch won't like you snatching

their spice trade from under their noses. Inspired thinking, though. Cut out the middle men. The Company will jump at that notion.' Already Kyd was impressed by the foresight of Light and his officers. They were forward thinking, developing the establishment to be far more than just a company port, with the sensibilities of merchants to the potentials of this untapped paradise. The location of the island might not suit Cornwallis' preferences, but British traders would be climbing all over each other to take their pieces of its pie.

They reached the town itself, a jumble of wooden structures set on impossibly narrow alleyways, a haphazard rabbit warren. Every available space was crammed with a functional purpose: dwellings, workshops, stalls, kitchens, warehouses, storerooms, almost every structure fronted by a shop of some form or other. Up until then Kyd had thought the island deserted – yet these streets told a very different story. Where the area around the fort had been tranquil in the early morning, significant activity was taking place in this hub of activity. The streets were rammed with people and abuzz with the bustle of trade. For the first time, the major appreciated just how many people had already arrived – and most appeared to be settlers. It was abundantly clear that, whilst Europeans might hold the authority, they were in a significant minority. The vibrant life of the island lay as much in the commerce of its natives as in the China trade.

Turning into a wider street, the level of noise ratcheted up several notches. Outside every building, lined up cheek-by-jowl, were a clutter of carts and stalls offering goods for sale, raising a bewildering din, each in counterpoint to its neighbour. Behind the stalls, a step or two up from street level, were the frontages of homes, each open to reveal the dwellings were also businesses: artisans, tailors, foodshops, provision stores, toddy shops, tea houses, coffin makers, ceramic wares, cobblers, basket makers, and many other trades Kyd could only guess at. Their signs, in garish red and gold Chinese characters, hung on banners over the entrances.

'China Street' announced Light. 'The very heart of the Chinese town.'

Kyd wandered along, astonished at the variety on offer as Light pointed out the delights of the stalls, mostly of an alimentary nature. String curtains of noodles on hooks were waiting to be thrown into boiling soup along with offal and greens, to be gobbled up by hungry workers who fed themselves by means of thin wooden sticks. Meat and vegetables were tossed into huge flat cauldrons of spitting oil over open fires by men dressed in little but scanty breeches. They stirred and scraped the fiery contents over a flame so high that it threatened to cause a conflagration, of particular concern due to the proximity of the people jostling to buy. Other stalls displayed impossibly high towers of woven baskets, containing steamed buns and dumplings. Piquant spices and overpowering aromas permeated the air, making Kyd's eyes water.

'Hungry yet?' Light grinned.

'I'm not sure,' replied Kyd, his nose wrinkling in distaste.

'You will be when you taste the fare,' he assured him. 'Come, a little further. I want you to meet someone.'

Towards the centre of the street, the general chaos thinned out around a double-storey wooden house painted white and festooned with various banners. Red lanterns hung from the overhanging roof; above the entrance was a black enamelled plaque etched in characters of gold. This was far grander than the other squalid dwellings, although similar in construction.

On a large mahogany chair inlaid with mother-of-pearl (a most incongruous luxury on this dusty and noxious street, Kyd thought) sat a sturdy Chinese man surrounded by attentive lackeys. Aside from the throne-like arrangement of the scene, the man's status was further demonstrated by his silken garb: a full-length coat with mandarin collar and a skull cap on his shaven head from which hung the pigtail of the China-born settler, marking him out as a trader of some wealth. Kneeling before the merchant was a humbler Chinese, little more than a boy, dressed in dirty and shabby attire. He was in the act of kissing a large jade ring on the finger of the merchant, as if to complete the effect of quasi-royalty.

'I take it, this is the gentleman to whom you refer?' Kyd muttered.

Light nodded by way of reply. 'Mr Khoh Lay Huan, leading Chinese trader and businessman. Known locally by several names, most notably Kapitan Cina, a position of authority in the Chinese community that I recently bestowed upon him.'

Kyd observed the ceremony of obeisance taking place with both interest and the condescension of one who regards himself vastly superior to those before him. Light recognised the arrogance of the recently arrived European. The young man was permitted to rise to his feet and, clutching the tattered bag that no doubt held the totality of his worldly possessions, he was explaining something to the older man. Even at a distance and without benefit of the language, Kyd knew the younger man was desperate; he was beseeching Khoh for some favour. 'What d'you think is happening here?' he inquired of Light.

Light shrugged. 'Any number of things. Khoh is the head of the Chinese community and all look to him for help, succour and advice. I suspect the lad is newly arrived and looking for work and accommodation. He appears hungry and needy.'

At that moment, Khoh nodded, whispering curtly to one of his attendants, who took the boy by the arm and led him to a nearby stall where he was provided with a bowl of food. He wolfed it down, bowing repeatedly in the direction of his benefactor. 'Does he assist every poor Chinaman who turns up at his door in such a fashion?' Kyd asked, rather bemused. 'He must be daily inundated with wretches off the boats, all looking for a free meal!'

Light frowned. 'It is their way. We might learn from it. The Chinese who are established overseas extend help to the newly arrived as a matter of course. Everyone at some stage was a migrant. It is a practice known as *kongsi*. Mutual help. The settler receives a job or small piece of land, enough to start him off, funded by members of the community who then share in his success. It is in their interests to keep him on the right road, or their investment will prove worthless. The benefactor thus receives the loyalty of a pool of retainers who owe their very existence to him. This arrangement is the key to the speed in which new settlers establish themselves and become useful members of the community.'

'He sounds rather like a feudal lord,' Kyd mused. 'Are these fellows little more than tribal chiefs? I would worry they might become so powerful that they disdain to follow the laws of the settlement!'

'How else might a penniless migrant ever hope to be more than a coolie without such a system? Are we so different? British men prefer their own and give a leg up to a countryman, expecting favours down the line. The Company is rife with such practices. Men like Khoh control the trade and the commerce, fund new businesses and developments – and they also control the behaviour of the people in their little kingdom. Anyone who breaks the rules, steals, or behaves in an unacceptable way is soon brought into line. As a result, the Chinese are the least disruptive and most productive community on the island. I include the Europeans, who can be a mighty source of nuisance. This is why I appointed Khoh as my kapitan cina.'

'The title is some sort of functionary?'

'A kapitan is the intermediary between his community and the administration; it has been a tradition in the Malay states for centuries when dealing with settlers from other parts. The kapitan also administers justice and keeps the peace in his quarter. It's a damn sight more functional than trying to curb the excesses of some of the other rogues who've washed up here already.' Light was thinking particularly the Europeans, from rapacious merchants to drunk and disorderly sailors and soldiers.

Kyd pursed his lips in thought. 'I would like to know more about "kongsi" and this man,' he replied.

'Oh, you will, sir. For you are about to meet him and I guarantee you will be intrigued. Khoh's a wily old fox but loyal and trustworthy in his fashion. We all have stakes in the same future thus his word can be relied upon. The Chinese rarely bite the hand that feeds. Their very survival in this region depends on the security that is offered through alliance with the British.

Come, I think it is time for our audience with the *towkay* –'

Although the two men must have stood out as the only two British in the entire street, Khoh and his people had so far shown little interest in them, nor had they acknowledged their presence in any way. Yet when they finally stepped forward, all eyes fell blankly on the interlopers.

'Selamat pagi, Superintendent,' called out Kapitan Khoh.

'Selamat pagi, Kapitan. May I introduce my friend, Major Kyd, sent from Calcutta by the governor-general himself. His purpose is to examine our progress so far. I hope you will consent to speak with him and answer his questions. I will provide an interpreter to assist you.'

Khoh weighed up the tall, fair Scotsman with a keen eye. 'His skin will burn like *char sui* pork,' he replied impassively. The conversation was entirely in Malay. Kyd presumed it was an exchange of formal politeness.

'He speaks no Malay, Kapitan.' Light answered with a twinkle in his eye. 'But you are not wrong. Our weather is not kind to those as fair as he.'

Khoh chuckled. 'Have you eaten? Come, let's go inside and take some food. Men cannot talk business on empty stomachs!'

Khoh rose from his chair and beckoned them inside the reception room at the front of his house, separated from the living quarters by an ornately carved partition. More mahogany and pearl chairs lined the walls in solemn attendance. In the centre of the space, a round marble-topped table was already set with bowls of steaming soup and platters of dumplings. Servants poured tiny cups of aromatic tea. Khoh took his place, indicating to the other men to join him.

Khoh gesticulated by taking up his chopsticks and miming the act of eating. Kyd picked up his set, and then placed them back down, looking helpless. Light grinned, took his own, and demonstrated. Kyd tried again and failed. With a wave of his hand, Khoh called for fork and spoon. An embarrassed Major Kyd suspected the whole charade had been done on purpose for the amusement of the Kapitan – and perhaps the superintendent, too.

As Light had said, the food was unexpectedly appetising: light, fresh, flavoursome, and oddly suited as breakfast fare. Even the perfumed tea complimented the dishes, cleansing the palate of the aromatic flavours. After they had done justice to their bowls – in silence for it seemed impolite to talk business during eating – cutlery was set down and Khoh folded his arms across his prosperous belly, ready to begin. Their conversation took some time, for each remark had to be relayed in two languages and occasionally a third, if Khoh could not express himself in Malay. In that case he brought over a flunky who translated into either fluent Malay or very poor English for their benefit.

The gist of the following audience was that Kapitan Khoh was willing to be interviewed about his community. He would provide guides to show the British major around the Chinese village. He was curious why the major had been sent from India, demonstrating his shrewdness; Khoh understood this was not a social trip.

'Your governor in Calcutta – why he not yet agree to treaty?' Khoh asked bluntly, unafraid to rush in where others feared to tread.

'These matters take time, sir,' Kyd replied guardedly.

Khoh harrumphed. 'Take too long then someone else will and island gone! Let me tell you something, Major. Many Chinese people come here. Work hard. They already live other places under Malays, Bugis and Dutch. They no want that anymore. But if your Company not make up mind trouble coming from outside. People will leave. You all fools to waste this chance! This good place. Superintendent Light good man. That is what Chinese people say.'

His case was simply made but who could argue with him? Light could scarcely restrain a smile at Khoh's accurate assessment. He had been saying much the same to the Council in every letter he wrote to Bengal. It was of particular significance that the same advice was now emanating from the leader of the largest community on the island. But then, Light had known exactly what Khoh would say. They had discussed this meeting at length in the days before Kyd's arrival. Not that Light had coached Khoh in what to say, very much the opposite. The Chinese leader had simply stated exactly what he believed. Laid down so bluntly, it validated Light's own entreaties to Lord Cornwallis.

'I would also very much like to consult with you on a recent legal matter. You have experience of administering justice in your own community, so your views are most welcome on the subject,' began Light at one point. The change of direction took Kyd by surprise. Was Light currying favour with the Chinese merchant or did he value his judgement – even in matters of legal decisions?

It transpired that recently two Siamese settlers had been arrested on charges of murder. They were accused of beating to death one of their own compatriots who – or so they claimed – had cheated them of all their savings. The men did not deny their involvement in the man's death, insisting that they had merely intended to recover their money by frightening him, but during the resulting scuffle, he had hit his head on a stone and died. Superintendent Light had no authority in capital cases; the two Siamese were to be dispatched to Bengal for sentencing. Yet before he did so, Light wished to examine the matter thoroughly, for the dead man had a reputation for criminal deceit and had been for some time preying on his unfortunate fellow countrymen. By all accounts, he had been a most despicable fellow, roundly condemned by all.

Khoh was familiar with the case and the concern it had raised amongst the Siamese, all of whom took the side of the two men. The lads had young families and were regarded as justified in their actions. 'English law no good for these men. Chinese kill Chinese – must judge by Chinese tradition. Same with Siamese. In Siam you cheat someone, then you die. No one blames these men. That man cheat many people. Got what he deserved,' Khoh reasoned.

'But a man is dead, Kapitan. Surely you cannot expect them to walk away free?' Light argued.

Khoh pulled a face. 'I know man is dead. I understand law is law. But if you go too hard, Siam people will be restless. They not understand why you see it different. To Siamese – simple: he stole money from poor people. They kill him. End of story.'

It seemed to Kyd that these people had no idea of civilised justice. But Light seemed intrigued by what Khoh had to say. 'Is there a possible middle ground, sir, in which we might ease the sensibilities of the Siamese, whilst addressing the requirements of British law? You have lived a long time in Siam, as have I. Manslaughter – even accidental – is usually punished in some form or other. What would you expect of a Siamese judiciary?'

Khoh thought for a while, sipping on a cup of tea, swirling the leaves thoughtfully. 'Slavery or hard labour for a period of time.'

Light concurred. 'I agree, Kapitan. I thought as much myself. Whilst it is hard on the families, these men might one day return when their sentence is served. I shall propose such a penalty to the Council when the time comes. This has been most helpful, Kapitan Khoh. Where possible, we should align our punishments with those natural to the native communities.'

Both men seemed satisfied. Light had given Khoh respect and had taken note of his suggestions. Kyd wondered how such a process would be understood in Bengal. Yet he could not deny that the riots and rebellions that occurred in India against the British usually began when local traditions and beliefs were denied or ignored. Perhaps there was something in this collaborative approach that they might learn from?

The interlude only served to increase Kyd's curiosity about Khoh's origins. The man did not seem educated or refined in any way – he was certainly no mandarin – but he was patently intelligent and had made a lot of money through trade. Kyd's only experience in the East so far was in Calcutta, where there were few Chinese. Those recently arrived were a secretive and reclusive lot. He wanted to know more about these enigmatic people.

'If I may ask, what brought you to the island, Kapitan Khoh?'

Khoh grinned. 'I have lived many lives in many places, Major. One day perhaps I tell you my story. For now, it is enough to know that I was living in Queddah where life for Chinese was uncomfortable. Captain Light – as he was known then – offered me and my people a safe place on the island. We owe him much. We repay him with our labour to build this fine new place.' Kyd suspected that behind the scant explanation lay a fascinating tale. He hoped Light might fill him in later.

With much bowing and ceremony, and a gift of an exquisite lacquer box containing preserved fruits, the audience came to an end. It was agreed that the following week, the major would spend some time in the company of Khoh's assistants.

As they left, Kyd observed to Light: 'Should I have bought a gift?'

Light shrugged. 'Probably. Next time. Khoh does not expect British people to know his customs. He's not like some of the locals who are mortally offended if their complex protocols are ignored. In fact, he is rather the opposite, keen to learn for himself how European society works. That is why he is so singular, for the average Chinese has great disdain for western ways. Perhaps Khoh does too, but he also knows that acquiring knowledge of our culture will serve him well in doing business with us. For he intends to, make no mistake. His new wife recently bore him a son. He told me that when the boy is old enough, he will learn English. That the child will play with my children and those of the other British on the island. He has high hopes for this boy in the next generation, able to deal directly with the British on equal terms. Chinese think ahead. Everything they do is for the future of their family. I respect his foresight greatly.'

Major Kyd thought it highly unlikely that Chinese gentlemen might one day dress in western clothes and grace the elegant salons of Calcutta. But such aspirations were beneficial if they opened trading links with these consummate Asian merchants.

Such men might be the key to dealing with China, that notoriously difficult environment for westerners. If, as a result, they chose to forsake their traditions and mimic English ways, so much the better. The Romans had recognised the value of winning over the local people; it was even more important than military conquest in the long run. A similar process was taking place in India where rajahs and nawabs fawned over the British and aspired to their gentlemanly lifestyle. Why not here?

As the two British gentlemen withdrew with as much stately courtesy as they could muster, soaked in sweat and red-faced as they were, towkay Kapitan Khoh observed their departure with wry amusement. He had plenty of time for Superintendent Light, but this major was another pompous fool whose long nose was perfectly shaped for looking down on others. No matter. Khoh would have the last laugh.

3

An Evening with the Worthies

Light Residence, Martinha's Lane, George Town. 29th May 1787

The family home of Francis Light was set some distance from those of the officers, a fair walk from the fort. It stood alone down a trodden path with an excellent outlook on the sea. A torrential shower had only recently eased, leaving the track puddled with rainwater, mud splashing on Kyd's freshly polished boots. Yet the afternoon rains were welcome, and the brightening sky already promised a balmy evening, ideal for dinner by the sea.

Major Kyd reflected on the house ahead, a bungalow charmingly decorated in what he presumed was the Malay style; he had noticed similar features on the house of James Scott. It was raised on stilts, encircled by a stout wooden veranda. The roof was high and gabled, tiled rather than thatched, setting it out as the house of a family of means. The main structure was flanked by smaller extensions as if rooms had been gradually added to the original shell. The wall panels were intricately decorated with carvings of a floral nature; the windows were framed by similarly ornate shutters; and bright arrangements of flowers dotted the exterior walls. As he was admiring the agreeable appointment of house, a squelching on the track to his rear alerted him to the arrival of another person.

'By process of elimination, you must be Major Kyd, by which

I mean I do not know you and, as the only doctor on the island, I can vouch for everyone else!' shouted a cheery voice. Kyd saw an earnest fellow, a little younger than himself, striding purposefully through the puddles to join him.

With his habitual charm, Kyd answered: 'May you diagnose your patients with the same exactitude, sir! I am indeed Major Alexander Kyd, the infernal nuisance sent by Bengal to interfere with your peaceful lives. Please call me Sandy. Everyone does,' and he extended a hand which the doctor shook warmly, a little too warmly perhaps. It was impossible to keep one's hands from sweating in this climate.

'Doctor James Hutton at your service. It's a pleasure to make your acquaintance. I knew your cousin Colonel Kyd when I was assistant surgeon in Calcutta. An admirable fellow.'

Kyd bowed. 'Another Scot then! By any chance are you related to –'

Hutton grinned broadly. 'Sadly not, sir. The great James Hutton, doctor and scientist, is not one of my kin, despite the similarity of our names. I am a mere ship surgeon from Lanarkshire with the good fortune to rise in Company service. You should feel at home here for the Scots are thick upon the ground on Prince of Wales Island.'

'We are a wandering tribe these days. You cannae walk a step either in Calcutta or here without bumping into an Hibernian brother!'

With that, the two men strolled in amicable conversation towards the entrance where their presence had already come to the notice of Lucy Ann. 'Major Sandy! Major Sandy! Welcome to our house!'

***

Miss Lydia Hardwick was in her element. Tonight's formal dinner was exactly the occasion she had hoped for: the bachelor community on display – and she the only female in sight. That is if one discounted the near-invisible Mrs Light, whose presence at dinner was, in Lydia's opinion, somewhat controversial. The superintendent's 'wife' should have remained out of sight with her children. Such a thing would never have occurred in Calcutta.

Having come down early with the girls who were now galivanting outside eager to spot their guests, Lydia had selected a shady seat where the late afternoon sun cast her fair skin in a diffused golden glow. A gentle breeze wafted her brown curls in a most becoming fashion. She waved her fan languorously, whilst adjusting the folds of her pale pink muslin to best effect – and waited for the gentlemen to arrive.

First the military: Lieutenant James Gray of the marines and Captain John Glass, commander of the garrison. Of the two, Gray was by far the more appealing, due to his handsome moustaches and bright blue eyes – and the fact he was an Englishman. Captain Glass was yet another Scot, acceptable, but not her first preference. Furthermore, John Glass had a chiselled hatchet of a face which constantly bore a stern expression suggesting a rigid man who would not be easy to influence. On the other hand, he held the senior position and was close confidant to Superintendent Light, so Lydia did not entirely discount him.

Behind came was Felipe Rozells with his genial smile. He embraced his nieces and bowed politely to Miss Hardwick. Her reserved tilt of the head was carefully orchestrated to discourage further conversation. Mr Rozells was not a candidate for her 'dance' card.

The arrival of Major Kyd caused a flutter of interest around the room, as well in Miss Lydia's virginal bosom, for not only was he an exceedingly fine-looking fellow (especially for a Scot) but he was from a family of note. Sadly, however, the major was already wed, reportedly smitten with his beautiful wife, even if she was half-native, or so they said.

Lydia gave only passing attention to Dr James Hutton who had followed unnoticed in Major Kyd's wake. He had little to favour him either in looks, fortune or origin, being an earnest but lowly Scottish ship doctor. On their heels came Mr James Scott – the richest man on the island – said to have several 'wives', although none 'official' in any sense that mattered. Miss Hardwick was not averse to marrying a man of mature years, however, even one as unappealing as Scott, if the fortune was sufficiently large.

That left the young writer, Mr Nathaniel Bacon, and the grizzled captain William Lindesay – the former young and penniless, the sea captain insignificant.

'May I offer you a glass of sherry, Miss Hardwick?' Lieutenant Gray approached, two glasses in hand.

'Why, how very kind of you, sir! Please take a seat – and Captain Glass, why don't you join us? This is such a charming spot to catch the breeze.'

***

The convivial evening commenced with aperitifs on the veranda with its excellent outlook where the party gathered around small tables on cane chairs scattered the length of the terrace. The young girls bobbed in and out or played on the sparse grass that fronted the property before it gave way to sand. They were allowed to attend the early part of the evening on the strict understanding that when the adults went in to dine, they would say their farewells and retire.

The superintendent circulated graciously, introducing Major Kyd before moving on lest the eager audience monopolise his distinguished guest. He steered the major carefully round James Scott, who nodded curtly from a distance, raising his Scotch in the direction. No doubt that interview would come later once Scott had taken his own measure of the man.

'Superintendent, if I may?' Dr Hutton drew Light aside while Kyd was speaking to the officers.

'Have we a problem? An outbreak of disease?' Light questioned anxiously.

Hutton shook his head. 'No, thank God. It has been relatively quiet of late at the hospital. I merely wished to inquire of your health. You've still not gained your full weight, nor can I refrain from noticing the dark shadows about your eyes. How are you faring?' A few months before, Light had been laid low with a particularly debilitating attack of fever, a condition that had plagued him off and on for years. This bout had been the worst so far.

'I'm as fit as a fiddle, dear James. Don't worry about me. It's not the fever but the infernal problems of governing without sufficient support or monetary provision that keep me up at night. I'm afraid I burn the candle at both ends just to keep up, unfortunately not in the sense of carousing as might once have been the case!'

Hutton shook his head in disapproval. 'Men have died from hard work too, Francis. You must beseech Calcutta to send more men. You cannot run this settlement singlehanded! It is not a ship.'

Light grinned wryly. 'A ship has a full complement of officers, dear Hutton. The captain is but the end of the line. Here on this island, I am superintendent, secretary, administrator, judge, architect, fiscal officer, and all! With a little good luck, however, I shall receive a few reliable fellows anon, although they may well be men for whom they can find no other use. An incompetent man is worse than none at all!'

The doctor agreed. He was constantly requesting doctors, but poorly trained orderlies were all he had received so far. 'Perhaps Major Kyd's survey will prove helpful in emphasising these issues to the Council.'

'We live in hope, sir. Now if you'll excuse me, I must ensure the major meets our other guests.' With that, Light moved away, leaving the doctor with the distinct impression that the superintendent's health was not a subject he wished to discuss. Hutton sighed and made his way to the decanters. He had tried his best. From now on, he would enjoy the occasion and sample the delights on offer.

***

Alexander Kyd assessed the dinner guests, approving of the array of the island's notables: soldiers, doctor, mariner, merchant, and Company man. There was also a local trader, acceptable for he was a Christian gentleman and a relative to the superintendent, but a native for all that. Kyd looked forward to an interesting exchange of opinions and, hopefully, adequate fare after several days of local food. The complementary beauty of the two ladies was also a treat for his eyes: pale, auburn-haired Miss Hardwick (whose rapacity for a husband was sadly all too obvious) and the delicate dusky fragility of the enigmatic Mrs Light.

His mood was subsequently improved by the unexpected quality of the food. After several days of curry and the like, it was a delight to dine upon western dishes: soup, fish, lamb and poultry washed down with excellent vintages. The dinner guests were soon enlivened by the fine cuisine and the liberal pouring of wine.

'Major Kyd, you must have your finger on the pulse. How fares the situation with the French these days? I hear they are beset with financial woes. Perhaps that will keep them out of our hair for a while?' asked Hutton as he tucked into a plate piled high with meat and vegetables; the limited budget allocated for the hospital and his personal living precluded him from such delights. His cheeks were already ruby-red from the wine.

Kyd put down his glass and leaned back in his chair, elegantly dabbing at his lips with his napkin. 'Never count out the Frenchies, sir! This is when they are at their most dangerous. There's nothing like a foreign adventure to distract the seething masses at home. Cornwallis is watching the situation, for whatever happens back in France is sure to be played out on the world stage by-and-by. I'm afraid we are not finished with their menace yet, good doctor!'

'I wholeheartedly agree,' broke in Light himself. 'I was once a prisoner of the French. Their ambitions in the East are deep-seated. I would never trust even the most genial Frenchman. Not even those in residence on Prince of Wales Island, for I have long suspected them of being in league with their navy elsewhere in the East.' Light took a sip of his wine before continuing. Every eye was upon him; it was rare for the superintendent to comment in public.

'The *Speedwell* was not only sent to India to collect my girls. On the way out, Captain Lindesay dropped off some of our French priests at Pondicherry, much to my relief. Monseigneur Garnault, the meddlesome leader of the Catholic community here is to become the Bishop of Siam and Queddah, and the initiation ceremony is to be held in India. Let's hope he stays there! Good riddance, I say. I don't trust any Frenchman in these waters, clerical collar, or no.' It was a mark of Light's deep mistrust of the priest, despite his wife's fondness for him. Kyd noted, however, that Martinha merely cast her husband an indulgent glance, as if he were a wayward child. Very little escaped the major's keen eye. Did she speak English? Perhaps she had not understood?

'Can't say I blame you, sir. The French are a menace. There's war ahead, I'm convinced of it. The last one did not resolve matters,' Kyd replied in full agreement.

For the first time, James Scott spoke. 'There's always war ahead, Major, and when it comes the French will invariably be in the pudding. You're astute in your judgement. I commend you most heartily, sir.' A frisson of surprise fluttered around the table at Scott's unusually fulsome approach. Before the evening had begun, he had been strictly warned by Superintendent Light to avoid offending the visitor whose good opinion was vital for the future of the settlement. He had been as good as his word. Scott smirked into his glass, aware this praise had been on the edge of unctuous, the better to keep to his brief whilst also demonstrating that his docility was under sufferance.

It was time for a change of tone. 'I've recently been in correspondence with your cousin, Major. He has great ambitions for a Botanical Gardens in Calcutta, I believe?' Light began. It was a suitably safe topic, one that flattered Kyd's family and gave him a chance to show off.

'The project is his great obsession. Robert hopes that not only will it create a veritable Garden of Eden, but it will also contribute to our scientific and medical knowledge. The forests of Asia provide a wondrous pharmacopeia could we but identify all the curative properties of its flora and fauna. What services does cousin Robert request, if I may ask, sir?'

Light responded with a roll of his eyes. 'Samples. A myriad different species, although Colonel Kyd did not specify the particulars as he is uninformed about the botany of the island. Thus, he wants samples of everything. Furthermore, he insists that we collect plants and trees *before* we clear each section of jungle lest we inadvertently cause irretrievable destruction to any one variety. It is the colonel's wish – approved by the Council – that seeds, spices, bushes and trees from all over Asia might one day be grown here, not only for the purposes of trade but also for medicine and science. It is a most worthy endeavour,' Light added as an afterthought in case he had given the impression that the request had been burdensome, although it had been in the extreme, another task loaded on his already full plate.

The major chuckled. 'I know my cousin well, sir. He can be devilishly single-minded. It would never occur to him that you have a thousand other duties to attend to, most of which somewhat more pressing than his botanicals! But, in his favour, I must add that I believe we need men of passion quite as much as men of business and war. For are we not put on earth to improve the lot of mankind as well as to benefit from its bounty?' he finished with a flourish that gained a buzz of approval from the other diners.

'Forgive me if I sounded peevish, Major Kyd. Scott and I are of the same mind about the suitability of the land here for sustaining crops indigenous to other islands –' Light observed.

'Although never let it be said that James Scott acted out of altruism!' Scott interjected with a gurgle of amusement. 'Where the colonel sees good works, I see Spanish dollars. Not all men can afford his scruples.'

'Quite so, quite so. It takes men of every ilk, no doubt,' Dr Hutton broke in wisely before Scott might have the chance to be even more scathing. 'And have you so far made much progress in assembling the specimens, superintendent?'

'Lieutenant Gray has been sending marines out daily. We have quite an array already. The colonel has given detailed instructions on how to protect the plants during the return voyage so we must construct various cases and prepare bottles. I wonder if you might look in at the warehouse and give the benefit of your knowledge, doctor? You may be able to identify some of the samples from your own experiments. The *Dolphin Hoy* sails next week.'

'I would be delighted, my dear Superintendent. 'I shall look in tomorrow and see if my scant knowledge may be of any use.' Dr Hutton replied. It would be a welcome change for venereal diseases and broken bones, he thought to himself.

'And may I speak for us all when I say many thanks are due to Lieutenant Gray and his worthy marines!' chimed in Miss Lydia

Hardwick, casting the said officer a winsome smile whilst raising her glass in appreciation. 'Such a great enterprise for the health of the nation!' she gushed excessively. Gray bathed in the glow of her approbation, oblivious to the amusement of the others.

When the congratulations had died down, Major Kyd ventured a question of his own. 'I had the pleasure of a morning walk with the superintendent today. We enjoyed an "audience" (I must call it that because the fellow had a distinctly regal court although in the most incongruous of locations) with a very interesting Chinese merchant. I believe "towkay" is the right expression? Name of Khoh. He's a significant figure on the island, is he not?'

Captain John Glass, the commander of the island's garrison answered. Not generally a man given to social intercourse, being of a reserved and serious nature, he felt on home ground when speaking of the island's communities. 'Khoh is a most useful person. As the Kapitan Cina, the Chinese community is entirely in the palm of his hands. As a result of his support, these Chinamen are the most biddable settlers on the island. They are also the most industrious. Their productivity and ingenuity are impressive. But Khoh needs watching. He would take us for a ride if he could. It would be foolish to accept these local fellows at face value,' Glass added gruffly.

Kyd caught the tilt of Light's chin at this remark. Light had already implied that there was not as much tolerance amongst the Europeans towards the native peoples.

'Do other settler groups have their own Kapitans, or is it just the Chinese?' Kyd added. He wished to pry open this subject further. It might be revelatory.

Glass nodded. 'Aye, sir. We have a Kapitan Chulia, as we

call him, who represents the Indian Muslim traders from the Coromandel, known here as Chulias. They are another community eager to work with the Company. They keep order amongst their people on account that harmony is necessary for good business. So far, I'm afraid we've had less success, however, with the Malays, the Burmans and the Siamese. They are not given to hard work and disciplined behaviour.'

Across the table, for the first time that evening, a frown passed over the perfect features of Mrs Light. Her lips tightened in annoyance at the captain's insinuation. So, thought Kyd, she does understand English. There was more going on inside her pretty head than he had at first considered.

'I beg pardon, Captain, but if I may take a different position? The Malays, Siamese, Burmans and others are small in number, mostly poor farmers or fisherman, whereas the Chinese and the Chulias are merchants and skilled craftsmen. We are not quite comparing like with like,' spoke up Felipe Rozells. He felt compelled to interject, not only for the sake of his sister's sensibilities, but also for his own. He was not as reticent these days as in his youth; proximity to the English had not endeared him to them. He was tired of their arrogance. 'In time, I am sure they will also organise in similar ways, but we must first attend to their basic needs and educate them if we wish for a useful population in which all communities have a place.'

'Quite so, Mr Rozells,' replied Kyd, eager to win the favour of the superintendent's wife. 'Exposure to the Christian missionaries will assist in civilising these peoples in the future,' Kyd suggested. He noted, however, that Mrs Light merely fixed him a piercing stare. His gambit had not worked.

'As long as the missionaries are not French, sir,' muttered Scott. 'That's all we need, the locals hands-in-glove with Frenchies!' A titter of laughter rippled around the table; the awkward moment circumvented.

The desserts eaten, Martinha rose to her feet, curtseying to the party and extending a hand to Lydia, who made a show of gathering up her fan and skirts with a giddy smile. 'Promise to behave yourselves, gentlemen! Not too much brandy, I pray!'

With only two ladies in retirement, the table numbers did not reduce significantly but the atmosphere took a distinct change. As Light circled the table, pouring healthy snifters of brandy and handing out cigars, the men gratefully unfastened buttons and cravats, mopped their brows, and lounged at ease in their chairs.

'Mr Rozells, you speak of a need for welfare and education, but your settlement is still in its infancy,' Kyd said, returning to the former topic. 'From my observations, there is much to be done on its immediate needs before refinements can be considered: the fort is in a dreadful state of disrepair, more roads and bridges are needed, and the agricultural needs of a growing populace must be provided. Superintendent Light spoke of current food shortages. Surely these are the primary aims in the immediate future?'

Scott took the bait, aware that the others – as Company servants in one form or other – would not feel at liberty to comment, whilst he loved nothing more than to pronounce on Company failures. 'The administration needs more investment from Bengal. In hard coin, Major. An establishment cannot flourish on promises alone. If development seems lacking to you, then it is because the funds have not been provided. I know for a fact that Superintendent Light is paid a mere pittance yet dips into his own purse to fund many of our projects. Take the shortage of supplies. Do you know why this has occurred? Are you aware of the Council's contribution to this state of affairs?'

Kyd, raised his hands as if to call a truce. 'Forgive me, sir, if I spoke from ignorance. I am indeed aware that the Sultan of Queddah is holding back rice and other food stuffs until the treaty is ratified by Bengal and he receives his due payment for the lease of the island.'

Scott grunted his acceptance of the apology. 'And who can blame him? The sultan has kept to his agreement. But not for long, I warn you. The Dutch are sniffing at his court promising inducements if he allows them to drive us out and hand the island to them. I beseech you, Major Kyd, to stress in your report that the treaty is a matter of urgency, or this new-born settlement will not survive infancy.'

The general intake of breath was appreciable, but nobody gainsaid his opinion. Nathaniel Bacon, the youngest at scarcely nineteen years old, on his first Company appointment, dropped his head in embarrassment, picking at crumbs on his side plate. He felt awkward at such a gathering, acutely aware that he was only there to make up numbers. This turn in the conversation only sharpened his discomfort. Yet one year on the island had shown him Scott's assessment was entirely accurate.

'But I hear the Hollanders have problems of their own these days,' Kyd countered, not to be entirely contradicted. 'Some matter of a Dutch fort captured by the Bugis? Perchance this will keep them occupied in the southern Straits and away from the island?' Kyd was well informed. He had spent the voyage reading reports on the island.

For the first time, Light commented. 'You are correct, sir. A Dutch possession in the Riau archipelago was recently taken by Bugis and Illanun forces. The Sultan of Johor may have played a hand in it, too. The Dutch may indeed be facing problems in the south but it does not follow it will end their northern ambitions. In fact, it may only increase their need for an island stronghold away from Bugis interference.'

Light point was incontrovertible. Kyd stroked his chin in thought. 'You mentioned Illanun? Who are they? I do not think I have heard of these people.'

The rest of the diners knew them only too well. 'They are pirates, sir,' piped up William Lindesay, captain of the *Speedwell*. As a seasoned trader in the region, the subject of the Illanun was close to his heart. 'Fearsome pirates. They hail from far in the east, in the islands of Sulu. Unlike the Bugis and the *orang laut* – who are given to brigandage at times – these fellows are warriors whose sole purpose in life is to raid and slaughter. They arrive each year on speedy perahus and bring terror into the lives of the people of the South China Sea. Their brutality knows no bounds. Their major booty is slaves; they are no respecter of persons. Many a British sailor has ended his life as oarsman on one of their boats.'

'If they are from Sulu then it would appear they are very far from home in the Straits,' observed Kyd.

'Just so, Sandy,' added Light, using his personal name for the first time. 'Perhaps we should fear this development more than all the infernal intrigues of the Dutch and French put together. Does it mean the Illanun have set their sights on the wealth of the Straits? They may be mere mercenaries for the time being, but like the Bugis before them, it may not be long before they develop a taste for settling. And if the Sultan of Queddah offers them employment? Where does that leave us?'

His concerns were shared by all. This was something new to Kyd – and of great significance to the future of the settlement. Cornwallis was reluctant to invest too much in Prince of Wales Island which he considered an unsuitable site for his much-needed naval base. Nor did he think the Sultan of Queddah much of an opponent for a few British warships and a platoon of marines. These Illanun pirates, however, posed a significant threat. On the other hand, the prospect of an indigenous conflict might deter Cornwallis altogether and lead to withdrawal from Prince of Wales Island. Who knew where his mind might go?

'Interesting information, gentlemen. I have much to learn, that is clear. Your intelligence is vital. I hope you understand my role here is not to increase your problems. The very opposite. This island is a pearl – and I have not yet embarked upon my survey! I will do all in my power to promote your cause. Superintendent, may Captain Lindesay be spared for a few weeks? He would be enormously helpful on the *Viper* when Lt Blair arrives. He knows these waters in and out.'

William Lindesay beamed with delight. 'I would be most honoured, sir. Superintendent –' His head shot in Light's direction for approval.

Light jumped up, decanter in his hand. 'I insist upon it! Lindesay's the man for the job! Who better than a country captain with fifteen years in these waters! Let's have another round to celebrate!'

If Light's manner was artificially gay, it was to be expected.

A potentially awkward evening had passed without major issue. Important matters had been raised and dealt with delicately. Major Kyd was more competent than Light had expected. Beneath the effusive charm and elegant manners, was a man of integrity. While Light did not intend to drop his guard, this visit might prove of great value. Even Scott had been more gracious than usual.

Playing up the Illanun threat had been a stroke of genius. It was vital to strike a balance in the dithering mind of Cornwallis between the suitability of the island and the potential threats to the China trade should the Straits fall into hostile hands. As the evening wound to its close, Light felt he had negotiated potential pitfalls. Major Kyd was a man with whom he could deal.

***

In the parlour, an uneasy silence reigned. Miss Hardwick made a few attempts at conversation with Martinha Rozells and her mother, both engaged in needlework, but her comments had been received with only fixed smiles. It was evident neither woman spoke any English. She herself knew no more than a few phrases in Bengali, enough to command the servants in Calcutta, but of Malay she understood not a single word. Nor did she have any intention to learn beyond what was strictly necessary.

There was no piano to amuse herself (and demonstrate her accomplishments) so instead she browsed the bookshelf, selecting a novel in English. Pouring out a glass of port, she settled down to read. It was odd that Superintendent Light should have such a book. It was not easy to imagine him reading Miss Burney's

Evelina, nor were his daughters old enough for such a tale. But who else might have any interest in the book in this household?

4
Family Matters

The Fort, Tanjong Penaga, Prince of Wales Island. Late July 1787

The *Viper* arrived and Kyd departed on his survey of the island. Light hoped for a spell when he might focus on the repairs to the fort that he and Glass had planned, a proposal that had gained the wholehearted approval of the major. For the time being, he would implement the changes at his own expense whilst submitting his claim to the Council citing Kyd's backing of the venture and his need to move rapidly before potential attack from elsewhere. Enough had already been said about the Sultan, the Dutch and the French to force the Council's hand.

But Light was not allowed a period of calm. The long-awaited arrival of the *Ravensworth* from Bencoolen brought further complications. The expected convict labour Light had been promised, earmarked for building and land clearance works, proved to be nothing of the sort. The superintendent was incandescent with rage to discover he had in fact been delivered 126 miserable slaves, not one a convict. These pitiful human beings had been selected merely because shipping them off to die elsewhere saved Bencoolen the expense of digging their graves. It was both a heartless act of inhumanity and a flagrant insult to Light. The Company was fulfilling its overdue promises in name only.

A small number of these sorry souls had died on the journey, or soon after disembarking; the rest were almost all in need of medical care, or at the very least rest and proper nourishment. Light immediately commandeered the services of the hospital and the good will of the Catholic community, led by Martinha and her mother. The admirable Dr Hutton attended to their needs with as much solicitude as he would have offered to the soldiers; he had been distraught at the flagrant abuse these poor unfortunates had suffered. It was to his great credit that he would not even allow them to be assessed until they were given time to recover and convalesce.

Light seethed at this extra burden on his already straitened treasury. A hundred and twenty-six new souls to feed and house, clothe and cure and not even one yet able to contribute! He spoke most sternly to Captain Roddam of the *Ravensworth,* who merely shrugged. He was but the messenger; the slaves had been in bad shape when they boarded. His men had done what little they could for them on the voyage.

Penning a stern letter of complaint to the Council, Light knew his case was futile. Even if they did address the matter, it would be weeks before it was tabled for discussion – and months more before he could hope for a response. Even then, it would most likely result in another exercise in the passing of responsibility onto others.

When Glass eventually interviewed the surviving Bencoolen slaves, he discovered that, of the fifty-eight men, over half were coolies, marking them out for heavy manual labour, yet Dr Hutton insisted only ten percent of the entire group was able for such work. A handful had useful skills: brickmakers, sawers, shipwrights, and boatswains known as *tindals*.

One fellow, Marlbro, was of particular interest; his given trade was 'doctor'. Marlbro had proved enormously helpful as an orderly around the wards, so Hutton suggested he might stay on in the capacity of assistant. The doctor also took some of the females, particularly the more mature ones, those who had shown an aptitude for caring. Yet Marlbro, a man in his mid-thirties of upright bearing and soft-spoken but reticent manner, remained an enigma. What manner of doctor might he once have been? A local medicine man? Or did he have formal training? Who knew what kind of man might wash up on a slaver?

But nevertheless, only twenty had any trade to speak of, with the rest largely unfit for hard labour, leaving thirty-eight men to be gainfully employed elsewhere. The majority were Caffrees from Africa, a further obstacle. There would be a reluctance amongst the island communities to accept such people as house slaves. The European belief that Africans were dangerous and unpredictable, especially around women, was widely held; even the Chinese and Indians were wary of them. It would not be difficult to find employment for the women and children – sixty-eight in total, although some were very young. Light had no wish to exploit little ones.

Light decided on a compromise that he hoped would sway local opposition. He selected those who might be seen as troublesome, either by dint of their age, size or general countenance, and brought them into his own household. He encouraged Martinha to do similar with the women. If they set an example, then others might follow. Domestic help was always in short supply. Furthermore, these slaves were free labour.

For his own part, Light had long had a mind to build an official residence near his family home. The recent influx of dignitaries, such as Kyd and Blair, had demonstrated that an *atap* dwelling at the fort – or even his own agreeable native-style bungalow – were inadequate if the island was to present an image of a thriving British establishment. These Caffrees would be ideal for the less onerous task of constructing a government house and laying out decent gardens. There were even bricklayers and sawers amongst them. Perhaps he might turn this sorry business in his favour after all?

It would be necessary, however, to keep a watch on those farmed out to residents. Many might presume they had carte blanche to take advantage, particularly of the women. He would not stand for that. It was yet another potential public order issue that might blow up like a mishandled powder keg, There were enough acts of civil disobedience and rowdiness already, particularly amongst the European community.

A polite knock at the door and the welcome voice of Felipe Rozells afforded him the opportunity to take a break from his concerns. Light was inordinately fond of his mild-mannered and steadfast brother-in-law. 'Come, come, dear Felipe! What say you to a glass of wine? Or would you prefer brandy?'

Rozells stepped in with a diffident smile. 'Wine for me, Francis. I hope I am not disturbing you. I merely wish to return those letters you asked me to prepare. I do not intend to keep you from your work –'

'Nonsense. I am more than ready to cast this all aside. The letters? You are the best of fellows, Felipe! I wish all my staff were as assiduous as you – and for all this, you receive not a penny in remuneration.' Light accepted the parcel of mail and set it down for later despatch. It would need little amendment. Felipe was never less than accurate in his correspondence.

His brother-in-law helped him where he could, mostly transcribing documents from Siamese or Malay, or preparing fine copy. His hand was much better than the superintendent's. Rozells was not officially part of the island administration, a mutual decision from the start. A Eurasian secretary would always be relegated to the position of lowly functionary within Company hierarchy; Francis had insisted it was time for Felipe to strike out on his own as a merchant trader. He had acquired the necessary skills in his years working for Light and Scott Esquires.

It had proved a wise decision; Felipe was making a good living from his commercial ventures, particularly in his dealings with the Chinese, Malay and Indian communities who respected his integrity. They were also drawn to him because he had the superintendent's ear. That could only be good for business.

'I hope you don't intend to sit at your desk all night, sir,' observed Felipe as he settled down with his glass of wine. 'Martinha tells me you do not take enough rest. Sometimes you work late into the night!'

Light scoffed away his concern. 'I spuddle away as usual, flitting from this matter to that, rarely completing anything to my satisfaction. Just as I set myself to one pressing task, another jumps up that is even more urgent. But I'm never too busy for family. Tell me, what news?'

Felipe sank back, took another gulp of wine, and rubbed a nervous hand across his jaw. 'As a matter of fact, my secondary purpose is to ask your advice. On a personal matter. If you can spare some of your precious time …'

It was evident from his hangdog look that Felipe was embarrassed, so much so he was unable to meet his brother-in-law eye-to-eye.

'Spit it out, Felipe! Whatever's gnawing your vitals, it's better out than in.'

'Er …'

Light leaned over with a brotherly hand on his shoulder. 'May I be so bold as to venture a guess? Does this matter concern … a woman?' It was unlikely to be a business matter, for Felipe was cautious and never took undue risks. But he was shy in his dealings with the fairer sex and had remained so far unwed, highly unusual for a man in these parts at the age of seven-and-twenty.

Felipe uttered a strange gurgling sound as if he were both choking and clearing his throat at the same time. 'Several, to be exact,' he muttered when he found his voice again.

'Several?' Light laughed out loud, amused by the unlikely notion of Felipe Rozells caught in scandalous business with several women. 'Good God, Felipe, are you catching up on lost opportunities?'

Felipe bridled at his brother-in-law's reaction. 'It's no laughing matter, Francis. I did not expect you to relish my dilemma.'

Francis forced his face into an expression of concern. 'Excuse me, dear brother, for I am lightheaded with lack of sleep. My remark was wholly uncalled for. Take a deep breath and tell me exactly what has transpired.'

Felipe nodded, took another drink, and proceeded. 'When I say several women, I do not mean I am involved with them in an amatory sense. Well, not all of them. Actually, none of them to be exact. I would never compromise a woman's virtue –'

'Felipe! Get to your point and stop rambling. List the women one by one and explain in what way they are causing you a problem!'

He filled up Felipe's empty glass in the vain hope that wine might loosen his tongue.

'Recently,' Felipe began, 'a number of families have arrived from Melaka, even though the Dutch have forbade migration to Pinang ... I mean, Prince of Wales Island.'

'No need to correct yourself, Felipe. It is Pulau Pinang to us. Go on ...'

'These poor folk are mostly Eurasians who have taken circuitous routes so as to not be apprehended by the Dutch authorities. We're doing all we can for them within the church community –'

'The women, Felipe? Get to the women,' Light reminded him gently.

'Ah yes, the women. Well, recently when I was in Melaka, I was approached by a fellow who claimed to be a relative. He wished my help to leave the port with his family. Initially I was sceptical for I had never heard of them before. So, I took down his name and promised to meet with him the following evening. The next day, I visited several Catholic churches until I found a priest who knew them. He assured me that the family was indeed named Rozells. They had often asserted that they were related to my father; distant cousins of some sort or other.'

Light listened carefully, keeping his face neutral so as not to deter Felipe. It would not go down well if it was discovered that the superintendent was involved in aiding and abetting migrants to flee from a Dutch establishment. Calcutta might baulk at that as an act of provocation. Yet, Felipe had his own life and responsibilities, regardless of the position of his sister's husband.

'I take it you offered them assistance?' Light prompted.

Felipe nodded. 'Juakim and his wife Andreza and four adult children: Jeronimo, Antoni, Thomas and Janeke. They are farmers. I smuggled them out aboard my vessel.'

'Where are they now?'

'Still aboard. I approached the church for help. They agree to take the parents due to their age and give them shelter and domestic work on church lands. The three sons are strapping lads, so I arranged for them to clear jungle on your plantation where they will live in the workers' quarters. But my problem is with Janeke.'

Light was puzzled. 'How so? Why is she unable to live with her parents? Would the church abandon a young woman to live alone in the settlement? I cannot guarantee her safety.'

Felipe blushed. 'Janeke was a housemaid for a Dutch family where she was wickedly abused by the master who threw her out of the house when her condition was discovered by his wife. He accused her of being a wanton when the poor girl had in fact been an innocent victim of his foul lusts!'

'Her life was ruined. No one will ever marry her now for she is considered spoiled. They believe she has brought shame on her family,' Light observed sadly. It was an all-too-familiar story. 'No wonder they wished to leave. It is hard enough living under the Dutch without being ostracised by one's own community!'

'The Catholic Church will not allow her to live on their grounds in a state of sin,' Felipe added.

'State of sin! Good God, Felipe, surely you don't regard the girl as a sinner! Why, Mary herself conceived the child Jesus out of wedlock! Without the aid of a good man like Joseph, she would surely have been tossed out on the streets! Does no Christian ever see the point of that story?' Light exclaimed.

Felipe sighed, utterly dejected. 'It is their way, sir. I would shelter her myself, but I only have a few rooms. It would be unseemly for me to take in an unmarried woman. There would be talk. They would say the child was mine, you know how people are.'

'I do indeed. We cannot let this poor cousin down. When Martinha and your mother hear of it, they will surely feel as we do. Have you discussed it with them?'

Felipe shook his head. 'I know they will embrace Janeke. They have tender hearts and have helped fallen women before. But I felt it was essential to speak to you first, for this whole sorry mess has other implications. It will be public knowledge that you have sheltered migrants from Melaka. I do not wish to cause trouble for you with the Council.'

'The Council be damned! This is a family matter. If they can ignore some of the flagrant acts of piracy that the Dutch have perpetrated on our vessels, then they can damn well turn a blind eye to this. We *will* take the girl into our household until the child is born. It's high time you had a decent home anyway, and not just rooms in Chinatown. Why not build a residence near ours? There's plenty of land this side. It all belongs to me, and I would gladly sign over a plot. Set up a decent household and perhaps Janeke and the child can be employed there in the future in some capacity? If you had a small staff, there would be no question of scandal –'

'Ah,' said Felipe. 'Which brings me to the second matter ...' He broke off, the diffidence returning. Instead of continuing, he fiddled with the cuff of his shirt. 'That is what I meant, sir, when I mentioned trouble with women. Apart from Janeke, there is another lady about whom I must speak...'

'Have you not adopted enough lame ducks already? Dear Lord, Felipe, do they see you coming?' Francis found is hard not to smile, even though he knew his brother-in-law was struggling with discomfiture and would not appreciate frivolity.

Felipe sighed deeply. 'The lady to whom I refer is not a "problem". Very much the opposite. Francis, I wish to marry. At last, I have found the right girl. She is quite lovely and, astonishingly enough, she is willing to marry me, although the Lord knows why such a perfect creature would find anything in me to love! I have approached her father and he is ready to give his permission to the union. But there are conditions –'

'Conditions?' Light interrupted with a gruff question. Had the hapless fellow been tricked into some ill-advised arrangement by a canny girl and her scheming father? Now that was a trap into which Felipe might inadvertently fall. He was an innocent abroad in the matter of feminine wiles.

'Her family is Chinese. The father accepts that his daughter must convert to the Catholic faith and raise our children as Christians, but he insists that we must live in her family home following Chinese tradition. He wishes his grandchildren to know their Chinese culture and language as well as western ways.'

'Western ways?' questioned Light. 'You are not a European, Felipe!'

'I am to a Chinese. Or rather my relationship to you and my Christian faith brings me into proximity with western circles. I speak good English, too. He is keen for his daughter and grandchildren to be familiar with British traditions.'

Something resonated with Light. He had heard similar notions of late from another source. 'Who is this girl, Felipe? What is her father's name? Would I know him?'

Felipe blushed again. 'Oh yes, sir. You are most acquainted with him. Her father is Kapitan Khoh Lay Huan. She is Khoh Lien Neoh, his daughter by his Queddah wife.'

Francis laughed out loud. 'That old goat! I should have guessed! Who better than Felipe Rozells for a son-in-law!'

Felipe was indignant. 'I met Miss Khoh by chance at the market. She was shopping with her maids. I was immediately entranced by her! Kapitan Khoh was not complicit in any way,' Felipe insisted.

Light leant over, his voice a gentle whisper. 'Do you think it likely that Miss Khoh is regularly seen in the market? An unmarried girl of a rich Chinese family? Such ladies rarely leave the house, other than to attend the temple! And how did you come to exchange words with her? I cannot imagine you approached the formidable Kapitan for permission to court her without some encouragement from the lady herself!'

Somewhat crestfallen, Felipe admitted that shortly after their eyes had met across the crowded market and the lovely maiden had smiled in response, before hiding her face behind her fan, he had been invited to dine at the Khoh household. His daughter had been present, sitting at a distance, her face demurely covered. Subsequently, Khoh had mentioned that his daughter was of marriageable age. He wished to marry her into one of the other communities on the island, in the interests of harmonic relations. Felipe had taken the hint and Khoh had welcomed his suit. From then on, he had been allowed supervised visits. Lien spoke excellent Malay, learned in Queddah. She was also receiving instruction in English, although her current level was rudimentary. When Felipe asked her if she might consider him as a suitor, she had received the request favourably, indicating to her father she would be happy to marry the young Eurasian gentleman.

'Then it is a *fait accompli*, my dear boy. You most certainly have my blessing. Your mother will be delighted, for she has long desired that you should take a wife. It seems you are making a choice similar to your own father, in the sense of marrying outside your community, so there should be no question of unsuitability. I wish you happiness with your young bride, and many, many children!'

Felipe flushed with pride. 'I will go and tell mother and Martinha, sir. Perhaps you understand now why I cannot bring Janeke and her child into my household. The Chinese are very traditional about such matters. They would be even more rigid in their disapproval than the Church.'

'Then we must find room for them in our own household, which is already expanding at an alarming rate. I cannot see how two mouths more will make much difference! And one a tiny babe, not yet born!'

And so, it was decided. For once, Francis went to bed that night with a sense of achievement. At least he still had some control in his family affairs if not the ever-increasing complexities of the island governance. With their support, the future for some of the island's most vulnerable arrivals might be eased.

***

Whilst her husband and brother were enjoying a celebratory drink in respect of the coming nuptials, Martinha and her mother were likewise in deep conversation. These days, with her husband rarely home at a decent hour, his wife spent most of her private time with Lady Thong Di. How she yearned for an evening alone with Francis, but such opportunities were increasingly rare. In his years at sea, Francis had regularly been away from home, an inevitability for a merchant captain's wife. But now that they were domiciled on the island, she had expected a more conventional family life. Yet he was as absent as ever. Sometimes she felt bitter, as if her best years were frittered away in the background, caring for children, running the household, endlessly sewing and mending, the only relief to the tedium of domesticity being her charitable works for the Church. But what of her own needs? What of his?

That night she was in a tetchier frame of mind than usual, having earlier caught Miss Hardwick in the garden, chatting with James Gray, when she should have been tutoring the girls.

'I must ask Francis to speak to Miss Lydia,' Martinha observed as they sat with a small glass of sherry. Thong Di was darning a tear in one of Lukey's dresses; Martinha was pretending to read.

'I think we need to send for the seamstress. Lukey needs some new clothes,' Thong Di replied as if she had not heard her daughter. Her hearing was poor these days – but it was also a useful excuse when she did not wish to engage in a particular line of conversation.

'Lukey ought to be more ladylike, then she would not tear her clothes so often!' Martinha snapped back, her daughter the butt of her anger when the real target was the governess. 'As I was saying, Miss Hardwick is becoming very lax in her duties. She is far too fond of her own appearance and of catching the eye of young officers!'

Thong Di was amused. 'The girl is young and all alone in the world. What else is she to do? Surely to seek a decent marriage is exactly what she ought to be doing at her age?'

Martinha tutted with annoyance. 'She has a job in this household. That is her first duty. She is a servant whose duties are to teach and accompany my daughters, not to romance young men!'

'You're too hard on her, Martinha. The girls are fond of Lydia. She acquits her responsibilities well. They do their lessons, and she is with them most of the day. Allow her a little relaxation.'

'Relaxation? Why are you not equally offended by her behaviour! Would you have allowed a servant in your household in Thalang to spend time chatting to young bucks over the fence! You would have chased them away and dismissed her!'

Thong Di put down her sewing. 'Miss Hardwick is not a servant, sayang. She is in employment in this house. If you are not satisfied with her work, then you must speak to her yourself. As the lady of the house, you should be the one to discipline her, not Francis. He has enough responsibilities already.'

'She speaks no Malay.'

'You speak good English. Why do you refuse to speak it with English people?'

Her daughter's face noticeably tightened. 'I find it better to pretend ignorance. In that way I both learn what they really think about me, and refrain from make idle chatter with such empty-headed people.'

'Oh, Martinha! You are so stubborn! You could be queen of this island if you had a mind to! Francis deserves more from you than this. It must embarrass him when you sit at the table like a mute. It only confirms their suspicions that he has allied himself with an ignorant local girl!'

They had repeated this argument at regular intervals over the past year. Martinha remained fixed in her determination to play little part in the island's social life unless it was on her own terms. Past experiences had taught her that, no matter what she did, the European community would always regard her as a woman of inferior birth. She preferred to keep an air of mystery about her than to pander to their unwanted opinion.

'I do not approve of Miss Lydia Hardwick.'

'Then you will be very pleased when she catches her officer and leaves your employ to marry him.' Thong Di replied, with the expression of one who has won her argument.

'Then what would the girls do?' Martinha asked. 'Who would be their governess?'

Her mother gave her a stern look. 'You cannot have it both ways, Martinha! Either she stays and annoys you, or she leaves, and the girls forsake their lessons. It won't be long until the new year when they return to Calcutta anyway. That will bring a natural end to all this.'

Martinha sighed deeply, resigned to the inevitable. She knew her mother was right. Part of her was trying to forget that the girls would not stay on the island forever. 'You are wise, '*bu*. I don't know what's wrong with me these days. I feel so angry all the time. Nor do I like young pretty women who flaunt their youth in front of me. It reminds me of that witch, Amdaeng Rat!'

Her mother burst out laughing. 'Are you worried that Miss Hardwick might catch Francis' eye? *Sayang*, that poor man has so much on his plate these days he barely remembers to eat, let alone romance nubile women!'

Martinha found herself smiling at her nonsense. 'I know he has no interest in her. In fact, he has no interest in anything these days. He staggers home exhausted and drops into bed, sleeping like a dead man,' she complained.

'Ah, so your unhappy state is in fact unfulfillment?' Thong Di teased with a saucy gleam in her eye. 'Is that the measure of it?'

'Mother! How can you talk of such things!' was her daughter's shocked reply.

Thong Di giggled. 'My dear, just because one does not discuss certain matters, does not mean they do not exist. Men and women need such moments together to rediscover their passion. Francis more than ever now that his responsibilities are so onerous. Perhaps you should find a way to tempt him from his office and take an early night's rest for once?'

With feigned shock, followed by a collapse into laughter, Martinha blushed and topped up their glasses. 'I think another glass and a change of subject is in order,' she announced. 'What is to be done with Felipe, Mother?'

The two women had been debating this subject for years. It was long past time for him to take a wife but, despite their best efforts, he had so far shown little inclination. This time, however,

Lady Thong Di did not respond with her resignation. In fact, she seemed even more playful than ever, smiling a mysterious smile as she feigned continuing her needlework.

'What is it, Mother? Why are you putting on that smug face? Do you know something?' Martinha was eager for news.

Her mother teased, laying down her task again and taking a sip of her sherry. 'I know nothing for sure, my dear, but I did glean a snippet of gossip from Askar Ali, the goldsmith fellow, who visited the house to repair a clasp on my necklace. He mentioned that Felipe had ordered a ruby brooch from him. He asked if I knew the purpose, so that he might ensure the motifs were suitable. I think he was fishing for gossip. Now why do you think your brother might require such a brooch?'

Martinha clapped her hands in glee. 'We must not get our hopes up! Yet, what else could it be? He must be up to something! Nothing stays hidden for long in Pinang, to be sure. Oh, I have quite brightened up at the prospect of finally seeing my dear brother wed! My mood is much improved. Let us drink a toast to that, Mother!'

They clinked their glasses in the English fashion. 'To marriage, sayang,' Thong Di beamed back, 'and I include silly Miss Hardwick in my wishes. That young lady needs a husband quickly, or scandal will surely follow!' Martinha was not wrong in her appraisal of the flighty girl. It was to be hoped that Gray was a gentleman. There was rarely much distance between good fortune and disaster.

5

Fanning the Flames

The Harimau, *Straits of Malacca. October 1787*

Perched on the prow, ruffled by a lively breeze, Soliman watched the dying embers of a blood-red sun slip beneath the horizon trailing a wake of burning orange fading through deep yellow into the purple bruise of evening. He breathed deeply of warm salt-tanged air – and peace settled upon his soul. His home since before he could remember, the sea was all he knew. There was no finer life than his, master of his own vessel, lord of his domain, answering to no man but himself.

Yet Soliman had not always been at one with his fate. Even now, the keen stab of regret sometimes pierced his heart. He would never know who he was or from whence he came. His memories of his father were so diminished that, even in dreams, he never saw his face, for only a vague impression of the man remained. And of his mother – nothing. Her short life had ended as his had begun, he presumed, for he was sure that if she had ever held him in her embrace, some sense would linger. He could not even recall his father ever speaking of her. It was one of life's great mysteries that, although he spoke the Bugis language almost as fluently as Malay, little else of those far-off days on a Bugis schooner was left to him.

His first clear memory was as a beggar child on the streets

of Madras. Had sailors put him ashore to fend for himself? Had he run away? Had he become lost after wandering from the harbourside? From what he now knew of sailors, it was unlikely he had been abandoned; a small boy was always useful afloat. Or was something sinister behind his plight? Had he been ill-used and fled the boat to escape? If that were so, he did not recall it, Allah be praised.

What guiding hand had led him, half-starved and close to the end, to fall asleep outside the lodgings of Francis Light? From then he had been reborn in the care of a good man who had cherished him. What were the chances of that happening to an abandoned child in this cruel life? And yet here he was, a young man with a settled life, one his poor mother and father could only have dreamed of.

Soliman had developed a deep abiding trust in God. In those years when he had struggled to know himself, stranded as he was between two worlds, chance had again directed him to the place he needed. Encouraged by his second 'father', he had spent many hours studying in a *madrasah* when in port in Queddah. Through his developing relationship with Allah, (*Subhanahu wa ta'ala!*), he had come to understand that He had a plan for him; he was safe in His hands. From that point on Soliman had embraced whatever life set before him and, in doing so, ceased to rail against fortune. He accepted that he was a Malay raised by an Englishman who had made it possible for him to be exactly what he was: an *orang selat*. The fact that he also read and spoke fluent English and Siamese was as happy a consequence as his knowledge of the Bugis tongue. All had proved of inestimable value to him as a trader in these waters, gifts from both his fathers.

Tonight, he was sailing back to his home on the island that these British called 'Prince of Wales', named for some unknown *rajah muda* on the other side of the world. It would never catch on, in Soliman's opinion. Names could never be imposed; they grew from the soil on which they were coined, watered by years of usage and tradition. This was Pinang, the island of the areca palm, where, in the little fishing *kampong* of Batu Uban, his own people now waited for him, the family he had created for himself. Nor did he forget his 'other' family, that of Captain Light, who had made his future possible. Soliman was a fortunate man indeed. His life was truly blessed.

Yet still, on evenings of pure joy like this, Soliman could not help but wonder, with the poetic soul of his people, whether he was not a poor foundling after all but a golden child, born of a fantastical coupling between a humble sailor and an enchanted princess, or some siren of the deep. Was this why his life had been so charmed?

His father-in-law, Ismail, had other notions. He believed that Soliman was in fact Minangkabau. 'You are too handsome to be *orang laut*! Look at your fine features and noble bearing! Only Minang men are so favoured – or how else would they catch Minang beauties?' When Soliman had finally plucked up courage to ask for Ismail's daughter in marriage, expecting to be chased away as a man from nowhere with no other distinction than still being alive, he had received an unexpected welcome. Ismail and his wife, Hasmah, whose approval was integral to the match in keeping with Minang *adat,* willingly handed over their precious daughter to this promising young sea captain. After all, it was known Soliman was close to the English governor. Rumours even claimed he was his adopted son. A very suitable son-in-law indeed. Whilst Soliman was shrewd enough to suspect his lofty connections might have had some bearing, it seemed yet another sign that God was blessing him. As for Aisyah, who had been making eyes at him for weeks whenever he was in port, he knew she wanted him for himself.

It was a happy marriage. They had found the perfect balance. Soliman was frequently away from home and Aisyah was used to that. Her father was a mariner himself, as were most of her people. In the tradition of her Minang folk, she lived in the family house of her mother and her new husband moved in. Men frequently travel overseas; it was better for peace in both the home and village for men and women to have their own worlds. Minang women were strong and opinionated; they knew their worth and their rights; they did not belong to anyone. Aisyah had chosen her own man and believed she had chosen well. With a baby already on the way, their marriage was sealed. Even better if it was a girl. Then Soliman would have proved his worth indeed.

A smile of contentment stretched across his face as he looked out over the obsidian shimmer of the night sea, the island already in view. The best of both worlds, as the captain would say. He could not wait to show his new-born baby to Francis. Light's first grandchild would be a child of the Straits people.

***

Satisfaction, however, is a perilous state of mind. A man less given to optimism than Soliman would not have tempted fate by relishing too much in his good fortune. On the following evening at the *pasar* in Malay Street, he received a stark warning of the potential hazard of his position. Soliman had accompanied his father-in-law, Ismail, whose duties included headman of the bazaar. For Ismail was otherwise known as Nakhoda Kecil, the *penghulu* of the original people of Pulau Pinang who had welcomed the British from the very beginning. In the early months of the settlement, he had organised his kampong to assist in the clearance of Tanjong Penaga and in policing the coast against Malay incursion from Queddah. Nakhoda Kecil was the closest thing to a leader that the Malay community had.

His family were one of distinction amongst the Pinang Malays. Nakhoda Kecil and his much elder brother, Haji Mohammed Salleh, had migrated from the Minangkabau heartlands in Payakumbuh, West Sumatra, many years before settling on the island when Ismail had been a little boy. His brother, a learned scholar who had devoted his life to religious teaching, had built the island's first mosque, Masjid Jamek, in the fishing village of Batu Uban. Whilst Ismail followed his family tradition and went to the sea to make his fortune, Mohammed Salleh had won his place in the hearts of the settlers as a religious leader, known as Nakhoda Intan, the Diamond Captain. The two brothers held great influence amongst the Muslim migrants.

George Town was a small place to contain so many different peoples without some measure of conflict. In the labyrinth of alleyways and the hotchpotch of buildings and shacks that had grown up haphazardly in the commercial heart of town, communities overlapped. On this evening, a rowdy group of English sailors wandered into the bazaar, looking for something to eat, or more likely mischief. They were well into their cups after spending the best part of the day in a Chinese grog shop a few streets away. Such sailors who had been weeks at sea would invariably make land, find a tavern, drink themselves into frenzy – then look either for a woman or a fight, one invariably leading to the other.

Whilst chatting with the cattle sellers at one end of the street, Soliman and Ismail were alerted to trouble by a sudden charge in their direction and shouting in a foreign tongue. It was not unknown to Soliman.

'What have we here, lads. Bloody little brown fellas, selling off their booty! This lot 'ere are all bleeding pirates, ya know? Seems to me we should 'elp ourselves to what we like as it was most likely thieved off one of ours.'

Whatever other profanities were uttered, they were lost amongst the ensuing chaos once the English sailors set to pocketing items willy-nilly. Stalls were roughly overturned, people mishandled. Malay vendors reached for sticks and keris ready to stoutly defend their wares. Women grabbed children and shepherded the old out of harm's way, stampeding down the alleyways. The drunken sailors pulled out knives and cudgels and a vicious mêlée erupted, where heads were bashed, and blood was spilt. Serious injury or worse was likely.

Soliman and Ismail waded into the panicked crowd, pushing their way forward whilst calling out for men to stand firm and hold their weapons. Soliman broke through first, hauling brawling men apart, as Ismail appealed for calm. Encountering one frenzied white man, big-bellied and all but incapacitated by rum, Soliman grabbed him by the neck and spun him round, a dagger at his throat. 'Hold! Enough! Stop your fighting, you louts! You've made your point. Now leave before we send for the guard!' he shouted out in English so well spoken that it stopped the sailors in their tracks. Even the Malays fell silent, wondering what had been said.

A small rat-faced man, with lank, greasy hair and spindly limbs, looked quizzically at Soliman. 'Where did a monkey like you learn to speak the King's English like a fuckin' gentleman? And who d'ya think y'are speaking to British tars like that? This 'ere is our bleedin' island. You do as we say, matey.'

'I 'ave a notion he's the superintendent's bumboy,' shouted one older man, who was mopping blood from his shiny bald pate with a dirty neckerchief. 'He's been wiv Light for years, so I 'ear. Fancies 'imself an Englishman.'

'Dirty little bugger, if y'ask me,' said ratface. 'We should show 'im his place ...'

Soliman reared up at the slur to Light's reputation, grateful only that the foul comments were unintelligible to the rest of his people. Mad with rage, he was on the brink of losing his temper completely, and – with a keris at the throat of the fat man – who knew what might have happened? The fact that the incident did not resolve in capital charges rested purely on the fortuitous arrival of the guard, further proof indeed that Soliman possessed a guiding angel.

The detachment was commanded by Captain Glass himself, with Lieutenant Murray at his side, accompanied by a troop of sepoys. As luck would have it, they were already out and about that night on the hunt for some sailors who had absconded from a Company vessel on the brink of leaving port. Jumping ship at the eleventh hour was a common problem. In most cases, absence was not discovered until vessels were out at sea; it might be several months, sometimes years, until they returned. Once ashore, the absconders would give a false name and make a claim for a piece of land with the intention of settling. Such practice was the scourge of Light's administration.

These men were always trouble once they received their allocation; they had no intention to farm the land, nor contribute to the island in any way. Living rough, existing on pilfering, gambling and cheating, they would sell their investment for profit some time down the line. In the interim, they were public nuisances, aware that the administration had few powers to restrain their excesses so long as they did not commit capital offences. Glass was determined to apprehend this gang before they disappeared into the underbelly and brought even more mischief to the peace and quiet of the island.

Shots were fired into the air. For a few tense seconds, the standoff continued, Nakhoda Kecil frantically begging Soliman to come to his senses and release the fat man. The younger man visibly shook with anger, his mouth drawn into a snarl, his teeth bared. No one had seen this side of the happy-go-lucky mariner. Good sense prevailed at last, however, when Soliman loosed his grip, kicking the terrified sailor back towards his comrades.

'What's the meaning of this affray?' Glass demanded.

It was Soliman who answered. 'These drunken sots have wrecked the bazaar, attacking traders going about their honest business. We are defending ourselves, which we have the right to do!' he shouted back.

Glass held up his hand for silence. He was a conservative man with no particular attachment to the locals, but he was known for his fairness. Yet he would not allow charges to be thrown about until he had thoroughly investigated for himself. 'Enough, boy. Who are you? On what authority do you speak?'

'Juragan Soliman of the *Harimau*,' he answered truculently, stressing his title of skipper of his own boat. He would not be treated like some ignorant peasant.

'Then hold your tongue, young man,' Glass answered in Malay. 'You'll have your chance to speak soon enough.'

The sailors stood in silence, their hangdog expressions betraying unease, sneaking sly looks at each other and muttering beneath their breath. Soliman wondered why they were not making accusations, blaming the Malays for starting the ruckus, answering his charges with a barrage of lies. That was the usual way when trouble broke out between the locals and the white men – and their versions of the truth were generally believed.

Turning to his men, Glass gave the order for the sailors to be apprehended then asked each for their names and vessels. None of them answered.

'Name? Vessel?' he repeated to each man in turn, his voice deadly calm, but all the more threatening for that. 'I have asked a simple question and yet you refuse to answer? It will do your case no good if you fail to cooperate. Am I to understand that what this man has said is true?'

One by one, they shook their heads. They did not dare admit that they were runaways. Better to be arrested for affray than desertion.

'Suit yourselves. But if you think this will result in nothing more than a night locked up in the fort for rabble-rousing, you are sadly mistaken. I know who you are. Captain Garrett discovered you were missing before he sailed. You're from the *Morning Star*, heading for Bencoolen. Before he left, Garrett gave me your particulars in detail, down to the very last missing tooth, hairy wart and disfiguring scar. Not only have you jumped ship – bad enough in itself – but you have subsequently caused a public order disturbance on the streets of the settlement. These are very serious charges. Enough to keep you locked up until the *Morning Star* returns when we may hand you over to your captain to deal with you as he sees fit.'

Glass indicated that Murray and his men should take over; the sepoys rough-handled the sailors back in the direction of the fort where they faced a miserable confinement for their pains – and worse when they were finally returned to Madras. As they were dragged away, Glass turned his attention back to the waiting crowd of Malay traders, for the most part in ignorance as to what had been said. An atmosphere of tension simmered; they were disgruntled with malice and on the brink of erupting once again.

Glass addressed them in Malay. 'Close up for the night, sirs. Go back to your homes. No more stirring trouble tonight,' he told them sternly.

Nakhoda Kecil faced him up, legs akimbo and hands upon his hips, striking a defiant pose. 'We are law abiding traders, Kapitan. We make our living honestly. Those ruffians attacked us. Look – our goods are spoiled! We demand compensation. We have the right to punish those who destroy our property!'

Glass nodded. 'I know you were ill-used by these men for which they will be punished. But this is not the time or place. You must take your case to the superintendent. He will listen to you fairly. I will speak in your favour. For now, please disperse.'

It was the best that they could hope for. Soliman was himself a witness, as well as a participant. The matter might be resolved in their favour this time. But it was unlikely that adequate recompense would be forthcoming – and what were the guarantees such things would not occur again? These *orang putih* were always drunk and violent. They preyed upon the local people for sport.

Eying up the British soldiers with a sneer, Nakhoda Kecil replied with vehemence. '*We* will not let this happen again. Next time, it is *we* who will run amok. Tell Superintendent Light to keep his people under control or you will see that that we are warriors too!' A cheer rang out from all the assembled traders. Malay town was a tinderbox that night.

Glass reflected on the warning. The penghulu was right. Until the island had its own law courts, there was always the chance that such grievances would result in fighting on the streets, one group against another. A judiciary was required, particularly when conflicts arose between communities. These native peoples might be meek and mild from day to day but when they rose up, all hell broke loose.

'I urge you not to make threats, Nakhoda. This is the time for cool heads. Do not stir up your menfolk. I promise we'll take account of your needs. We share your concerns. But let us deal with these bad fellows, I beg you. According to *our* laws.'

The nakhoda raised his hand to still the jeering of the crowd and commanded everyone to leave the street. He stood with Soliman whilst each merchant packed up his scattered belongings and righted the overturned tables. One by one the crowd dispersed, trudging away until only Glass and two sepoys remained. Then, with a curt bow, Nakhoda Kecil himself turned and led Soliman away, both deep in conversation.

The younger man had much to think about. Although his unusual relationship with the superintendent might raise his esteem amongst some of the island's dwellers, there were others who regarded his position unacceptable, even an abomination in the order of things. He must tread carefully. The Europeans would not tolerate a Malay they deemed acting above his station.

Only then did Captain Glass breath a long sigh of relief. The crisis was averted, at least for one night. He turned back towards the fort, mentally compiling the report he would present to Light and the letter he intended to compose for the Council, urging them immediately to expand the powers of the island government. So deep in thought was he, that he did not hear the muttered comments exchanged by the attendant sepoys.

'Muslim dogs. We should have fired at them, not in the air. That would have chased them quick enough!' they sniggered. The problems of public order did not solely exist amongst the local people. The military were amongst the worst offenders, regularly abusing their power behind the backs of their officers – and in some cases with their tacit approval. As well as traditional enmities between the different communities, fierce rivalries lay between religions. The sparks of conflict were igniting randomly around the settlement. Only a slight breeze and the flames of discord would burst into conflagration.

6
The Poisoned Chalice

Scott Residence, Light Street. October 1787

'Quite like old times, Francis?' James Scott observed as he poured out liberal measures from a crystal decanter. Of late there had been little time for such indulgences.

'True enough, my friend, but mind the measures. I have papers to go through before I retire. My head must be reasonably clear,' Light added ruefully.

'Papers, be damned, Francis! A fellow must loosen his belt from time to time. And drink until he falls from the table. It is the eleventh commandment!' he chuckled.

Light took a swig and swallowed deep, murmuring in pleasure as the fiery liquid warmed his vitals. 'In truth, I often take refuge in the bottle these days. Drinking alone, however, is a miserable pursuit. I miss our times together, Jamie. Even if you always drive me to frustration in most things!'

They both laughed, wholly at ease, familiar enough to allow for silence while they enjoyed the moment. Sometimes a trusted friend nearby was enough.

The two men were seated in the atrium of Scott's commodious residence. Although the magnificent wooden home, known locally as the 'Istana' appeared from outside to be of Malay construction, many of its internal structures borrowed from features more commonly seen in Chinese or Siamese houses, with separate pavilions arranged around a central courtyard. To those familiar with the Straits, this residence was a fascinating mélange that mirrored the rich heritages of its many different peoples.

The tiled floor lay beneath the stars, adorned with plants in large vases set around a small sunken pond. It was not quite a garden but much more than an air well, although both functions were intended. Scott had observed this fashion in Chinese merchant houses in Melaka. Even the Dutch now favoured the style. All the rooms skirted this space, each with a distinct purpose of its own, separating private from public; office from recreation; working quarters from living; children and women from the world of men.

Scott's wife, born Anna Julhy Burgo, a woman of mixed heritage from Jangsylan like Martinha herself, was a Catholic Eurasian with a Chinese mother. Anna Julia, as Scott called her, was a markedly different woman from those with whom Scott had kept company in the past, not the least because they had undergone a Catholic marriage in Jangsylan back in 1780. Even then, Scott had not entirely abandoned his taste for concubines; he had kept an unofficial 'wife' in Queddah at the same time, who had born him two daughters.

This rival had not escaped Anna Julhy's notice. Whether she had given her husband an ultimatum or welcomed his other family willingly, Mee Ngah and her daughters now shared the house – and, by all accounts, the two women lived harmoniously. How Scott achieved this unorthodox arrangement was a mystery to Light, although Martinha, who was close to Anna, insisted that Mee Ngah no longer 'consorted' with Scott. Light was dubious, knowing his friend's predilections, but it had to be said that, since the joint baptism three years ago of Mee Ngah's daughter, Mary, and Anna's daughter, Sophia – along with Mee herself – no further children had been born, other than to Anna Julhy. Perhaps Scott was indeed behaving himself these days.

The two women had become like sisters, raising their brood jointly. The little ones were often at the Light household where the growing gang of children – steps and stairs from one to ten – played happily together. Anna Julhy was a delightful lady, voluptuous and cheery, rarely without a smile upon her face, in direct contrast to her cantankerous husband.

Yet one might be misled by her apparent geniality; Mrs Scott was as tough as nails, a businesswoman herself through and through. Indeed, it had been her commercial acumen that had introduced her to Scott. Even now, she maintained her contacts in Siam, traders of great significance to her husband's business – and her own. It was a happy marriage, even if Scott pretended his wife an encumbrance, while she merrily chided him nonstop for his irritability.

Anna was nowhere to be seen. She was in confinement awaiting the imminent birth of their fourth child. For all her Christian beliefs, Mrs Scott was traditionally Chinese in her attitude to the childbed. It was unlikely she would appear again in public before the end of the year.

'How do you manage it?' Light asked, his hand to his ear, listening carefully on the quiet night air.

'Manage what, pray tell?' smirked Scott, who knew well what Light referred to.

'The absence of the infernal din of children! To my knowledge you have at least six young 'uns in the house and not a peep from any of them!' Light grinned. 'My home is the very opposite. Either William or Mary is screaming blue murder, or the older girls are stampeded around like a herd of Indian elephants!'

Scott tapped his nose, his eyes crinkling in amusement. 'It's the women who do it, Francis, not I! I made sure to choose two women of the people, not fine and dandy noble ladies like Madame Martinha and Lady Thong Di, who rely upon the services of maids to discipline the little ones. Servants inevitably indulge the bairns and pander to their whimpering. My ladies have the knack of charming children to sleep – or scaring them rigid! Furthermore, my Caffree girls are proving equal to the task of childrearing without spoiling. For which I have you to thank, sir!'

The experiment with the Africans had been successful, at least within their households.

'How goes it with the men?' Light inquired. Scott had taken over a group of young males to work on his fledgling spice plantations. It was not onerous work as the land had already been cleared, nor did long hours in the open worry these men.

Scott gave a grudging nod of approval. 'They're shaping up so far. I've a Chinese *mandor* who runs a tight ship. He has his own stake in the venture having borrowed a sum of money from me at unusually favourable rates to buy a few plots for himself. I find this method efficacious in ensuring loyal service. If my crop does not thrive as well as his, then his debt will be called – an incentive for diligence, I find.'

Scott was a fiendishly clever businessman. Light suspected that as the years rolled on, he would make as much money as banker to new migrants as he would in his commercial enterprises

– in which he made a fine profit already. 'I would never criticise a man making profit who also enables others to make their way. I, too, am satisfied with these Caffrees in the main. The experiment is turning out rather better than I expected. I wish I could say the same for the European hordes who wash ashore these days. There are far too many ruffians and deserters, not to mention drunk and disorderly sailors and miscellaneous ne'er-do-wells. I fear we're heading for a crisis. The locals will not stand for it if no action is taken against their lawlessness,' he complained bitterly.

'That business last month in Malay town was a disgrace. At least Glass apprehended the renegades.'

'We must do more to contain it,' Light insisted. 'I've set up a gaol on the corner of Lebuh Pasar, a designated prison for miscreants with a guard company on hand at all times to nip disorder in the bud. Sergeant Major Gregg is appointed provost to lead the night watch and administer to the rowdies. We must be seen to take action, Jamie! The Malays were ready to run amok the last time. Soliman was there. He warned me how close it came to boiling over. There's no use appointing local kapitans if we cannot regulate our own people!' The alcohol and the presence of an old friend were loosening the usual restraints on his tongue.

Scott nodded his agreement. 'Aye, but watch those damned sepoy guards, all the same. They're too much above themselves. I hear they run their own gambling and whoring establishments. Every woman who arrives is preyed upon – and some are bought and sold like cattle. *Quis custodiet ipsos custodes*, eh?'

'Virgil?'

'Juvenal, ya blockhead. Did ya never heed your lessons,

Francis?'

Light laughed out loud at Scott's jibe. 'Not one, I'm afraid. I invariably recognise the gist but cannot for the devil tell you who said it! But you are right. These soldiers are a bloody law unto themselves – and not only the sepoys. But Glass is a good man and has a firm hand on it. He's ready to flog any soldier if he comes across infringement. Yet it cannot continue like this. I need judicial authority to enable me to bang a few heads together, not send them back to Calcutta where they invariably talk their way out of the charges.'

'No luck with Cornwallis?'

Light scoffed. 'I write each week with a list of requests but have yet to receive a response. One good piece of news – Kyd's excellent report. We couldn't have asked more of him. He's wholly convinced of the island's prosperous future and recommends immediate investment, with the fort particularly stressed as an urgent priority. As for the island's potential as a naval base, Kyd agrees that Pulau Jerajak is the perfect location, off shore and flanking the coast south of George Town. So, all in all, we seem to have won that argument successfully.'

'I'll drink tae that,' replied Scott, refilling Light's glass beyond the moderate thimbleful he indicated. 'D'you think Cornwallis might be convinced?'

'I wouldn't hope for too much from that quarter. The Governor has a notion that to best protect the eastern seaboard of India, a naval base must be situated closer. One report will not sway him. You know these aristocrats. They presume that a bevy of titles guarantees their genius, setting them above the rest of us mere mortals. They need learn nothing, for God gives them omniscience on account of their blue blood. I do not imagine Cornwallis takes much notice of anyone but himself, however compelling the scientific or military argument.' Light's earlier good humour was quickly subsiding as the weight of his problems settled back upon his shoulders.

Scott gave the matter some thought as he sipped upon his whisky. 'And where might he prefer to site his naval establishment? Some godforsaken island in the midst of nowhere?'

'Andrew Ross writes he's heard whispers of the Andaman and Nicobars,' he admitted.

'Sweet Jesus! Do they want to feed the cannibals with English beef? Those islands are good for nothing but a landing for water and then off again as quick as you like!' Scott asserted. 'Does Cornwallis merely stick a knife into the map without consultation? Those islands are also fever pits. Surely, he has heard of the failed Danish experiment?' Scott was so incredulous that he felt obliged to drain his cup and pour another huge measure.

'With the usual arrogance of his class, he believes Danish failure has no bearing on British success. I could weep when I think of all we might achieve if Prince of Wales Island was accorded sufficient investment!' Light exclaimed bitterly.

The two men were in agreement, but only to a point. Scott could not help but remind Light of his earlier counsel, warning him of this very possibility. 'You're naïve if you didn't expect this outcome from the start. I cautioned you this island was a poisoned chalice.'

'I disagree, old friend,' Light bit back, with more than a hint of annoyance. 'We simply need money. And money can be found. There are other ways to raise adequate funds should Cornwallis refuse to open his coffers. This is a successful trading port. If we but introduce a moderate customs duty …'

'Over my dead body!' Scott erupted, banging his fist upon the table. 'This island is a free port. It is what the Company decrees – and it is what we always wanted! Why do you imagine this island, in its infancy, attracts such a glut of trade already? It is because we welcome all, and everyone can trade free of constraint. That is why they flock here from every other landing in the region! Profit is not made by levying tax but by conducting business, as you once knew yourself, Superintendent!'

Light returned the fiery glare with his own cool stare, green eyes glinting with an unfamiliar steel. 'I do not run this island for the benefit of your profits, James. As superintendent, I am not here to make any man's fortune, but to ensure the population lives in safety and security the better for us *all* to prosper. This is not your personal pot of gold!'

His friend grunted his anger. 'I haven't yet seen you turn your nose up at your share of the spoils! Don't act the saint with me, man! You're grabbing prime land as fast as everyone else, maybe more so. We deserve this, Francis! Without our endeavours, this island would never have become a Company establishment. It would still be a desolate place with a handful of fishermen eking out a humble living. We've made of it a treasure house for all! Any fortune that we make is our just reward!' Scott spluttered.

'As far as I'm aware, sir, I am the superintendent. This is no Triumvirate –'

'Duumvirate, ya fool! Triumvirate implies three,' snapped back Scott stony-faced. He paced around the atrium, his hands behind his back and his eyes to the heavens. Light noticed him gripping and loosening his fingers, as if trying to control his fists.

Once his temper cooled, Scott continued, his voice as tight as a bow line. 'I fear we may fall out over this matter, Francis. Nor do I appreciate you pulling rank. I've been as responsible as you for the accomplishments we have made here. Without the money I have made on your behalf, you would already be bankrupt on the pittance they pay!'

An uncomfortable silence reigned, Scott's raised voice reverberating in the stillness of the warm night. Light chose not to reply immediately. The two friends were at a crucial moment, one he had anticipated for some time. The wrong word now could forge a break between them that would be difficult to mend. James Scott was not a man he desired as an enemy.

Light held up his hands in surrender. 'I apologise for my harsh words, old friend. The very last thing I wish is to quarrel with you, for in the main what you say is correct. You have been my right hand for many years and without your acumen, my fortune would already be gone. But the fact remains: if I am to continue as governor of this establishment – and fulfil my duties honourably – there has to be a reckoning. I can no longer juggle two distinctly opposite careers: trader and administrator. It is impossible to govern if I am also committed to my own profits. To put my fortune above the office would be the very definition of corruption. I cannot make decisions with one eye on my own purse at the expense of fair government.'

Scott heard his words out, swilling the dregs in his glass thoughtfully. 'It appears you've given the matter some thought, Francis. Exactly what do you have in mind? How will you and your family survive without the profits trade brings in? Have you given adequate thought to that? Damn it, man! The Company is all about independent merchants carving up trade for their own profit! It's a merchant company – that is the very nature of it!' His voice began to rise again as he stirred himself back to anger.

'By regulation, an officer should not be encumbered with personal interests that may affect his loyalties or use the office as a means to fund his own trade. Hastings established that well enough and Cornwallis is also of that mind,' Light replied quietly.

Scott spun round, splattering whisky from his glass in the process. 'Hastings was impeached for it and bloody Cornwallis is a poppycock who thinks all men have his fortune!'

'Nevertheless, probity requires me to –'

'Probity, be damned. Francis! We are a partnership! We work well together and have done for many a year. Are you about to tell me you wish to sever our links?' Scott was almost pleading. Light had expected anger but had not anticipated the desperate appeal he heard in his friend's voice. The full extent of Scott's attachment to him lay revealed. It reflected his own feelings, for Scott was the closest thing he had in life to a brother.

'Jamie, you are my greatest friend. I wish for nothing more than to continue in your good graces. But we must be realists. Before our enemies use it against us, we must change the nature of our connection. I must stand down from all involvement in the partnership. We must dissolve our active association, so that in future I have no part in daily decisions. Thus, no charges of favouritism can be levelled. I may, however, remain as a sleeping partner, allowing you to manage my investments, and receiving my annual share of the profits. I cannot deny that without them, I would struggle. This compromise must shape all our business relations. And I must exclude you from intimate knowledge of Company affairs in future. It must be demonstrated that you do not have access to confidential information that you might use for your own advancement.'

Scott breathed deeply but appeared to be calming down. 'If you think that you can forgo nights like this, then you are sadly mistaken, Francis. A man needs a friend he can trust, or he will go mad – especially one as burdened as yourself. My door is always open. But I bow to your judgment and accept the inevitable with a sad heart, for I think no man other than you would make such a foolhardy gesture. For my part, I shall draw up the documents to dissolve our active partnership forthwith. You will, however, remain an equal shareholder.'

'I am not sure equal is just, James. You are shouldering the load alone. Yours must be the greater share.'

Scott shrugged. 'I'm sure we can accommodate something to suit us both. Let's set our accountants to work and see what they come up with. Agreed?'

He extended his hand. Francis looked at it before lunging forward to clasp him in his embrace. 'This is not the end, Jamie! It is just a new road we are embarking upon. This is as much about how we are perceived by others as anything else.'

'And no more of your bloody nonsense about duties – unless levied only on the Dutch or Bugis! Mayhap sometime in the future we will be in a place to introduce such measures – but we must not kill the golden goose before she has even laid her eggs!'

They both laughed at his summation. 'Calcutta wouldn't countenance it anyway,' Light admitted. 'But I shall toil away until the day comes when we can charge levies to finance our own future growth. Once I have a notion, I am the very definition of dogged.'

'I'll not argue with that, my friend. Now let us sit back down and no more protestations about drinking in moderation. You're no Presbyterian, sir. Tonight, we'll drown our partnership in Scotch whisky while you tell me all the private matters that I am shortly not allowed to hear.' The glasses were replenished – with no argument from Light this time.

'I do reserve one area of the administration where your assistance would be mightily advantageous, however,' Light began. Scott looked sharply at him, eager that some leverage might still remain.

'Go on.'

'The delicate matter of the unresolved issues with Sultan Abdullah. There will need to be negotiations behind the backs of both Calcutta and the other players else it will be impossible to find common ground. Would you be my envoy to the court when the time comes? I cannot be seen to bend and scrape but Abdullah would accept an approach from you. He knows how close we are.'

Scott's smile was as wide as the cat who stole a lick of cream. 'Most assuredly, Francis. I offer my services as go-between with the local potentates. It would be to all our advantages to be a fly on those particular walls. An excellent compromise to seal our new situation. What of Perak? Have you any joy of Sultan Ahmauddin?'

Light stretched back in his chair, savouring the belt of Scotch he had just imbibed. 'A few letters have passed between us. He needs rice, I need tin. The same old story. But he's reluctant to enter into open trade, for his Dutch masters are breathing down his neck. His letter was amusing – I rather like his style. He cloaked his response in a lurid analogy about a beautiful woman (ergo Perak), a jealous and brutal husband (the Hollanders) and the engaging new lover whom she prefers (that would be me). Fear of the husband's retribution is the only reason she refuses to dally with her beloved. But it indicates nothing. The sultan is probably just romancing us all with his blandishments.'

'He's another canny old rogue. He outlived his older brothers and has been playing politics all his life. But he didn't chase you away. That signifies his interest. While we're on the subject of rogues, a word about this new appointment in Thalang. It would appear Lady Chan's toadie, Phaya Thukkarat, has not been confirmed as governor as he promised. I went with the guns and gifts for the king they expected us to provide *gratis* but not even as much as a sniff of the promised tin. My patience is wearing thin with the lot of them.'

It was not unexpected. Light had received the usual begging mails from the acting governor, Chan's nephew, full of obsequious prattle and lofty claims. Despite her ennoblement at the hands of King Rama, Chan's once unassailable position was in decline. Jangsylan was firmly under royal control; the new governor would likely be a royal appointee. King Rama would never allow a local to hold the sort of power Chan had once enjoyed. The lady was aging, her health beginning to fail. The destruction of Jangsylan had sapped the last of her indomitable spirit.

'She intends to visit Bangkok for an audience with the king. She believes he will allow her control of the tin trade on account of her record – and his love for her son. I suspect she will be unsuccessful. But we must not forsake her. She still commands respect on the island – and deserves our support. We may never see the tin, or if we do, it will be at a premium, I fear.'

Scott responded with a glower, tossing a leather wallet upon the table. 'Your "private" mail. My clerk passed it to me. Not suitable for the official post, he said. The usual gaggle of ladies: Chao Chipat, Chao Bun Chan – and the notorious Amdaeng Rat, as well as Lady Chan herself. I think it's high time you disassociated yourself completely from the lot of them, saving Chan herself. It's not only your wife who would take umbrage at discovering the secrets of your past amours, Francis.'

Light blew out his cheeks as he snatched the wallet. 'They've suffered hard times. Who can blame them for reaching out, even though our "association" is years past. They hear of my good fortune and hope I remember them kindly.'

'Not to mention the child you have there,' Scott countered.

'I send money regularly for Georgie. I provide rice and cloth for all of them. But I do not answer their missives. I will not open myself to extortion.' Light pointed a finger direct at his friend: 'Nor should you be challenging my parental responsibilities, when you yourself have at least a dozen bairns scattered up and down the Straits. Look to your own affairs, James, before you criticise me,' he rebuked.

Scott mimed a slap on the back of his hand at Light's reproach. 'As you yourself have only this night reminded me, Francis. I am not the governor of a British establishment but a ne'er-do-well merchant without a shred of integrity. It cannae work both ways, laddie. My scandalous behaviour is openly acknowledged. It is you that must be clothed in white and play the sanctimonious governor. Take care you're not found out for your less than virtuous past!'

By response, Light burst into laughter. 'Oh, but we had some fun, didn't we, Jamie? Back in the old days when we did what we pleased, and the devil take the hindmost. I don't regret it. Sometimes I long for the freedom. I haven't sent foot off this island in well over a twelvemonth. No wonder my feet are itchy and my temper sour!'

'The only cure is a belly full of liquor.'

Light rubbed his hands together in agreement. 'Fill my glass then, *Doctor* Scott, if that's your medicine for melancholy! I will drink a toast to friendship and how deftly we've avoided bloodying our noses this evening. It is a testament to our bond that we can find our way past even intractable problems.' He held up his glass. 'To friendship, James!'

'Ya cannae sup Scotch whisky without toasting in Gaelic, man! *Slainte mhath,* my old friend. And if we drink much longer, I may even be persuaded to sing one of my favourite airs. What say you to a few verses of *The Morning Dew*, eh?'

PART TWO

The City and the Island

(1788-1790)

7

The Art of Illusion

The Prince Henry, *Hooghly River, Calcutta. Late January 1788*

An interested observer on the riverside jetty would have been intrigued by the motley band of travellers disembarking from a trading vessel moored midstream. The *Prince Henry* – owned by James Scott, merchant – was commanded by James Glass, a doughty sea captain who regularly took great personal offence when confused with John Glass, the garrison commander of Fort Cornwallis. The two were very different men: one a humourless Scottish soldier, the other a hearty Irish mariner.

It had been an interesting voyage, a world away from his usual crossings. The two parties under his charge, namely women of Superintendent Light's family and envoys from the court of Terengganu, had made for an uneasy atmosphere. The Malay officials were silently offended to share the restricted space with women. But Glass, a man who thrived upon a challenge, believed he had deftly handled the sensibilities of all.

Sarah and Lucy Ann Light were returning to school accompanied by their mother and grandmother. Miss Lydia Hardwick was no longer their governess after marrying the 'dear' lieutenant. Her goal accomplished, she was now busy establishing herself as doyenne of the island's fledgling society. No one had been much surprised. It was a relief that scandal had been so adroitly averted.

The envoys were known to Captain Glass, who was often a guest at Sultan Mansur's court. The sultan of Terengganu had come to the same conclusion as the sultan of Queddah: the British were ideal allies against his local rivals, particularly as they both shared a common enemy in the Dutch. For some months now, Sultan Mansur had been making approaches to Superintendent Light. His persistence had finally borne fruit, for Light had dispatched the royal envoys to present their own case to the Council, with Glass as interpreter. They offered generous trade monopolies in return for a moderate supply of opium. Sultan Mansur also offered the inducement of installing a British Resident, suggesting Captain Glass himself for the honour.

Light was fully aware that the Company had no interest in Terengganu; the proposition would never be accepted. Yet it was not in his interests to be the harbinger of bad news. He did not wish to lose the support of a regional sultan well-disposed towards him. Thus, he had passed the matter on.

A certain amount of legerdemain had been required on board to keep apart the parties, especially as the Light girls treated the ship as their personal playground. Their mother, however, was not insensible to the predicament, so restricted them to one side of the vessel. The worthy envoys generally remained below, emerging on deck only in the early morning or the cool of the evening. On alternate nights, Captain Glass invited one or the other to dine in his cabin. The Mohammedan gentlemen would never sit at table with women. Thus, the first hurdle had been accomplished. The next two months in Calcutta would be a constant to-and-fro between chaperoning the ladies and pandering to the envoys – but Glass was ready for it. This was a chance of a lifetime for the ambitious Irishman.

***

Despite her dislike of sea voyages, Martinha had been delighted to accompany the girls back to school. There was no question of her husband travelling at this time; his presence was required upon the island. He did, however, promise to make the trip as soon as he could, perhaps the following year, so that they could once again enjoy the delights of the great metropolis together.

Martinha was not entirely sure that Calcutta was a place she wished to visit regularly, other than to see her daughters. The memory of her first foray had not endeared her to the place. There she had first come to realise the inferior status in which she would always be regarded by the British. So deeply had the experience affected her that she limited her social contacts with Europeans, even to the extent of feigning not to understand the English language. She would not submit to haughty English disdain. Yet, in Calcutta she could not continue this pretence, for few here knew her language.

With this commission, Francis was forcing her hand, demonstrating it was impossible for a woman in her position to bury her head in the sand. She must accept a public role for her family's sake. Well, let them try to demean her this time, she had decided; she was older now and more than equal to the task. Never again would she be treated as an ignorant native. In fact, she had one indisputable advantage: if there was one thing these white people respected, it was aristocratic birth. Mostly, because so few Company people had it themselves.

The heritage of the peoples of the Straits was a tapestry woven from its many diverse cultures, little understood by those outside. Martinha's Malay grandmother had been a Queddah royal, her grandfather a Siamese noble, her own father a wealthy Christian Eurasian. How one chose to portray oneself was a matter of perspective. She had learned that much from her husband and his contemporaries who regularly assumed different guises: merchant, envoy, soldier, master, ally, friend. If rumour had it that Mrs Light was a Malay princess, then so be it. She was as much that as any of her other faces.

During their stay, they were to be the guests of the Pigou family. Captain Peter Pigou, now sadly deceased, had been an old friend of Francis in his Madras days. His son, Thomas, had recently become Light's assistant, at the personal request of the superintendent himself. The family were honoured to host the Light family in their home, grateful for the patronage he had offered young Thomas that had led to such prestigious advancement.

The Pigous did not live amongst the lofty palaces of Chowringee but on the southern bank of the Hooghly, Garden Reach. Impressive mansions were already springing up along the river frontage of this soon-to-be fashionable district, but the Pigou residence was situated several streets away in the older neighbourhood, where lowly mariners and traders traditionally resided. Although a socially acceptable address, the humble villa betrayed the lesser fortunes of the Pigous, particularly since the loss of their father. Peter Pigou, an enterprising and eternally optimistic East Indiaman captain, had been known more for ambitious schemes than sound money-making. His widow Catherine had been left only an inadequate legacy and a small Company pension with which to raise their three children.

Yet Calcutta was not London where such a family might have been forced into penury. In India it was possible to retain a household on only a small income, society connections and good favour. Huguenots by origin, the Pigou clan had sought their fortunes out East, scattered throughout the commercial cities of India. Uncles Frederick and Crommelin, both influential Calcutta traders, had done their best to support their poorer relatives, ensuring the children were decently educated, introduced into society and, in the case of Thomas Pigou, a position in the Company. That Thomas had seized the opportunity only added to their prestige – and ultimately their fortunes. The investment in the cadet branch of the family had not been wasted. *Quid pro quo* was the lifeblood pulsing through the veins of British India.

From the moment they stepped into the Pigou household, Martinha and her mother were swept up in a dizzying whirl. Sarah and Lucy Ann, already familiar with their hosts, bounded forward, delighted to be free of the constraints of shipboard life and back with friends they had known for years. The small hall echoed with the screams of children and the shrill chatter of the adults. For the first time Martinha observed the full extent of the assimilation of her children, instantly able to slip from one culture to another, as easily as they could switch languages. Her girls were different in this place.

Mrs Catherine Pigou was an extremely round lady, all dimples and dumpling rolls, with high swept copper locks arranged in kiss curls around her chubby face. She clapped her bejewelled hands together in delight – and launched into a series of complicated introductions. Several members of the immediate family were present: her sister-in-law Mrs Chitty and brother-in-law William, whom Martinha at first presumed were married but later discovered were cousins. It was very confusing. There were also two daughters, Louisa and Harriet, and other children, second cousins to Loulou and Hatty apparently, but the adults were not their parents. This information was relayed with little attendant explanation. Thong Di looked at her daughter helplessly; Martinha shrugged back her bewilderment.

'Oh my, oh my!' twittered Mrs Pigou at their blank expressions. 'You must be bamboozled listening to my silly nonsense! Forgive me, dear ladies, for I am a notorious chatterbox. Once I start, I gabble on and on, thirteen to the dozen. I am known for it all over town. Especially when cock-a-hoop with excitement. To think I am entertaining the family of the famous Superintendent Light! Such an honour! Who would have expected that young rascal would do so well!' Her splendid bosom quivered as she executed an odd half curtsey, before she collapsed into giggles, much like a child herself.

Martinha understood the gist of Mrs Pigou's ramblings, but what 'chatterbox', 'bamboozled' and 'cock-a-hoop' were, she could not say. And were there not twelve in a dozen? The English language was a very strange tongue. Why did they not simply say what they meant in words that everyone could construe? And who were Loulou and Hatty?

An awful thought dawned on Mrs Pigou. 'I presume you speak our language?' she exclaimed with abject horror on her face. Even if honoured to host these distinguished foreign guests, it was already a moot point how they were to 'fit' in with society and with whom they might 'mix' during their stay. If they were unable to speak English to boot, that would really put them beyond the pale.

Martinha returned a weak smile. 'I do speak English, Madame Pigou. My mother understands it well enough but struggles to pronounce the words. However, she tries. For my part, I believe I am quite fluent.' Or so she had thought until she visited the Pigous.

***

Too soon the day dawned when the girls returned to school. Sarah and Lucy made a dramatic show of weeping and wailing, before dashing off with scarcely a backward glance, full of stories to share with girls who had remained shut behind high walls while they had been gadding around the Indies. It was not goodbye, of course, for they were to see each other every Sunday while Martinha and Thong Di remained in the city. It did much for Martinha's spirits to see how settled they were. Francis and she had done the right thing by them, no matter how hard it had been to let them go.

It was not so easy for Martinha and Thong Di to adapt to their surroundings. The city had grown only more sprawling and crowded since their earlier trips. Life was eternally hectic, every moment of the day accounted for, an empty existence of socialising, gossiping and self-indulgence. It was a life of extravagance, or so it seemed to Martinha. Catherine Pigou constantly pled poverty, yet she had upward of twenty servants. Gowns were changed several times a day; food and drink were plentiful; gambling on card games was popular in the evenings. It was not privation as Martinha understood the word.

Yet, although they were constantly feted by their generous host, guests never reciprocated. Martinha and Thong Di did not receive a single invitation to dine, left behind at home when the Pigous had social engagements. If friends of their daughters visited on Sundays, they arrived with only their nannies. It soon became apparent that without Francis, Martinha's position was not recognised in Calcutta society as other than a curiosity.

Mrs Pigou held several gatherings in Martinha's honour, where the guests were invariably women of mixed heritage, daughters of British men and their mistresses, or the local wives of army officers and sea captains. Sometimes, they were the *begums* of Indian nawabs, those considered respectable and wealthy enough. Men never attended, unlike at Catherine Pigou's open house events, when even unattached gentlemen called and sat at table with unmarried ladies.

On one particularly hot day, her maid Esan informed Martinha that she had a visitor. It was a curious time to call, for it was early afternoon when everyone retired to their rooms to sleep during the hottest hours. The calling card read 'Mrs Eliza Kyd'.

A short while later, Martinha presented herself in the drawing room, smoothing back her hair and straightening her sarong. Mrs Kyd stood in the centre of the room still as a statue, as fresh and cool as an English summer day. She was possibly the most beautiful and polished woman Martinha had ever seen. After a month or so of well-fed Pigous whose gowns could scarce constrain their girth and whose white-powdered cheeks wobbled as they preened, Eliza

Kyd was a different species, a goddess amongst women. Lissom and slender, skin like creamy milk, gown draped to perfection, her shining chestnut ringlets framed features so perfect they might easily have been sculpted.

'Mrs Light! How good of you to receive me at this inhospitable hour! I must apologise but I was unsure how long you intended to remain in Calcutta. Pardon my presumption!' Her voice was as perfectly modulated as the rest of her, a mellifluously enunciated English that was music to the ears.

'Please do not apologise! I am delighted that you called. Come, sit down. My girl will serve refreshments.' Long glasses of cool lemon tea were handed out as the two women took to the shady veranda, fanned by one of the houseboys.

'My husband Major Kyd has spoken most highly of you, Mrs Light. He so enjoyed his time on Prince of Wales Island and has most particularly insisted that I introduce myself to you. I fear he is occupied these days as surveyor general and the commander at Budge Budge or he would have accompanied me himself.'

It was likely to be more excuse than explanation, but Martinha responded in similar fashion. 'Major Alexander has been a good friend to our island, Mrs Kyd. Superintendent Light was delighted with the outcome of the recent survey.' But, despite the graciousness of the exchange, the two ladies were aware that each was assessing the other's mettle.

Eliza jutted her chin forward with a hint of playfulness, looking Martinha up and down. 'I must say that I wholly agree with my husband's assessment.'

'It is a most prosperous settlement –'

'I do not speak of the island, my dear. I was referring to you.

Major Kyd mentioned that you prefer not to speak English, yet he was convinced you understood all that was said. And he was right! Your English is perfectly acceptable,' she continued gaily, amused by her own wit.

Martinha was less entertained. She would not be a figure of fun for another silly English woman. 'Yes, I understand your language well enough. But it is not my inclination to indulge in idle gossip around dinner tables with gentlemen. It is not acceptable in *my* culture to do so,' she added brusquely, as if admonishing the British for their laxity in morals.

Mrs Kyd gave another of her mysterious smiles before peeling off one of her lace gloves, tossing it onto her lap. To Martinha's astonishment, the ivory skin of her extended palm was intricately embellished with henna motifs. 'I think I must explain. I do not mean to tease you, my dear. The very opposite. I show you my hand as proof that we have much in common. I am, as you, a child of two heritages. I have broken with etiquette and called in the heat of the day because I wanted to meet with you alone, away from the prying eyes and itchy ears of tittle-tattlers. I wish to extend the hand of friendship in the hope that I may make your stay more amenable, as your husband did for mine. I know that you must find your position in Calcutta untenable.'

Martinha listened in amazement. 'Two heritages? But, you are so, so …' It seemed impolite to continue.

'So white? Yes, I am, am I not? And God be praised, so is my son, James. You can imagine how the vultures were circling to catch the first glimpse of him,' she chuckled, mirthlessly. 'In Calcutta, if a woman is remarkably beautiful and knows how to play the coquette, it is possible for her to create an "illusion" of acceptability. I look and speak like a perfect English rose. In fact, I am the darling of this town! Until my back is turned, of course,' she shrugged as if it was of no concern, but there was bitterness all the same. 'The illusion is but transitory. My true story is suspected by all.'

'You – a Bengali woman? How can this be?' Martinha asked.

Eliza did not offer an answer, but instead put her own question to Martinha: 'I believe you too have an interesting origin. First tell me of your background and then I promise to be honest about mine.'

Martinha obliged. 'My father was a Portuguese Eurasian whose grandfather was French. My mother is the daughter of a Siamese nobleman and a Malay princess. My husband is English.'

Eliza clapped her hands. 'What a wonderful story! Quite like a fairy tale. No wonder your skin is so pale, your hair so lustrous and your figure so willowy! Your history is even more exotic than mine!'

Martinha had a thousand questions. 'Who are your parents? Where were you born? Are there others like you?'

Mrs Kyd smiled broadly, not the practised smile of earlier, but a wide infectious grin that made her look younger, revealing the girl behind the elegant façade.

'My father is an English gentleman, my mother is said to have been an Indian *rani* – a princess, like your grandmother.' Eliza paused and winked. 'All pish posh, of course! My maternal grandfather was a Bengali cloth merchant with mixed blood of his own. My poor mother (known for her light complexion) became concubine to my father, Mr Horace Wagstaff of Derbyshire. After her death, and on account of my apparent lack of native features, my father insisted I should be raised by an English governess. Thus, he could pass me off as English and my mother's origins forgotten. Although I may present myself as the quintessential English gentlewoman, I am, in fact, nothing more than the illegitimate daughter of a Company officer and his bibi.'

It was a revelation to Martinha, even more surprising when she learned that there were others living in similar dissemblance. Many Company people had such skeletons in their cupboards. 'The henna?' Martinha asked hesitantly, wondering why Mrs Kyd had taken the chance of revealing herself by this distinctive adornment.

'It is my small act of rebellion! From time to time, I ask my girl, Parvati, to paint my palms with henna. On Indian high days and holidays, for festivals and the like. I do it for my poor mother who gave her life to bring me into this world but never had the chance to teach me her ways. Shame on me to hide it beneath my gloves! I do not possess the courage to declare myself openly before the world,' she admitted, with an unexpected hint of shyness.

'Does Major Kyd know?' Martinha wondered. 'Forgive me, if I am too forward, madam.'

'Of course, he does! Alexander is amused by it. He says it "adds to my allure". Gentlemen worry far less about such things than prim ladies of society. Their morals are more "accommodating" where the exotic is concerned. But make no mistake, if my skin were browner, or my eyes were black, then I too would be confined to the *zenana*. Even by dear Major Kyd,' Eliza added softly. 'On the other hand, Mrs Light, you comport yourself in a wholly different manner, if I may say so. You wear your native cloths with pride, you ride about in public with your mother. You have the courage not to pander to society. I am captivated by your audacity!'

That the alluring Mrs Kyd might find a simple girl from the Straits an object of admiration, came as a profound shock to Martinha. 'It is not courage, Mrs Kyd,' Martinha insisted. 'I come from the Straits. It is very different there. Our people have mixed for generations. Once, I tried to wear European attire, but I felt uncomfortable. I prefer to be what I am. If that is not acceptable in Calcutta, then so be it. I will soon enough return where I belong,' she explained in her guileless fashion.

Eliza shook her head sadly in response. 'But I have nowhere else to go, I'm afraid, so must continue on this merry dance. Please, call me Eliza. And may I call you Martinha? You may be the only person in town with whom I might truly be myself!'

***

The household was agog at the visit of the captivating Mrs Kyd. That the leading light of Calcutta had been in their drawing room was news on its own, but that she had been there to visit Mrs Light had thoroughly astonished them. Nor did it take long for the intelligence to circulate. Martinha's diary soon filled with invitations, with Captain Glass in demand as her escort. Mrs Kyd's approbation had been sufficient to raise Martinha's esteem.

Yet, although Martinha was grateful to Eliza Kyd, she could not say she found her visits to the theatre, dinner parties, assemblies and balls quite to her taste. She was still treated as a curio and felt awkward in company: baffled by the plays, tongue-tied at the table, and quite unable to participate in their unseemly dances.

At one such gathering at the house of Mr John Ogilvy, the father of Sarah's best friend Margaret, Martinha encountered William Fairlie, a man she disliked intensely, for he had once made it obvious that she was a woman of no consequence who should be kept out of sight.

They exchanged a stilted greeting. Fairlie asked her about her husband. Moments later they were joined by Ogilvy.

'I was just chatting with the charming Mrs Light,' began Fairlie. 'She spoke of her husband, my dear friend Francis. We are well acquainted. He banks with us in Calcutta.'

John Ogilvy, a balding Scot sporting a fine growth of black sideburns, feigned surprise. 'I had no idea, William! Why, wasn't I just saying to Pigou before he left that I should dearly like to find out more about the place? I've a notion to invest there. Perchance you could mention my name to your husband, Mrs Light?'

Martinha nodded demurely. 'I will indeed, sir. Mayhap you would like to visit us and see for yourself our fine new settlement?'

Ogilvy beamed. 'Maybe I will, dear lady. They say it is a pleasant voyage. It would also be a fine thing to visit young Pigou. Mrs Ogilvy and I have high hopes that he may one day be our son-in-law. He is promised to our daughter.'

Martinha glanced across at little Margaret running around the garden with her own two girls. 'You have a daughter older than Margaret, sir?'

Ogilvy appeared confused. 'Margaret is my only child save for our bairn on the way, pray God for a safe delivery.'

Although not unused to little girls being married off to old men, it came as a surprise that such practices occurred amongst the British. Margaret Ogilvy was not yet nine years old, whilst Thomas Pigou was two-and-twenty. She tucked the information away as something to discuss with Francis on her return.

'We will look forward to your visit then, Mr Ogilvy. Thank you for inviting us to your charming home. My daughters are very fond of Margaret.'

The two gentlemen cleared their throats, looking for an excuse to withdraw. Just then, on a cloud of perfume and silk, Mrs Kyd swept by, taking Martinha by the hand. 'I'm very sorry, gentlemen, but I really must speak to my good friend Mrs Light.'

'Those two old bores,' whispered Eliza as they found a quiet corner. 'I couldn't possibly leave a dear friend alone with them!' It was Mrs Kyd to her rescue yet again. 'I can't talk long because Alexander insists that I do the rounds. Let's meet up tomorrow. May I call early morning? Dress formally – there's someone you simply must meet!'

***

Clad in songket, Martinha stepped from Mrs Kyd's bright yellow landau onto the delightfully named Mangoe Lane, the eponymous golden fruit trees that lined the road complementing the carriage to perfection. Their destination was a pretty chunam terraced house belonging to a Mr John Hill. Mrs Kyd led the way up three flights of stairs, refusing to reveal the purpose of their visit, yet noticeably bursting with anticipation. Martinha's curiosity was piqued. She found herself caught up in the expectant mood, as giddy as one of her daughters.

'Welcome, dear ladies!' called out an affable female voice.

They entered a bright and breezy reception room, with floor-length windows opening out onto a small wrought-iron balcony festooned with flowering plants. In this pleasant spot, seated on low cushions, they sat down to tea and cakes. 'A tidbit before we start work, eh?' their host announced mysteriously.

Her name was Mrs Diana Hill; she had been in Calcutta almost two years. Similar in age to Eliza, the two could not have been more different, although they were close intimates. Diana Hill was lean and boyish, with unruly flaxen curls carelessly knotted in a silk bandanna. Her face was angular but full of character, exuding an air of self-assurance. It was in her dress, however, that her singular nature was revealed, for she wore men's garb: a long tunic over cotton pyjamas. Furthermore, her feet were bare, with ankles adorned with bracelets that tinkled as she moved, like a Hindu dancing girl.

'I must apologise for my attire, Mrs Light! These are my work clothes. Gowns are too constricting in the heat. I find kurta pyjamas ideal at home, both for the climate and the atelier.'

'Atelier?' The word was entirely new to Martinha.

Mrs Hill waved her finger in mock reprimand at Mrs Kyd. 'Naughty girl! Have you not informed Mrs Light of my profession? Tut, tut. You are too playful, Eliza!'

'I wanted to surprise you, Martinha! I shall now reveal all. Mrs Hill is a prominent miniaturist! She has exhibited in London where she won prizes for her art. Recently Diana painted one of me so that Alexander may carry my image on his next voyage. Miniatures are all the rage these days, don't you know? You might like to have yours painted. It would be the perfect gift for the superintendent!'

'Miniature?' Martinha could only echo the word. She was completely at a loss.

The women exchanged amused glances before Mrs Hill dashed into the adjoining room. Martinha glanced across at Eliza quizzically, but her lips were sealed. Moments later, all was clear. Mrs Hill was an artist who painted tiny images of people in oval frames as gifts for their loved ones. Diana laid out examples on the table.

She was extraordinarily talented. Her intricate brushwork and luminous colours created astonishing likenesses. There were three subjects: a pale, dreamy lady with brown ringlets in a peach silk dress; a pink and chubby child with an angelic froth of ginger curls; and a gentleman in brilliant crimson jacket, bouffant hair powdered white, his liquid blue eyes and full lips marking him out as a man of sensitive emotions.

Eliza clapped her hands. 'I recognise them instantly! Why, the lady is Mrs Graham – such a delicate soul! And her little son, the fragile darling! And this, of course, is your broody brother-in-law, Mr Hill. He has the soul of a poet, don't you know?'

Martinha picked up each in turn. She had never seen anything like them. That such precise features, such glorious colours – even the very secret soul of the sitters – could be rendered on a miniscule scale! Turning over the small oval ornament, she smoothed her finger across the back. 'Ivory?' she enquired.

'Yes, I prefer to work on ivory although some are copper. They are meant to be no bigger than one's palm so that one may gaze upon them daily and hold them close to one's heart. Some keep theirs by their bedside or escritoire, for their eyes only. Even though many miles may separate two hearts, your loved one is with you always!' Mrs Hill explained with dramatic flourish.

'I have never seen such beauty! Are they very expensive? I so desire one for my husband!' exclaimed Martinha.

'Not so very expensive. I feel sure he would think it worth the price!' Eliza assured her.

'Then it is settled.' Mrs Hill tilted Martinha's chin so that the sunlight fell directly upon her upturned face. 'Extraordinary features, my dear! Your skin is porcelain, but your eyes are warm chocolate. And that hair! May I unknot it?' Martinha pulled the pin; it fell about her shoulders, a curtain of obsidian. 'We must paint you in the sunlight to capture the perfection of the blue-black sheen!' the artist insisted.

Soon the three women were settled on the flat roof above, shielded from the sun by a large white canopy. There, in the languid heat, Martinha sat as Diana sketched, listening to the conversation of the two women and occasionally making her own observations. Bathing in the atmosphere, Martinha began to understand the friendship of women. All her life, she had been surrounded by family and servants, her only friends being members of her own household. The unfettered freedom of idle conversation with intelligent females made a deep impression on her. Where she had judged the English ladies of Calcutta as silly gossips, Martinha recognised that this was merely a facade. Men might reign over them in all things, but in their private world, they had the licence to speak their own minds.

Diana Hill was a widow with two children left behind with her mother-in-law in London, the terms upon which the family had given her permission to leave. Before her marriage, she had been a student of miniature painting and now, freed from marital responsibilities, she had resumed her profession. Artists were ten-a-penny in London, where it had proved nigh impossible for a woman to secure regular commissions. Then Diana had heard about the enormous demand for such portraits in India, ideal for sending home or carrying on long voyages. Through her benefactors in the art world and her contacts in the Company, she had been granted permission to make passage to Calcutta. It had helped enormously that her brother-in-law, John Hill, was a successful junior merchant. And here she now was, making not only a living, but a name for herself. Diana had even painted a miniature of Lord Cornwallis himself, about which he had complimented her most kindly. No wonder so many ladies – and gentlemen – were flocking to her studio.

'Isn't it wonderful, Martinha? A lady able to earn her own way in life! Who has ever heard of such a thing!' gasped Eliza.

Martinha gave it some thought. 'In your English society, women have little freedom. In the Indies, however, married ladies are accustomed to engage in commerce. Of course, we spend most of our lives in the home, but it does not mean we are denied a place in public life. My aunt has held the trade of Jangsylan in her hands for many years and, through her husband the governor, she was for a long time the real power on the island. My mother herself was once an ambassador for a sultan.' Martinha realised how sheltered she had allowed herself to become. Unlike her mother and her aunt, she had never exercised that sort of influence. Francis preferred she spend her time in charity work and household matters. He did not approve of her meddling in his affairs.

'How interesting!' Eliza commented. 'Our British men are

patriarchs who keep their women like dolls, with nothing of consequence to do but bear children and fill their lives in idle pursuits! They're just as bad as Indian rajahs with their women in seclusion!'

'The other day at the house of Mr Ogilvy, I heard something that surprised me.' Martinha's tongue had been loosened, aided by a few glasses of wine. 'He spoke of Mr Thomas Pigou, that he was promised to Mr Ogilvy's daughter, Margaret. She is only nine years old. I did not know such things happened in England!'

Diana grunted in disapproval. 'To hear them pontificate about Muslims and Hindus bartering young girls around as wives, one might imagine the practice was an offence to them. But women are in short supply in Calcutta. Acceptable women, that is. Once upon a time, the British took local "wives" but things are changing. Too many aristocrats are gobbling up the senior posts these days, bringing their pompous wives and rigid sensibilities. Now one must "prove" one's Britishness or risk the loss of one's livelihood.'

Mrs Hill shed more light on the changing social climate in the city. 'Every ship that arrives is full of marriageable English ladies looking for husbands. They call it "the fishing fleet". Poor things. At home they face either spinsterhood or dreary lives as governesses and companions. What else can a decent young woman without an income do? I shudder to think of the alternative. So off they sail to India, to be mocked for their desperation, when all they are doing is seeking their fortune just as any British man! These girls end up on display like prize cattle, "sitting up", as they say. Men who already have local woman, now find that they must have a British wife to ensure their future. Not that anything will change, of course. We all know where most of them choose to sleep at night!'

Martinha's eyes were truly opened in the days spent on Mrs Hill's roof. She felt some regret about her treatment of Lydia Hardwick, another woman trying to better herself, no different from Mrs Hill, the professional artist, or Mrs Kyd, the illusion of an English lady. Her mother had understood what she had not. One day Sarah, Lucy Ann and even little Mary would find themselves in this arena. Would they be bartered for their beauty, affecting to be what they were not their whole lives long?

8

Unfinished Business

Kuala Bahang, Queddah. June 1788

Almost two years had passed since Soliman last docked along this familiar jetty. Since then, a marked change had been wrought on the once-bustling port. It was now a forlorn backwater of canoes, fishing smacks, sampans and riverine dugouts. The only sea-going vessels appeared to be from Siam or Sumatra. It was as if their new island settlement had sucked the lifeblood of the place, leaving only its frail bones.

He had come for rice in exchange for opium. Food was scarce on the island. Soliman planned to circumvent the official market and supply his people direct by appealing to his brothers across the channel. Francis would not approve, but there were hungry mouths to feed in his kampong, and the conflict between Queddah and the British was not of their making. It would not be the first time Soliman had indulged in smuggling; he had done it often enough for Light himself in the past. Not that he regarded his action as illegal. Trade was trade. If they had rice to sell and he had goods to exchange, what was the issue?

The story put about by Queddah to explain the trickle of rice to Pinang of late was that the harvest had been poor and there was hardly enough to feed their own population. It was nonsense. The rice fields of Queddah were as abundant as ever and even more important now that the British island had lured away their other trade. The sultan was using food as a lever to force the hand of the British. The treaty remained unratified; the lease had never been paid. There was great discontent amongst the Malay people who regarded Light as a cheat who had betrayed them with clever words.

Leaving his crew aboard, Soliman did not wish to advertise his presence so had dressed simply with his long hair left unbound, hoping it was enough of a disguise. He was well known in the port on account of his connection to Francis Light and did not wish to draw the anger of embittered citizens upon himself.

His desire to remain incognito failed almost as soon as he stepped onto the land. As if from nowhere, palace guards ran forward with their weapons drawn. In moments he was seized, rough-handled, the keris concealed in the waistband of his sarong confiscated. At first, he struggled until his own keris, polished to a lustrous finish and rubbed in arsenic, was held to his own throat. He did not relish the irony of being slit by his own weapon of destruction.

'*Lepaskan saya*!' he shouted but they would not let him go. Instead, he was dragged through the streets then thrown onto a bullock cart, tied like an animal for slaughter. Surrounded by hostile guards, he was rattled along dirt tracks out of town and up the hill until his bones were sore and his wrists burned from the rope. He could see nothing, for he had been forced onto his face, a rough foot pressing on his spine to hold him down. The sun burned; his sweat ran in pools beneath him. He could taste its salt.

After an interminable while, the cart came to a sudden stop and Soliman was unceremoniously dumped onto the ground. As he struggled to his feet, still shrugging off opportunistic blows, he observed that they were in the grounds of an elegant Malay home, as grand as any palace. It was black-timbered, with carving on the finials of the roof and the windows and doorways. The grounds were beautifully kept, lush with flowers and abundant with trees and fruits.

'Lower your head, traitor!' shouted one of the guards who pulled him along by his hair. Stumbling forward, he was led to the rear, thrown into a room at the top of a stairway in a section of the house that was connected to the main residence by a narrow-stilted passageway. He had been expecting a dank prison cell, but to Soliman's surprise, he found himself in a richly decorated chamber. It was sparsely furnished, containing only an ornate desk and chair, and bound books on the shelves. The walls were decorated with wood panels adorned with motifs of *awan larat,* a stylised riot of intertwined vines and flowers bordering sacred Quranic script etched in golden. This was the private room of a man of substance.

Someone entered from the inner room. 'Release him, fools. He's not a prisoner. Bring refreshments and bandages for his wounds. Then leave us alone!'

Hesitantly, Soliman raised his head. This time it was not slammed back down upon the floor. His interrogator was a man he recognised. It was Tunku Ya, the Laksamana of Sultan Abdullah. Soliman had been present at negotiations before the settlement, not that he expected the great man would recognise him. He had been at the back of a group of mostly British men.

'I see you know who I am,' the Laksamana said. The expression on his stern face was unreadable. He was viewing Soliman with the usual disdain of a noble towards a man he considered far beneath his rank.

Soliman dropped his head. 'Yes, Tunku. You are the Laksamana. I am not worthy to –'

'Cease!' He held up his hand. 'Consider the polite addresses have been done. I do not have time for pleasantries. You have been ill-used and for that I apologise. It was not my intent. I asked them to bring you to me as soon as you reached land. Their treatment indicates how much anger is simmering against the British. You are known to be a Malay who lives amongst them. They think you a traitor to your people. Perhaps it is just as well I have brought you here, for who knows what might have happened in Kuala Bahang without my intervention?'

'I am no traitor!' Soliman raised his voice, his anger rearing up.

Tunku Ya pulled a small stool out and placed it before him. 'Be quiet. Sit down. You would do well to measure your words with care. I am not a man to insult.' He took a chair for himself and placed it across from Soliman. 'Tell me a little about yourself, young man.'

Soliman took a moment before answering. 'I live in a kampong on Pulau Pinang amongst Minangs, but I am not of their race. My father was a Malay sailor. He died and I was abandoned in India. Francis Light took pity on me and raised me as his son. I owe him much. He is a good man.'

Tunku Ya nodded. 'This much I know. Do you have family in the kampong?'

'A wife. A daughter, recently born. I am a trader with my own vessel. I take no part in the affairs of the island.'

'But you are close to Superintendent Light?'

Soliman paused. 'I see him from time to time,' he added.

'As father to son?'

Soliman shrugged, recalling their last meeting. Light had come to the village to bring a golden bangle for his new-born daughter, referring to little Nuraini as 'my first grandchild!' Yes, he thought to himself. As father to son.

'I will never betray Francis Light, nor will I betray my people or my religion,' Soliman insisted, ignoring the question asked.

Again, Tunku Ya demonstrated his tolerance by patting the young man on the hand, almost in avuncular fashion. 'Let me explain something so that you understand what I seek. The promises made in the treaty remain unfulfilled. The British occupy our island and yet no lease has been paid. Furthermore, our enemies circle us, but there has been no sign of military support. In the treaty it states that the British would "defend the coast of Queddah". Are we to presume that Captain Light – our *wakil* in Calcutta – lied to us and never intended to honour the treaty? Or …' he stopped speaking as Soliman attempted to interrupt, holding a finger to his lips '… or, has the British Company reneged on its promises? Do they think that there is nothing we poor Malays can do but accept our losses? For, if the latter is the case and your Light is powerless, we must act before too late. We stand at a crossroads, Juragan Soliman. It is vital we understand the true situation so that we can make the right decisions. What happens next may cost us all a great deal in human life – as well as money.'

The alarm in Soliman's eyes showed his grasp of the situation. 'War?' he gasped. 'Queddah may go to war with the British? They would send their warships and destroy you all!'

The Laksamana sat back in his chair, his hands clasped over

his belly, his elbows resting on the arms. 'How interesting that the British are unable to supply warships to fulfil their promises, yet ships appear as if by magic when they fear their own interests are compromised!' He chuckled but his face was grim. 'What you must understand, Soliman, is the British have enemies, too. Two years ago, they were the saviour of the Peninsula, a breath of air after the evils of the Dutch and Portuguese. They offered hope against the Bugis, their very presence enough to deter the Burmese and the Siamese. But things have changed. The kitten has become a tiger, as the old saying goes. Now, they turn their backs on old friends and prove themselves worthless liars. One by one, those friends are abandoning them. The Sultan of Selangor has sent back the British flag and refuses to trade with them. The Sultan of Perak is losing patience and threatens the same. The Sultan of Johor lingers in exile in Siantan, his letters to the Company ignored. The Sultan of Terengganu has been waiting for months for the return of his envoys from Calcutta. Meanwhile Dutch fortunes are rising. Soon the Malay kingdoms may choose them over the lying British. So, perhaps when we face British warships, we may do so with the might of the Belanda!'

'But the Dutch would seize Pulau Pinang for themselves!'

'And we would have our revenge and the protection of the most powerful Europeans in the region. Is this what you wish for your island home?'

It was a vision of a nightmare future not only for Light and his settlement, but also for his own family. What chance they might be spared if the combined forces of so many enemies were to attack Pinang? 'But what can I do? I have no influence in these matters,' Soliman mumbled helplessly. 'How can I help prevent this disaster?'

The other man laughed softly. 'Of course, you cannot. This is not what we ask of you. We know many things, but we cannot be sure where the fault lies. Is our enemy Light or the Company? If Light still wishes to honour his treaty, then we are ready to open negotiations – with the added incentive that we will starve the island and ally with his enemies if a speedy resolution is not found. If we are to reverse the inevitable, time is short. Our chance to claim back our sovereign rights will soon pass, and we shall be the slaves to British greed forever. If any man can discover Light's intent, we believe it is you. Would you act as our mediator? Carry private messages to Light? Vouch for his character to the sultan?'

'I will not act against him,' Soliman stated firmly.

'Nor will we ask that of you. What do you say?'

'If I refuse?'

The Laksamana grunted. 'You would not be welcome in these waters again.'

'If I agree?'

'Your vessel will be loaded up with rice at very favourable prices.'

The two men contemplated each other, the younger searching his conscience for the right path. Soliman closed his eyes and prayed silently for divine help. Tunku Ya bowed his own head in respect.

Soliman had made his decision. 'I will help bring peace. That I am willing to do.'

***

The subsequent audience with Sultan Abdullah was held in his private quarters, away from the prying eyes of the court who had their own opinions on approaches to the British. There was growing resentment and calls for war. Not only were commercial activities in their port stagnating now that the vibrant bazaar of George Town attracted both foreign and regional trade alike, there was also the matter of injured pride. Pulau Pinang was theirs. It had not been abandoned to the British, merely leased. No payment had been made. They felt doubly cheated, particularly on account of the preferential treatment Francis Light had once received at court. It was as if they had been betrayed by one of their own.

Soliman was relieved that he did not have to stand in the *dewan* before the assembled nobles. It was bad enough that some knew of his associations with the superintendent of Penang without announcing it to all and sundry. Yet, a private audience was even more intimidating. Who was he to converse with the sultan of Queddah?

The reception chamber was small but elegantly decorated. The walls were wood panelled, wondrously carved in forest flora surrounding sacred golden *surahs*. On a platform before a silken hanging of bright yellow sat Sultan Abdullah resting on a saffron divan. Tunku Ya introduced Soliman who remained head bowed, struggling to still the trembling in his legs. Such was the respect that was owed to God's chosen representative on Earth. He thought himself unworthy even to share the same air.

'Bring him closer,' the sultan replied.

The laksamana nudged him; Soliman stumbled a few steps until he reached a cushioned mat and dropped to his knees.

'Raise your head, boy. I wish to look at you. It is the eyes that reveal the measure of a man,' Abdullah pronounced.

Soliman slowly raised his head, blinked a few times, and then looked the sultan in the face. He raised his chin, a hint of bravado to mask his discomfort. The two men held the gaze for what seemed to Soliman an inordinate length of time. But he dared not look away.

The sultan was much younger than Soliman had imagined, for in his head such lofty persons must be venerable old men. Before him sat a small man with handsome features already beginning to run to seed; his skin was pale and bloated. Despite the elegance of his fine songket, the sultan's body showed the signs of fine living, with a belly that his narrow shoulders did not carry well. In all, he did not look a well man, whether from indulgence or cares, Soliman could not tell. Yet, he was the sultan all the same.

'You're a handsome rogue, I will admit,' Abdullah spoke. 'I had expected a more brutish man. Tell me something of yourself. I wish to learn about you.'

Soliman took a swallow more akin to a gulp before commencing. 'I ... I am a sailor, *Tuanku*. I have a *padewakang* and I trade in the Straits: Melaka, Aceh, Bintang, Pinang, Ujung Salang, Mergui. That is all. I am a humble man,' he added.

The sultan gave him a sardonic look. 'Oh, you are much more than that, young man. Do not be coy. What of your wife?'

'She is Minang. The daughter of Nakhoda Kecil, the headman of our people on the island,' he replied.

'Not of our people. He is *pendatang* from West Sumatra. These Minangs think to settle here and take land from us. They are as greedy for what is ours as the English,' the sultan pronounced. Soliman winced. This was not a good start.

'What else? Make sure to tell the truth. I already know things about you. I will not take kindly to lies.'

For a few moments, Soliman paused. There was no avoidance. He must continue.

'I was an orphan child on the streets of Madras, starving to death. Captain Francis Light took me in and cared for me like a son. I owe my life to him.' As he spoke the last words he raised his head, a hint of defiance in his eyes. To his surprise, the sultan chuckled.

'Good, so now we are being honest. You are close to this British governor. He talks to you?'

Soliman shrugged; Tunku Ya slapped his head. 'Have more respect!'

The younger man raised his joined hands. 'I beg your apology, Tuanku. I visit the superintendent from time to time. He gave my daughter a gift when she was born. But he does not confide in me on matters of state.'

'Nor would I expect him to!' The sultan snapped back. 'What kind of man would you say he was?'

'Francis Light?' Soliman gasped. 'Why, he is the best of men. A good man. A true friend.'

'So, he has no flaws?'

'No man is perfect,' Soliman admitted.

'Then tell me his.'

A shadow passed over Soliman's face. 'I cannot do harm to him. He has been a father to me. Please, Tuanku, do not ask this of me!'

The sultan sighed in annoyance. 'Fool! All I ask of you is to answer a few simple questions. Is he a man we can trust? Once we thought he was. Now his behaviour suggests he is a traitor who lied to steal the island and never intended to honour his promises. You know him best. Is he capable of deceit?' There was anger in the sultan's voice at the mention of betrayal.

It seemed to Soliman that perhaps this was a chance to heal the rift between Queddah and the island. What he said next could calm the stormy waters and allow the resumption of peaceful trade, a benefit to all. This was not the time for him to be reticent or faint-hearted. He might aid Francis, not harm him.

'My lord, I swear that Captain Light, although he is a clever merchant and governor who drives a hard bargain, is first and foremost a man of his word. He believed that the treaty was the beginning of a new era between Queddah and Calcutta. But the Company are deceivers. They make promises and refuse to honour them. They have done this everywhere in India. The biggest victim is Francis Light himself, who is caught in the middle. They give him little support either in money or arms. It is not the fault of the superintendent, but the faithless British!' Soliman insisted with vehemence.

'Interesting. You believe that your Light would make good on his promises if he could? Or is he more interested in making as much profit for himself and his compatriots as he can? They say he has claimed all the land on the island with Captain Sakat.'

'He makes no such claim, Tuanku. He gives out parcels of land to anyone who settles. He treats everyone with fairness, whether orang putih, Malay, Chinese, Chulia, Arab, whatever. He keeps the peace. He raises kapitans from the local communities and allows them to govern their own people. Superintendent Light wishes all to live in harmony. Yet, the orang putih are not in agreement. They treat the local people like dirt beneath their feet.'

'And what does the superintendent do to stop this?' The sultan queried.

'Whatever he can. But he has no rights to punish orang putih. He sends letters asking for judges so that those who break the peace can be punished. He asks for more money, but nothing comes. Most of the buildings come from his own purse!'

Both the Sultan and Tunku Ya noticeably relaxed their guard at these revelations. The tension in the room began to dissipate as if they were hearing what they had hoped to hear. Soliman gleaned that they were desirous of a peaceable resolution too.

'And what of the treaty? Why are we still awaiting ratification? What has Light to say on that?' Tunku Ya had one more serious issue to settle.

'I know little of the matter. It is not something the superintendent would discuss with me. But I have seen him lose patience with the Company many times. He warns that Queddah will not tolerate the situation. But his letters go unanswered for months and when they reply, they say nothing about these matters. I have seen him throw letters across the room in anger. But that is all I can add. Superintendent Light is a discreet man. He does not even confide in James Scott. They are no longer business partners. Such is the honesty of Francis Light that he will not take advantage of his position. He calls that corruption.'

It seemed to the sultan and his senior minister that Light's distaste for taking advantage of his situation was exceedingly strange. Why else would one take on the onerous responsibilities of governance if not to build one's own fortune? Yet, they could not deny, this did not sound like the behaviour of a man without integrity. Sound judgement, perhaps.

His tongue now loosed by the positive reaction of his betters, Soliman expanded on the fine qualities of Francis Light. He launched into a robust retelling of the recent attack at the Malay bazaar, which gained even more gore and brutality in the retelling, as is the way of a good story. The sultan was impressed to learn that the English sailors had been held prisoner and sentenced to hard labour for the benefit of the whole community. Light had ensured that these rowdy louts pay back for the disruption of their riotous behaviour.

It was an enlightening conversation, giving more of an insight inside the workings of the fledgling settlement than they had gleaned from all their many spies. Perhaps it was time to lay down the gauntlet and adopt more pacific methods so that the two parties might come to terms.

'Go back to your island and tell your superintendent that we wish to find a peaceful way forward. Tell no one other than Light. Carry a letter for us with the offer of the hand of friendship.'

***

From the Ruler of Queddah, the Abode of Peace.
Al-Mustahaq

This letter of love and affection is sent by us in the spirit of everlasting sincerity to our distinguished friend, the Superintendent of Pinang Island

Firstly, we speak of the Great Treaty that was agreed between our two honourable nations. We now wish for a lasting agreement so that all our obligations and promises may be honoured for the benefit of both our peoples. It would please me greatly for an understanding to be achieved so that our friendship may be restored.

Then we may return to the matter of rice and cattle. We wish to supply the entire amount you require but the poor harvest last year caused great hardship. Furthermore, the Dutch have sent messengers and are seeking rice from us for their people. They offer a high price. As you know we did supply the rice to Melaka, but we purchased it from Siam and made profit from the trade. Thus, we may reserve enough of our own crops to feed your island, once all that lies between us is settled.

Then it came to our attention that our noble brother Sultan Ibrahim Shah of Selangor, the Abode of Sincerity, has turned his back on our noble English allies and returned your flag, refusing further trade with the Company. Others amongst our brother sultans are also contemplating such actions, some even promising their loyalties to Belanda. Queddah remains your friend during these times of difficulties. We trust our devotion is in accord with your own.

Thus, we honourably beseech our dear friend to inform his admirable associates of all that has come to pass so that they may see fit to restore the harmony between us.

This is my wish.

Written in the year 1202 AH, the 29th day of Shaban.

9

Across the Blackwater

Tulloh Jelutong, Prince of Wales Island. September 1788

It began with the disappearance of a few goats from the farms that fringed the forest across the Ayer Hitam River at the western limit of the settlement. At first it was presumed theft. Many newly arrived settlers could not afford meat, even more so now that food was in short supply. Prices had risen sharply on account of the Queddah embargo. Then scattered scraps of hide and gnawed bones turned up, which suggested a different explanation. Concern grew. Fences were found pulled down and trampled. More animals were taken. A plantation worker vanished. At twilight and early dawn, a shadowy beast was sighted, lurking on the perimeter of the plantation. It walked on four legs. The more gullible spoke of forest demons taking revenge on humans for encroaching on their territory. Those of more sense suspected something real and much more terrifying – a rogue tiger.

Until that point, no tigers had been sighted on Pinang. Yet they were a common nuisance on the mainland. The channel between was narrow; tigers were known to be strong swimmers. Howsoever it had arrived, prompt action was required to catch the predator and mollify the burgeoning fears of the population. The confidence of the settlers had already been shaken by food shortages and the threat of conflict with Queddah.

In some ways the tiger was a godsend for it presented Francis Light with a welcome escape from the burdens of his office. For months he had been encumbered with one crisis after another whilst not yet entirely recovered from debilitating illness. Martinha had returned invigorated from her Calcutta visit and now seemed quite renewed. She had more confidence these days, even to the extent of embracing her position as First Lady of the island with more enthusiasm at last. It was time for him to embark on a timely diversion to refresh and repair his spirits. All work and no play maketh Jack a dull boy, or so they say. What could be more revitalising than an exhilarating hunting trip?

Light had always found that a stimulating diversion works wonders to turn the restless masses from contemplation of their real problems: poverty, insecurity, starvation. It was often demonstrated in the navy. *Panem et Circenses,* Bread and Circuses, as the Romans used to say. Those emperors had been masters at the art of distracting the mob. If Superintendent Light could assemble settlers to embark on this dangerous expedition – and even better, return victorious with the carcass of a tiger – opinion might swing back in his favour.

Mutual cooperation was the key. It was already demonstrated by the migrant communities, something from which they might all benefit. Malay kampongs were beautifully kept, their houses swept, and their compounds well maintained. Everyone took responsibility: the plants and orchards were tended; the men cleared undergrowth to ward off snakes and rats; the entire village collectively built houses and community halls. This communal responsibility extended to other areas, such as patrols, catching marauding crocodiles, sharing irrigation channels, and access to fresh water. As a result, kampong life was generally harmonious for all. No one was left alone or in dire straits without the support of their neighbours. In much the same way, the Chinese had their kongsi system. These two very different traditions sprang from the same instinct: if all members contributed to public welfare, then all would be uplifted.

It was this spirit that Light wished to harness in his tiger hunt: the people working together to protect each other, not only to kill a dangerous wild animal, but to forge bonds between them. The residents of the island shared more in common than the differences that lay between them.

In the deepest dark of night, before the first trace of dawn hinted at the day to come, the volunteers assembled on open ground near the superintendent's new residence. Light had arranged bullock carts for transport; others had brought their own wagons. Most, however, walked. The roads to the west were little more than tracks trodden through usage; at many points they would abandon their rides to plough through *belukar* and forest on foot.

Upwards of fifty men assembled that morning, more were probably waiting at the Blackwater River itself. Perhaps it was too many; in the noise and confusion a wily animal might go to ground. But in many ways, participation in this hunt was more important than victory. Everyone wished to take part in this crucial right-of-passage. How would one stand before one's neighbours if your son, husband or brother had not done his share?

Despite the early hour, women, children and old folk lined Light Street to watch the procession move off, heading away from George Town towards the rickety bridge that crossed the river about three miles away. Standing out amongst the apprehensive spectators, Mrs Lydia Gray made a particular spectacle of herself, wailing with theatrical abandon for her husband to return home safe. Lt Gray kept his eyes firmly on the road ahead, his embarrassment revealed by the high colour of his cheeks. His men were mightily amused, sniggering and aping Mrs Gray's tender entreaties behind his back.

At the head of the column rode Light alongside Thomas Pigou, with several Company men in a cart behind: Nathaniel Bacon, John Chiene, John Henderson and Dr Hutton, his assistant, Marlbro, by his side. Behind marched the artillerymen under Lt Gray, who were expected to fell the animal once it had been driven out of hiding. Then came a large group of plantation workers and Caffrees whose function was as beaters; Light had offered them a monetary reward for success in locating the beast and driving it towards the guns. As all they had by way of weaponry were stout staffs, they were in the greatest danger. They could not be expected to risk their lives without compensation.

Behind them sauntered the Malays, led by Nakhoda Kecil and Soliman. They were mostly young men, simmering with excitement to prove themselves, confident they would be the ones to kill the tiger with their bare hands, for this was their terrain and they knew the forest better than anyone. Some had spears sharpened to fearsome tips; most carried keris tucked into sarongs. Their mood of celebration infected the whole party. Men broke into song while others talked and laughed, their merry sounds carrying far on the still air. Gray observed to Light that once they neared the forest, that would all have to stop – or the tiger would be well gone. But for now, Light did not wish to pour cold water on their gaiety. Time enough for fear when they sighted their prey.

In smaller bands came Burmese sailors and Christian Eurasians, Siamese traders and Indian shopkeepers, carrying any tool or stick they might use as weapon. Bringing up the rear was a well-armed group of stern Chinese sent by Kapitan Khoh, some even bearing rifles, which initially caused some consternation amongst the Europeans. Light had allayed their fears; these men were from the Kapitan's personal bodyguard or sentries from his warehouses. The superintendent could personally vouch for them.

It was Light's intention to reach the crossing point at dawn with the cool of early morning ahead. Breakfast was to be served, a further inducement for the poorer folk to join in, before they set off over the river into Light's plantation which he fondly called 'Suffolk Estate'. On the limit of his newly cleared forest and that of James Scott's rival plantation, 'Scotland', they would enter the 'hunting grounds' of the tiger where bones had been located. Trackers had also found prints and fresh dung.

The jollity that marked their departure soon faded away as the trundling carts lumbered over the difficult terrain and those on foot began to struggle at the demanding military pace. As the comparative safety of the town receded, the reality of their mission sank in. Somewhere out there awaited a giant predator, strong enough to take down several men, even if wounded by rifle shot.

Inevitably, there were those who claimed this was no ordinary beast. The Malays spoke of a man-tiger, the spirit of the island, bent on revenge against those who had taken land owned by the creatures of the forest. Such were-tigers possessed unnatural strength and unearthly powers. They could appear or vanish at will and were able to assume human form. It might even be disguised as one of them, lurking amongst the hunting party itself.

The Chinese equally regarded tigers with fear and awe, for in their culture he was the king of beasts with powers to ward off evil. It was said a tiger lived for hundreds of years; to kill one must be done with great respect or evil luck would befall them. Likewise, as the vehicle of Durga, the goddess of destruction, the Indian labourers held the tiger in reverence. To shoot a rogue animal might be necessary but must be accompanied by rituals lest the awesome cosmic power of the beast be directed against those who sought to do it harm. Many of the hunters carried talismans, each particular to their own beliefs. Several holy men also travelled along whose function was to say the prayers and incantations to protect them, including Nakhoda Intan, Fr Michael Rectenwald, the new Catholic priest, and a Burmese monk.

'Should we be fearful? Do you expect fatalities?' Thomas Pigou ventured as they led the head of the column towards the river.

'You need to ask? I would have thought you were a veteran of tiger hunts,' Light grinned at the younger man, whose normally cheerful disposition was unusually serious.

Pigou shook his head. 'I was never asked to such events, nor did I ever desire to be involved,' he answered ruefully. 'On such jaunts, it was the rajahs and nawabs in the company of the high and mighty members of the Council. I am more of a man for sitting behind a desk than riding into battle against fierce predators,' Pigou added with an attempt at light-heartedness that was belied by his anxiety.

'Then you can take my place at the desk any day, sir,' Light responded with a sardonic chuckle as he stared about him at the surrounding tree cover, so dense in places that they had to raise their swords and hack at overgrowing branches to cut their way through. Despite regular usage, the jungle had encroached the track; it could be swallowed up in days. Light breathed deeply of the refreshing moist air, sensing the almost imperceptible change in the forest fragrance as night slowly faded into morning. I was not made to be shut indoors pushing a pen the whole day long. This is where I belong. Under the sky. In the fresh air, he mused, almost thinking aloud.

'But you have not answered my question, sir.'

'Is this a dangerous pursuit, you mean? Good God, yes. The people in these parts have many folk superstitions about tigers, but if you've ever tangled with one, you would soon recognise that these animals do indeed have preternatural senses. They are wise and cunning, immensely strong, and formidably courageous. Even dying, they can kill a man with one savage blow. We will be fortunate indeed to slay this fellow without a substantial butcher's bill. Keep that to yourself, man. This bravado will soon enough turn to terror when the beast is sighted. We must keep our heads and behave as if everything is under our control. Much as we always do before these people.' Light rolled his eyes and put a finger to his lips. It did not reassure Pigou.

But he found his nerve. 'It is important that we are seen to be leading the attack, I think. The white people, I mean,' he added awkwardly.

Light flashed Pigou a thoughtful glance. He was fond of this young fresh-faced boy with his enthusiastic and sunny nature. Thomas was both a fine accountant and competent administrator who had made a huge difference to his own workload since his arrival – but he was still unsure whether he could trust him in all things. Pigou was a Company man through and through. It was likely that he had been enjoined to report to the Council behind his back. Who could blame him? He had his own career to tend, even more so now that he was the breadwinner of his family.

'It is equally important that *all* communities are here today. We are still strangers to each other, uneasily inhabiting an island together. If we are to create a success of this settlement, we must create bonds of loyalty that transcend our individual origins else I fear the tensions that lie between us might grow strong enough to erupt into bloody hostilities.'

Pigou considered Light's words. 'In my humble observation, our masters prefer that very stress and strain. Divide and conquer. I dare say forging a harmonious society is not on their list of requirements for Prince of Wales Island, sir!' It was a surprisingly incisive comment, which might almost be taken as criticism of his employers. Or was it a clever ruse to catch him out?

'The Company does not always have the best understanding of the realities of its foreign settlements. The traditions and cultures of the Straits are not the same as those found in India,' Light answered obliquely.

'Indeed, sir. I have observed this very fact myself these months. I believe your vision for Prince of Wales Island is farsighted. You are an enlightened man, Superintendent. I am learning much about leadership and governance in your service. The Council would be wise to listen to you and act upon your suggestions. This island could become a pearl in the crown if they took your advice.'

If this was flummery meant to coddle his pride and encourage revelation, Pigou deserved a medal. Light did not believe him capable of such cunning. While Thomas might report their conversations to the Council, he would not purposely entrap him. 'There are times, Pigou, when it defies belief that Britain has ever made a mark upon the world led by men of such little vision,' he opined. 'My navy days demonstrated that well enough – and I have seen no reason since to change my opinion.'

They were still some distance from their destination, well out of earshot. In fact, despite the quiet of the dawn, this was probably the most private place in which the two men had found themselves since Pigou's arrival. It made confidences possible.

'May I ask a question, sir? Please do not answer if I take liberty in posing it,' Pigou ventured.

'Go ahead, lad,' Light replied.

'This business with the Sultan of Queddah. You received a missive from him. Are you now on better terms? Is the king willing to trade with us again? I fear that unless the treaty is ratified soon, we may find ourselves facing a local war. Yet, I believe the sultan has some grounds for his resentment. Surely there should be compensation for ceding the island. It seems immoral to lease the land of a sovereign state and pay nothing for it.' It had been on Pigou's mind for some time.

'Your instinct is right, sir. The matter must be resolved. Approaches have been made of late. Even as we speak, James Scott is on his way to Queddah for discourse with Sultan Abdullah.'

'James Scott?' exclaimed Pigou. 'I thought he'd gone to Jangsylan?'

'Indeed, he had. After which, he intends a short visit to Alor Setar on his return journey. He speaks on my behalf. I have made a proposal and have informed Calcutta.' Light did not enlarge on either.

'This is good news. I'm sure an agreement amicable to both parties will be reached! Well done, sir. It's an important step forward!' Pigou was impressed.

Light was less confident. 'A lot of water must flow beneath the bridge before a settlement is made. The governor-general is ambivalent about the future of this island. He may just as easily decide on whim to abandon it. I cannot see him honouring most of the sultan's demands.'

'Can the sultan be persuaded to ask for less?' Pigou asked.

'Perhaps. Cornwallis has finally agreed to pay no more than ten thousand Spanish dollars and only for ten years, a third of the original demand. The sticking point is not so much the lease itself. I believe Abdullah would agree to a reduced amount. It is the arms and men the sultan insists the Company must supply to protect him from his enemies that will be the hindrance. The Council will never accept those terms.'

'But if conflict in the area threatens trade? Would that not change their thinking?'

Light shrugged. 'I am not convinced they give a damn for the security of the Straits. Furthermore, times are changing back in Europe. The Dutch are no longer the enemy, so it seems. Everything is upside down these days. So perhaps we must also change our principles. We shall see, we shall see,' was Light's evasive answer.

'You would forsake your commitment to Queddah? Risk the outbreak of hostilities? It could be disastrous!' Pigou gasped.

'Can you think of a better way to bring warships from India?

Cornwallis might refuse a few soldiers and weapons to a minor monarch in a backwater kingdom, but you can be damned sure he'll come down like the avenging angel on any who attack a British emporium. I would not be at all surprised to see British warships in the Straits, but none of them will ever fire a shot in defence of a Malay sultan. You could wager the family silver on that, Thomas.'

Not much further along the path, the forest thinned out again as they wound down towards the river crossing. The bridge was rudimentary, a rickety wooden structure lashed together by rope. It would not bear many transports at one time. From this point they were to proceed on foot. Light called the company to halt; they would break fast here and leave all the horses and vehicles. Once they crossed, they must be unencumbered.

The men threw themselves down upon the river bank, drawing water for the animals and mopping themselves down. Even at this time of the morning, the heat was on the rise. Mosquitoes swarmed the stream, attracted by the sweat of men and horses. But once the banana leaves had been unwrapped, the men tucked into their rice and *sambal* regardless, discomfort temporarily forgotten.

Work on the new estates had been temporarily halted due to the tiger, so there was no activity in the surrounding area. Light and Gray, accompanied by Raban and a few soldiers, sauntered across the bridge onto the estate grounds until they were out of sight of the party whose voices soon receded, deadened by the thickness of the trees. After a short distance, they reached the cleared ground where smallholdings had been leased to settlers growing agricultural produce or raising herds for local consumption.

The best land belonged to Light and was intended for plantations. A variety of local spices and fruits were being grown, but it was early days and much of the work was still in land clearance and laying irrigation channels. It was quiet today, however, with most of the workers having either joined the hunting party or taken their families into town away from danger.

The morning mists cleared to reveal the distant peak towering over dense, unexplored forest teeming with life, its verdant symmetry hiding its secrets. Their task was formidable. Somewhere in the tree cover between them and the mountain top above, the tiger was most probably watching them. What were the chances that the animal might reveal itself?

The officers crouched together on the ground, tracing a battleplan in the reddish-brown mud while the soldiers stood to attention, rifles primed. From this point on, the tiger might appear at any time; they must not be complacent. With his knife, Light drew a semi-circular arc indicating where the beaters were to wait until the signal was given to advance. Meanwhile, slaves would tie a few kid goats at the very edge of the forest to lure the tiger into their clutches. Once it was disturbed, beaters should drive it forward towards the troops. If they made enough noise and beat down enough undergrowth, the startled animal would surge towards the open ground – where the guns would be waiting.

It was a simple plan that would have been more effective if they rode elephants as in India, for even an enraged tiger would hesitate from charging one. But there were none at present on the island, an omission Light intended to resolve in future. Elephants could contribute much to the heavy clearance work, as was common in Siam and Burma.

The men, now rested and fed, were drilled on their allotted tasks. An arc of beaters was sent into the forest, each placed in sight of the other, primed to close the net. Artillery and local men were ranged in a phalanx, guns alternating with spear, dagger or sword. It was a fearsome battle line.

The entire gathering then settled down to wait, aware that hours might pass before activity occurred. Time passed. Men became restless, stretching stiff limbs and scratching insect bites, wandering off to relieve themselves, whispering together until taken to task for inattention. The sun was already high in the sky and their cover was scant. Any noise from the scrub or the jungle gave cause for alarm. A large snake disturbed one cluster of men as it slithered by; there was much alarm as they pounded it to pulp, their excessive reaction indicative of the tension of the hours of waiting.

When the first intimation of danger was sounded, however, it came from an unexpected source. They heard a distant flurry of raised voices that quickly became shrieks of terror. Then a single shot reverberated throughout the silent forest – followed by silence.

'Behind us!' Light shouted. 'The wagons!'

Across the bridge, where they had earlier taken breakfast, a small group had been left behind to guard the animals and vehicles. Most were old or very young, men not considered fit for the fight, lightly armed with sticks and knives, except for John Henderson. He was a Company writer, recently arrived from Madras, who had volunteered to take responsibility for the safety of the camp. He claimed to be a decent shot, so had been supplied with a rifle.

The religious men, the doctor and his assistant had also remained behind with the supply carts.

'Keep the beaters in place,' Light commanded. 'Half of the artillery, follow me! Gray, hold the position here with the rest.'

They ran hell for leather back across the estate in the direction of the bridge. Perhaps someone had been startled and discharged a gun by mistake? Had a wild boar or a crocodile surprised them? Would the tiger have ventured so far out of the forest to the other side of the river?

As they neared the bridge, their panic returned when they heard more raised voices and frantic movement. Thrashing through the bush, they eventually burst out onto open ground to behold the devastation before them: overturned bullock carts, at least one badly injured beast, and others charging about in frenzy. Dr Hutton and Marlbro were on their knees attending to several wounded men. 'What the devil happened?' Light shouted.

'All's well, sir!' shouted John Henderson. 'It's a hell of a mess but appears far worse than it actually is.'

Dr Hutton looked over his shoulder, nodding his agreement. 'Just minor cuts and sprains. Perhaps a broken wrist. We've been inordinately fortunate, Superintendent. If not for Mr Henderson, I shudder to think what might have transpired!'

It took Light some time to gain his breath, so mad had been his dash back to the camp. 'The tiger?' he finally gasped out.

'Indeed, sir. And a mighty brute it was as well ...' Hutton drew Light's attention to a circle of men beyond the wagons, all gathered around staring at the ground. Whatever it was, they kept their distance, as if they expected it to rise and attack again.

Light pushed his way past – and there was the tiger, more

huge in death than in the imagination. It lay slumped on its side, as if sleeping. Only the spreading pool of blood oozing out beneath its giant head revealed its fate. 'Sweet Jesus!' Light cried, advancing tentatively. He drew his pistol; like the others, it seemed a wise precaution in case the beast might have one final almighty assault left in him. Kicking out at its belly, he tested its response. Nothing but a lifeless mass remained. 'I heard only one shot!' Light exclaimed in wonder. 'How was he felled with only one shot? Who is the marksman that took him down?'

'That would be me, sir,' John Henderson spoke up. He was a softly spoken, laconic young man, small in stature and of an undistinguished appearance. His hair was mousy brown, his moustache a wispy affair, like the first growth of a youth. If not for his deep voice, Henderson might have passed for a boy. Henderson was American, itself somewhat unusual in these parts, appointed by Madras to serve in the superintendent's office. Light had suspected that it was another example of the Company sending only those they could not find a use for elsewhere.

'Good God, man. Where did you learn to shoot like that?'

Henderson grinned shyly. 'I've been shooting grizzlies since I was a little boy, sir. I tell you, even a tiger ain't got nothing on a mad bear. Right between the eyes. Do not miss. That's what my father used to say. You'll only have one chance, so make damned sure it counts!'

The tiger must have already left the cover of the forest well before they had arrived, perhaps even crossing the bridge at night, or wading the river. In fact, while they had been taking breakfast, it must have been watching from the belukar, until only a few remained, largely the less agile and battleworthy. Just as a predator shadows a herd until the young and the infirm fall behind, so the tiger had bided his time. And once those left had begun to doze in the late morning sun, he had struck.

No one had observed his presence. There had been no great leap or roar. One moment all had been quiet then suddenly the horses had reared, whinnying and smashing their hooves into the carts, desperate to break their reins and escape. The bullocks had also tried to stampede, overturning their wagons, which had only served to drag them down. In an instant, the tiger had savaged one poor bull and then turned to challenge the petrified onlookers, most of whom were all but turned to stone.

Until John Henderson had jumped atop one of the mangled carts, raised his rifle and faced the mighty tiger straight on. The tiger had crouched, ready to leap up and devour him. Then just one shot – and the animal had crumpled even before it could let out its final roar of victory.

Light searched the colossal head for the entry wound. Right between the eyes. Dead centre to its brain. The tiger had died in an instant, moving from life to death even before it had been aware. It was an astonishing act of marksmanship.

'Good Lord,' Lt Gray shook his head in disbelief at the evidence of Henderson's skill. 'I have never in my life seen such a clean shot in the face of imminent peril! Sir, you have missed your calling. You should be an artillery officer!'

Henderson seemed embarrassed by the admiration. 'Where I come from, it's nothing much. You learn to shoot – or you don't survive long. I'm just thankful I was here when I was needed. Else I think we would have lost more than a bullock to this fellow!'

'It's no wonder that you Yankees won the war against us, Mr

Henderson, if every boy can shoot as straight,' Light laughed. 'I'm heartily glad that America was on our side this time!'

It was quite a while before they could even comprehend how much danger they had been in, and what might have happened had they not set out that morning. The tiger had been on the move. Had it continued on its track, it would not have been long before George Town itself was at risk.

Soliman slipped quietly to Light's side. 'It was God's will, sir. Allah has other plans for us.' Father Michael had just said much the same.

'God's will or the Devil's luck,' Light muttered softly. 'We've escaped a terrible threat by the skin of our teeth and no mistake. More vigilance is needed as we clear further into the jungle. In future, we must organise patrols and post watches for such killers. For this is not an old, lone tiger. He was in his prime. There may be others. We must be ready for them.' Light again raised his eyes to the thickly forested peaks that rose above them. What else lay out there? Enemies both within and without. They must not rest upon their laurels, for who knew from whence would come the next jeopardy?

All the same, today they had won a significant victory. Members of the different peoples of Prince of Wales Island had killed a predator that could have brought disaster upon them. The tiger's carcass was handed over to the people with the caution that the animal was deserving of respect and honour, for he was a great spirit of the island. The Chinese claimed the eyes, the fat and other organs for medicine. The Malays and Indians prized the teeth and claws as talismans. The tiger skin was to hang upon the wall at the entrance of Government House, as an emblem of the island united. Every single part of the animal had its use: its great rib bones were carved into knife hilts and ornaments, hair fasteners and buckles and other purposes, both ceremonial and useful. Everyone returned with a memento for their families, even if it was just a single whisker or a scrap of bone.

As the company wended its weary way home, overjoyed at the fortuitous results of the day's activities, raucous cheers were raised to Mr Henderson and his magic power with the rifle. He was the new hero of the hour.

'You were right, sir. Look at them. You've made a unity of this divided settlement. Truly remarkable. What a day, sir. What a day!' proclaimed Thomas Pigou, his usual geniality returned.

Light's high spirits had dissipated, however, as he returned to the more introspective mood of earlier in the day. 'It is the outcome I had hoped for, I cannot deny. But we must not be overconfident. One swallow does not a summer make, I fear!'

'Aristotle, sir?'

'Was it? Well, I'll be damned. There is still learning left in my head!' he chuckled. 'But without pouring cold water on our present gaiety, we must build upon such moments. Good will is hard to win but may be lost in moments. There is still much for us to do. And just as other tigers may lurk out there in the forest, so our enemies still circle – both outside and within. Today was indeed a step forward. To keep within the classical vein, may I suggest we "*festina lente*", as Julius Caesar was wont to say.'

'It was Augustus, I believe, who thought it prudent to "hurry slowly". Julius never took his time at anything, I'm afraid. He was always in a hurry.' Pigou responded with a grin.

'Indeed. And look how he ended up, eh? A lesson to us all.'

10

Baptism of Fire

George Town, Prince of Wales Island. 23rd April 1789

It had been the two of them for dinner, served under a canopy on the flat roof of Government House. The night was cool following early evening rain, the scent of jasmine wafting over them on the breeze. Lanterns cast the marble-topped table in a soft glow. Francis had gone to some lengths to impress his wife – and show off this imposing new residence, the largest edifice on the island. It was not quite Belvedere, the great estate where Warren Hastings had lived in Calcutta – but they had come far since the humble wooden dwelling that had been their first home on the island.

The food, local dishes in keeping with Martinha's preference, had been delicious; the cooks had taken great pains to entertain their lady. The servants had kept a discreet distance to allow the couple privacy. Mrs Light was greatly loved. Her unseen hand influenced many of the measures that the superintendent had introduced to benefit them all.

'Well, what do you say to this place, Martinha? Why not consider this our family home? Your mother can remain mistress of our kampong house. It is but a step away from here; the children can run back and forth at will.' He dearly wished she would consent to moving in. The governor should reside in Government House along with his family. It would further enhance Martinha's standing amongst the British if she entered public life by his side. Otherwise, she was just his mistress hiding away in purdah.

Martinha sighed in contentment, her perfect features flushed with wine, her eyes mellow in the candlelight. 'It is a very beautiful place, Francis. You have achieved so much in a few short years. I promise we shall keep an apartment and stay here when it is appropriate to do so. Yet, I find these English buildings so forbidding; there is too much plaster and marble, solemn art and statues. Our little wooden "palace" is heaven to me. And I believe it is for you, too.'

She was right. Their home, on the track already known as 'Martinha's Lane', was the only place he truly felt at home, free from care and surrounded by love and peace.

'You are wise, my dearest Martinha. I agree it is enough that this should be our official home when dignitaries visit, and we must host dinners and perhaps the odd ball or two. On such occasions, we must show a united front. Yet it is preferable to retreat to our little nest the rest of the time. Let's drink to that, eh?'

He called a servant to bring the flagon of sweet white wine that she loved; it was wrapped in wet cloths to keep it chilled. They toasted to their future in the magnificent building that was now the focal point of Prince of Wales Island, worthy even of entertaining the governor-general himself. 'Pigou is as pleased as punch with his apartment, as are the writers. It's a sight more amenable than the paltry rooms they used in town!

'I hear they have Mrs Gray to keep them entertained. Lord, how she must love to flaunt her airs and graces in a great mansion!' Martinha chuckled.

'Indeed, although she has already set her sights on a property of her own no less. Gray has obtained the neighbouring plot and intends to build a pretty house with a fine sea view.'

'She thinks to outdo the governor himself?' Martinha gasped, still given to annoyance at Lydia Gray's social climbing.

'Hardly. It is but a small piece of land and the house will be humble enough. I could not deny them, my dear. They are our first married couple. She is the only English woman on the island, so it seems only fitting that we give them a decent place to live.'

Martinha's pout suggested otherwise. 'There are many good women on this island who deserve a pretty house by the sea. I do not see you worrying about the tawdry rooms they must endure,' she responded tartly.

Francis sighed. He took her point, but it was simply the way things were. English ladies were deemed too delicate for the rigours of this climate.

'I see Thomas has found himself a local wife,' continued Martinha, her tongue still sharpened to the task. 'Fortunately, he has not seen fit to move her into his apartment in the residence.'

'Martinha! Be reasonable! Government House cannot be a bordello for Company men! Ady Bonsu, whilst a perfectly charming young lady, is a woman of scandalous reputation, who has previously shared her favours with any number of the island's residents. Would your own father, for example, have allowed her to share the same table as your mother and the rest of the family?'

Martinha grinned coyly. 'I expect not. No one of any race or creed in these parts would welcome her openly in good company. But she's with child already and Thomas is very fond of her. Ady is a sweet girl who has had a hard life. We should not judge those more unfortunate than ourselves. I hope he sees fit to look after them properly. As a good man should ...' There was a hint of irony in her comment. She knew of her husband's other women and the child he had fathered, now in Jangsylan. It was a pointed reminder of his responsibilities, although she would never address the subject openly.

Her artful reproach amused him. 'Pigou's a decent fellow. And he's head over heels in love with Miss Bonsu. Yet, I fear she must accept the limitations of their alliance. Whilst he will always look after them, she can never be acknowledged or return to Calcutta with him. Such things are simply not acceptable these days.'

Martinha was reminded of the gossip concerning Thomas Pigou she had heard when in Calcutta the year before. 'Not the least because he has a wife waiting for him there,' she observed wryly.

'Pigou is married already?' Light exclaimed.

'Not married, but there is an understanding, I believe,' Martinha replied with the smug satisfaction of the bearer of tittle-tattle. 'I quite forgot that I was reliably informed in Calcutta that Pigou was promised to a young lady when she comes of age. It will be a fortuitous marriage for him. She's of excellent family with a sizeable dowry.'

'Who is this girl?' Francis was curious now. Pigou's contacts might be useful to him too. Such was the way society worked.

'I suspect you will be as shocked as I am. It is none other than Margaret Ogilvy, Sarah's schoolfriend! The girl is barely ten years old!' Martinha rolled her eyes in mock horror.

'Well, I'll be damned!' her husband exclaimed. 'He's never mentioned a connection to John Ogilvy to me. Ogilvy's on the

Council, you know?"

Martinha tutted loudly. 'Is that all you can say? Your only thought is how this might benefit you? How would you feel if Sarah was promised to a man already four-and-twenty?'

That brought a frown to his brow. 'I hadn't thought if it like that. She is but a child. It is entirely improper that young girls should be bartered in this way. I have never liked the practice of arranging marriages.'

Martinha clapped her hands together in glee. 'From the gentleman who married a young girl merely to improve his own business connections with her family!' She laughed broadly at his hypocrisy.

Francis grunted. 'That is entirely a different matter! Your mother came to me out of her concern for your wellbeing. And I accepted her offer because I respected both your poor father and your fine mother and wished to extend them my support!'

She reached across the table, patting his hand affectionately. 'I'm merely teasing you, *sayang*. I understand how these things work, but it still comes as a shock that before too long, men may be looking at the daughters of the eminent superintendent of Penang as suitable wives. Imagine that!'

Francis shuddered at the thought. 'Not for a very long time, I hope. I intend to chase away any suitors for at least another ten years. Which brings me to another matter we must discuss. Our visit to Calcutta. What say you to November? Then we may celebrate Christmas together as a family. I plan to lease a house for four months. Bring our own servants. We deserve a little luxury.'

'That would be so wonderful! The whole family this time! Even little Willie. He will love to sail on a ship!' Martinha was delighted.

'It will be more than a pleasure trip, mind,' Light admitted. 'Cornwallis will damned well have to hear me out face to face. The news is daily more worrying. I have just been informed that Archie Blair has been charged with founding a new establishment in the Andamans. They intend the naval base to be situated there – and you can be sure that plenty of money will be found for that endeavour. I must make the case for Prince of Wales Island once and for all before it falls into oblivion.'

'And demand the monies owing to you,' added Martinha with vehemence. 'You cannot afford to provide from your own pocket. Why, you have paid for the entire building of this residence so far. Not to mention the bricks you're shipping over from China and the brick kiln you have built in town.'

Francis' face grew sombre. 'The transport ship went down on route, I'm afraid. Ten thousand bricks already paid for! I also advanced five thousand Spanish dollars to Sultan Abdullah as part payment of the lease. Cornwallis has finally committed to the sum of ten thousand per annum. I have not yet revealed to the sultan, however, that the Company intends only to pay for ten years. After that time, Prince of Wales Island will be deemed entirely British property.'

It did not come as a surprise. Martinha had begun to doubt whether any monies would ever be forthcoming. 'At least if the decision is taken, it suggests the Council is ready to commit to the island?'

'They've not sent a single penny yet. I've attempted to force their hand by offering this first tranche. They damn well better make good on it, for if they do not, my funds are quite depleted.

Without Jamie Scott, we would be facing ruin!'

'Is it really that bad?' she cried. He rarely discussed financial matters with her; she knew he struggled on the pittance provided by the Company, but it had not occurred to her that they might be destitute.

He stood up, pulling her to her feet gently, regretting his outburst already. 'Let's walk awhile. It is not that serious, my dear. I've a substantial deposit of funds in the care of William Fairlie in Calcutta. Whatever happens, our family is secure. And I am sure that the Company will eventually make recompense. But the wheels of the Council grind slowly. I write a letter and receive a decision nine months later. In Bengal, perhaps we may proceed at a more acceptable pace. Don't worry, dear girl! I regret having raised the subject at all.'

They had taken the steps down from the roof then out of a side door into the grounds. Servants with torches followed at a discreet distance perusing the grounds for evidence of danger: snakes, giant monitor lizards, even wild boar might lurk in the garden after dark. Finally, the superintendent and his lady emerged onto the silent sands drenched in moonlight, the lights of the residence flickering in the distance. The tide was high; waves crashed on the narrow shoreline in sprays of saltwater that licked at the dry sand before racing back to the sea. Hand in hand, they set off towards their family home.

'Have you heard Felipe's good news? Mother is delighted!'

'About the baby? Yes, he told me himself this morning, but since then I have heard it from a number of other quarters. It seems Kapitan Khoh is pleased as punch and has been boasting around the town.'

Martinha giggled. 'Poor Lien has been sneaking off to our house whenever she can to escape from her mother and their slaves. You know what the Chinese are like about expectant mothers! She must not eat anything "heaty", she must take rest, she must drink special soups and medicines, she must not do this or that. While she is with us, Mother makes sure she eats her fill of forbidden fruits and cakes, and we go for long walks on the beach to take the air. I like little Lien very much. She has a mind of her own. Felipe is very happy.'

'Yet another little one to add to our growing household. Janeke has settled in well, hasn't she? And baby Anneke is a delight,' Francis observed, pulling Martinha gently round to face him. They stood there, relishing the beauty of the evening together, a rare opportunity to set their cares down and devote themselves entirely to each other alone. 'Perhaps it's time we should think of adding to our brood? Before it is too late?' he murmured soft and low, his lips grazing her cheek as he whispered his desire in her ear.

'What's that?' Martinha gasped, pulling back from his embrace. Francis stared at her, momentarily bemused, until he followed her pointed finger and saw what had alarmed her. Off in the distance, somewhere above the town, a glow lit up the night sky, yellow and red, orange and gold. Specks like frenzied sprites danced amidst the colours, soaring skyward. For a few brief seconds, they stared spellbound until the first acrid stench of burning drifted on the night air, carrying with it screams of terror.

At the self-same moment, all the watchers woke from their shocked state; Light, Martinha and the entire staff dashed forward, drawn like moths to a candle. And then they heard the dreaded sound: three rounds of the signal gun: FIRE. The most dreaded enemy of a shanty town.

A lone rider appeared, galloping towards the residence. Jumping from his horse before it came to a halt, he stumbled in their direction. Eyes rolling in panic, his young face was smudged with ash. 'Fire, sir. A huge inferno in the town! It's spreading fast. Captain Glass is calling for every hand on board. They are forming chains for water ...'

***

If Light had wished to galvanise the settlement, the great fire surely had that effect. Every member of the island community raced to defend George Town; even the young and old were out to do their share. Soldiers organised water chains that stretched from the jetty to town, any container available passed frantically down the line. Side-by-side, residents of every social class worked as one machine, a host of Davids struggling vainly against the Goliath that threatened to overwhelm them.

Teams of soldiers with grappling hooks and stout tree trunks as battering rams pulled down buildings at the perimeter of the fire, those bound to be destroyed, to create a waste ground in which the flames might burn themselves out. Those unfortunate residents whose properties were endangered – or selected to be forfeit – risked their lives to salvage their precious goods, until the guards forcibly dragged them away. Their entire lives were in those buildings; they would rather die than lose their investments. Most of the Chinese, however, were stoic in the face of loss. Their houses could be rebuilt. If they lived and saved most of their goods, they would start again. They had done it before.

The fire had taken a strong hold, fanned by the land breeze of the night. As far as one could tell, it had broken out in the Chulia quarter. As the wind blew the flames towards the sea, the entirety of George Town was at risk. The Chinese streets were next in line. It was only a matter of time before they too would be swallowed up.

The skies were clear; there was no prospect of rain. Would the wind die down or blow all night? Their only weapon against the complete destruction of their town were puny buckets of water, slopped on to the edges of the blaze. It was a hopeless task, but still the people toiled, for there was nothing else that might save them. The old and young were herded towards the beach, clinging to their meagre goods: a doll, an iron pot, a basket of food, a few personal heirlooms. Whimpering and moaning could be heard on all sides, but it was muted. Even those who had lost homes or businesses were too shocked even to complain.

Light sent men to ensure his own family was safe. His residences were not at immediate risk, so he ordered the vulnerable to shelter in Government House, where his servants were instructed to provide food and shelter. Dr Hutton led a field team while orderlies carried the seriously wounded to the hospital at the fort. And then the superintendent – with the rest of his household and Company staff – joined in the chains. Martinha wrapped her hair in a dampened shawl and knotted her sarong like a dhoti, working side-by-side with the rest.

With no time to dwell on the hopelessness of their task, the people worked tirelessly for many hours. Their faces were black with smoke and ash, their bodies drenched in water, their arms aching with the endless effort – but still they battled on. Those who collapsed from heat and exhaustion were carried back to the rear, while others rushed forward to take their places. Many were singed from proximity to the flames but refused to seek treatment despite their burns. Only the helpless wails from those who toiled in full knowledge that their own livelihoods were already gone rang out, but even they were almost lost amidst the explosions and the crashes of the fiery onslaught.

It took hours, but at last there was a halt to the advance of the flames. Although at the centre of the inferno it still burned like the fires of hell, the flames no longer licked and jumped at the surrounding areas. The line was at last beginning to hold back its progress, even slow it down. But still the water was passed and poured, until – God be praised! – the wind died and Light called a halt. The night air was still. No breeze stirred. Even the fire subsided to a less threatening crackle.

The throng ceased its frantic charge, stepping back from the still-fierce heat to watch the miracle as it happened, most barely able to stand for their exhaustion. Moments passed, then minutes, until they dared to hope that the worst had indeed passed. Teams of the most able-bodied were assigned to carry on through the night but at a slower pace, in rotation so that rest periods were possible. Although the blaze itself was now contained, at its heart the fire still burned strong. Here and there sparks reignited and sent fresh flares flickering.

These dying embers would remain dangerous for days. Ultimately, only a deluge might put an end to it. Everyone prayed for rain, each to his own god. Father Michael led the Christians in a prayer of thanks; Nakhoda Intan did the same for the Malays, while Buddhist monks and Hindu priests gathered their people to chant their rites.

When it was safe to do so, Francis Light took a break from his endeavours, at last submitting himself to Marlbro to tend his burns with salve. Beneath the smudgy layer of ash, his face was set rigid, a combination of exhaustion and despair. He had feared the settlement gone. Would he have possessed the will to carry on and start anew? Now, in the aftermath, he felt numb. The town was saved but the cost to at least one community – the Indian Muslim traders who contributed so much to the welfare of the emporium – was great. George Town had survived, but the task of rebuilding would be costly – and who would foot the bill?

Glass approached the medical tent, himself in need of assistance. Blood streamed from a head wound caused by a glancing blow from a falling timber. 'How do you fare, sir?'

Light viewed him, sighing deeply. 'Rather better than you, John, it would seem,'

'It's naught but a scratch, sir. Head wounds bleed like the devil. The town is saved. It is a wonder.'

Light nodded. 'We have again escaped ruin by the skin of our teeth. Maybe there is something in the people's belief that God has chosen us. Which God, however, I do not know, for tonight the Chulias must wonder what it is they have done to displease theirs so much. Tomorrow we must launch a thorough enquiry into the circumstances. I need to ascertain how the fire began and whether this event was malicious or accidental.'

'Assuredly, sir. I must also inform you there has been some looting, although the majority has behaved well.'

'Without the general population, we would never have

overcome this blaze. Whilst I will bring any culprits to justice, we must not be seen to attack the ordinary folk, for they have played their part as much as we. And they have sustained the greatest losses. But we shall make examples of looters. They must be held to account,' he shouted, whether from his burns or from his anger it was hard to tell. 'Now get yourself bandaged up and take some rest. Our work begins in earnest come daylight.' He patted the captain on his back, thanked Marlbro for his gentleness, and eased his tattered shirt back on.

Just then, Martinha arrived, leading several women for treatment. Light had forgotten all about her in his urgency. 'Good God, Martinha! Are you still here?' he exclaimed. 'Have you been hurt?'

His wife held out her arms to still his fears. 'I am well, sayang. Calm yourself. It is these poor women in need of help. They've worked alongside the men and proved their mettle tonight.' Dr Hutton himself came forward to attend them, leaving her in the midst of the milling throng with her husband.

He tilted up her face with a soothing caress. 'By the look of you, I believe you've done the same. You had no need to take such risks. What if anything had happened to you?' Light said, tenderly brushing dirt from her cheek.

Martinha smiled. 'I am a woman of this island. These are my people. What kind of example would it set if the superintendent's wife had shirked her duty? I may not be the best host at your dinner parties, but I do know how to stand by our settlers when the time comes. Am I not a daughter of Lady Thong Di and a niece of Lady Chan and Lady Mook! And what about my grandmother, Tengku Mahsia? Would she have run from danger?'

Light drew her into his arms, heedless to the crowds of people who were privy to this moment of intimacy. On a night such as this, barriers were shattered; all over town men and women were holding each other, either in sorrow or in joy. 'No matter what losses we have suffered this night, we have also gained much. The people have shown their strength in unity. But most of all, you have risen to the place you were destined to hold. You are the Lady of Pinang, my love. The very Pearl herself.'

Martinha threw her head back and laughed. '*Cakap kosong*! Nonsense, Francis, you silly man! I was only doing what every able-bodied person has done. Do not raise me above the others. There were many pearls tonight who toiled to save their island!'

'But none so fair and bold as you!' he whispered as he threw his arm around her waist. His mood had suddenly lightened, a lingering echo from earlier. Martinha, too, seemed oddly gay.

'The title is already claimed. The self-styled Lady of the island is Mrs Gray herself, or so she believes,' Martinha giggled. 'I am but a lady of dubious local birth,' she added tartly.

Francis gave her his roguish grin. 'Ah, but where was Mrs Gray this night? I have heard that at the first alarm she hurried straight to Government House where she insisted on the rooms usually reserved for visiting dignitaries. There she withdrew with her maid. And as far as I know she is still abed, without a single care for her poor subjects.'

'Oh, Francis, I do believe you are being catty. It does not become the superintendent. Think of the poor woman! She has a delicate constitution. After all, she is but an English woman ...'

The superintendent threw his arm around her shoulders and together they sauntered through the damaged streets of George

Town as the first streaks of dawn pierced the smoky sky. They bestowed consolation on the tragic victims and gave thanks to those brave citizens still tending to the fire, without whose sterling efforts an unthinkable disaster would have occurred.

***

The initial blaze had broken out in a textile shop, unoccupied at that time of night. The owners were most insistent that no burning candle would have been left unextinguished, for the stock was largely cloth and trimmings, the most combustible of goods. Even so, the proprietor and nearby residents were questioned in the hope that one might be induced to inform on another, in the case of malicious intent. Yet, despite all threats, no such claims were forthcoming. The detainees were eventually released. Suspicions lingered, however, and rumours ran rife for weeks. Most believed the fire had been set by a rival trader who had not anticipated the scale of the mischief he had done.

In total, the Chulias lost fifty-six properties, an enormous cost to a community numbering less than two hundred souls. A few Chinese houses had also been destroyed, but by-and-large Chinatown had been saved. By a further quirk of fortune, no fatalities were reported, although many injuries, burns and broken bones had been recorded. Light's office assessed the cost of the fire at 20 000 Spanish dollars, an extraordinary sum. It may well have far exceeded that.

The consequences did not end there. As soon as the blaze had first been brought under control, Light had ordered Lt Gray to mount a watch on the port, banning any vessel from leaving.

First thing next morning all ships and perahus were searched. A significant amount of stolen goods was retrieved, some compensation at least for the Chulias who had lost so much. One Acheen vessel particularly loaded with loot caused some surprise. Its captain had been centre stage during the fire, originally proclaimed the hero of the night. He had in fact been taking stock of prime properties for his sailors to raid in the pretence of lending a hand. His punishment was a heavy fine and permanent banishment from the island, the penalty for any foreign ships involved in such opportunist thefts.

Some of the looters had been local. Not every citizen was upstanding. To Light's surprise, however, these were mostly turned in by their own communities, an indication of the success of the kapitans in policing their own. The punishment was public flogging.

It was a popular spectacle. Prompt justice dispensed before all the people went a long way to assuaging their anger. The sterling actions of the troops in marshalling the response had also impressed. This dreadful calamity had served its purpose in the greater scheme of things. When Superintendent Light instructed that the town should be rebuilt in brick – this time nobody objected.

11

Burrah Din

The Garden House, Middleton Row. 13th December, 1789

Lucy Ann Light's tenth birthday dawned on a sunny Sunday morning in Calcutta at the beginning of the Christmas holidays. This auspicious anniversary, the attainment of double figures and her departure from childhood, was to be marked with festivities: presents, new clothes and a party.

The Lights had leased a charming garden villa east of the Maidan, owned by a senior merchant currently on leave. It was an extravagance; such properties rented at a premium. Light could have secured a house more easy on his purse further out of town. Yet he deemed the expense worth it; a visible demonstration of wealth and status was requisite in this most cupidinous of cities if a man wished to be taken seriously.

Behind the façade of a warm family reunion to celebrate a traditional Christmastide, the visit had another purpose. No less personage than Earl Cornwallis himself had summoned Light to Bengal to defend his new island settlement. The directive was an ultimatum, the last chance for Prince of Wales Island, yet Light chose to regard it as a timely opportunity. The governor-general would never be more accessible than during the Christmas festivities for which Calcutta was famed, where night after night the notable residents held balls and dinners, each grander than the last, culminating in the grand Governor-General's Ball on Christmas Day.

There would be no better chance to make his case than in person, jaded as he was of writing endless letters that fell on apparently deaf ears. Face-to-face, Light believed he could secure a commitment for the future of the settlement. He was always at his most persuasive when able to shake a man's hand and look him straight in the eye. Even the most sceptical had been won over in the past. Sir Warren Hastings, a first-rate judge of men if ever there was one, had taken a fancy to him once they met. Surely Cornwallis would be an easier nut to crack? Yet they had already been in Calcutta nigh on a month – and still not a peep from Government House.

The day began with a visit to the Catholic chapel at Burra Bazaar where Mass was said by an Augustinian friar. It was, of course, St Lucy's Day – hence the child's name. Light declined to join them; he was not a churchgoer by nature other than when propriety required it. Nor did he wish to suggest Papist sympathies, especially in Calcutta itself. So, off the women went alone, the girls delighted, for at school they had to attend dour Anglican services; Catholic Mass was always much more entertaining. Even more so on this occasion, since the young Italian curate took St Lucy and her tragic life as the focal point of his sermon. It appealed to their romantic natures.

On their return, young Lucy Ann bounded from the carriage where she found her father reading in the garden, making the most of a few hours of quiet and his brand-new reading spectacles, his first purchase in the city. Dr Hutton had urged him to make eyeglasses a priority. The superintendent had been suffering headaches for months. The glasses had already proved their worth.

'Papa! We had the best sermon today!' she announced, trailing the rest of the family behind. 'It was about my namesake, Santa Lucia. That's what Padre Giovanni called her. Don't you think "Lucia" sounds much more amenable than Lucy? I think, perhaps I will insist I am Lucia in future!'

Martinha sank down into a chair, grateful for the cool glass of lime juice provided by the servants. 'Lucy, allow your father his peace! Go upstairs and change for breakfast,' she chided fondly. 'Dear Francis, the priest made such an impression on the girls. Despite their Anglican schooling, they're still Roman Catholics at heart, you know?' Satisfaction was writ large upon her face; it was a further sign that their English upbringing in Calcutta had not entirely dislodged the values she had inculcated.

Francis muttered, 'Smoke and mirrors, I believe they call it nowadays. Incense, candles, costumes and overpainted statues for the gullible. Not to mention a heavy reliance on magic and miraculous tales. Exactly what would appeal to childish minds!'

It was his typical response and made Martinha chuckle. 'Better a belief based on faith rather than propriety, my dear. I fear you Protestants have all quite missed the message of the Lord.'

Lucy was in no mood to be quietened, launching herself into the gory details of the gruesome martyrdom of her namesake. St Lucy, a Roman maiden, had refused to accept the hand of a suitor. In revenge he revealed her as a Christian. The pitiful girl was sentenced to burning at the stake.

'But she was so holy that the flames shied away from her body and refused to burn her. The Romans were so angry that a soldier dragged her off the fire and slit her throat.'

'Ah, so she died anyway, poor child. Iron must be less affected by goodness than fire,' Francis commented drily, suppressing a smile in the face of his daughter's dramatic monologue.

'It is so very sad, Papa! She was beautiful and gentle, always taking care of the sick. May I change my name to Lucia? It's so much more fashionable than boring Lucy!'

Her father raised his hands up. 'How many names will you have, young lady? Ann, Lucy, Lucy Ann, Lukey, Lukey Ann – and now Lucia. We cannot keep up with you!'

Lucy was already on another tangent. 'Do you know Lucia means light? What an extraordinary coincidence because my surname is also Light. Furthermore, I was born on the exact day that St Lucia died! I feel most connected to her. I believe I would like to follow in her footsteps –'

'You wish to be a martyr?' Francis asked aghast.

'Papa! You're making fun of me! Of course, I do not wish to be a martyr! St Lucia was known for her kindness to the poor and unfortunate. She is the patron saint of the blind. I would like to be good like she was!'

'Then merely a saint, perhaps? We must be grateful for small mercies. I presume apprentice saints keep their rooms tidy and play kindly with their siblings? And never, ever act unladylike?' he jested.

'Oh, Papa!' Lucy shrieked, already falling from goodness at the first hurdle. 'Today is my birthday! Must you torment me so, even today?'

He pulled her onto his knee, his book slipping to the floor, as he tickled her until she squealed even louder. 'I am indeed a wicked father, but I love nothing quite so much as my daughters' laughter. Come, we waste the day. Let us partake of the wonderful breakfast that your mother has planned for you. I believe there are also some parcels waiting at the table! And then a gentle stroll on the Maidan before your friends arrive and the real entertainment commences. Today is the first time in a very long time that I have been on hand for your special day – I intend to make the most of it. But be warned! There may be teasing ahead!'

***

Unlike on her previous visit, when Martinha had discovered herself a social pariah, this time was entirely different. The weeks of December and early January were a procession of social engagements, each more ostentatious than the last. Christmas, known locally as *Burrah Din*, 'The Joyous Day', was the most important festival in the Calcutta calendar. In the desire to recreate the season in the image of an English Yuletide, the Christian community, whether Anglican, Catholic or Orthodox, foreign or Eurasian, had raised it to new levels of extravagant excess.

The Lights attended numerous 'winter' balls, rubbing shoulders regularly with old acquaintances and meeting new ones, increasing their public prestige as they widened their social circle. The rumour mill fed upon distinguished new arrivals, especially those who already had the eye of the governor-general. Yet still no invitation arrived for the long-awaited audience. As the days passed, Light's frustration grew. He had been in the same position before; the Company delighted in keeping its servants on a leash.

At the home of William Fairlie, who always hosted one of

the grandest events of the season, they enjoyed an evening of astonishing magnificence. His home was decorated for Yuletide in the 'Calcutta' style, holy plantain trees trimmed with wreaths of exotic blooms flanking doorways, and kissing boughs of fruits and spices replacing mistletoe and holly. A great yule log burned in the wholly redundant fireplace.

Long tables draped in finest white linen and lace groaned under dishes of every meat and delicacy imaginable: venison, beef, goose, fish, great Christmas pies stuffed with poultry and game, steaming cauldrons of spicy turtle soup, and platters of grilled fish and crustaceans. The dessert table, piled high with gorgeous fruits, was rich in the traditional Christmas sweets: minced pies, plum pudding and elaborate sugared cakes. This abundance was washed down with cups of spiced punches or *lumba pillans* of 'loll shrub', tall glasses of red wine.

The grand buffet was followed by dancing in the ballroom to music provided by a string quintet. The floor was thronged with eager participants whether for a stately minuet, favoured by the older guests, a lively gavotte for the youngsters, or an intricate quadrille for the experts. Francis and Martinha declined to join in for fear of revealing how little they knew of society's current fashions. Instead, outside in the spacious gardens lit by dozens of lanterns, they sauntered in the evening air, making small talk with other guests.

Major and Mrs Kyd soon joined them, along with Fairlie and a few others. Eliza immediately drew Martinha away on the pretext of meeting some of the ladies. The gentlemen stood by an ornamental pond where they were offered fine French cognac in crystal rummers.

'D'you think the recent news about Archie Blair might sound the death knell on your island, Francis?' Fairlie enquired. He affected concern, but it was hardly an innocent comment. Kyd winced.

'Archie Blair? Of the *Viper*?' Light asked, feigning ignorance 'He surveyed our island. Good man. Meticulous. Wouldn't you agree, Kyd? You know him better than I. What news?' His insouciance was deliberate; inside his stomach churned.

Alexander Kyd nodded his agreement. 'Fine fellow indeed,' he replied but made no elaboration.

'You were in the area recently with William Cornwallis, surely? You must be *au fait* with the latest developments?' Fairlie would not let the subject lie, prodding further.

'I was indeed in the Nicobars of late. Blair's doing sterling work there,' was Kyd's brusque reply.

At the very mention of the remote island chain in the Andaman Sea, Light knew in an instant that Fairlie's apparently innocuous remark concealed a new revelation. He was being excluded from something important.

'I'm afraid you have the advantage of me, sirs. News reaches us very tardily in Prince of Wales Island. What exactly has Blair been up to?' Light turned his attention to Kyd, with barely concealed resentment. Was he playing him out?

'Lt Blair has been engaged on a long survey of the Andaman and Nicobars on behalf of the governor-general. He presented a very detailed report last summer. As a result, the GG asked me and his brother William to take a peek. I have not long returned to Calcutta.'

'William Cornwallis, Commander-in-Chief of the East India

fleet? Taking a "peek" at the Andamans? So, the governor-general has decided to site his naval base there? Is that what I am to understand?' Light responded tartly. 'Yet no one thought to send me a note?'

'Please, Francis. It is early days! No decisions have been taken. Blair set up a small redoubt on south Andaman and continues his mapping. William and I were there merely for an opinion. The commodore has his eye on another harbour further north, so Blair has been instructed to scout it out. This in no way impinges on Prince of Wales Island. There's no intention for the Andamans to become an emporium. It is well established that your island is the most fitting location for a port and trading establishment.'

This was not the place for a heated discussion, particularly as they were already drawing an audience who anticipated Light might make a public criticism of Lord Cornwallis. Fuel for gossip was meat for the table quite as much as roast beef. 'Of course, you're right, sir. This has no bearing on Prince of Wales Island. We wish you every success in your new endeavour, Alexander,' Light forced a reply through gritted teeth. Fairlie's eyes glinted with something akin to pleasure. It was hard to know whether his purpose was to support him or enjoy his discomfiture.

'Hardly *my* endeavour, Francis. It is all down to Blair and his phenomenal abilities. I promise to keep you informed of any new developments, my dear fellow,' Kyd added with his polished charm, a friendly hand on the superintendent's shoulder. The gesture irked Light intensely although he struggled not to betray his annoyance before these people. Instead, he inclined his head in acknowledgment – and swallowed down his ire.

Other gentlemen joined them, including a familiar face from

his past. It was William Hickey, who had once shared Light's imprisonment at the hands of the French. On that occasion, Light had judged him an odious social climber, but the other men received him well enough. His years in Calcutta had been kind to him. He was now a well-established advocate in the office of the Chief Justice. Hickey, for his part, greeted Light warmly as an old friend, where years before he had dismissed him an insignificant country captain.

Light acknowledged Hickey's excessive display of camaraderie with a mere polite nod. 'I recall the French were remarkably hospitable,' Light remarked when Hickey mentioned deprivations. 'We were hardly thrown into dungeons. The food was remarkably palatable as I recall.'

'Just so, sir. Yet, no amount of fancy sauces may replace a man's freedom. I never did have much affection for the French, but that period of my life made them my enemies for life. Have you heard the news from France? Most alarming. Yet I cannot conceal a certain pleasure at their recent calamities. The more the damned Frenchies are embroiled with their own commonfolk, the less those Froggies are able to poke their tiresome noses in these waters!' Hickey replied, well pleased with his own wit. Light found no reason to change his original opinion of the man. The others, however, were with Hickey to a man.

'Lafayette has found himself a new revolution,' commented Kyd. 'First America and now his own nation. The man's a turncoat of the worst order. No respect for his class. The next thing, he'll be preaching his sermon on the rights of man in London, God rot his bones!'

It was generally agreed that, however much it amused them

to see the French government attacked from inside, the example of a nation turned against its nobility was a dangerous one. 'It changes everything, of course. The Dutch are with us now. They'll not support treachery in Europe,' observed another.

'Then the Dutch will have to change their tune in the Straits,' Fairlie guffawed. 'They might hold half the Indies, but they're the little tiddlers of Europe. France will eat 'em up if they don't watch out!'

It was another pressing reason to resolve matters with Cornwallis. If the Dutch were to be placated, might Prince of Wales Island be sacrificed to the alliance? So many complexities and possibilities threatened at every turn.

Desirous of a change of subject, aware that his manner towards Hickey had been discourteous, Light ventured some pleasantries. 'And how fares the lovely Mrs Hickey. Has she taken well to life in India?'

An embarrassed silence fell over the listeners. Hickey assumed a lugubrious expression. 'My dear Charlotte died six years past, at not yet one-and-twenty. The privations of the journey and her sufferings in captivity took a great toll on her delicate constitution. I will never recover from my loss. When she left this world one Christmas night, the light of my life was extinguished forever. The festive season brings such painful memories. It is impossible for me to embrace the merriment of the season. We keep a quiet time in my household out of respect.' Even this sad revelation annoyed Light. Hickey relished the role of bereaved widower with too much melodramatic self-regard. It smacked of playacting.

'My condolences, Mr Hickey. A tragic loss, to be sure,' he replied with politeness.

'Most kind of you, dear Francis. You must visit our home this Burrah Din during your stay! Bring your good wife! Jemdanee will be delighted!' Hickey's moods changed quicker than the monsoon weather. He was already beaming at the prospect of entertaining. So much for solemnity at Christmas time.

'Jemdanee?' Light found himself asking, although he immediately regretted showing any interest in the dreadful fellow.

Hickey – with no sense of the absurd – replied with a self-satisfied expression: 'My beautiful wife. The love of my life! The most beautiful Bibi in all Calcutta!'

***

Meanwhile Martinha and Mrs Kyd were enjoying cups of punch, strolling about the garden arm-in-arm. Eyes greedily followed their progress although direct contact was avoided.

'They're bursting with curiosity but dare not show it!' Eliza whispered in glee. 'Take a look around and count the number of native women here tonight and you will understand why. Of course, many ladies have 'interesting' backgrounds, but few would be prepared to admit it,' Eliza added with a wink. 'Including me, of course. Yet there you are with your exotic features, walking brazenly amongst them wearing cloth of gold. The cat amongst the pigeons!'

Martinha furrowed her brow. 'I hardly think so. I feel more like a tiny bird stalked by a host of cats! But tell me, dear Eliza, will Mrs Hill be in attendance? I would so like to meet her again. I wish to commission a family portrait.'

'Of course, she will, my dear! Everyone who matters is here

tonight! Why, I believe I saw her earlier across the ballroom. Diana loves to dance, don't you know? Let's go and seek her out.'

Diana Hill was indeed on the floor, dancing a ponderous minuet with a handsome officer. When the music ended, he escorted her with tender solicitude to an armchair, before rushing off to fetch a cooling drink.

'My dear Diana!' called out Eliza Kyd, ushering Martinha along. 'You look quite done in, poor thing!'

Martinha would not have recognised the unconventional artist in this elegant society lady draped in silk and jewels. 'Mrs Hill?' she gasped.

Diana face broke into a smile, amused by Martinha's surprise. 'You surely don't imagine I wear pyjamas in society, my dear Martinha? Whilst I may court controversy from time to time, there's a limit to my audacity! I must inform you of a significant change in my status. I had the good fortune to remarry a twelvemonth ago. And as you may perhaps have suspected from my delicate demeanour, I am presently *enceinte*, thus my dancing is limited to a slow-paced stroll about the floor.'

'On sent?' replied Martinha somewhat confused.

The two ladies giggled. 'With child!' Eliza murmured in her ear. 'It is considered impolite to mention such matters directly in public. We use the French word or "an interesting condition" or such like.'

The English language never ceased to amaze Martinha. Or was it more a case of prudish English convention? The voluminous fabric and the fussy pleating of Diana's ball gown had successfully concealed her expectant state. How strange that a pregnant woman was deemed embarrassing to men's eyes! Martinha had never yet met a man who baulked at what lay beneath a woman's skirts, regardless of her 'condition'.

Congratulations duly shared, Diana's new husband was formally introduced, the attentive soldier, Lt Thomas Harriott of the First Bengal Infantry. Harriott, an aloof Englishman, was diffident in his manner, replying to their conversation with a single word whenever possible. After a few pleasantries, he left his wife to her friends, grateful for the opportunity to join the gentlemen for a serious drinking session outside.

'Thomas is the sweetest man, but still thinks himself a bachelor, poor fellow. He was a soldier for so long that he's quite out of his depth in the company of ladies. If I hadn't given several nudges in that direction, he may never have had found the nerve to propose!' Diana's irreverent sense of mischief revealed itself at last.

'Are you sure it's reserve, Diana? Perhaps he finds your friends as unsuitable as your profession?' Eliza responded with a knowing pout.

Diana blushed. It fascinated Martinha how English skin was so pallid that it revealed one's inner thoughts. She had no wish, however, to see her friend embarrassed by the prejudices of her husband. It seemed an appropriate moment to make her request.

'My husband and I are in Calcutta for some time yet, Mrs Harriott. Would you consider allowing us to sit for a family portrait? Or perhaps you are in no condition for such an undertaking at the present time?' Martinha wished for nothing more than to hang a family portrait in at the superintendent's residence in the English custom.

Diana's smile faded. 'My dear, I no longer take paid work,

I must confess. Thomas wholly disapproves of my profession for a married lady. He says it reflects badly upon his reputation that he should put his wife to work.' she sighed. 'However, I do occasionally paint as a gift for my close friends. And I do consider you a dear friend, Martinha! Nothing too grand, though. Perhaps some miniatures? Or would you prefer I recommend another artist? There are many talented ones in Calcutta in need of work.'

There was a false note to her gaiety. How unfortunate that such an accomplished woman was no longer allowed her art, all because her husband – no doubt once drawn to her for that very singularity – now felt he must restrict her freedoms.

Eliza agreed. 'I simply do not understand why you were so keen for this marriage in the first place, Diana! There you were in a successful profession, renowned amongst the most notable families in Calcutta, building up an impressive reputation. Only to throw it all away for love!'

Diana smiled sadly. 'My life may have appeared to be an idyll from the outside, but little is ever as it seems. My brother planned to marry. His prospective wife – and her pompous family – was offended by me. She said I was an 'insult to the female sex'. What else could I do? An unmarried woman cannot set up house alone. No one in society would have attended unless I had a male chaperon. Nor could I afford to support myself without a man's assistance. Art is not as remunerative as you might think. Many of my clients fail to settle their accounts before returning to England. Sometimes I wait for months and months for payment; it is deemed "impolite" for a lady to dispatch bills. Not only that, but commissions do not come by every day. *C'est la vie,* ladies. I am luckier than most. At least Thomas has a decent income from his inheritance as well as his excellent commission. My standing in Calcutta has risen greatly during the past year. All in all, a wise decision.'

Martinha could not help but compare Diana to the formidable women of her own family. Many women of the Straits were downtrodden and had restricted lives, but their husbands rarely complained when they showed an aptitude for commerce. In contrast, these supposedly enlightened English women were allowed little of value to do with their lives, their talents choked off as soon as they began to flower. Were their menfolk so threatened by them?

Had Francis ever felt the same about her?

This gloomy train of thought was interrupted by an announcement from Mr Fairlie. Calling everyone to charge their glasses for a loyal toast, he embarked – in his strident and tuneless baritone – on a hearty rendition of Christmas carols. Various soloists then took their turns with "The Holly and the Ivy" and "Unto Us a Boy is Born", received with boisterous applause and drunken merriment from throats well-oiled. Finally, to a stirring version of the "Boar's Head Carol", servants carried in a platter with an actual boar's head replete with apple in mouth to herald the serving of the late supper. More food appeared on already laden tables.

By midnight, Francis and Martinha made their farewells, abandoning the festivities whilst still in full swing. It would be dawn before the final guests took their leave. Entertaining in Calcutta required the sturdiest of constitutions and a very strong head for liquor. Their quiet island life had left them quite unprepared for the arduous task of social intercourse.

***

A continuous volley of cannon ushered in the birth of the Saviour on Christmas morning, sending the Light children into a frenzy. Sarah and Lucy teased the little ones that French warships had attacked; Mary and William bawled. It required a great deal of persuading to calm them down.

A huge breakfast was held at the Court House, the only building large enough to open its doors to all, followed by a sumptuous luncheon at Government House for senior officials and other people of distinction. From the roof top of the official residence, the assembled guests watched a further royal salute from the Grand Battery on Lal Dighi, each burst of fire requiring the downing of a lumba pillans. As if that was not enough eating and imbibing, the evening was crowned by a Christmas Ball in gardens illuminated with enough lanterns to turn night into day. There was a display of fireworks over the river. Every single family of note was in attendance, the ladies decked out in their finest, a riot of glittering gem and fabric to rival the pyrotechnics.

Martinha had never seen the like. The fireworks scared her. The crowds intimidated. She longed for her little garden house and a quiet family occasion as the Christmas season should be celebrated. Yet Francis relished it. On all sides were Council members, army officers, rich merchants, bankers, shipowners, architects. This was the reason he had come to Calcutta – to rub shoulders with the high and mighty.

And then came the moment he had been waiting for. An equerry appeared at his side. 'The governor-general wishes to speak to you in the parlour, sir.' Such an occasion was a significant moment for an official audience.

The parlour, a large, airy room far grander than its designation suggested, was a distance from the noise and excess of the party. Light was asked to wait outside before being formally announced. The governor-general was with a group of men each holding glasses of brandy. He immediately felt like an interloper, excluded from the camaraderie of the important guests. No one offered him a drink.

The earl was an impressive figure, tall and upright of bearing, clad in scarlet-trimmed black and gold, his greying hair well curled. His face was oddly oval, the lower jaw hanging heavy beneath his high-domed forehead. His pointed nose was full of disdain, his lips were fleshy, and his eyes unreadable. It was a face perfectly formed for effigy. The great man stared at him with only the merest hint of an acknowledgment. His companions likewise surveyed him impassively. It was a most intimidating experience.

'My Lord? Francis Light, Superintendent of Prince of Wales Island.'

'I know who you are.' It was a curt response. Moments ticked by marked only by the clock on a mantelpiece. The faint noise of the gathering spilled distantly into the room: music, laughter, singing, the bursts of fireworks.

'I wished to see you for myself,' Cornwallis finally spoke. 'I believe one is able to tell much about a man by observing the cut of his jib. Once the actual jibber-jabber begins, one can lose sight of the real person behind the mask, don't you know?'

Light was unusually discommoded by Cornwallis' words – and suspected that was exactly what the great nobleman wished for. It was inordinately difficult to make any sort of good impression whilst being examined like a fish on a slab. It was, however, very easy to look like a fool. 'You are most perspicacious, my Lord. There has been too much talking already. I am a man of few words and far prefer action ...'

'Then hold the clever words yourself, man! Perspicacious, eh? Are you a flatterer, Light? Do you think to win me over by toadying?' Cornwallis gave him the benefit of a sardonic stare, his cold eyes hardly blinking. The companions tittered, the very embodiment of sycophants.

'No, sir. I do not seek to flatter. The truth, however, may also be complimentary. My Lord.'

Silence reigned for an instant – and then Cornwallis laughed. It was a mirthless sound, but a laugh for all that. 'I never doubted for one moment you were a clever fellow. I learned that much from the endless missives I've received from your little island paradise these past years. Superintendent Light is never short of words, I can vouch for that, whatever he proclaims. You will join us for a glass of brandy, sir?'

Light was glad he had only drunk sparingly so far, unlike the other guests. His head must remain clear in this maze of contradictions. A man servant handed him a crystal goblet containing a liberal measure of an excellent French brandy. Cornwallis held out his own glass. 'Those bastard French know their wines and spirits, I'll give them that. How fitting we raise their cognac to our English monarch. The King!'

They all repeated the salutation and drank down a toast. 'I expect you're wondering why I've summoned you tonight. Before we sit down to talk, I wanted to get your measure. For talk we must, sir. The problem of your island must be resolved.

It has gone on far too long. I'm damned tired of it. Let's hammer something out whilst you're in town. I'll discuss no business at Christmastide, though. Let's meet after Twelfth Night at which time I shall expect a definitive report. My officers will arrange the details. Now drink up and get back to your wife, there's a good man. Leave your betters to their own celebration.'

It was the most discourteous of dismissals, but Light shook off his annoyance, gulping down a swig of brandy before replacing the still full glass upon the proffered silver tray. Earl Cornwallis was one of the greatest aristocrats of the land. One had to swallow down the haughty and boorish arrogance. It was fed to the upper classes with their mother's milk. Pride must not ruin this long-awaited opportunity. The game was on.

12
In Flagrante

Tanjong Penaga, Prince of Wales Island. Late December 1789

The night chose itself. Heaven-sent for righteous punishment, a tropical storm of fierce intensity had kept all good souls at home. None but those with nefarious intent would venture out amidst the lightning and lashing rain. Thus, shielded by the elements, Captain Glass, Lt Raban and a troop of handpicked men gathered to the west of Chulia Street, seeking any shelter they might find under the scrubby trees that edged the hilly rise.

Once assembled, bedraggled and blown, Glass ordered them to proceed with stealth, but at a brisk pace. Boots mired in sludge, they splashed along a lane already swirling in water and mud. With cloaks sodden, they trudged miserably along the deserted street, taking the back alleys to ensure they could not be observed from the fort.

The shanties that lined their route were dimly lit by candle glow, the muffled hum of voices faintly audible, but doors and shutters firmly closed. On Beach Street, they turned north, stumbling almost blind but in a familiar direction, grateful for the anonymity of the darkness.

A sudden flash of lightning illuminated the stark outlines of a row of *gudangs*, locked and bolted for the night. There was no sign of any guard, although these warehouses were the property of James Scott who employed nightwatchmen. Such was the foul nature of the weather, it would seem, even they had found shelter, regardless of Scott's wrath. Glass made a mental note to inform the senior merchant; such laxity benefitted no one.

Not a single other soul was abroad. So devoid was there of of any sign of life in those streets, the men wondered if the tempest might even have discouraged their quarry. Perhaps Captain Glass had misjudged the situation. Glancing at Raban, whose sour expression suggested he feared the same, Glass pushed down his own uncertainty. Raban did not share his enthusiasm for tonight's action. Soldiers never enjoyed acting against their own. But young George Raban would do his duty. It was in his nature to follow orders, regardless of his opinion of them.

Along the jetties, junks and skiffs tossed in the surging waters, their rigging creaking ominously. Trees bent at alarming angles. The air swirled with fronds and branches large enough to knock a man senseless, snapped off in the violent blow. The wretched band carried on, stumbling out on to the muddy beach where crashing waves sprayed them with thunderous foam. Adjacent lay the swamp, its banks overflowing, forcing them to wade through gushing channels pouring towards the sea.

There was something eldritch in the air increased by the poor visibility and the intermittent sheets of lightning exaggerating every lurking shadow. This nightmarish version of a place they knew so well in daylight heightened trepidation. It brought to mind tales of supernatural beings said to dwell in darkness in these parts. On such foul nights, demons walked abroad, waiting for unwary folk fool enough to venture forth.

A sudden shriek – animal or human? – further fed their

febrile imaginings. Were they stalked by a bloodthirsty *pontianak* wishing to claim their souls? Live too long in these primitive parts, the local folklore ate into one's brain. There was so much here that a Christian could not fathom. Glass muttered the Lord's Prayer under his breath to drive the evil conjuring from his mind.

Not before time, on the quayside south-east of the fort, they saw the outline of a row of wooden sheds that housed the marine and customs stores, a repository for seized contraband. There was no denying a certain genius in this choice of location.

There was no visible lookout; if watchmen had been posted, they had deserted their positions. Their approach was unobserved. Yet this place was definitely occupied for as they grew near, raucous laughter reached their ears and the glimmer of lanterns shone dimly through the pall of rain. Ordering a few men to the rear against any who might try to flee across the muddy beach or were prepared to take their chances in the rising swamp waters, Glass and the rest burst through the front door, howling fiercely and waving swords, eager to vent their frustrations on the criminals inside.

The unsuspecting gathering fell into a shocked silence. For moments their brains did not comprehend what was happening. So over-confident had they been, they had allowed themselves to be taken red hand in the very midst of their crimes.

The outer room had been cleared of stores, all bales and crates stacked up against the walls, In the middle ground large barrels served as tables, each one bearing the tell-tale signs of gaming. Jugs of beer and flagons of spirits were plentiful. Through a doorway, a crowd of young Malay boys, jars of palm toddy in hand, were watching a cock fight. In those first moments, vicious squawks were the only sound to pierce the rooms.

All walks of island life were represented: Chinese coolies, Malay fishermen, foreign traders, lascars from all parts. Most surprising were the number of apparently upright British settlers, including a few employed in the administration itself– albeit in junior positions– such as the young up-and-coming merchant William Nason. Human frailties crossed all social ranks, it would seem.

After the initial immobility of surprise, the miscreants scattered. Everyone made attempts to flee, a futile skittering here and there. Men ducked around the barrels in an instinctive urge to run, no matter how hopeless their chance of escape. Some swept up coins; others cut their losses and ran – but there was no way out.

First, Glass dispersed the Malay boys with a stout kick up the rear. It was enough they lost their meagre sum of coins and faced Nakhoda Kecil when they reached home. The Europeans were given a curt dismissal in the full knowledge that public humiliation and private censure would soon follow. The sailors and merchants were herded into the back room where their names and ships were recorded. Should they be seized in such an establishment again, they would be permanently banned from the island.

While all this was accomplished, the motley group of errant soldiers responsible for this shameful commerce was brutally rounded up. The guards who had endured this unpleasant duty were determined to take their woes out in full against those who shamed their company. The culprits showed little sign of contrition. Despite their predicament, they still swaggered and sniggered, nursing their bloody noses and bruises, as if they expected little more than a sermon from the commander and hard duties back at fort.

Meanwhile, Glass and Raban made a thorough search of the premises, ascending to the upper level, a floored space under the rafters meant for marine stores. There they made an unexpected discovery. In the far corner, five distraught girls huddled together in abject fear, like deer in the gaze of a predator, too afraid either to run or cry out. Glass knelt before them – they shrank against the wall – and attempted to address them in as gentle a voice as the usually gruff officer could muster. He spoke first in Malay, then Tamil, assuring them that he meant no harm. There was a distinct relaxing of their shoulders – but no one replied. The two officers surveyed them bleakly. They had anticipated prostitutes, but these women were no seasoned whores. They had the appearance of recently arrived migrants. Had these unfortunate girls been seized on arrival to be sold to the highest bidders in a lewd auction? If so, this was the worst of the crimes on display tonight.

One young woman stood out amongst the rest, distinguished for her composure as well as her astonishing beauty. The others looked to her when Glass spoke as if she were the leader or an older sister figure. They awaited her response. The captain repeated his words directly to her, but she only shrugged her shoulders. She did not understand. The others attempted to explain, but she remained unmoving, staring directly at Glass, proud despite her predicament.

To his discomfort, John Glass found he could not tear his gaze away. The woman held her head high, all the while protecting the others with comforting arms. At last, she acknowledged him with a slight incline of her head. Amidst all the drama taking place below, the captain remained transfixed, quite at loss to proceed further.

The girl was of a dark complexion, her skin like polished ebony. She had high cheekbones so chiselled that they might have been shaped by a rule. A tangled brown-black profusion of thick locks tumbled around her elfin face. Even her stained and torn clothing could not hide her natural grace. Yet it was her eyes that bewitched him from that first moment: pale emeralds casting a startling luminosity from within her sultry darkness.

'Er ... Captain? Perhaps we should wrap cloaks about these ladies and take them to the infirmary? Dr Hutton will ensure they're well cared for until we know what we might do with them,' George Raban interrupted hesitantly, unusually decisive for this meek young officer.

At that, Captain Glass recovered his senses, immediately relaying the information to the women, assuring them that they were safe now and no further harm would come to them. They would be fed and clothed. Their injuries would be tended. One by one, they warily helped each other to their feet with little other choice but to trust these men. The soldiers helped the girls descend the rickety ladder, handing over their damp cloaks to cover their rags.

Regaining his lost composure, Captain Glass reasserted himself. 'Well done, lads. A good night's work. Raban, haul these brutes off to the gaol in town. The rest of you accompany the ladies to the infirmary. Send word to Dr Hutton. We can house them at the hospital for the time being. I fear these unfortunate innocents were to be victims of debauchery. Our arrival was timely indeed.'

***

A few weeks later, John Glass stepped out of Government House. It was the time of day following the rains when freshness lingers, and blue skies chase off the angry grey. A glorious evening beckoned, a welcome fillip to his mood.

The recent months had been particularly wet, even for the season, incessant rain for weeks on end with little sign of respite. And it was still over a month to the Spring Festival when the hot dry weather would commence. Until then there was little sign of the storms and floods abating. Some said that the new Year of the Dog would bring stability and calm; others that the return of Superintendent Light would set the island to rights. All Glass knew for sure was that his tenure as Acting Superintendent would then come to an end, much to his relief. He was unsuited to the complex challenges of administrative office. Military command was a far straighter road to travel.

As Glass made his way towards the town along the still-waterlogged thoroughfare of Lebuh Light, he surveyed the shambles that the heavy rains had wrought. They were struggling to right the damage. Temporary repairs to the fort had crumbled. Wood was rotting, riddled with mould and overgrown in foliage that burst forth thicker after each downpour. Even stone walls had crumbled, metal rusted away, and the gullies ran high with stagnant floodwater, undermining foundations. Erosion along the northern littoral was exacerbated by the higher-than-usual tides, the sea edging ever closer to the land. The deputy superintendent had taken immediate action with sandbags and extra channels, but it had achieved little more than wrapping a bandage around an infected limb. The fort was no longer a stockade worthy of its name.

George Town itself had likewise been affected. Before, fire had been its greatest enemy, now it was the turn of floods in the crowded, badly drained streets that lay so close to the beach. There had been a significant death toll. The many streams and creeks that fed into the sea had been transformed into fast-flowing rivers as torrents discharged from the mountains, carrying off unwary victims. Crocodiles washed into town on floodwaters had claimed more.

If that had not been enough, the Sultan of Queddah had taken it into his head to cut food supplies again, taking advantage of Light's absence. They were now more vulnerable than ever. It plagued John Glass that he did not have the skills of his superior to tackle so many different crises at one time. His respect for Superintendent Light had risen even more these months.

At least he took comfort in his one successful action, spurred on by a visit from Nakhoda Kecil, with whom he had always shared a good relationship. The Malay leader had been concerned that some of his young boys had fallen under the malign influence of soldiers. The bad fellows had encouraged the boys to behave in a manner unbecoming by selling them alcohol and tempting them to gamble and whore, practices that were *haram* in the Mohammedan religion. Hapless parents constantly complained of sons who returned home drunk, their pockets empty. The nakhoda had begged Glass to take immediate action against his men, both Indian sepoys and English privates, for running these illegal activities. These gambling dens were conducted in public view, the soldiers behaving as if they were untouchable. The situation was adding to the growing lawlessness of the island.

Glass had prohibited such illicit practices several times before, only to find them springing up again behind his back. Stern lectures and minor punishments had failed to make any mark. The dens were running again, the flouting of military discipline more brazen than ever.

Although Light shared Glass' concerns, the two men had disagreed on the necessary solution. Light insisted that the only viable sanction would come with the establishment of civilian courts, to which even military or Company men might be summoned if their crimes impinged on the local community. The island needed its own judiciary if it were to exert real authority over all inhabitants. He would bring this up during his trip to Calcutta.

Glass did not share his views. Soldiers must face discipline in timely and punitive fashion, dispensed by their own senior officers. Military punishment should never be a matter for the civil authorities. Furthermore, to wait for Company approval might take years. In the meantime, they needed to apply stout military censure, make examples of a few of the worst offenders, and even knock a few civilian heads together into the bargain. With the superintendent absent and Glass in charge, he had an opportunity to prove his point once and for all.

It was a familiar story of corruption and the abuse of authority that were perennial problems throughout the ports in India. Soldiers acquired a sense of entitlement over the native population – even those who were Indians themselves – particularly in Bengal, where they were generally recruited from higher castes. Exploiting their position and mishandling those beneath them was virtually inbuilt into the system, for what could these pathetic natives do against British troops on a British island? Nor was it merely a matter of illegal gambling dens and unlicensed alcohol – bad as that was – but the dens were also brothels, where unfortunate migrant women were forced to work, seized from their families on arrival as some sort of 'tax' for entry. The soldiers also sequestered goods – including alcohol – from merchants who were bullied into paying these 'terms' for permission to import their wares.

Glass had received further complaints from Kapitan Khoh. Official liquor licences were only granted to Chinese. This illegal trade in contraband undercut the prices charged by these local innkeepers, who paid rents and taxes to the administration for the privilege. Thus, revenue was lost, as well as business! No one, however, had seen fit to complain about the aspect that had most troubled the puritanical Glass: the abuse of the women who were forced into degrading commerce against their will. Not only was it morally wrong but it was also tantamount to slave trading.

When credible intelligence finally reached his ears, Assistant Superintendent Glass taught a harsh lesson to the contemptible scoundrels who had shamed the army's reputation. The offenders were given the harshest of military punishment, including public lashing, before dishonourable discharge and transport back to Bengal, where further disciplinary measures awaited. The incident served as a dire warning to others if they continued in criminality unbecoming of the British army. Glass still recalled the night with unbridled pleasure; it was the one solace in these months where he had been swimming against the tide.

The success of the raid, however, was only part of it. Something else had occurred that night to rob him of his habitual melancholy. Sarippa had entered his life. Her presence had demonstrated to this lifelong solitudinarian why men search for their whole lives to find the perfect soulmate.

It seemed to Captain Glass that he had met Sarippa amidst such degradation that only the unseen hand of a benign God could have ordained it. He had always been a religious man, staunchly Presbyterian by both nature and upbringing, with enough simple faith to believe in divine miracles. On the night of his greatest achievement, amidst the apocalyptic storm that surely was a significant portent, the Lord had seen fit to reward him for his uprightness.

The women had been temporarily housed at the hospital while investigations were made to return them to their families. Most had been forced off boats at the jetty, their families given no choice but to accept, although they had received a small recompense for their loss, with a bill of sale which rendered them unable to complain. Those girls were now returned to their parents or husbands, although it was unknown if they had been welcomed back. It was likely they were regarded as soiled goods. Nor did anyone ask the women how they felt that their loved ones had sold them to pitiless soldiers, merely for the right to settle.

Sarippa, however, had nowhere to go. At first it had been impossible to discover anything about her for she did not understand anything that was said to her. Nor did she even try to speak in her own tongue. It was even suggested that she might be mute. Dr Hutton's medical assistant, Marlbro, however, finally broke through her wall of silence. Sarippa was a Sinhalese woman of Ceylon.

Although African in appearance, Marlbro had been born in Batticaloa on the east coast of Dutch Ceylon. His first language was Tamil, but he also had a smattering of Sinhala. Under his gentle questioning, Sarippa proved eager to share her tale. With her two elder brothers, she had fled their homeland after Dutch reprisals on their village. It had not been their wish to take her along, but they had reluctantly let her follow.

When the soldiers seized her, her brothers had gladly bartered her away for a few paltry coins to set them up in their new life. Now Sarippa had no wish to be reunited with them; she refused even to reveal their names. Instead, she asked if she might take employment with a local family. She would make her future on her own.

Marlbro found the solution. Sarippa was a bright girl, a quick learner – perhaps she could assist at the hospital? Until her Malay was proficient, he could translate for her, whilst teaching her the language at the same time. Dr Hutton agreed, amused by the thought that his serious-minded orderly might have taken a personal liking to the girl. Furthermore, such a beauty left alone would always be at risk of unwanted attention. If any feelings should develop between the two, it would be an excellent development. Marlbro deserved a wife.

That was not how it transpired. The hospital, located at the edge of the compound of the fort, offered an irresistible lure to the already-smitten Captain Glass to find regular excuses to pay visits to Dr Hutton. At every opportunity, Glass made a beeline for Sarippa, eager even for a distant glimpse of his goddess.

The woman visited the market daily to buy food, accompanied by a Caffree slave, in order for her to practice her new language skills. Thus Glass began to take a morning stroll at the same early hour, telling himself he was merely concerned for her safety but, in his heart, aware his obsession was much more than that. For days he struggled with his conscience, whilst battling the pressing problems of his onerous responsibilities. Sleepless nights finally drove him to approach Sarippa in person; he could endure it no longer. One day as she was fetching water from the well, sunk not far from Government House, Glass rushed forth to greet her, before he had the time to change his mind.

'Why, good morning, Miss Sarippa! What a pleasant surprise to see you here. How do you fare?' Glass asked her gruffly in Malay, unsure if she would understand him.

'Good, sir,' she answered brightly. 'Thank you for your kindness. I like the hospital. Everyone my friend,' She flashed him a broad smile, a different woman now from the haughty girl he had met that first night. 'The doctor and Encik Marlbro are very good people.'

Glass had steeled himself for silence, or perhaps a mere nod by way of reply. Her easy conversation took him entirely by surprise. He cleared his throat to win time to think as he struggled to proceed.

'My goodness, you speak Malay already! Very good. Excellent. Well done,' Glass jabbered inanely.

The woman surveyed his discomfort with amusement. 'Encik Marlbro teach me. Is easy. Many words same like my language.' She gave him a coy but knowing smile.

Sarippa hoisted the full water jar smoothly onto her shoulder; it was time to leave. There was nothing more to say. Yet she lingered, watching him through green eyes that danced with playfulness. Was she toying with him? What might he say to keep her there?

It was now or never. Sarippa had given him an opportunity – he must take advantage of it. Plucking up his courage, Glass indicated that Sarippa should go first, and fell in alongside her. They strolled in an awkward silence side-by-side until they reached the path that led towards the grounds of Government House.

'Well, it was very nice to see you again, my dear,' Glass said, inwardly cursing himself for his awkwardness. Sarippa made as if to carry on her way, when out of his mouth, almost as if his subconscious was speaking for him, he heard the words: 'Miss Sarippa? May I call on you one afternoon after your duties? Perhaps we could take a walk together?'

She spun to face him in a movement as lithe and elegant as a dancer and made a slight curtsey. 'I very happy to walk out with you, sir.' Then she continued on her way, hips swaying with new emboldenment, carrying the jar as proudly as if it were a crown.

That had been the beginning. Once Glass had breached his own walls, a floodgate of emotion replaced his earlier hesitancy. He no longer cared to hide his feelings, meeting her in full view of the public – who missed nothing, of course. The captain and Miss Sarippa were the talk of the town.

Tongues wagged, but no one dared raise the matter to the captain's face. After all, he was deputy superintendent. Many officers kept local women, so it was not so remarkable. Even Thomas Pigou shared a few rooms in Chinatown with his lively Indonesian lady, Miss Ady Bonsu, the mother of his child. It was generally deemed preferable that the dour Captain Glass was at last behaving like a normal soldier. A military man of his age without a woman was seen as an aberration. It brought his manhood into question – was he a sodomite, perchance?

Their incipient relationship had remained entirely chaste. Glass suspected that Sarippa might be amenable to his advances but he had not acted upon his own amatory urges lest it seem advantage-taking. Who could blame a girl in her predicament for offering herself? What woman would not cling to a senior British officer, more than willing to accept his inevitable liberties if only to ensure her safety? Honourable Captain Glass would not countenance it. It would make him no better than the soldiers who pandered vulnerable women, or the coarse men who used them! A senior officer must be above reproach.

But they could not 'walk out' forever, like two lovesick, moon-faced adolescents. Marriage to a native girl was completely out of the question for a British officer. The Council would not tolerate it, even if men were encouraged to keep concubines. This thorny problem occupied Glass's thoughts during those weeks of high command quite as much as any of the administrative issues that plagued him.

That afternoon the answer came to Glass out of the blue, like a sudden flash of lightening in a clear sky. His perplexity thus illuminated, his way forward became clear. Why had it taken him so long to resolve his dilemma?

Superintendent Light was married to a native! Mrs Martinha was of the Roman Catholic persuasion. To his knowledge, no questions had been asked in Calcutta, where even now she was graciously received. Light's 'wife' was Christian – thus saved – and her position as a decent woman established. Of course, her status was legally nothing more than mistress, for no Protestant banns had ever been read, nor special licence granted. Yet Catholic nuptials had satisfied Mrs Martinha's family and the honour of Francis Light. They gave legitimacy to his children without ruffling Anglican sensibilities. It was the perfect solution.

Sarippa must be accepted into the Catholic Church. Glass would approach Fr Michael as a matter of urgency. The padre was a decent fellow. He would be amenable, particularly if it meant another soul for his ever-growing flock. Then, when the moment was ripe, he would inform the superintendent, sure to be supportive in the circumstances, and their unorthodox – but holy – matrimony would be realised.

Glass raised his eyes to the heavens, where cerulean patches swept away the last of the dark clouds, as if the heavens themselves were blessing his epiphany. This was surely a harbinger of God's eternal plan, in an accidence of many such of late.

13
Jemdanee

Government House, The Esplanade, Calcutta. 11th January 1790

The interview at Government House stood in stark contrast to Light's previous audience with Warren Hastings four years earlier. That had been an intimate affair in an unassuming private study. The two men had spoken as equals. Governor-General Earl Cornwallis, however, was accustomed to lesser mortals bowing and scraping in his august presence. Such men take their infallibility for granted, a natural endowment of their birth right. Despite having summoned him to Calcutta for this very meeting, Cornwallis had ignored him for weeks, leaving Light idling away, his worries mounting. No doubt it amused the governor-general to let him stew. Lesser men must wait on the grace and favour of their masters.

For more than an hour already Light had found himself waiting amongst a host of other petitioners, all of whom were called before him. Cornwallis was still demonstrating his supreme authority. Finally summoned into the inner sanctum, Light stepped into a lofty hall sumptuously furnished in the grand manner, another reminder – if it were needed – that Cornwallis was second only to the king in the Indies. Several assistants were in attendance as well as a corpulent, bewigged gentleman, dressed in sober but expensive cloth. His face was round, his features doughy pastry, small shrewd eyes set in a sea of baggy wrinkles.

'Good morning, Superintendent Light,' Cornwallis pronounced with weighty formality. 'May I present Mr Joseph Price?' Light should have guessed his identity. Once the advisor to Governor MacPherson, Cornwallis now kept him close to hand, one of the few merchants he trusted. Price, a former sea captain who had made his fortune in Bombay and Calcutta, was one of the most influential voices on the Council.

Light greeted them with due deference and was directed a seat. 'Let us cut to the chase, sir. Describe the main matters for attention and your most urgent needs. No flim flam, please.' Two clerks settled at escritoires flanking the governor's desk, ready to transcribe his every word. Company records were painstakingly meticulous, their archives a labyrinth of parchment.

Whilst gathering his thoughts, Light surreptitiously wiped away a drop of sweat that had formed upon his upper lip. He was intimidated. 'First, may I thank you for the honour of this private meeting, sir –'

'Get on with it, Light!' Cornwallis' highhanded manner was already on display.

Light nodded meekly, straightening his shoulders. 'In the few years since its establishment, Prince of Wales Island has demonstrated prospects far above expectation. The volume of traffic per annum has increased from a handful of vessels to hundreds, drawn from all quarters of the globe: Europe, China, Siam, Burma, Java and the Arab world. We are now the preferred landing in the Straits and the ideal way station for Company ships on the China passage. Favourable reports from all those who regularly use our emporium abound. The population of the island has swelled, migrants in their droves providing an essential supply of labour.'

Cornwallis harrumphed. 'This we know already, man. It's a damned free port. Of course, the merchants will flock there! Especially as the Dutch have been grinding their noses into the ground these many years. I'm fully apprised of the suitability of your little island for trade, but in what way has that contributed to the Company? So far, Prince of Wales Island has been nothing but a drain upon our Treasury – and from your constant begging letters, it would appear the place will continue to be so for some time yet!' It had not begun well. Cornwallis deemed the island not worth the investment.

Just then, the grand double doors were flung open. All eyes turned to the cause of the interruption. In strode a bluff man with a purposeful gait, an expression of contrition on his large face, a hand to his heart in apology. Something in his facial characteristics recalled the governor-general himself.

'My sincere apologies, gentlemen. An urgent matter at the port.'

The governor-general broke into an unexpected smile of such warmth that it entirely changed his stony visage. 'William! No need for apologies for we've barely begun. Superintendent Light – please meet my younger brother, Commodore Cornwallis. William, I believe you wish to make the superintendent's acquaintance?'

'I do indeed. Delighted to meet at last, sir! I've followed your career with interest. You and I have much in common – two navy men in the Indies,' he said, shaking Light's hand firmly. William Cornwallis may have resembled his older brother, but in personality they were complete opposites.

'Thank you, sir. Your reputation precedes you. The honour is all mine.' His reply was without exaggeration. Commodore William Cornwallis was much admired. Perhaps he might find an unexpected ally in this quarter?

'Gentlemen, please continue.' William Cornwallis seated himself in large armchair, his hefty bulk overflowing its sides.

The Earl continued. 'I was saying that, despite the trade in and out of Prince of Wales Island, we have yet to see a penny profit. Furthermore, it is not yet clear if the said island even has the means to support its growing population or to provide the necessary to our ships. Does it have suitable timber for repairs? Is there sufficient land for grazing to provide meat for our fleets? Can the island grow enough to sustain all the demands upon it? I hear food has been in short supply this year.'

'You are well informed, sir,' Light answered meekly, without pointing out that this intelligence had originated from his own office. 'The island is in the process of substantially expanding its agricultural land. But these things take time, for clearance of the forest is no easy task. More land is now under cultivation – with much more to follow. Timber is plentiful – every type and species of wood grows there – and we are logging apace. The more settlers we receive, the greater our ability to cut trees and plant food. The root of our current food problems lies not in our lack of effort or suitable resources, sir. The Sultan of Queddah has taken it into his head to refuse rice and other food stuffs. He uses these exports as coercion to force the Company's hand over the matter of the ratification of the treaty.'

Cornwallis jumped to his feet, beating upon the oak desk with his large hands. 'That old saw! We cannot allow an insignificant chieftain in his jungle lair to make demands upon us. I will not be held over a barrel by such rogues!'

The room fell silent. William Cornwallis approached his brother, resting a supportive hand upon his shoulder. 'Do not rile yourself so, dear Charles. Sad to say we are always at the mercies of these people. However, it is incontrovertible that the treaty is still to be ratified nor has the sultan received his due. One can hardly blame the fellow grasping at straws after all this time. Mr Light, perhaps you could outline the main issues again for us?'

Light bowed. 'I've been in private negotiations with the sultan through an intermediary, my former partner James Scott. The sultan has agreed to re-open trade links on the understanding that payment will soon be forthcoming. I have suggested an interim sum of five thousand Spanish dollars per annum. It is substantially lower than the original amount demanded. Scott has delivered the first payment, which I have made from my own pocket. I dared not leave the matter unattended in my absence.'

Cornwallis was now deep in thought, resting his chin on his hand. 'I concur that we need to settle this once and for all. I suggest we double the figure – ten thousand per annum for a period of say, ten years? After that, he can go to the devil. We will have spent ten times that sum in developing his desert island. It's all he can expect. No need to clarify those terms at this juncture, naturally. Let him think it's ten thousand in perpetuity. That should calm things down.'

It was a complete betrayal of the spirit of the agreement, typical of the ruthless pragmatism of the Company. What indeed could the sultan do in future against a well-fortified British port?

'And if he does not accept? What if he resorts to violence to reclaim the island?' Light asked, although he already knew the answer. Notwithstanding, he wanted it on official record so that blame for a future conflict could not be lain at his door.

Cornwallis shrugged in disdain. 'Let him try to attack a host of British warships. He will lose all if he does. The aces are in our hands, Light. Surely you can see that?'

'Indeed, sir. You have a fine grasp of the situation. But if I may ask – the island is currently in need of much investment. The fort is in a state of disrepair. The only improvements we have made thus far have come largely from my private funds. There is also the pressing need for a designated wharf sufficient to accommodate naval vessels. I believe Major Kyd recommended Pulau Jerejak for an East Indies naval base.'

'Your question, sir? You have merely set out a list of demands, all of which come at an exorbitant expense. I take it you're making a request for funds in your meandering fashion?' Cornwallis sneered.

'Dear Charles,' broke in William Cornwallis. 'Superintendent Light has already shown his commitment to the island, having depleted his own fortune in the Company service. It is only fair the be fully recompensed. No new territory is ever settled without initial outlay.'

At least the governor-general seemed prepared to listen to someone. 'Naturally, we are grateful for your service, Light. The monies outstanding will be remitted in due course, have no fear. The fundamental question, however, remains. Is your island the best place to situate a naval base? It may be a useful trading station, but I do not believe it serves our navy best. The Straits is too far distant from India in the event of war. Our urgent requirement is a safe harbour for our navy within striking distance of the enemy. If subsequently the decision is taken to locate the station elsewhere, then it would be wholly profligate to bankrupt our treasuries by sinking more funds into your island now. Let the private merchants who benefit from trade put their hands into their purses. Encourage local traders to do their share.'

The fate of Prince of Wales Island hung precariously in the balance.

'If I may make a suggestion?' chimed in Commodore Cornwallis. 'As Commander-In-Chief of the East Indies squadron, I would very much like to visit the region to see for myself the opportunities it might afford. Mr Light, I'm sure you're aware of our surveys in the Andamans? It seems entirely appropriate that I should compare the two before our final decision. What say you, Charles? Wheresoever we ultimately plant our flag, that settlement will require great sacrifices in time and money. Perhaps we should not reject out of hand the devil that we know, rather than the one that we do not?'

A wry smile crossed Earl Cornwallis' face. 'As ever the diplomat, dear William. I wholeheartedly agree. The Andamans may be nearer, but they are isolated and troubled by natives and disease. We would be remiss not to consider an established port. When do you leave for home, Mr Light?'

'February, sir. A few weeks hence.'

'Then perhaps William might travel on your ship? It would provide an excellent opportunity to familiarise him with the particulars.'

It was a valuable concession, the best he could hope for. Light owed William Cornwallis much. Why had the Commodore interceded on his behalf? He suspected he would soon find out.

'And now to other matters. Is there tin on the island?'

The swiftness of the change of topic left Light momentarily lost for words. 'I … I believe so, sir. The topography is much the same as the rest of the coastline. Tin is plentiful throughout the Peninsula and Siam.'

'But you have not found any deposits as yet?'

'No, sir. None of significance. But should they exist, it most likely lies in the hills, as in Jangsylan. Much of the interior has yet to be surveyed. Nevertheless, we expect tin to be an asset in the future. For the meantime, we are laying plantations. The climate suits all spices; it is our intention to be self-sufficient in the major crops. By this means we may undercut the Dutch and avoid long journeys to the outer reaches of the archipelago to acquire them.'

For the first time, Joseph Price spoke. 'An interesting commercial venture, Mr Light, and one of which I wholeheartedly approve. We merchants should be progressive in our thinking, creating markets that suit our own needs instead of allowing ourselves to be prey to the greed of others. And yet, the tide is turning vis-à-vis the Hollanders.'

Cornwallis nodded gravely. 'The news from France grows more unsavoury by the day. We've recently had word King Louis was arrested whilst fleeing. It's a bad business. God knows what those wretches will do to him. No European monarch will stand for it! It will mean war, especially if the royal family is badly used. Even the damn Hollanders have respect for nobility! And should there be conflict in Europe, I'm sure you understand the consequences for the Indies?'

'There will be conflict here, sir. It is always the way,' Light answered.

'Indeed. Yet I refer in this instance to our relations with the Dutch. If we should come to blows against the French, we would find ourselves on the same side. Such an alliance would change every aspect of our foreign policy. The erstwhile enemy now becomes the friend. Do you apprehend the significance?'

Light understood far better than most but was loath to speak the words out loud. 'In future we must not upset the Dutch and they must allow our shipping to pass unmolested.'

'Exactly. Why then should we sink money into an island that is no longer of strategic importance? It's a lucrative port, I'll give you that, but as a British colonial establishment, it would be surplus to requirements if we were now welcome in Malacca.'

It was a crushing blow to Light's aspirations. 'The Dutch are not our only enemy in the Straits, sir. They are but one amongst many, and even now they deal behind our backs with Queddah. We must approach an alliance with vigilance. Furthermore, should the Dutch lose their hold on the Straits, or even fall to the French in Europe, it will be open season on their territories. The entire sea lane might be closed to us. The Straits becomes more dangerous every year. We may never have greater need of a fortified stronghold in the region.' It was a bold assertion but warranted in the circumstances.

'Fie, man,' interrupted Joseph Price. 'Who might fill the void? The local rulers? You sent those envoys from Terengganu. We've examined their proposition – and denied their appeals for alliance. My own agency is more than able to conduct such trade without having to deal with their tinpot king. It is my belief that these local sultans are wholly incapable of understanding either trade or politics. Nor can they be trusted to keep their word. With the combined vessels of Britain and the VOC, they would be powerless to stop us.'

The rejection of the alliance sought by Terengganu came as no surprise to Light but the ignorant belief that a merchant from Calcutta had a better grasp of the internal politics of the Peninsula was arrant nonsense. Maintaining peaceable relations with the kingdoms was key to the Straits. Were they willing to risk the ire of the sultans at this delicate juncture?

'There's more to this than local politics, sir,' Light countered. 'The Straits has always been plagued by piracy of one form or another, although few rulers consider it as such. Raiding is an ancient practice in these waters when they deem there is no other option. Every island, coastal settlement and river village will turn to brigandage if threatened. More than that, we have the Bugis, who will rampage in the south should the Dutch turn their eyes elsewhere for but a moment. And now an even fiercer danger raises its head, the Illanun of Mindanao, the fiercest raiders in the East. They not only prey on ships but also offer their services to the native kings as mercenaries. If we turn from our alliances, we might face hordes of these ferocious killers in the pay of the sultans we have shunned. An East Indiaman would not stand a chance against them.'

William Cornwallis spoke up. 'Light is correct. The Illanun are a dangerous menace. So far, I have only heard of them as raiders, but as mercenaries or settlers, they would present a formidable challenge. We must not act in haste, Charles. It is too soon to withdraw from Prince of Wales Island. Let us wait until my survey is done and events in Europe are more apparent.'

'There is more, sir,' chimed in Light, grateful to ride the wave of the commodore's support. 'We must as ever pay heed to Siam and Burma. Those two empires may be more inclined to fight each other, but now Siam is in the ascendancy. King Rama is not satisfied with unifying Siam. He wishes to claim his suzerain rights in the Straits. If we withdraw our friendship, the sultans will have no choice but to open their doors to Siam. And I assure you, Siam will close the Straits. Remember, they have two coastlines and sound internal routes from sea to sea. They could completely dominate if it pleased them. I would not ignore their ambitions. Rama has no love for Europe. He would relish closing down our trade –'

'And we would be squeezed between the Asian hordes ...' Cornwallis muttered, rubbing his chin in thought.

'Not to mention the French,' Light added.

'The French?'

'What if they should offer support to Queddah or the other sultans? Perhaps Johor at the very entrance of the Straits? To my knowledge, they have made advances to Sultan Abdullah, perhaps other sultans, too.'

Silence reigned in the great high-ceilinged room; even the clerks paused in their scratchings, watching for the governor-general's response. The warm air hung heavy with expectancy. Sweat peppered every brow. The future of British trade might rest upon the next few moments.

'You've raised some valid issues, Mr Light.' Lord Cornwallis finally admitted. 'We must not ignore the years of experience you bring to this table. A hasty decision would be a mistake. But I must stress that, whilst your little island means the world to you, it is but a speck in the ocean to the Company, as are all the insignificant chieftains of the Straits who give themselves the lofty titles of sultan and rajah. Do not lose sight of the important matters of this world, Superintendent Light. Your horizons have become too small, sir. And remember, no action that might jeopardise the intimate relations now established between Britain and the States of Holland will be countenanced. Nor shall any military support ever be provided to the kings of the Malay states.'

The decision had been taken, or rather deferred until a later date. Light felt fortunate to have received even that much. Cornwallis had taken heed of his argument, even if his preference inclined elsewhere. Prince of Wales Island had been foisted upon him by a previous administration. He had no wish to glorify the reputations of other men.

His brother, however, was a horse of a different colour. Although both William Cornwallis and Alexander Kyd had stakes in the Andaman expedition, there was evidence that neither was entirely convinced by the remote island location. There had also been an assurance of financial compensation. He could at last approach the sultan of Queddah for a settlement.

***

It was late afternoon when Francis Light ran up the stairs of their fine villa, ruffling up William's hair as he passed him on the upper landing. The child had just awoken from his nap and was being carried downstairs for milk and biscuits by Esan, tantamount to a second mother to their little boy. Willie was wrapped around her shoulders, still bleary-eyed and grumpy. He was not yet in the mood for his father's boisterous affection.

Their temporary residence was the home of Sir Elijah Impey, the former Chief Justice of Bengal. Impey had fallen along with Hastings; both were currently fighting impeachment back in London. A property of such grandeur was hard to find in Calcutta these days, for demand was high. Fairlie had arranged the lease on Light's behalf.

Entering the lofty private quarters, Light found Martinha surrounded by a bevy of servants. She had adjusted to the vast household army that came with the property rather better than he. It irritated him that he could barely move without falling over someone in attendance. Not so his wife. Once Martinha had lived a life of unimaginable privilege as the granddaughter of Siamese nobility on the island of Thalang. He was proud to finally offer her the comforts she deserved.

Martinha's private dressing room was spacious, grander even than the reception room of his official residence. Lofty ceilings and tall windows rendered it airy and light, although the wooden shutters were closed against the afternoon sun. The furniture was a typical blend of restrained English drawing room and opulent Indian luxury. The entire floor was covered in a silk carpet resplendent in red and gold images of flowers, birds and forest. Heavy brocade curtains framed the windows, lace hung in folds from the elegant French dressing table; a serpentine walnut commode graced a wall. His personal dressing room – and bed – were in an adjoining suite, in the aristocratic fashion where husbands and wives rarely slept together. Light did not use it other than to change his clothes.

Martinha perched regally on a low stool in the centre,

selecting fabrics from an array of samples laid out before her. Several servants stood by, far more than necessary for the task, but that was the way in India.

'You're home, dear Francis! I have almost finished. These textiles are so wondrously rich and intricate. I simply cannot resist them. Allow me a moment!' Martinha exclaimed, flushed from the pleasurable experience of shopping in the comfort of her rooms. He gave her a fond smile. To see her so enjoying her stay in India warmed his heart. She was growing more confident daily. Although they had never discussed the subject, it was his desire that when his duty was done, he would return to Suffolk with his family as a man of means on his own country estate. This pipe dream was far from realisation for he did not yet possess sufficient fortune to accomplish it. Nor was he entirely sure how Martinha would regard his fantasy.

'How was your audience with the governor-general?' she asked. The merchant and his boys had packed up their wares and were *salaaming* as if Martinha was a rani. Light waved his hand to dismiss the house servants. He did not trust them. Servants were known to sell nuggets of Company information to feed the appetite for gossip in the city.

'The best I can say is that it was "interesting". Cornwallis is a damned difficult man. He has no desire to learn from those who are experienced, for he believes he knows everything. But we made some headway. He promises more money for the island and has committed to an annual payment to Abdullah. It should be enough in the short term but his bloody obsession for the Andamans still blights the horizon. Must everything I do be confounded by men of ignorance and privilege?' Francis poured a glass of wine from the decanter on the commode and drank it down, slumping into a delicate chair with force enough to snap its spindly legs. His mood was decidedly sour.

Martinha carried her stool to his side. 'Dear Francis, do not be dejected. There is still hope. We've always known that the way ahead would be full of challenges,' she consoled. 'But don't forget, it is you yourself who never chooses the easy path! *Kalau takut dilambung ombak, jangan berumah di tepi pantai*!'

Her witty retort, quoting an old Malay proverb, brought a smile to his face. 'Will you not even allow me to wallow in my misery for a little while? But I must admit, that saying is particularly apposite. "If you fear the waves, don't build a house upon the beach". Martinha, you have ten times the wit of most of these fools! How I love you!' He swung her onto his knee, while she playfully struggled against him, squealing for him to 'desist' and 'let me go!' Yet she willingly accepted his embraces, curled up on his lap, the cat with the cream.

Murmuring in his ear, aware that he would not be best pleased, she whispered: 'Sayang, we have an invitation this evening. I know you have no mind for socialising tonight, but I rather think we should attend. It would take your mind off all these problems. What say you?'

Francis sighed. It was the last thing he wished for, yet he could refuse her nothing, especially now that she was openly engaging with Calcutta society. If one day they should return to Suffolk, the more Martinha was familiar with English culture, the better. 'Whatever you wish, my dearest. It would do me good. No use maudlin all night long. At whose home do we have the pleasure?'

'A rather interesting gentleman with an even more fascinating wife. Eliza insists we must meet them before we leave. Jemdanee is the talk of Calcutta!'

'Jemdanee?' Light replied, rolling his eyes to the heavens. 'We're dining tonight with that damned toady, William Hickey? Could this day be any worse?'

***

Contrary to expectation, Light enjoyed his evening at the Hickeys. Firstly, if one discounted his loathsome host, a most engaging group of people had gathered around the large dining table in his well-appointed residence in the heart of town. William Hickey had done well for himself. Amongst the distinguished guests were the Kyds; a flamboyant Irishman, Thomas Hicky; the ubiquitous William Fairlie; a jovial architect Richard Blechynden; and none other than William Cornwallis himself. Only three ladies were present: Martinha, Eliza Kyd and William Hickey's mistress, the mysterious Jemdanee.

Jemdanee was unique; no other women like her existed in the whole of India. She was a Hindustani woman of extraordinary beauty who, if not for her black mane of hair and native attire, might have passed for a European woman, perhaps from Spain or Italy. Her skin was flawless, milky cream with honey sheen. Her eyes, large and brown, danced with spirit. The lady had lips of such perfection that her admirers wrote poems to celebrate them. Although diminutive of stature, with delicate ankles and tiny hands, her figure was curvaceously bountiful. Had she been borne through the streets on a palanquin, no one would have doubted her a queen.

The lady was swathed in layers of Bengal muslin as delicate as gossamer, over *sulhanki* trousers of the finest silk. Her body was adorned with every form of jewel: anklets and bangles; rings and earrings heavy with gemstones; chain after chain of golden necklaces with ruby and emerald pendants. From her brow hung a braid of pearls.

It would have been enough to sit and worship this effigy of near-divine beauty, but Jemdanee was no marble statue. She presided over the gathering like the lady of the house, which indeed she was. Her wit was as sharp as her loveliness was soft.

William Hickey introduced her as 'Fateh Jemdanee, queen of Bengal!' in his usual effusive style although, for once, it was hard to disagree with him.

'My darling Fatty!' chortled Thomas Hicky, an Irishman, no relative to William, although they were close acquaintances.

'Wah!' replied Jemdanee. 'You naughty boy! Is you who are the fatty at this table! Look at your belly! Is round as a drum!'

The other guests knew her well enough to tease. Although her heavily accented English was laboured and peppered with Bengali words and phrases, she made herself understood – and even grasped the nuances of English humour well enough to throw it back at them. Jemdanee was a delight: a clever, spirited woman who knew her worth and relished in it. Both Light and Martinha were intoxicated by her captivating charm.

'Willie!' Jemdanee called to Commodore Cornwallis, whose red face beamed back at her. 'Why you still no wife? A big handsome boy like you? You want Jemdanee find you pretty brown girl?'

'Why, madame, if she resembles you in the slightest, I would be most honoured!' he answered, dropping to his knees to kiss her hand. 'Beg pardon, ladies,' he added as he struggled back to his seat, bowing to Eliza and Martinha. 'Madame Jemdanee loves to pull my leg. She thinks it high time I took me a wife. But what's a sailor to do? I spend my entire life afloat. Who would have me?'

Martinha was sure every unattached woman in Calcutta would count themselves lucky to have such a husband, a decorated naval officer and brother to the most famous man of the day. It was a merry evening, full of such nonsense, quite unlike the usual formal dinner parties they had attended. It felt more like a group of old friends, like the old days gathered around the table in Queddah when they had caroused with fellow country captains until the wee hours.

When the women withdrew, Jemdanee led them to her private parlour that was decked out in exotic finery like an Ottoman harem. She settled down cross-legged upon a silk divan and motioned for the others to join her. Martinha had little problem, for sitting in this manner was the Malay way, but Eliza made hard work of it. 'Tsh!' exclaimed Jemdanee. 'You are too English. You not know how to bend your knees! Must practice or your bones go old and dry!' observed Jemdanee with a grin. 'See how Mrs Martinha can. She Indies girl. Moves with grace. You want wine, ladies?'

Jemdanee indicated to a servant to pour two glasses. 'You do not take wine, Mrs Jemdanee?' Martinha inquired.

She shook her head. 'Haram. You know this word, Martinha?' she asked.

'Yes. My people also say haram. You are Mohammedan?' Martinha asked.

'Of course. Maybe not very good one but I try. I never take liquor. Or pork. These things I cannot do. Why you drink wine?' Jemdanee questioned.

'I am Christian although my mother was Muslim. We once lived at the court of a sultan.'

'Wah! Then you rani, too! We can be good friends. You must come see me often!'

Wonders abounded in Calcutta, but Martinha believed that nothing was quite as breath-taking as Fateh Jemdanee, the self-styled queen of Calcutta. Between her and the bewitching Eliza Kyd, Martinha's eyes had been opened to notions quite beyond the narrow horizons of her old life. She did not know how it might affect her in the future – but she was sure it would. As St Augustine had once said: 'The world is a book and those who do not travel read but one page.' Without Francis, her life would have lacked such rich experiences. Few women from Thalang had the opportunities that she enjoyed.

Yet she understood the frustrations her husband must feel now he was no longer free to roam the Indies as a merchant captain. No wonder he felt chained by the responsibilities he had assumed. It was a small horizon for a man like him, despite the honours he had gained. For the first time it occurred to her that perhaps they might not stay in the Straits forever. One day, she was now sure, Francis would go home.

Of course. Maybe not very good at [illegible], but they [illegible] [illegible] Oxford. [illegible] came [illegible] [illegible].

[illegible] Christian [illegible] should [illegible] [illegible] lived [illegible].

[illegible]

[illegible] [illegible] [illegible] [illegible] [illegible] [illegible] [illegible] [illegible] [illegible] experiences for women [illegible] [illegible] [illegible] that [illegible] enjoyed.

[illegible] [illegible] [illegible] [illegible] [illegible] [illegible] [illegible]

PART THREE

The Gathering Storm

(1790-1791)

14
Hobson's Choice

Government House. George Town, 21st March 1790

'It has been my pleasure, dear Francis!' William Cornwallis clinked his glass and toasted his imminent return journey to the Andaman Islands to rendezvous with Blair. His flagship, the *Crown*, had finally arrived to collect him for duty. This sojourn had been a rest cure after many months at sea with the fleet or playing politics in Calcutta. The island life had its appeals, but he was ready to return to his vagabond existence. A few more days would be perfect, while the *Crown* revictualled and repaired, stocking up on a few luxuries for what would be a lean season on the remote Greater Andaman Island.

'How do you cope with the life of a landlubber?' Cornwallis asked, his train of thought already drifting to departure. 'My feet itch after a few weeks in one location.'

Francis sighed. 'Not as well as I ought to. The first few years were particularly hard. I'm a sailor at heart, Commodore. I thought that I would end up buried at sea, but it looks more and more likely that my old bones will moulder in a grave out here, with all manner of fearsome insects chewing on my sorry remains.' He made a joke of what Cornwallis suspected was far from that.

'I'll warrant it's no worse than being food for fish and crabs, dear fellow!' he replied with merriment. 'Surely, though, you plan to return to Suffolk some day?'

The superintendent concurred. 'If God spares me, that would be my wish. But it will be a while yet, I fear. This island is at a crossroads, Sir William. I would see this endeavour through to its conclusion first. Pray God, for a successful one.' The two men refilled their glasses and toasted to a speedy resolution.

It had been a fine evening, the rain bringing freshness to the humid air. A bright moon cast its silvery glow over the sea; the sky was blush in gold and purple. On such a night, it was difficult to imagine that across the narrow strait on the opposite shore, a threat was lurking.

'At least we shall ensure the fort is strengthened, you have my promise! Whilst that may not entirely allay your fears, it will at least repulse any attack those heathens might muster,' Cornwallis observed.

'Undoubtedly. I've requested twenty thousand Spanish dollars from the Council for that very purpose as a matter of urgency,' Light replied.

'And I've demanded all your requests be honoured. My brother can be a difficult man, but not unreasonable. In his defence, we must remember that his remit is broad. Great responsibilities lie upon his shoulders, far weightier than this small island. He has already suffered one great failure in his career and is determined never again shall British possessions suffer humiliating defeat.'

The loss of the American colonies had not previously featured in their conversations; Light had no intention of picking at that particular family sore. But Sir William was right. Cornwallis, like Warren Hastings before him, had wider responsibilities that were quite lost on a sea captain who had spent most of his life in this far off corner of the globe.

'You are, of course, entirely correct. One tends to become obsessed with local politics, forgetting the outside world where greater matters are afoot. But by the same token, the reverse is true. Those at a distance can overlook the vital part this region plays in our fortunes. The more harried Britain is abroad, the more her control of eastern trading routes becomes vital. A mere happenstance has made these little islands the centre of economies far distant. We must never underestimate their importance.'

'Indubitably, Francis. And that is why you have enticed me here. In my capacity of naval commander, my vision looks to a wider horizon than those who dwell on land. I, too, believe our future prosperity depends on the security of our overseas ambitions. Tell me, what do you consider your most pressing challenge in the next few months?'

Light weighed the question. 'In one sense, I must answer by saying – where to begin? The fort is a key, but we now have hopes to set that right before the year is out, thanks to the Council. Food is another major issue, for the people are struggling; the prices of basic commodities rise daily. Pigou has already observed a decline in the numbers of ships and people arriving, which is a matter of concern, for it suggests word is out of impending trouble. We need more people, sir. Without them, how can we ever hope to be self-sufficient?'

Cornwallis nodded thoughtfully as Light continued: 'At the heart lies the treaty itself. Sultan Abdullah waits on our decision and he will not wait forever. This current sabre-rattling demonstrates his patience has run thin, nor is he powerless to wound us. He has his own cards to play. I cannot say I do not share his concerns. Promises were made –'

'By you, sir, not by the governor-general. You acted without formal ratification. My brother is bound to nothing.' Cornwallis was brusque in his admonishment. In legal terms, he spoke the truth.

Light placed his hand on his heart. 'I do not deny it, sir, other than to say I was given little choice. Our position was perilous. But surely the subsequent success of the settlement has proved me right. It was worth the deception!' It was a weak argument, but the only one Light had.

Cornwallis held up his hands. 'I'm not arguing against you. I believe you acted in good faith, but the matter of the treaty remains. It isn't about the lease, Francis, you know that. My brother has already shown his willingness to pay, at least for the time being. The crux is that we will never supply military aid to fight on behalf of any local ruler, regardless how cleverly you argued your case to convince that dunderhead MacPherson.' Cornwallis gave Light a meaningful stare that lay somewhere between a smile of approbation at his audacity – and the frown of a disciplinarian.

It brought a grin to Light's face, as well as a flush of embarrassment. 'I admit I went too far. Sometimes a desperate man overreaches …' he confessed.

'It's done now, Light. We cannot go back. Everyone makes mistakes in life. The measure of a man is how he deals with them. Choose a side, man. Are you with us or does your hankering for these people mean you will forever pander to their needs? I know you sympathise with the plight of the sultan, but it's time to cast aside other loyalties. You're an Englishman, goddamit! Your very future and that of your family and fortune are at stake. Choose a side, Light – but make sure it's ours!'

'A Hobson's choice, sir?' Even now, Light could not resist a provocative reply. Cornwallis merely shrugged – and emptied his glass.

His impassioned plea still hung on the night air unanswered as Light returned to the decanter to refill their glasses. It gave him time to think. Not that he needed long: pragmatism and quick thinking had always been his nature. When a decision must be taken, he never wavered from the unpalatable choice, should it be the only route open. In truth, he had made his mind up in Calcutta weeks before.

'You may be assured, Commodore, that I will not divert from Company policy again. We will forge an acceptable treaty – or we will give Queddah a bloody nose. My loyalties will never again be divided.

'Good man! I never expected less. I'll make sure my brother is appraised of my opinion on your fine character. You know that you always have my support.'

Francis extended his hand in friendship. 'You're a true friend, sir. I consider myself fortunate to have had this time to know you better. I must admit when I first stood before your brother in his grand office, I thought my cause was dead in the water. Then you strode in and saved the day, as I know you've done in many a sea battle!' The two men shook hands heartily.

'My brother's bark is very much worse than his bite. He's a stickler for formality and all that feudal nonsense, always was. But he's a man of vision and prudence. He will not make decisions without careful consideration. Take heart, Superintendent. This island is too good to lose. Let's survive the next few months and do not dwell on the worst possible fate. If it comes to war, then so be it. Worrying about it will not change a thing. Death only visits once, sir. Anything else we can survive.'

***

Later that night in the comfortable rooms allotted to him in Government House with the best view he had ever enjoyed on shore, William Cornwallis settled down to write a letter. The delicate chair beneath him sighed as he lowered down his considerable weight.

Written this 21st day of March 1790,
Prince of Wales Island.

My dear Brother,
The weeks on this island have passed most pleasantly. I find myself in an amiable and refreshed state of mind, quite restored. Although not much given to sedentary activities, I can honestly attest that I have enjoyed myself greatly in simple pursuits that would mean little to a man such as yourself, accustomed to the grander life.

We sailed around the island on genial Surveys, enjoying dips in Seas of cerulean blue as warm as bathwater, fished for our own dinner, made a few hunting trips into the Interior and dined – quite well if somewhat plainly – on local food and traditional British fare. I have eaten rather more Fruit than is my usual inclination and drunk an equal Excess of decent wine, more than I anticipated having been warned of shortages. Thank God, French Wines and Brandy are not supplied by the detestable Sultan of Queddah, so that is one blessing.

On the subject of the troublesome Mohammedan ruler across the narrow Strait, I must reiterate what good Superintendent Light has already related in his reports. Sultan Abdullah is a duplicitous fellow whom I believe has made recent advances to the Dutch for weapons and troops with which to wrest Prince of Wales Island from us. It is fortunate indeed that the Hollanders are currently on their best behaviour, or they would have already launched a concerted attack. The damn Frenchies are also in the stew somewhere. Such is the danger of the current position.

The Sultan continues to besmirch the character of Englishmen by his false Declarations, ignoring the issue of the exorbitant figure of ten thousand Spanish dollars per annum promised for possession of said island and refuses to give back the value that we are owed by denying basic Food and other Commodity. Superintendent Light's position is untenable. We must extend support, for to lose this jewel of a Possession would be a serious blow. Furthermore, and I say this as a naval man, we have need of this island if we are to retain our passage through the Straits. I do not need to remind you what the loss of such a sea lane might mean to our trade with China, even more deleterious at a time of imminent War with the French, which would place enormous demands on our Treasury.

I must impress upon you, dear Charles, what a fine man Superintendent Light has proven to be. I have come to greatly admire him. We are fortunate to have such a man in place on the Straits – his understanding of the people and his political connections are invaluable. Most of all, I believe he is a Man of Ability and Principle, one in whom we can place our trust. I am not one to shower praise lightly, as you know, so you will take my opinion of him to heart.

The night is late, and I am soon to bed. The 'Crown' is in Port taking on supplies and water. I depart in a day or two for Great Andaman where further adventures await with another Admirable Fellow, Archibald Blair. I shall write as soon as I find a Ship there to convey my News. Until then, may God keep you in His Grace.

Yours in obedience and love,
Your brother, William

15

Strange Bedfellows

China Street, George Town, Prince of Wales Island. 6th June 1790

On any typical day, Kapitan Khoh strode through his fiefdom on foot, greeting his clients, enquiring after their families, crouching with them by the wayside over bowls of noodles. He was a man of the people, not a remote mandarin who would not dirty his feet on the mud of humble streets. He had fled from such tyranny.

Khoh was an example of enforced migration. Once, another life ago, he had been a young rebel fighting the hated Manchus. As local commander of *Tian Di Hui,* the Heaven and Earth Society, he had led his band on several raids until the inevitable happened: their cabal was betrayed with brutal consequences. Khoh had been one of the few to escape execution, forced to flee from T'ung-an to Siam and then the Straits, never to return. He believed himself the living embodiment of what was possible if lowborn peasants were given a second chance. His very existence was an example to all.

On the other hand, he could not deny that the grovelling that graced his progress gave him satisfaction, just as the passage cleared through the crowds to ease his way seemed wholly deserved. It is the nature of Chinese to respect their superiors, especially a philanthropist who has extended help and financial support to the newly arrived poor. Few in Chinatown had not profited from his patronage. It carried weighty responsibilities for the benefactor, but also brought great benefits.

Yet on this day, Khoh had chosen a litter, that most ostentatious mode of transport, imperially draped in red and gold. For this visit was not a patriarchal perambulation; today his pre-eminence was purposely on show to court the conventions of a very different world. He was on his way to Government House for confidential talks with Superintendent Light.

Kapitan Khoh Lay Huan recognised the respect that Francis Light was extending. In return, he tolerated the obligatory *kowtows* to British sensibilities, even if subservience was neither his nature nor inclination. It preserved the 'illusion' of superiority so valued by these *ang mohs*. It bemused and amused him in equal measure that the British failed to see that when Chinese made their obeisance, they did so in silent disdain of their arrogant European frailties. How could such an uncultured race ever hope to equal the civilisation of China?

Not that he saw Superintendent Light in that regard. Alone among his countrymen, Francis Light had genuinely won the admiration – even friendship – of the Kapitan. He respected his astute commercial acumen, a quality that he greatly valued. Light and he were men of similar ilk, quintessential merchant traders, born to lead, far ahead of the common hordes in reading the mood of the times. The superintendent was also a man of justice who supported the migrant people as much as he was able, often at the expense of his own credibility with his superiors. Now that he had need of more support than ever, Khoh was determined to be the man to supply it. It was not altruism: the Kapitan rarely took any action without his own fortunes being centre stage.

Of late his relationship with the superintendent had taken a favourable turn, not entirely to be laid at the door of coincidence, for it was in the main the result of Khoh's own machinations. His daughter's marriage to Light's Serani brother-in-law, Rozells, had produced the desired result in double quick time: the first child had arrived exactly nine months to the day of their marriage! It was an auspicious outcome, aided by the chosen date for the wedding – the first day of the Rooster year. The little girl was thriving and his daughter, Lien, was already carrying another, hopefully a son this time.

The alliance had been felicitous in every way. Marriage had transformed Lien, his shy and obedient daughter. She was now a married lady of position and influence, well accepted in Light's *tsap tsing* family, that was oddly open to all comers in Khoh's estimation. Whatever disapproval most Chinese felt in tainting the purity of their blood with that of other races, Khoh felt vindicated. His decision had been wise. He now possessed the most binding of connections with the man at the very heart of the settlement – an irreversible bond of blood relationship. It was always preferable that business should be conducted within the 'family'. Furthermore, the prestige Khoh gained as a merchant who mixed freely with Europeans and knew their ways, was priceless.

Light also recognised the new opportunities that the marriage offered. Indeed it had been the superintendent himself who had first approached him with a suggestion for a closer partnership. Recently Kapitan Khoh had been despatched to Achin as unofficial ambassador to the court of Sultan Alauddin on the superintendent's behalf, with strict instructions to keep the matter to himself. No suspicions had been raised, for Khoh was a regular visitor to the Islamic kingdom. He knew the sultan well; having traded in Kutaraja for many years, regularly performing 'favours' for the sultan for which Alauddin had kept him well supplied in textiles, pepper and tobacco. The pretext of today's official visit might be to deliver in person his regular report in his capacity as Kapitan Cina, but the real purpose was, of course, to reveal the results of his secret embassy.

The vestibule of Government House was unimpressive to Kapitan Khoh, who found its pale walls and wooden floorboards stark and inharmonious. There were few decorative motifs, save a British flag, royal insignia, and the large tiger skin stretched above the entrance. The staircase faced straight on the entrance doors. Very bad *feng shui,* a sure sign that luck would fly from the building; it was no surprise the administration was in peril. Yet Khoh shrugged aside his reservations – and made a mental note of the architecture. The lofty ceiling made the building a welcome haven from the heat outside, as did the large, shuttered windows that could either let in light, or cast welcome shade. As he waited to be received, Khoh pondered the possibility of building a fine house that blended the best of European techniques, elements of indigenous style and the feng shui of the Chinese tradition. Such a residence would impress all the elites, both western and eastern.

A short time later, he was disturbed from his reverie by the appearance of an officer, Mr Nathaniel Bacon, who welcomed him in Hokkien. Khoh was pleasantly surprised and made a mental note to learn more about the fellow. Mr Bacon was obviously keen to make his way in the world, presumably hoping to leave his clerk's position and become a merchant. Whilst not fooled that Bacon's effort was any more than commercially driven, Khoh approved of any fellow who acted out of calculation. A man had to place a stake on the table if he wished to win.

He was led into an airy office to the rear of the building with a splendid frontage facing out to sea. Between house and shoreline, a garden had been planted with young saplings and hardy bushes as well as flower beds, tended by Light's Caffree slaves, who had originally caused such a stir in town. Khoh had to admit they were doing a fine job; they had built this house and were now keeping it in perfect order.

The superintendent was already on his feet behind a large untidy desk. Advancing across the room, he extended his right hand. Khoh paused, momentarily hesitant, and then held out his own. 'Welcome, welcome, dear Kapitan!' Light began with a broad smile, grasping his hand in a firm shake.

Khoh tested the unfamiliar English syllables on his tongue in reply: 'I am honoured, my superintendent.' And gave a bow.

On a cabinet behind Light, Khoh's sharp eyes picked out a series of tiny oval paintings set in ivory frames. They were Light's children, rendered in astonishingly detail and wondrous colours. These Europeans were masters of the figurative arts, unlike the stylised Chinese fashion constricted by ancient rules of harmony and form. He was impressed. They captured the likeness of a loved one forever.

Light noticed his interest. 'My children, Kapitan, our pride and joy. They were painted during our Calcutta trip. My three daughters remain there for school. It's comforting to have their images with me whilst I work. Although I must say they are a good deal more well-behaved up there on the shelf than when they are present in the flesh!' he grinned with the fondness of a devoted father.

Khoh chuckled. He had almost lost count of the number of his children – perhaps ten? Long ago there had been a wife in Fujian province with one child and another on the way until he had been forced to flee. They had been childhood lovers. It was his one regret. His other wives had been more for expedience than pleasure. A man is better unencumbered by the hindrance of love, he now believed. There had been his Siamese wife, daughter of a local leader; she had given birth to three living children, although he had also kept a few concubines there whose offspring he may well have fathered. Later in Kuala Muda, he had married his Queddah wife, Guan Boey, the daughter of a previous Kapitan Cina, who had given him two sons and his daughter Lien. This marriage had raised his standing in the local community; he had inherited the role of Kapitan when his father-in-law had died. Although Boey had accompanied him to Pinang, she had proved amenable to him taking a new young local wife, Saw It Neoh, who had added to his brood. Her family were Babas from Melaka – Khoh wished to embrace her Nyonya culture.

The two men strolled out onto the commodious balcony where a pair of large cane chairs were set beneath flowering vines, a sea breeze cool upon their faces. A terracotta flask, teardrops of condensation running down its bulbous body, waited on a marble-topped table, flanked by two paper-thin Chinese cups. 'Rice wine, cool against the heat. Will you join me, sir?'

Khoh was unaccustomed to cold drinks, considered by Chinese doctors to be deleterious to the body, but he made an exception out of politeness – and curiosity. Taking a small sip, he found it surprisingly refreshing.

'Is good,' he answered gruffly, before taking a second sip.

Light raised his own cup. 'To friendship!' he toasted. 'I must say, dear Khoh, your English is much improved, whilst my Hokkien remains very poor, I'm afraid.

'Me not so good in English, Superintendent. Speak Malay?'

It was agreed. They would both revert to the comfort of the traditional *lingua franca*.

Light knew well enough not to charge straight into the matter in hand. 'Your granddaughter is growing fast, so I hear. With another on the way. A great blessing, sir!'

'Most auspicious,' replied Khoh. 'Your wife has been good to my daughter. I thank her for her kindness. We are well pleased that both families are in good accord,' Khoh answered formally.

The two men nodded, Light refilled cups.

'Your house is very beautiful, superintendent. It is good for our island that we have great buildings.'

Light looked about him. 'It's a decent enough place. Nothing to compare with Calcutta, though. The palaces there are magnificent. But we do our best. This is an acceptable residence in which to entertain foreign guests. Yet I do not really live here, although I have an apartment above. I prefer to walk across the beach to the atap house –'

'Your wife's house, on Martinha's Lane?' Khoh interjected.

'Indeed. My dear wife even has a road in her name now! It speaks to how kindly the people think of her,' he replied.

'She is a good woman. Helps all the people. Everybody loves her.' Khoh's compliment was noteworthy; he was not a man given to praise.

Etiquette and family matters discussed, the conversation steered inexorably towards its true destination. 'Speaking of building, I've recently completed a small house on my lands in the interior, the estate I refer to as "Suffolk" after my English home. My Caffrees are proving to be excellent craftsmen, well suited to construction.'

'A new home for your family, perhaps?' asked Khoh.

'No, it is little more than a *rumah kebun*, a garden house for pleasure trips. The land itself is cleared for agricultural purposes.'

Khoh smiled. 'I may have the ideal proposal to make good use of this land.' The way ahead was now clear for the real negotiations. 'You suggested I might have discussions with his Highness Sultan Alauddin on my recent trip to Achin. The sultan is most interested in our island and indicates his desire to aid our progress, both out of his true friendship and for the benefits Pinang might bring to the trade of his kingdom.'

Khoh paused while Light acted as if this was the first time that he had heard the suggestion. The game was now afoot.

'The sultan was particularly impressed by the welcome the island has extended to many poor Achinese, driven out by the Dutch, who have reported of their prosperity here. He also showed concern at the hostility of the sultan of Queddah and bemoans our recent difficulties.'

'The sultan is most generous to think of us,' Light responded.

'He did not merely feel sorrow on our behalf,' Khoh continued blithely. 'The sultan insisted I carry back 400 *maunds* of rice, which he can scarce afford, as a mark of friendship between Achin and the British Company.'

'Excellent news, Kapitan Khoh! This is indeed a gift from God in our current plight! I trust you will take responsibility for distributing rice fairly amongst all our communities. With the usual commission for your efforts?'

Khoh made a stately bow, bathing in the benevolence of his act, which was in fact no more than trading in rice at officially sanctioned inflated prices, only to be expected in the current situation.

'The sultan made another generous offer,' Khoh added, as if in afterthought. 'He has heard we have a mind to plant spices on our island. As you are aware, Achin has an abundance of pepper, which is why the Dutch press the kingdom so hard. He believes it is in the interests of both Achin and Pinang that he should supply us with pepper plants, so that together we may control the trade on both sides of the Straits and strangle the Dutch monopoly.'

Light considered his words carefully. 'I must advise you, sir, that political events have taken an unexpected turn. The Hollanders and the British now find themselves in accord; the Company instructs us against obstructing their interests. But a gift is a gift after all; it would be churlish to refuse. One cannot blame the sultan for his lack of insight into the affairs of Europe. I presume you have offloaded the pepper plants?'

'Indeed, superintendent. They are waiting in my gudang.'

'Then we must not let them shrivel and die. It would be intolerable to treat a gift from a foreign king with such disdain. My Caffrees await at the Suffolk estate. If you would be so kind as to transport the plants immediately, I will ensure they are in the ground as soon as possible.'

The two men were both fully cognisant that behind the courtesies (necessary both to save face and confound any eavesdropper), this plan was the fulfilment of long preparation. Light had entered a partnership with Khoh and provided land to the wily Chinese merchant for their first foray into plantations. Khoh had put up the rest of the investment, making use of his ships and his Achin network. The rights to import rice at a price set by Khoh himself had been a clause in the agreement.

As in his arrangement with James Scott, Light intended to continue taking the profit he was due from the island. He felt no sense of duplicity in this secret deal. Most of his fortune had been depleted establishing the settlement, with only a fraction of it ever likely to be recouped from Bengal. It was only just that he should reclaim a portion through judicious investments, particularly those that also benefitted the island.

'This matter will remain confidential between the two of us, Kapitan Khoh?'

'Assuredly, honourable Superintendent. It is a family matter. No need for others to know our business, sir.'

'Another cup to seal the agreement before the wine loses its chill?' Light suggested. Khoh accepted a third cup, his cheeks already flushed red from the earlier two.

'Anything else to report from your community?' Light now turned to local affairs.

Khoh shook his head. 'Everything quiet. Small matters only that we can deal with ourselves. But people are worried. Everybody talk about Queddah. What is happening?' As circuitous as he could be, Khoh could also be alarmingly direct.

The superintendent sighed deeply. 'Not good. Hostilities continue. Calcutta has sent the funds to repair the fort, but it is never enough. I will instruct each community to play their part, for the governor-general insists that the locals contribute towards the fortifications. Instruct every Chinese male to supply one *tiang* for the stockade, fifteen feet in length. I will demand this also of the Malays and the Chulias. Are you in agreement?"

Khoh nodded. 'This we can do. I must warn you, superintendent, there are spies on the island. Chinese from the mainland have been offering money to my people to foment riots to aid the Queddah attack.'

It was of little surprise to Light. 'Have you dealt with them?'

Khoh laughed coldly. 'They will not be causing trouble anymore. Not without their heads, I think. That may keep the Queddah agents at bay for a while but there are always some willing to be traitors. They do not see it as betrayal. Many say: "What do we owe these British? Why should we fight and die for them?" I cannot blame them. You owe the sultan money. A debt should be paid.'

Light stood up and stared across the narrow strait, rubbing at his forehead to relieve the band of tightness that was his companion these days whenever he thought of the threat across the water. 'I agree with you, Kapitan. But it is not my choice. I have already sent monies over to the sultan, but it is not enough. Give me some time. I guarantee I will find a way to end this uncertainty. But it may come to hostilities. Are you prepared for that? People will die.' He turned round on his heel and looked Khoh directly in the eye.

Khoh sat ramrod still, his gaze impenetrable, as if meditating. Until: 'You must choose your side, Superintendent. My instinct tells me you are standing between two worlds, trying to appease them all. This is impossible. You will lose the support of both. Then all you have done will come to nothing. Choose your side! People can make their own minds up once you raise your banner.

Most have nowhere else to go. The poor follow no cause; they cannot afford such principles. But they know their chances with the British are always better. The Company will send warships with many guns. If you act now. Too late, and everything gone. The people will leave like rats on a sinking ship. And who could blame them?'

Khoh's opinion was an uncanny echo of the commodore's advice. Two men from different backgrounds but with common ground between them all the same: they knew human nature. Did he himself lack the ruthlessness required? Was he too much of an optimist, ever relying on charm and persuasion to achieve his aim? What was he waiting for?

'Will you back me up in this, Kapitan Khoh? If it comes to war?'

Khoh rose to his feet, extending his own right hand willingly this time. 'I put my trust in you some years ago. You have never disappointed. I am a man of my word. Besides, we are now family. Blood ties cannot be broken. My people are your people. I will do whatever I can to take your part. This is my promise, sir.' It was more than courtesy; it was the symbol of an unbreakable pact between them. Light was not insensible to its significance.

Later as he watched his new partner climb into the sedan chair below, Francis Light could not help but shake his head at the peculiar quirks of fate that brought him trusted allies in the most unusual of places, whilst he struggled to win the confidence of his own people. Khoh was a valuable associate, capable of turning any endeavour into gold. There was no better partner, an asset beyond measure. Furthermore, both men were equally reliant on the patronage of the other. There was a certain comfort in that.

17

Strawberry Hill

The Royal Palace, Alor Star, Queddah. October 1790

The Sultan of Queddah's patience had been sorely tested. Four years since the British occupation, still he waited for the treaty promises to be honoured. He was heartily tired of the endless visits from James Scott and that sweet-natured Pigou boy who was charming enough but looked like he expected to be eaten whole. The British delivered a sum of money here and there, but it was little more than a bribe to keep him quiet. Although constantly assured Light was doing his best, the superintendent's credibility at court was waning fast.

To add insult to injury, his Laksamana's agents in Achin had brought news that Sultan Alauddin was supplying rice, pepper plants and other commodities to Pinang. 'Alauddin needs an ally against the Dutch. The British wish to control Queddah. Together they each benefit, especially now Holland has made peace with Britain,' the Laksamana pronounced.

Sultan Abdullah banged his fist against his palm. 'The Company would not have ordered this; they know little of Achin. This is Light's own doing. He stirs the pot to suit himself. We've been taken for fools! Light abandons us to placate his Company masters. We must end this pretence. The problem now is Light himself.'

Laksamana Tunku Ya remained his usual composed self, nodding wisely in agreement, whilst inwardly daring to hope that at last the wretched boy had woken to the truth. If prompt action was not taken, the British would send the ships and troops they had once promised Queddah to use against them.

'I fear your assessment is entirely correct, my Lord. Your esteemed brothers in the other Malay states have similar criticisms. The Sultan of Terengganu is affronted that his offer to the Company was rejected, blaming lack of support from Light. The sultans of Selangor and Johor are no friends of his and offer us their help. Furthermore, the British alliance with Achin concerns the sultan of Siak who fears they will close the Straits to all but their own traffic. Even Rembau is willing to supply troops.'

The sultan raised an eyebrow. 'It seems you have been busy, Tunku. I should have been informed before you made advances to my brother sultans! However, in this case, I will make an exception. Time is important, as you say.'

The Laksamana bowed deeply. 'My apologies, my Lord. As you say, I did not wish to waste a moment. There is more, however. Our friends in Riau have made an approach through Sultan Ibrahim of Selangor. The Illanuns they employed against the Dutch remain in the Straits. He suggests we might wish to engage their services against the British ...'

'Those pirates? You mean he is unable to make them leave now that his use for them is done, so foists them onto us? You think we should bring those devils into our waters?'

For once the sultan had read the situation correctly. The Bugis did indeed wish to rid themselves of the volatile Illanun. Even better to ship them off to Queddah in the guise of friendship to cause mayhem in the northern waters. Yet, without such a force of warriors, famed for their skills in sea battles, Tunku Ya feared that even the growing alliance against the British might fail.

'I share your disquiet, your Highness,' Tunku Ya responded, eager to placate his young protégé. 'Your wisdom is unparalleled. We must consider the unpredictable nature of these savages. If we were to take this course of action, the terms of our contract with the Illanun must be strictly enforced. They would not be allowed entry into our ports or rivers, or anywhere along the coastline of Queddah. I suggest they be offered anchorage off Pulau Bunting in the north until they are required. If they should become restless and prove too difficult to control, we can send them in the direction of Ujung Salang, where their pickings will be so much greater than the nearby islands. That would be enough to distract them from our settlements. The lure of Pulau Pinang should also keep the Illanun devils to your terms.'

It was settled. The largest Malay alliance in many years was to be assembled across the strait from Prince of Wales Island. It was estimated that 400 perahus would be provided by the Illanun alone, not to mention vessels from Riau, Siak, Johor and Terengganu with a land force of ten thousand armed men. The tiny island of Pinang was about to be swamped by a mighty onslaught.

***

As soon as Soliman left the Kuala Queddah estuary, he was already alert to the two ships on his tail. As surreptitious as he had tried to be, it was unlikely that his presence had not been detected. Spies abounded and his boats were well known. For days he had been constantly followed, but violence would not be directed against him on land, for he was officially under the protection of the sultan. But once he took to the seas, it would be open season for anyone who wished to take their chances and ensure that this Malay captain would never reach Pinang with his intelligence. Despite his uneasy pact with the sultan, Soliman was under no illusion that his usefulness to the court was now over.

These boats had been sent to slaughter all on board then scuttle the ship in open water. If they succeeded, their bodies might never be found or would be washed so far from their origin in such a state of decay that it would be impossible to identify them. Soliman did not relish such an end.

Which is why he had left port on a late afternoon when only a fool would have sailed out. Dark threatening clouds were racing across an angry sky as he sailed out into the open sea, the high churning swell revealing that the storm had broken ahead of them with a vengeance. They were sailing into a maelstrom.

Soliman appeared complacent. These conditions lay at the heart of his strategy, his mastery over wind and wave unassailable. Heading straight for Pulau Payar, the tiny southernmost islet of the Langkawi archipelago, he intended to outrun both the storm and his pursuers, refusing even to consider what might happen if he failed. It was not an option.

As the heavens roared and the lightning flashed, only his instinct and the efforts of his skilful crew kept them on course. It was impossible by now to check the progress of the boats on his tail; he must look only to his own efforts. At last, almost too late, the thickly forested outline of the island was revealed momentarily by a fortuitous streak of lightning. Manoeuvring as best they could around the headland, fending off the rocky outcrops with their oars, they began the slow progress of rowing around to the other side of the island.

It was a perilous journey against currents that seemed hellbent on crashing the humble padewakang to its doom against the cliffs. By the time the storm had diminished and the worst of the winds ease, the night was thick dark, the stars masked by their heavy cloak of grey clouds. Finally, out of this inky blackness, the welcome bulk of a large ship emerged. It was the *Indus,* Light's snow-brig. They were safe. In minutes, Soliman clambered up the rope that swung and clattered precariously against the side to be greeted heartily by William Lindesay, his old captain.

'You cut it fine there, my boy. We thought you were a goner and no mistake,' William grinned as he threw a blanket around Soliman's shoulders. The young man was soaked to the skin, shivering so hard his teeth rattled in his head. 'You wouldn't last a day in the North Sea, my lad, if you think this is cold. Let's get something warm down you. Your men need anything? I'll send a few lascars over to sort them out. Then we'll set the watch and you can all get a few hours' sleep until the dawn.'

The next morning, with skies so clear it was nigh impossible to recall the misery of the night before, the horizon shimmered clear on all sides. With any luck their pursuers had broken up and were now lying on the bottom of the sea themselves. Of course, it was equally possible that they were lurking just around the headland. But it mattered little. With the escort of a British ship, the *Harimau* was safe from harm. The *Indus* might only carry 8-guns, but it was eight more than any local perahu. The return trip to Pinang would be a pleasant jaunt.

***

On reaching the island, Soliman's first stop was Martinha's house even before he had eaten or changed his clothes. The intelligence he carried was of the highest importance. He must reach Francis before any rumours began to circulate.

Martinha sat in the shade of her garden surrounded by a gaggle of children and some women. Despite his urgency, Soliman could not help but join in the fun and games, crouching down amongst the children who were soon leaping over him as he tickled and teased. Mary and Willie already knew him, but this was the first he had seen of little Anneke Rozells, their distant cousin, baby Maria Rozells, Felipe's daughter, and her pretty mother, Lien. There were also the offspring of various household servants, including a little curly headed Caffree boy. It warmed Soliman's heart to see them growing up together, children of every creed and colour, chattering in a colourful blend of languages. It gave him hope that they might grow up on an island that gave no consideration to the colour of a man's skin or the nature of his religion. It was what he wanted for his brood.

When he had finally extricated himself from the rough and tumble, Soliman joined Martinha who was watching fondly from her cane armchair. She made a discreet sign to her women to take the children inside; it was hot, they were sweaty, and it was time for a snack. Once they were alone, she rose – a little unsteadily, he observed – and indicated they should stroll on the beach. Martinha held a parasol to protect her fair skin from the burning sun.

After they had exchanged a few pleasantries about his own

growing family – a baby son now as well as his playful two-year-old daughter, Martinha's face clouded over. 'You have news from Queddah?'

He nodded curtly. 'For the superintendent's ears only.'

Martinha sighed. 'Not good news, then?' Soliman's shrug confirmed her suspicions. 'He's on the hill today up Macpherson's Track. We're building a house at the summit, above the waterfall. It's his latest obsession.' Martinha indicated the series of peaks that rose above the settlement. Soliman glanced up instinctively. 'He is alone?'

'Yes. Just Francis and some tindals. With bearers and a couple of sepoy guards. He'll be back by nightfall, if you wish to wait.'

Soliman shook his head. 'It will be the best place to meet with so few to observe us. Do you have a cart that I might borrow? It would speed my progress.' He was exhausted and a four-mile walk followed by a demanding uphill climb would finish him off.

'Even better,' Martinha replied, 'I will send to the fort for the superintendent's horse; he went on the wagon with the others. I will pen a note saying he has asked for it to be delivered to the waterfall for his return journey.'

It had been some time since Soliman had been on horseback, but as soon as he threw his leg over the saddle, it was as if he had never been away. As they trotted along under a hot sun, he found himself lulled almost to a doze; the dramatic escape of the night before and a scant few hours of sleep had taken their toll. He had to struggle to keep his eyes open at times. Despite the purpose of his journey, Soliman could not help but delight in the beauty of the forest as he rode the several miles along the well-trodden path, bestowed with the grandiose title of 'The Macpherson Track', after the governor who had first granted Light leave to settle the island. The tranquillity of the forest stood in stark contrast to the imminent danger they all faced.

When at last the Great Cascade came into view, Soliman found himself pausing for a few moments to wonder at its majesty. To think, this creation had stood deep inside the forest unseen by human eyes since the beginning of the world! And here he was to witness its magnificence. Nature was surely the greatest glory of God! The mighty cataract flowed down a deep cleft studded with huge boulders like ancient guardians, worn into amorphous shapes by the unseen hands of time. At the midway point, the slope reached its limit and the gushing waters cascaded over the ragged edge into a foaming torrent of sweet mountain water that thundered into the pool below. Amidst the dappled sunlight of the forest the scene cast a magical golden glow, as if a thousand fireflies were lighting its descent. Droplets of spray hung in the misty air, cooling the body as the sight refreshed the spirits.

'*Berhenti!*' A coarse voice shattered his tranquil moment. Soliman's head shot round to see a surly Indian sitting on a flat boulder by the side of the waterfall, resting his back against a large tree. The man was armed, his hands on his rifle in warning.

'The Superintendent sent for me,' Soliman replied, his mind running over a likely excuse. 'He wants my men to cut down some trees up there.'

The sepoy sneered. 'He got big black men. No need for little Malays.'

Soliman swallowed down his anger. 'Malays know how to bring down ironwood better than anyone. We can fell ten trees at once – it is skill, not size that makes us better!'

There was little arguing with that. It was a well-known fact that the Malays were second to none at clearing jungle. They had refined their methods in the forests long ago, learned from the indigenous people. Even great axes struggled with hardwoods. They, however, did not use brute force but teamwork of which they were particularly capable – as well as ingenuity.

The sepoy received Soliman's lie with a hunch of his shoulders. It sounded plausible enough. 'Tie your horse up over there. You must walk the path from here. Only one way up. Stick to it and you won't get lost.'

The track was scarcely deserving of the name. Most of the way was uphill at a steep gradient, boulders taking the place of stairs. Here and there wooden step bridges had been strung up, attached precariously to the trunks of trees, to aid the litter bearers who carried up materials. The temperature grew cooler as he ascended. Towering trees clustered so close together that their foliage let in little light, the humidity rendered the interior dank and cool. The soldier had been correct. The track was clearly marked. It was not difficult to find his way.

By mid-afternoon when he reached the plateau, he found Superintendent Light under a canvas awning, poring over plans with a few of his slaves. The group was startled by his arrival, all eyes swivelling in his direction. Soliman raised a hand in greeting; Light returned a broad smile of welcome.

'Soliman, my lad! What the devil are you doing up here? Come, let me show you around my new domain!'

Although Light must have suspected the reason for his sudden appearance, he showed no sign other than pleasure. Instructing his men to pack up for the day, he threw his arm around Soliman's shoulder and led him forward to enjoy the view. 'What do you think? Look at it, Soliman! Imagine, every morning opening one's eyes to this?'

There was no denying that the vista was breath-taking. Before them lay the narrow channel between Pinang and the mainland, the distant coastline misty in the haze. The great mountain, Gunung Jerai, soared over the flat landscape of Queddah, the two hills greeting each other, twin giants in a world of ants. The sinuous channel of silver sea sparkled under the afternoon sun, dotted here and there with vessels, whose slow progress at that distance was soporific. It was much cooler at this height, despite the sun overhead, and the air was fresh and breezy. Soliman inhaled, taking a full deep breath. 'Almost as good as the sea,' he murmured, looking sadly over to his father.

'You're right. This is the next best thing. Once upon a time, I used to run away to sea whenever troubles confounded me. I no longer have that option, so I intend to hide myself up here with the family when I can no longer stand the heat, miasma and concerns waiting down below. It's good to see you again, my boy. No one other than my dear wife knows me quite as well as you.'

Light led him back to the shelter, where he poured cups of water and offered Soliman some bread and fruit. And while he took his ease, Light chattered on about this and that as if he hadn't a care in the world.

'I will build a fine bungalow here, one in which Martinha will feel at home, but perhaps a little grander than her current house. Two storeys so that the bedrooms will share the excellent view. There will be extensive gardens, lots of flowers and bushes, for in this more temperate spot, many plants thrive that will not grow in the lowlands, especially not near the sea. I have always cherished a notion to bring plants that grow in my dear mother's garden back in Melton – she loves to surround herself with blooms. Roses would do well up here and so would strawberries. Soliman, I'll warrant you've never tasted a strawberry! There's no fruit like it in the world. And Suffolk strawberries are the queen of them all. I have sent for a consignment and shall plant them here to remind me of my home.'

Soliman smiled dreamily. 'I should love to taste this strawberry fruit.'

'And you shall. You shall take home punnets from my garden to feed to your babies!' A shadow suddenly darkened across Light's brow. 'I remember as a child on summer days, my mother would spoon juicy red strawberries soaked in thick cream into my mouth. It was my favourite food. It is as if that were another life, you know? I am fifty years old this month. Imagine, I have lived on this earth for half a century! And half of those years away from Suffolk. I fear the mail each time it lands upon my desk. Every letter may bring the tidings that I most fear. My dear mother even now may already be gone. And here I am, halfway up a mountain on the other side of the world, and still the taste of strawberries lingers.'

Soliman was unsure what to say in answer to his sudden change of mood, especially with the knowledge of what he had to report. 'You may yet live to see her, dear Francis, if God wills it.'

'Indeed. If God wills it, dear boy.' They sat for a while in silence, both deep in thought: Francis of fond reunions, Soliman contemplating final partings should his father ever choose to leave.

When next he spoke, Light's thoughts had moved on. He was now ready to broach the subject that he had avoided thus far. 'You were gone too long, Sol. I've been worried. Thank God, our rescue plan worked. I never wished for you to become embroiled in all this, you know? If I hadn't been entirely desperate, you would not have been used this way,' Light began, running his hand through his hair, a nervous habit of his. 'I would never forgive myself if you were to pay the price for my mistakes.'

Soliman looked up at him. 'So, you admit you made mistakes?' he asked bluntly.

Light did not accept he had entirely been at fault. 'I would not have done any different even had I known the outcome, I must confess. I made my choices and now I must meet the consequences. You have news?'

'It is not good. The sultan has lost faith in talking and has made up his mind. He builds an alliance of the Malay states. It is whispered abroad that Selangor, Johor and Rembau are with him, as is the sultan of Terengganu –'

'Damn that bloody Joseph Price,' spat out Light. 'What would it have cost Cornwallis to agree to the sultan's demands and place John Glass there? I'm sorry, Sol, carry on ...'

He continued. 'As is to be expected, Selangor has brought in Riau-Lingga and Siak. The word has gone out that the sultan of Achin is with you, and they fear you will close the northern straits between you.'

Light groaned. 'Is it impossible to keep a secret in these waters? Kapitan Khoh assured me that no one would know about our dealings!'

That brought a grin to Soliman's face. 'You know better than anyone that someone always talks. The news probably came from the sultan himself, for he will want to crow about his alliance with the British so that the Dutch will find out!'

'I must be losing my touch, Sol. Getting old, I suppose. I expected it would eventually be common knowledge, but not quite so fast! The ink is barely dry on the agreement.'

'There's more, Kapitan. Even worse.' Both men grew sombre. 'Riau has offered the Illanun force that they recently employed. It is said to be over 400 war perahus.'

Light massaged his forehead, whispering curses under his breath. Then, as if his mind had suddenly been decided, he stood up and straightened his back in defiance. 'He leaves us no choice. Perhaps it's for the best. The more his alliance threatens, the more strength in my argument to the Council. I will have the ships and troops I need. Then I swear I will blow Abdullah's army to Kingdom Come and his pirate allies with them. No more dillydallying with pretended niceties and emptying my pockets to appease him. There is only one course of action that anyone understands in the end – war!'

17
Home Truths

Martinha's House, Tanjong Penaga, Pinang. November 1790

Just before the onset of the rain, at its steamiest time of day, the bride and groom made their fond farewells as they led the procession from the reception to their house near the fort. Captain Glass, commander of the fort, had married his beautiful Sarippa. A convivial wedding breakfast had been hosted by the superintendent and Mrs Light in the grounds of their own family home, a significant honour for the Catholic community. The congregation of the Church of the Assumption was out in force.

The Portuguese Eurasian community was well represented, and they were renowned for boisterous celebrations. The guests on Captain Glass's side, however, were thin on the ground: apart from the Lights, only Pigou, Scott, Dr Hutton and William Lindesay had attended both the service and the festivities. A few other notables had shown their faces but by and large the occasion had not been marked in any significant way by the captain's peers. It was probably for the best. Their approval was sought by none.

Martinha breathed a sigh of relief as she waved off the merrymakers accompanied by the players and singers. Most of her household followed the procession: Janeke and a few maids took the children along. Even Felipe joined in, his little daughter in his arms. Lien was in confinement awaiting the imminent arrival of their second child.

A welcome calm now enveloped the house as the hurdy gurdy of celebration receded into the distance. Fr Michael stood to take his leave, red in the face from too much wine. Martinha stayed him; there had been little opportunity to chat all day.

'Tea, Father?' The padre gratefully accepted, settling back in his chair. Moments later, Superintendent Light joined – and they were three.

'We did well by them, don't you think? Glass is still beaming like a fool. Never have I seen such an expression on the man's face. He's entirely besotted. Not that I blame him. Sarippa's a beauty!' Light broke off, aware his comment was inappropriate in the presence of a man of celibacy. He quickly changed the subject. 'Father, may we extend our deepest gratitude to you for your sterling support? It has not been easy for them to accomplish this marriage. We appreciate your kindness.'

The German priest waved his hand blithely. 'Why would I not wish to assist? Captain Glass is an honourable man and deserves to be happy. As for Mary, as dear Sarippa now wishes to be called, it is no more than my vocation to bring unbelievers to the Lord. She already shows deep devotion to the Mass. I cherish a hope that in time she may bring the captain himself into our Communion.'

Light chuckled. 'Don't expect that to happen soon, dear Padre. The Company may tolerate a Catholic wife, but his career would come to a dead halt if he turned to Rome.'

'One cannot place earthly triumphs before one's immortal soul, Superintendent,' the priest retorted with a smile. Light had great respect for Fr Michael Rectenwald, a welcome alternative to his previous French colleagues, in the superintendent's opinion. As he often observed to his wife, you knew exactly where you were with a German, even if they were as a race given to gravity, whereas who knew what was going on in the mind of a Frenchie? Where Fr Antoine Garnault had been arrogant and condescending, Rectenwald was humble and amenable. Furthermore, Padre Miguel, as his parishioners called him in their patois, had won the love – rather than the awe – of his largely Portuguese Eurasian congregation.

Light teased back. 'It appears your spiritual mission is as successful as our trading enterprise. The little chapel was bursting its seams today!'

'Father Michael hopes to build a bigger church as soon as the current crisis is over.' Martinha boasted. It was her new project; she was already raising funds.

'Make sure you build in brick next time,' Light counselled. 'Every new construction should have a brick base at least.'

'Of course, *mein lieber* Superintendent. It is an essential requirement, although inevitably raises costs. Are there no plans yet for a Protestant house of worship?' Fr Michael enquired with a hint of mischief. The Catholic community never tired of remarking that there was still no Anglican church on the island. It was left to Light to read a few chapters of the Bible on high days and holidays, much as he had done aboard ship in his seafaring days.

'Are you so eager for competition? Light grinned back. 'It would be my wish to build a chapel, of course. Land has already been set aside with that purpose in mind, but I fear it will not be a priority for some time yet. Our energies must be on our immediate needs, namely the fort and the safety of our inhabitants. Even when this confrontation with Queddah is resolved, there will be other requirements: a courthouse and a hospital to name but two.'

'I would have thought that the English merchants might at least set aside some monies from their profits to erect a small chapel. Surely the Company would supply a pastor?'

Light made a gesture of frustration. 'One would imagine so. But it appears that not one of our successful businessmen is prepared to lay down a penny of his own fortune to finance a church. As for the Company, it has no interest in such things. "What for?" they would say. "A captain can say the necessary words over the dead and read a verse on a Sunday. If there is a desire for God, then build your own Church!" It is a curious circumstance that although our people have spent most of their history fighting over religion, we remain a singularly ungodly nation,' Light observed wryly.

His comment rang a chord with Fr Rectenwald. 'The British upper classes tend to conflate God with King and Parliament, or so I've found,' he replied. 'As a result, as long as they raise a glass to his Majesty, their observances are fulfilled.' Martinha was not sure she quite understood the joke, although Francis found his remark most entertaining. The European sense of humour confounded her.

'Superintendent and my dear Mrs Light, I thank you both for your generous hospitality in opening up your home for the celebrations,' the padre observed.

'It should have been at Government House,' Light insisted. 'Glass is the Commander of our military forces as well as my Deputy. Yet even he asked me not to hold it there. The British community disapproves, I'm afraid,' Light added by way of an explanation.

Fr Michael sighed. 'At least Mr Pigou showed up.'

'Not to the church, though!' He left his own Miss Bonsu in her advanced condition to represent him!' Light fumed. 'Those two men are close friends and colleagues! Could he not set aside his prejudices even for one day to support John Glass?'

'Francis, please! Do not shout!' Martinha broke in, her hand on his arm in restraint. These days her husband's temper was volatile, reflecting the mounting anxieties that were never far from his mind. 'I fear Mrs Gray has waged a campaign of opposition, which has quite gone round the town. She is a great influence on opinion ...'

'She's a harpy!' Light snapped back. 'We welcomed her to this island, she married one of our officers with our blessing – and now it is she who is the arbiter of island society, such as it might be. I will *not* have this petty English snobbery on Prince of Wales Island! It's rife in India, but we will not stand for it here!'

Even the kindly priest found himself defending the situation. 'I'm afraid it's almost impossible to prevent such notions, sir. Once they find their way in, these prejudices pervade everything. Even those who are not inclined to agree feel it is better not to speak out, thus power is given to the small minded. Glass himself is above such things. He's an excellent fellow and cares not a fig for snobbery and unkind remarks. Mary is a sweet-natured girl, who feels blessed in her good fortune. Ignore the naysayers, sir, for it is their loss.'

Light could not argue with his good sense. 'Father Michael, if that is not a quote from the Sermon on the Mount, then it should be. For you have added to the wisdom of Jesus Christ himself!' His cheerful mood had been restored. 'May we also extend our heartfelt gratitude for your efforts for the poor? You live in the image of Christ, sir. No wonder people flock to your altar, for you alone bestow your charity on all comers, regardless of origin or belief. Even Kapitan Khoh has remarked on your kindness to his people. Your little school is another godsend. Not only does it teach the migrant children, but it frees their mothers to make a few coins here and there in the day. Not to mention that you fill their little bellies at lunchtime with a plate of vegetable rice!'

'I could not do it without Mrs Light and her dear mother. Their support is essential, as is their service.' Women who could read and write gave a few hours of their time to the school, organised by Martinha and Thong Di. Families also donated meals on a rota. Martinha funded the church's charitable work; her husband pretended not to know the extent of her donations. It was his wife's commitment, just as he had drawn heavily upon their funds for the sake of the island itself.

'I fear I may not be able to visit for a while,' Martinha said, glancing over to Francis for permission to speak, which he freely gave. 'I'm expecting another child next year. Dr Hutton has warned me that I should not mix too freely with the poor for fear of infection.'

'My congratulations to you both!' Fr Michael exclaimed. 'What wonderful news! I shall keep you in my prayers. Dr Hutton is entirely correct. The town is far from sanitary. Do not worry, Mrs Light. There are many ways to lend your support, not the least through prayer. The petitions of women are the most pleasing to the Lord! Would you allow me to say private Mass for your family here on Sundays after the main service until you are recovered from the birth? The chapel teems with worshippers; swamp fevers are on the increase. I would wish to spare you and your family from contagion,' he added.

'Most kind of you, sir.' Martinha responded. She had hoped he would make this suggestion. Not only for herself, but for her mother too. Thong Di's health was not as robust as it once had been.

Francis echoed her sentiment. 'I too would feel much relieved if the family could attend services either at home or in Government House, if you need a larger space. We're quite a Roman community in our household these days. I feel myself surrounded!'

Father Michael's droll expression did not require comment. It was not just the soul of Captain Glass he sought. On that diverting notion, the priest took his leave, chuckling to himself as he strolled back towards Christians' Place.

***

Finding themselves at last alone, a rare occurrence these days, Francis and Martinha sat in companionable silence as the day waned. It would not be long before the rest of the family returned. Martinha decided to seize the moment.

'Francis, while we have this chance, there's something I would ask but I fear it may upset you. Your moods are so capricious these days,' she began uncertainly.

Light levelled his gaze at his wife and feigned a serious frown, which entirely failed to convince. 'Since when has my beautiful wife learned such words as "capricious"? This must indeed be serious. Yet I cannot help but be charmed by her remarkable eloquence.'

'Don't make fun of me! I am serious. Today I overheard something that has preyed upon my mind. I do not wish confusion to lie between us, especially in my present condition –' she broke off as if still unsure quite how to proceed.

'Pray continue, my dear. I do not mean to make light of your worries,' he added contritely.' You know, you can ask anything!'

Martinha folded her hands nervously on her lap, biting on her upper lip. 'I know it is unseemly to eavesdrop, but I could not help but overhear Mr Pigou in conversation with Mr Scott. You know how loud James Scott can be! Mr Pigou even had to caution him to lower his voice.'

'I imagine Scott was already a few glasses along by then. What did the old fool say?'

'Thomas observed that it had taken Captain Glass long enough to work out that he might surmount convention if his beloved were to become a Catholic, like Mrs Light and Mrs Scott. The ladies would be satisfied that they were married in the eyes of God, yet the Company would not care. Scott answered him thus: "To them, a Catholic wife is nothing but an ..." She paused, stumbling over the word, "... an *a-din-a-ton*. A pig might as well fly."' She looked quizzically at her husband.

He winced but did not answer. Martinha would not let it lie. 'What means this word in English, Francis?'

Rubbing his bristles with his hand, he gave a low moan. 'The word is Greek. Not English. *Adynaton*. It means something that is impossible. Like in Malay: *tunggu kucing bertanduk*. When a cat grows horns ...'

Martinha's face was impassive. She had deduced the meaning for herself already. Perhaps some part of her had hoped she might be wrong, which is why she had asked him so bluntly. He wondered in passing if he ought to have lied.

'So, marriage in a Catholic church is not legally binding to your people.' She spoke softly but he recognised her simmering anger. 'In the eyes of the British, I am not in fact your wife at all. I never was, despite the *three* marriage ceremonies we have had: Muslim, Buddhist and Catholic. None has any legitimacy in the eyes of your people. To them, I am just your mistress. Your Bibi. Your *mia noi.* Your *gundik.*' She spat out each insult with contempt. 'Is this how they have thought of me all along? Is this why they show no respect for me in Calcutta?'

He let the words fall without interruption. Even after she finished, he remained silent. There was little he might say by way of explanation. Martinha was entirely right in her assumptions.

'I should have told you long ago,' Light finally admitted, reaching for her hand. She did not draw it away but neither did she respond to his caress. 'I cannot change the way my people see the world, much as I wish I could. You are my one true wife, Martinha. You do understand that, surely?'

She contemplated him for a moment. 'Why did you not marry me in your church?'

'There are no Anglican churches here.'

'We have visited Calcutta together twice. There are many churches there.'

Light sighed. 'You know we could not marry in Calcutta.

Even if I found a preacher who would have consented, a licence would never be granted. And even if I did, it would do no good. It is not socially acceptable –'

'But to keep a whore is?' she reverted to Malay as if she did not even wish to speak his language anymore.

He winced. 'You are not my whore! You are my wife! Yes, they are amenable to a man keeping a mistress, but they will not allow marriage between a British subject and a native. It is Company regulations. And I am a senior officer of the Company.'

'I hate your damned Company! I regret the day that you took office with them!' Martinha's voice wavered on the edge of tears. He did not wish to upset her, especially in her condition. 'What of our children? Are they legitimate? Would they have any claim on your estate if some day in the future you married an English wife and had proper English children with her?'

'I will never marry another woman! All these years we have been together, there has never been anyone but you! You know my feelings, Martinha!' Francis was aghast that she might doubt his love.

She called his bluff. Martinha was in pain; he deserved to suffer, too. 'No one but me, you say. What then of Amdaeng Rat and little Georgie? Do you not still maintain your other little family in Thalang? For if you do not, then it means you have let down another woman to whom you made promises.'

Martinha sat back, triumphant in the knowledge that his former mistress's name had stunned him into silence. Francis opened his mouth, but words almost failed him.

'Amdaeng Rat?' he whispered. 'How did you know?'

Martinha waved her hand dismissively. 'It does not matter

how I know. Do you really imagine a woman does not know when her husband betrays her? She knows – but chooses *not* to know. I also know that Rat was not the only one. You were never faithful to me when you were away from home. I have accepted that long ago. Yet it seems I must accept now that my position is even more fragile than I believed. You should have told me, Francis. I would have accepted had you told me.'

Martinha rose as if to walk away but Francis caught her arm. He would not let her leave with such bitter words between them. 'Stay, Martinha! Give me a chance to defend myself. I know how many times I have failed you in the past. I swear I have put those days long behind me. There are many things I should have told you over the years, but I never had the courage. Yet, you must believe me when I say that never will I leave you. Everything I do is for you and the children. Everything I own is yours. If I have failed as a man, I swear I have never failed as a husband and father. Nor will I ever!'

His desperate pleas rang out around the room. Servants paused their chores to listen, construing enough of the mixed English and Malay to understand the gist. Ears edged closer to walls and windows to gather riveting nuggets of gossip. The captain and his lady were having a disagreement! Thong Di working at her tambour, set down her frame. Her room was directly overhead; she could not help but hear their words. This exchange had been brewing for some time; Francis had been too remote, Martinha too fragile in her condition. Everyone was on high alert, watching for signs of trouble from across the strait. It had taken a wedding to finally cause the pot to boil over.

'What would happen if you lost this island?' A different

consideration occurred to her, one that had never been voiced between them. 'I keep my eyes and ears open, Francis, even if you keep the details from me. I know it is by no means certain we can withstand an onslaught from the Malay states, especially if the Company does not lend its full support. What if the worst was to happen and we were driven from our home?'

There was more to her concern than legal quibbles surrounding their marriage. Even he had been loath to contemplate the realities that lay ahead if everything he had been working towards these many years came to nothing.

'We will prevail,' he muttered. 'We must prevail.'

'And if we do not?' Martinha insisted. 'You must have given thought to the alternative. Where do we go if all else fails?'

Francis had never once proposed to his wife the ultimate future that he planned. Yet his dream would cost her the most. 'If we leave this island, there is only one place I would wish to go. To England. To my beloved Suffolk.' Finally, he had admitted it.

'And what of me and the children when you return to Suffolk?' she put to him.

A crease in his brow indicated the extent of his surprise. 'Why, you come with me, of course! We would buy a fine estate and live like a lord and lady, with our children the toast of the countryside!' There was a wistful faraway expression in his eyes. Her own misted over with tears at his pipedream.

'The wife you do not dare to marry in a Protestant church. You think to bring her to an English village? I am a native of the Indies, in your own words, Francis!'

'They will love you as I do!' he murmured, taking her in his arms. 'It is different there. In London or Calcutta where only society matters, such things cause scandal. But not in a country village where everyone has known me all my life. You would be a curiosity for a time, but then they would come to accept you. My dearest wish is for you to meet my mother. Pray God she lives long enough!' Francis exclaimed.

Martinha's next reaction mystified her husband. The minds of women were truly unknowable. 'I'm so happy we've had this talk, Francis!' she gasped.

'Happy?' he repeated. It would not have been his choice of adjectives to describe the bloodletting of the past half hour.

'I needed you to say these things. I have long ago forgiven you for infidelity. I always understood our marriage was unusual. I've spent enough time in Calcutta to realise how your society thinks. It is not so different here. Each community has its own traditions and does not respect those of others. But I have been worried for some time that perhaps you may one day decide to return home – as many of your countrymen do – and leave behind your local wife and family. When I heard Scott and Pigou talk like that, I could not help but wonder ...'

'You silly goose! Just because Scott has abandoned families in every damned port in the Indies, does not mean I will do as he. In some ways, you are more protected than a mere wife. They believe you a Malay princess, no less, they do not wish to offend your people. As long as you are my beneficiary, then you are safe. One thing the English always respect is a legal document,' he smiled, as he dabbed at her tears with his kerchief.

The lively sounds of children running towards the house brought them back to reality. 'They are home. We have said enough for now. Come my dear, we'll talk anon. But one thing

I must impress upon you. We are not going anywhere for quite some time. This island is ours, and ours it will stay. My word on it, my dear.

18

Noblesse Oblige

HMS Crown, *Pinang Roads. 8th January 1792*

It was late morning when Superintendent Francis Light boarded HMS *Crown,* as it lay at anchor resplendent in its glory. Commodore Cornwallis had arrived the day before, fresh from his survey in the Andamans. He had been sent by the governor-general to render assistance in respect of the imminent threat from Queddah. Calcutta had finally acknowledged the danger.

The superintendent was piped aboard with the traditional salute reserved for naval captains in respect of his past service. The old familiar tradition brought the sweet pang of memory, each whistle and command recalling Light's youth as vividly as yesterday.

As he eased himself over the rail onto the deck, accompanied by Pigou and Glass, he gave himself a moment to gaze about the majestic frigate. The *Crown* was a fine 64-gunner, a warship of the line such as he had served on as a young officer. He could almost reach out and touch the world that once was his – and might still have been, had he been born on the right side of the blanket. A different life arose before him, one of naval battles and military command, of promotion and distinction. By now he might have been an admiral.

The cheery greeting of the ship's captain awakened him from

his idle musings. 'Welcome aboard, Superintendent Light. Captain Maurice Delgarno of HMS *Crown* at your service. Commodore Cornwallis has instructed me to escort you to his cabin.' Delgarno led them towards the poop deck astern into the spacious gallery below where the quarters of the commodore were situated.

William Cornwallis sat in his oak-lined cabin at a table laid for formal lunch, replete with white linen, silverware and gold-rimmed wine glasses. Through the bowed windows behind him, sparkling waters and forested peaks shimmered in the heat. The incongruence of the tropical background against the magnificent interior of polished wood, brass, crystal and silk was not lost on the visitors. How could two such different worlds exist in one place?

The two men greeted each other fondly. Introductions were made, glasses were filled and a fine lunch was served for six: Light and his two deputies with Cornwallis, Delgarno and Captain Edward Osborn of the escort ship, *Ariel*. By the final course, when they had toasted in the newly arrived year of 1791, formality had been replaced by conviviality, as was invariably the case in naval gatherings.

'Quite like old times, Light?' Cornwallis smiled in acknowledgment of Light's former rank.

'Indeed, sir. I need but close my eyes to recall the nights of my youth spent dining in the captain's cabin. Save for the tropical surroundings, for I spent most of my navy days in the Americas,' Light agreed.

'As did we all. Those days are well behind us now,' Cornwallis added in a reference to the loss of the colonies, in which his famous brother had paid such a central role. 'But there are always battles to fight, so bold sailors never go to waste. Which brings me to our current situation, dear superintendent. You understand our presence in these waters is not to wage war but to assure a peaceful resolution? It is the wish of the governor-general to end this nonsense with Queddah. We must finally come to terms. No one wishes to be embroiled in petty local fights. Not when real wars loom at us from all over the globe!'

Light concurred. 'War is the last thing I desire, sir. For one thing, it is entirely bad for business, which is the very lifeblood of Prince of Wales Island. There comes a time, however, when a sharp shock achieves more than endless jawing around a table. These Mohammedans have kept us on a hook for far too long. Every time we come close to hauling them in, they squirm away with yet another preposterous demand. I fear we have no alternative but to show our teeth. As of December, all ports of the mainland have been closed to us. The channel teems with hostile prows, the marauding Illanun of Mindanao the most threatening. Commercial shipping bound for the island has been deterred.'

'I see no sign today of such threat,' Cornwallis observed, indicating the lazy view from the cabin window, of craft bobbing around from ship to shore, no apparent enemy in sight.

'On account of the recent action we have already taken – and your current imposing presence here,' Light replied. 'For months we've been patrolling and building fortifications. The settlers have assisted in reinforcing the outer wall of the fort and a Bugis chieftain, Dato' Punggawa Tillibone, has set up a battery on the coast to the south. From there, they observed the increased presence of Illanun pirates. At the same time, we've received reports of attacks on the coast of neutral Perak. I was not prepared to sit and wait from them to land on our beaches – so I have already taken measures.

Cornwallis approved. 'You intervened? Good man.'

Light nodded. 'I commandeered two vessels stranded in port by the blockade: the *Greyhound* and the ketch *Princess Augusta,* instructing them to patrol the waters to the south and keep an eye on things. They were involved in a few skirmishes, enough to disperse the prows further down the coast. Meanwhile, I armed the *Dolphin*, the *Royal Admiral* and a few cruisers, and we held the northern entrance to the channel. For a few days we played cat and mouse with the Illanun but they scattered after a few broadsides. I doubt they expected resistance. I hear the pirates have taken themselves off to the Boontings, a small archipelago to the north. It's typical of brigands to lie low until the threat dies down. You've arrived not a moment too soon. I'm not sure how long we could contain them. Only a frigate will dissuade them in the long run.'

The table was cleared while Pigou spread out a chart, placing cones of sugar to indicate current positions. Cornwallis and the other captains familiarised themselves with the location. 'It strikes me these Illanun devils are here primarily for their own gain,' Cornwallis observed. 'If they don't make booty soon, Queddah better watch out. The dogs will turn on their master. These natives can never keep an alliance for more than a few weeks,' Cornwallis observed.

Light agreed. 'They're already plagued with rivalries, even within the camps of the sultans. But they are past masters at hiding and reappearing the moment one's back is turned. We cannot afford to be complacent, even with a frigate and armed cruisers in the channel.'

'It is the ideal moment to parley. I shall lead a delegation to the sultan. My name's Cornwallis after all. The sultan will think the governor-general himself has honoured them with a visit; I doubt he could distinguish one Cornwallis from another! Let's see if I can't talk some sense into them. My brother is willing to make concessions. After all, the sultan has waited nigh on five years for his treaty. He has some reason to be disgruntled. It's the money he wants. He'll back down once he sees coin upon the table,' Cornwallis assured them.

Pigou and Light exchanged a meaningful glance. The lease had never been the sticking point. It was the armies and weapons that divided them, a requirement that Cornwallis would never even acknowledge, let alone concede. 'I propose Mr Pigou and Captain Glass accompany you. They know the lingo and the necessary court etiquette. I beseech you to be wary. They're slippery as eels. Money is only part of it. The sultan wants our commitment to arms and men for his personal defence.'

Cornwallis mocked very idea. 'Then I will quickly disavow him of that notion. The only arms they shall see are those aiming at their prows if they don't come to their senses!'

It was worth a chance. Perhaps Sultan Abdullah would be satisfied with a Cornwallis in his palace and a lease paid in full. At the very least, the Commodore would learn the intractable nature of the Malay temperament. The irascible commander would not stand for the sultan's machinations for long. Either way, they were closer now to resolution than at any time in the last few years.

'If I may raise another, rather delicate matter, sir?' Light said as the decanter was passed around once more. 'Although we are most grateful for your presence, the arrival of your ships has added an extra burden to our already straightened circumstances. The *Crown* alone has five hundred men aboard, not to mention the *Ariel* and the other ships I have commandeered. Dr Hutton informs me that twenty critical patients have been admitted to the hospital, with countless others arriving daily for minor treatment. His meagre allowance does not stretch to these extra numbers.'

'Forgive me, Superintendent Light. I have been thoughtless. Please inform the good doctor that I shall order an immediate sum to be paid to the infirmary to cover medications, food and other necessities as well as Hutton's services. I will also send our doctors over to assist. I do not wish to overburden your resources more than is strictly necessary. I am already in your debt for the fresh food you supplied to the Andamans last month. It helped stem the tide of scurvy. It is not my intent to take advantage of your generosity!'

Not for the first time was Light grateful for the support of William Cornwallis. There were few men of his class who showed such consideration for those beneath them. They were fortunate indeed to have his patronage.

***

Light kept his own counsel during the short crossing back to the island, undisturbed by Glass and Pigou both nodding off in the heat, unaccustomed to imbibing in such quantities at lunchtime. The liquor had the opposite effect on him however, bringing a certain clarity of mind. *In vino veritas* had rarely seemed so pertinent a maxim.

His interlude aboard the warship had left him awash in contrary emotions. The nostalgia for his boyhood was lanced through with bitterness that this world had been snatched from him, despite his aptitude for the sea and command. Yet, it was the manner of his rejection rather than the loss of his naval career that grieved him most. He did not regret abandoning the navy for the Indies. His life had been the richer for it. Imagine having spent the past quarter century a slave to the Royal Navy! The freedom and adventure the Straits had afforded him, not to mention the fortune he had accumulated, were more than compensation. His eyes had been opened to the world, freeing him from the heavy chains of society's conventions. Nor would he have met Martinha.

The visit to the *Crown*, however, was a vivid reminder that he was a veteran of sea battles, having served in wartime under the finest commanders of the age. He had the skills for battle. War might be bad for business for a country ship captain, but it was the best course of action for a superintendent. For years he had teetered on thin ice to keep the peace against the intimidations of Queddah and the lack of action from Bengal. Now it was time to don his other badge of office. He must strike first while the iron was hot.

William Cornwallis could exercise diplomatic skills all he liked but he was out of his depth. At least the illusion of negotiation would have been maintained. The sultan enjoyed the distinction of direct talks with a British nobleman. Yet from this moment on, Light would use this lull to lay the ground for the inevitable attack that he would make, in his own time, at the location of his choosing. Decisive leadership meant neither looking to others, nor seeking the easier path. It lay in seizing the moment when your enemy least expected it: the art of misdirection, smoke and mirrors.

His newfound resolve was tempered by his other allegiance that answered neither to national nor commercial considerations. Parting from his colleagues at the jetty, Light returned directly to his family home on the pretext of sleeping off the heavy lunch, to which the others were heartily in agreement. While they strolled amiably homewards, Superintendent Light set off at a brisk pace that belied his claims of torpor.

Quiet in the languorous heat of the afternoon, with only the thwack of a *cangkul* thrashing the undergrowth and the rhythmic crashing of waves pounding on the shore, the household was at rest, sleeping away the fierce humidity. Francis found Martinha in her room by the open window, fanning herself whilst dabbing perfumed water on her neck. She looked pale and drained, her face grown thinner even as her belly had swelled.

'Francis! What a surprise! How was the meeting with Cornwallis?' she asked, although her listless manner suggested her interest was slight.

He took the cloth from her hands, refreshed it in the bowl, dabbing her head and neck. 'How are you, my dear? This damned heat is cruel, is it not? Perhaps you should try and nap awhile until evening?'

Martinha's answer was tetchy. 'I would sleep if I but could! The babe wriggles incessantly each time I close my eyes and then I toss and turn for hours, drenched in sweat. Would that my time had already come!'

'I wish I could take it from you, my love. This has been a difficult time. It is more than just the heat and noxious maladies.

Martinha, we are living in a time of great anxiety. Day by day, the reckoning approaches. We must prepare for the inevitable ...'

'Has something happened, Francis? Are we under attack?' she cried out in alarm.

He rested his hand on her arm, calming her distress. 'No, nothing like that. Everything is exactly as it was. We are still in stalemate. Which is why we must act now when we have the opportunity. Martinha, I wish for you to take your mother and the children to Calcutta. I shall arrange a lease on a house for the rest of the year. You will be with the girls and can deliver our baby with the best medical care available. Mary also needs to be placed in school; this would be the ideal opportunity –'

'NO!' Her reply was definitive, enunciated in terms that brooked no opposition. 'I will not leave Pinang at this time. Do not ask this of me again!' Her disagreeable mood had turned to outright anger.

'But Martinha ...'

'... No! There is nothing you might say to persuade me to leave. This is my home. Dr Hutton is a fine doctor. There are experienced midwives here. I will be fine.'

'Your mother –'

'My mother is not fit to travel. She is getting older. It is better that she stays at home.'

'Your mother is my age. She's as fit as a fiddle,' Francis countered.

'I do not think a sea journey will be good for me in my condition.'

'If you leave now, there will be no problem. I have already asked Hutton's opinion and he recommends it. He suggests sending one of his women from the infirmary to attend you.'

Martinha bridled. 'You've discussed this with Dr Hutton before me?' she snapped. 'Am I to be ordered around like one of your junior writers?'

Francis bit his tongue. It would do no good trying to reason with his wife in this mood. Women in her condition were given to hysteria; rational thought generally eluded them. 'Dear Martinha, please do not agitate yourself. I meant no harm. We are at a dangerous moment. My mind would be at ease knowing my family was safe from harm. You are everything to me, surely you know that? I am near besides myself with worry that something will happen to you all!'

His desperate words soothed the worst of her high dudgeon. 'I too am sick with worry. We're so vulnerable here! Do you remember the early days? Little Mary at my skirts and baby William at my breast – and who knew if Queddah would attack? Yet it came to nothing. I believe in you, Francis. Queddah will never prevail against you. Especially now with Calcutta taking notice at last. The governor-general would not send his own brother unless he was determined to support us.'

Francis was not so convinced that the presence of the Commodore was any more than a sop to his desperate appeals. William Cornwallis was stationed at Port Blair along with the fleet. The Council clearly favoured it for the naval base. What guarantee did he have that this current crisis might not convince the governor-general that Pinang ought to be abandoned? 'Cornwallis is only here to assess the situation until reinforcements arrive. Do not hold out too much hope, my dear.'

His wife sighed gently, idly stroking the swell of her body.

'What do we ever have but hope, sayang? This child has a dangerous journey ahead even to reach the light of day. There are no certainties in life. We must trust in God alone,' she murmured. Martinha prayed even more than usual these days. How little he considered her worries, so occupied had he been with his own.

He ventured on a different tack. 'Lydia Gray has sailed with Lindesay on the *Indus*. She plans to stay with friends in Alipore until things calm down.' It was not a persuasive argument.

Martinha could not resist a smile at the mention of the lady. 'So, I have heard. It didn't take long for Mrs Gray to desert her darling husband and the social whirl, did it?'

'James says his wife is of a delicate constitution. She has been laid low by anxiety the past months. He fears it will be injurious to her health.' Even he could not keep the sarcasm from his voice.

Martinha rolled her eyes. 'Lydia Gray is hale and hearty, as well you know. The opportunity for six months preening in Calcutta playing the victim is too good to miss. That is exactly my point, Francis. If Lt Gray is sending his wife away, then there is real cause for concern. It unsettles the community and leads to panic when those in authority expect others to make sacrifices they themselves are not prepared to make. I could not live with myself if I abandoned our people at this moment.'

'No one would blame you, Martinha! You are with child!'

'I am not the only woman on the island in this condition! But even if they did forgive me, I would not forgive myself. I am the wife of the superintendent. I come from a family who has wielded power for many years in Thalang. Did Aunty Chan or Aunty Mook take flight when the Burmese invaded? No, they stayed to show an example to others. And so shall I. Noble birth has its advantages, yet it carries heavy responsibilities. This was taught to me by my own people since I was a little girl.'

Light expected the same from himself and others, why would Martinha not feel the same? She was a woman of distinction in every way. He could not deny her the right to make her own decision. 'You put me to shame, Martinha. Just like you, I was taught that with rank comes responsibility. I will not force you to leave. Stay by my side and we shall ride out this storm as we have sailed through many others in our life together.'

'I have no doubts on that score. Know this – you will prevail. There is nothing in this world can stop you. Haven't you proved that time enough already?'

***

It was a less phlegmatic Commodore Cornwallis that sat down to dinner at Government House a few weeks later after to-and-froing between the sultan's palace and the island. No sooner had the desired agreement seemed close, they had been plunged back to the beginning, without a single jot of ground gained. Over dinner, he raged about the hopelessness of dealing with such adversaries, who did not understand the first thing about the art of diplomacy.

'After indicating that a sum of 5000 Spanish dollars per annum would be adequate compensation and promising to end the food embargo, suddenly the figure of 10,000 is back upon the table and only the promise of arms and men acceptable! Time and time again we have indicated that our government cannot provide military support for a foreign ruler. There's no rhyme or reason to their argument! Once they smell a whiff of concession, they renege on all agreement so far and ask for something more!' Cornwallis exclaimed, thumping the table in frustration until the wine glass threated to overturn. 'No wonder you've been at your wits' end these five years!'

'I've written to Abdullah in the strongest terms this very day,' Light countered. 'The ports must reopen immediately, or we will regard it as an ultimatum. Let's see what he has to say about that!'

'It's all bluff, I'll wager. I hear the Illanun are causing mayhem in the north. If this stalemate goes on much longer, their motley alliance will collapse under them. I'll make a few more sorties to keep the matter dragging on, but make no mistake, this will come to naught. We'll have this island *gratis* if the wooden-headed sultan doesn't see reason!' Cornwallis assured him.

'Nevertheless, I have also written to your brother seeking leave to poke the tiger. I will threaten war if immediate settlement isn't reached. I want the Earl's permission to run our own gauntlet on Queddah trade, closing their ports with a parallel blockade. If I can keep the Chulias and the Siamese out, the sultan will soon feel the pinch. Let's see what sinking a few of his prows or raiding the Laddas does to his damned alliance. It's time to raise the stakes on this endless bargaining!'

By March, neither permission from Calcutta had arrived, nor the expected attack. Spies reported quarrels in the rival camps; the alliance was on the verge of collapse. Meanwhile the Illanun, tired of inaction, planned to take their services elsewhere – or raid the lands of their erstwhile allies. Abdullah encouraged them to target southern Siam to distract them. Suddenly the invasion seemed less threatening. Cornwallis believed the conflict had been averted. When an East Indiaman arrived loaded with armaments, supplies and three troops of sepoys, it seemed his work was done.

On the 15th of the month, Cornwallis re-joined his fleet at Port Blair with confidence that war had been averted. Abdullah would accept terms, his coalition dead in the water. James Scott was directed to deliver an initial payment of good faith, on the understanding that the balance would be due once the Illanun had withdrawn. After that, Abdullah would accept what he was given.

Four days later, much as Light had warned, reports of large force, even greater than the original, was reported heading for Prai across the strait. Meanwhile Illanun prows had mysteriously reappeared as if from nowhere. The rumours of internal disagreement had been exaggerated. The sultan had been leading them along, waiting for the departure of the warships to return even stronger than before. He called for Light to appear before him and do fealty for the island. It was tantamount to a declaration of war.

19
The Little Pirate

Boonting Island, Langkawi (the Laddas). 12th April, 1791

Langaon stood astride his canoe, hair streaming in the wind, breathing in deeply of the coral-gold dawn. It felt good to be raiding again. For too long the brothers had lingered without purpose, confined like disobedient children to the northern islands. If the Sultan of Queddah was too craven to strike against his British foes, preferring endless parley, then he deserved to be disobeyed by his allies for whom he showed such little respect.

Pickings had been slim for months. Since their leader Si-Tamburan had decreed that all slaving should cease until the war was over, the men had lived a tedious existence, fishing for sustenance with only the occasional miserly raid on a local island to alleviate the boredom. Nor did the Laddas possess much worth taking; even once-golden Ujung Salang had been much reduced by the Burmese. Still, passing trade had kept them occupied; there was always opium and pearls from merchant vessels fool enough to cross his path.

Langaon was a young warrior in his third season, captain of a *garay* in the Illanun fleet in the service of Sultan Abdullah of Queddah. As one of the many nephews of Si-Tamburan, he had been singled out for distinction, chosen to head a vanguard action to scout the southwest channel ahead of the main squadron. Their wise admiral did not underestimate the English officer who ruled the island of Pinang. This Kapitan Light would not sit at home waiting to be slaughtered in his bed. British warships would be on their way to stop them; it was Langaon's task to seek them out.

Nor was Si-Tamburan satisfied with the bounty promised by the sultan. Not even the prospect of slaves from the well-fed population of Pulau Pinang, nor the treasure from its coffers, was enough to slake his appetite for booty. Battles were unpredictable. Who knew if the British might prevail? Si-Tamburan would ensure an Illanun triumph regardless of the outcome for Queddah. The brothers had been patient long enough. From now on, everything that fell into their hands was fair game.

While the main fleet sailed south through the conventional channel past Pulau Langkawi, Langaon had been sent around the outlying Boontings to the west to intercept the British should they attempt a surprise attack from the rear. Then would the chaser become the quarry.

His four nimble *salisipan* skimmed over the churning waves, war canoes built for speed and manoeuvrability manned by Illanun oarsmen. Much praise was heaped on their mighty *lanong* warships and the smaller garays, but Langaon believed the salisipan was their greatest accomplishment. No ship of any nation could hope to keep up with this sprightly craft in full flow. Narrow enough to slide into tiny creeks and inlets, fast enough to outrun any pursuer, able to twist and turn with the dexterity of a serpent when fired upon, the salisipan appeared out of nowhere – and then was gone before the enemy had time to act.

From his position on the rudder oar, Langaon proudly scanned the seas about. Garbed in a distinctive scarlet jerkin and chequered sarong, with a knotted head cloth shot through with thread of gold, he stood out as a man of nobility. Hanging from his belt of silver dollars was his precious *kampilan* sword ominously adorned with hanks of human hair, each corresponding to the many notches on its blade. Thrust into his *sablay* was an ornate golden Bugis keris, plundered in an earlier Riau campaign. Langaon's reputation was already well-established; he hoped to increase his glory in the coming action – and his wealth.

The wind was in their favour, the single sail swelling as proud as the belly of a man of substance. The rowers pulled steadily, well within their compass, ready to raise the tempo at a moment's notice. Little sign of shipping other than a few junks and perahus had been sighted; all kept a wide berth. He was not interested in such small fry.

And then he saw it, the glint of reflected light dancing off distant metal. Shading his eyes, he strained until he could pick out a blurry outline that could only mean a vessel of some size. Langaon shouted to his men who turned as one to follow his raised arm, immediately recognising what he had already observed. Instantly the mood changed. Drawing themselves up taller in their benches, they heaved to a more robust rhythm as Langaon raised the beat. They sped on, faster and faster with every stroke, until the far-off smudge grew more distinct, enough for these expert mariners to identify it. Not a warship but an East Indiaman heading out across the Andaman Sea, no doubt loaded in cargo and men, attempting to flee before battle commenced.

There was no time to lose. Langaon called his men to reverse direction, which they did with dexterity, altering the stroke with astonishing precision. They would rendezvous with the main fleet.

A lone slow-moving merchant ship without an escort meant these waters must be free of Company frigates. Wherever the British were, they were not heading north; an unmissable opportunity had sailed into their path.

***

Soliman was conflicted. In general, he despised the British – all Europeans – but he believed Francis Light to be a man of principle who would honour his promises, especially those made to friends and allies. The Honourable Company – wholly misnamed in Soliman's opinion – had twisted and turned for years, refusing to abide by the terms of the treaty of Pulau Pinang. In the meantime, Superintendent Light had tried his best both to placate the sultan and convince his British masters, while the faithless Company had closed its ears to his entreaties.

Suddenly everything had changed. For the past few months, Commodore Cornwallis had been in constant talks with Queddah, but it had been nothing but misdirection to lull the Malays into false hopes. Had the superintendent planned all along to launch a surprise attack? Perhaps there had never be any intention to broker a settlement? For the island was to be wrested by force from Queddah with the full weight of British military might.

Soliman's loyalties were sorely tested. The sultan had been patient for years; he had sought every opportunity to search for common ground. He could vouch for that for he had been the go-between. Who could blame Sultan Abdullah if eventually he resorted to a hostile alliance to threaten the British into submission? How long was the sultan expected to suffer the arrogance of the Company, which made a huge profit from the new trading emporium, whilst ruining the economy of Queddah with no recompense? The Malays of Pinang were worried for the future; if the British lost the island, Queddah would not forgive their support of Francis Light. There would be slaughter. Some secretly colluded in the hopes they would be spared. But Soliman's family would never escape the revenge-taking. His personal connection to Light was well known.

What was he to do? His allegiances were divided between what was right and what was expedient, between his sympathy for his people and his love for his adoptive father. When the superintendent asked for his assistance in the coming action, Soliman spent hours searching his conscience before making his decision. He had even considered taking his family and fleeing the region, perhaps to Ujung Salang or Sumatra until it was safe to return. But, in the end, he could not run away. It was neither in his nature nor how his benefactor had raised him. 'I will help you if I can, but I will not fight Malay people. Do not ask that of me.'

'I would never ask that of you, Sol. Such a thing would be unnatural. I wish for you to stay away from the main conflict. Except for this one service. Would you act as lookout? Warn me when the Illanun are close at hand? Then your work is done. I promise that when we strike, it will be fast and furious. This stalemate has gone on too long. There can only be one end. Sometimes one must go to war in order to bring peace.'

'Easy for you to say,' Soliman retorted. 'You have warships.'

'You and your people should thank your God we have. No one on this island is safe from the wrath of Queddah. You chose your side long ago when you threw yourselves on my mercy and settled this island without the necessary agreements. Now we must ensure that as few as possible suffer for the chance we took.'

So Soliman complied as he had always known he would. His destiny imprisoned him between two opposing worlds, the price he had paid since a small child for the gift of life. God willing his own children would not share his fate once this final betrayal was complete.

The night before had been spent at sea, circling the waters north of Pinang, watching for any hint that the Illanun were returning to these waters. The day had barely dawned when he espied distant Illanun scouts. It was as Francis had predicted, an advance party searching for enemy warships. Any innocent merchant vessel, particularly a lumbering East Indiaman, would be a temptation too great for them to pass. Thus, giving the impression of a local perahu wishing to keep out of trouble, Soliman had immediately fled in the direction of Pulau Perak, a rocky islet in the channel nearby. The Illanun had paid his boat no heed.

As soon as he was in sight of the island, he ran up the agreed flag, signalling to the watchers on the peak. Then Soliman bolted for home, his part accomplished. Whatever happened next, his only purpose now was to safeguard his own.

***

In the somnolent hours before dawn under the ethereal light of a cloud-obscured moon as their only guide, a silent company of men boarded a motley of vessels moored between Prince of Wales Island and the mainland. With a few naval cadets to command the gunboats, accompanied by troop barges and a punt loaded with a weighty 18-pounder, Glass, Raban, Mylne and 600 sepoys slid out under the cover of darkness, using only the currents and the night breeze to ferry them across to the opposing shore. They drifted towards the northern promontory of the river Prai where a few wooden stockades had recently been erected to serve as forts. There was no apparent sign of life. Not a single guard patrolled the ramparts, no one observed anything amiss. No alarm was raised.

In sight of the marshy mangroves riven with streams and inlets, 400 men slipped onto the barges and, under the protection of four gunships armed with small cannon, they were conveyed to land, hauling the punt and its sturdy 18-pounder. Once disembarked, the remaining sepoys and sailors under Lt Raban's command, quietly withdrew back towards the island. In the middle channel, however, they raised sail and headed direct for the Malay fleet moored in the entrance of the estuary. The combined merchant fleet of Scott and Light Esquires, the *Indus*, the *Bristol*, the *Prince Henry* and the *Speedwell* were off to war.

The marines on land found the early going hard. Creeping at stealth through the swampy hinterland, amidst a skeletal forest populated with deadly snakes and predators, they feared that any moment their presence would be detected, and they would be sitting ducks. Perhaps they were being enticed into a trap. Any moment fierce keris-wielding warriors might leap upon them to leave their mutilated bodies in the brackish mangrove as food for wild beasts.

Their fears were unfounded. Finally, they reached firmer ground from where their progress accelerated. Shortly afterwards, they were in sight of the forts. The troops of the allied states were camped further along the river. By the time news reached them of the British attack, it would be too late.

At a given sign, they divided into two platoons. Glass made for the larger fort, the furthest from their current location, while Mylne surrounded the nearby stockade with the rest. It was integral now that they kept their nerve; anyone who moved too soon would ruin the element of surprise that was their greatest weapon.

Time ticked by; minutes dragged like hours, hearts thumping in a heady blend of thrill and fear. Then the sign they had been waiting for. A sudden mighty explosion shattered the eery quiet, and a crackling, smoke-encircled glow brightened the dark sky. Fire had broken out on the river. The punt, loaded with gunpowder, had been floated into the tangled jumble of prows and galleys ranged haphazardly along the mouth. For several heart-stopping minutes, its burning taper had threatened to peter out, but at last the dying sparks had reignited – and the charge had blown in a mighty explosion that was heard on Pinang island itself.

The result was mayhem. Malay lascars ran hither and thither attempting to staunch the flames as the British fired their cannonry at will. Volley after volley smashed into the helpless perahus, until those on boats realised their only option was to swim for shore, for it was impossible to sail from the conflagration amidst so much debris and confusion. Within a short time, the armada was in ruins.

The attention in the forts was directed towards the river. The British were destroying their navy! Soldiers ran for weapons, dragging cannon into place to set about their defence. With all eyes elsewhere, Captain Glass made his charge, blasting through the timber walls with the might of the 18-pounder as easily as a knife through butter. A parallel assault on the second stockade was launched by Mylne, the far-off shrieks and booms revealing a similar result. Within a few hours, both forts had been reduced to ashes and the Malay navy was destroyed. Only then did the guns cease and the British troops pull back, returning to their ships in the channel.

The war was not yet over but the first battle had been decisive. The coastal defences and the strait were now in the hands of the Honourable Company. Fort Cornwallis and the island remained untouched, protected by the artillery ranged along the foreshore led by Lieutenant Gray and the local militia under Kapitan Cina Khoh, and the penghulus, Nakhoda Kecil and Dato' Punggawa Tillibone. Such was the completeness of the victory that not a single defensive shot had been required. The Company casualty list was low: four dead and a dozen wounded, set against a huge death toll on the other side. The Perai shoreline was littered with corpses, body parts washing in on the morning tide, the river choked with broken boats and charred spars.

The sultan and his court fled to join the remnants of the army downriver, still clinging to the hope that the huge Illanun fleet would arrive any moment. Then the Malay Alliance would take revenge on the British for their cowardly attack under cover of the nightfall.

But the Illanun did not appear.

For the next few days, several attempts were made to reclaim the shore, each assault repulsed by the sepoys who were now in charge of all defensive positions. Rumour began to seed panic; either the Sulu pirates had deserted or – incredible to imagine – Light had defeated them at sea. On the third day, British scouts reported that the allied states had withdrawn. The huge coalition that had taken years to assemble had broken up in days. The writing was on the wall for Queddah. It was time for strategic withdrawal. *Sauve qui peut.*

***

His visit to HMS *Crown* had planted a seed in the superintendent's mind, the missing card in the deck, so patent that he wondered why he had not seen it before. Was age clouding his brain, or had the years of administrative duty dulled him to his true nature?

He was an experienced veteran of naval warfare and a sea captain for many years in these self-same waters. Therein lay the resolution to the murky impasse. Cornwallis had sent sepoys for the land fight – the domain of Captain Glass and his marines. He had also sent a frigate with extra cannonry and armaments. By imaginative deployment of their own vessels – and any others that happened to be in port – what more did a naval officer need to knock wild, marauding brigands out of the reckoning?

The Illanun had many qualities to be feared – fast ships, fierce warriors, well-tried tactics – but they had not studied naval stratagem. They had never sat in dusty classrooms listening to vivid accounts of Hannibal and Alexander the Great, the only part of history to which he had ever paid attention. In his years of service as a midshipman, the battle tactics of countless generals and admirals had been dissected and discussed until they were second nature. On this day, it would finally come to roost. Light planned a two-pronged attack by land and sea, straight from the annals of Antony and Caesar and the bravado of Sir Francis Drake. He would bring the battle to the enemy, the last thing they would expect.

For the first time in years, Francis Light felt buoyant, despite the danger into which they sailed. He was on home ground, or rather home waters. Succeed or fail, it was on his own terms. Not that he seriously considered anything but victory. Once he had made up his mind, his certainty had been unswerving. Each turning point of his life had rested on such moments. If he trusted his instincts, the victory was already won.

With the assistance of an East Indiaman, the *Bombay Castle*, currently stranded in port, Light set his trap. It was an aging vessel at the end of its useful service, which consideration played some part in its involvement. With assurances that no real harm would come to it, its captain had agreed – gallantly, some might say – to become the necessary bait in the trap.

Yet the vessel was not entirely without defences, being a 28-gunner with extra cannons in reserve. Indeed, Captain Hallam fully intended to use them whether strictly in the plan or not, for he had tangled with Illanun brigands several times before and possessed an inveterate hatred for them. And so, the cumbersome vessel had ambled from Prince of Wales Island at the slowest speed he could safely maintain, doing everything he could to suggest a ship hardly fit for such a voyage, but desperately attempting to flee.

The appearance of an Illanun fleet on the horizon, even one expected, still had the capacity to chill the very marrow of one's bones. Every instinct of each man on board screamed out to raise sail and flee. Instead, the captain and crew made a seemingly futile pretence of running for the shelter of Pulau Perak, the only landfall for miles, drawing the pursuers further and further to the northeast of the little island.

The ruse was working. The Illanun fleet divided into two

sections, each aiming to surround the East Indiaman from opposing sides, then choke it in their net. By the time the pirate devils realised the danger, it would be too late. They would become the meat within the pie themselves.

From the other side of Pulau Perak, three British warships, *Dolphin*, *Princess Augusta* and *Atalanta* slunk unseen, advancing in arrow formation, widening their arc as they neared the prey. So intent were the pirates on the lumbering merchant ship almost in their grasp that no notice was given to their rear, from which direction the speedy warships were now steadily gaining on them.

The first intimation of trouble came when a single brig, the *Greyhound,* appeared from the eastern side of the small islet, veering towards the *Bombay Castle*, as if in its defence. Yet even then the Illanun were not dismayed. A cheer went up. Two ships! The lanongs and the garays sped faster, their forces further splitting to surround both vessels at once. So fixed on their prizes were they, that they had neglected the most basic rule of battle. Protect your backs.

And then the warships let loose a cannonade. Every advantage that the Illanun had possessed – momentum, agility, and surprise – was lost in that instant. Although they were many, their vessels were small fry in confusion, trapped in an ever-decreasing net closing from behind, before and in the centre. Whichever way they twisted and turned, they collided with their own crafts. Crippled perahus rammed into those still in the fight, causing fatal damage. And still the superior cannonry bombarded them from a greater height. Even the *Bombay Castle* now felt safe enough to reveal its gunnery and take free aim.

Aboard the *Indus*, Light ran from gun to gun, shouting

encouragement, utterly at home amongst the chaos, smoke and deafening blast, expending the frustration of years in this bloody reckoning. The much-feared double-oared lanongs and elegant speedy garays that had wreaked havoc over the entire East Indies were helpless, children's toys on a duck pond. Light watched in awe at the simple majesty of battle – and the awful deadly triumph of superior firepower.

A single garay broke from the confusion, slipping through a gap in the milling throng to strike a course straight for the *Indus*. In one futile act of reckless bravery, its captain – a stocky young warrior marked out by his scarlet vest – waved a polished sword and screamed nameless curses as his swift bark advanced on its suicidal path. Francis Light locked eyes with the young man recognising the same unshakeable resolve that had once propelled him to jump from the deck of a sinking ship into a maelstrom of water, or set foot on an island without formal sanction, knowing it was his last chance. His heart went out to the lad. But not all acts of insane bravery result in victory.

Light raised his gun, aimed – and shot him clean through the heart. The young man's body tumbled dead into the water, now as scarlet as his coat. His men took fright, veering away from collision, leaderless and defeated, and made for the open sea. Light indicated to his gunners to let them go.

Si-Tamburan, commander of the Illanun, watched helplessly as his mighty armada was destroyed. He gave the signal to withdraw. They would lose no more men and boats today in the service of the Malay sultan. Setting a route to the west, some headed for Sumatran waters where they might rest and recoup, others fled north back to the Laddas. They would return, perhaps tomorrow or the next day – but when they did, Light would be ready for them.

***

Retaliatory raids took place over the following days from an ever-decreasing Illanun fleet until the last of the survivors finally dispersed, pursued by Light's ships for several miles until it was evident that they were departing the region. On April 19, a mere week since the first shot had been fired, the Laksamana of Queddah approached Light's flagship bearing the surrender. The sultan wished to sue for peace.

His terms were robust; Sultan Abdullah held Light entirely responsible for what he deemed an unnecessary assault on a kingdom in the process of negotiation. Queddah would cede Pulau Pinang to the Company for a lease of 10,000 Spanish dollars per annum. Light granted him 6,000. No further commitment to supply Queddah with military aid was included. Food supplies were to be reinstated immediately, nor was any other European nation allowed to trade in Queddah, especially enemies of Britain. The sultan had no option but to agree. Representatives from both sides were tasked with drawing up the treaty to be sent to Calcutta. Ratification would be swift this time. The Honourable Company had what they wanted.

With complete capitulation at such little cost, Francis Light returned to his beloved island, accompanied by his victorious men. The people of Prince of Wales Island, who had watched from their beaches with ever-growing confidence throughout seven days of war, welcomed the conquering heroes in triumphal fanfare. Settlers of all communities lined the streets; services of thanksgiving were held in temples, mosques, and chapels; and an atmosphere of celebration filled the air with expectation and hope for the future.

The superintendent finally headed homewards, bone-tired with weariness. The fervour of battle had gifted him inhuman strength. Now his old bones were paying for it. All he wanted was to curl up with Martinha in his arms, and sleep for days.

It was not to be. The house was oddly quiet, unlike everywhere else on the island. Calling out, suddenly afraid that something untoward had happened in his absence, he was answered by a gale of excited shouts. Mary and William charged down the stairs, followed by Janeke, Lien and a host of servants.

'The baby has arrived!' Mary screamed in delight. 'A little boy! He is so beautiful. So tiny! We have another brother!'

'I'm a big brother now!' announced young William with no other thought than his own, as if his father's return from a cataclysmic battle was nothing to remark.

'And mother?' Light gasped, scarce able to believe that any more blessings could be showered on him. Would there be a price to pay, the worst cost of all?

'Martinha thrives! An easy birth!' Janeke replied with a broad smile, her own little daughter clinging to her hip. 'Come, sir, and meet your little boy!'

With the other children hanging off his arms, Francis entered the stifling bedroom, where servants even now cleared away the debris of childbirth. Martinha was propped up on a bank of pillows, pale but happy, a tiny boy suckling fiercely at her breast.

'Francis! My love!' she exclaimed. 'Look, we have another

son! My own little Francis! Named for you on account of your great victory!' she added.

Light fell on his knees, the emotions in his breast so powerful he could not speak. So much blood and death and – amidst it all – new life! The baby boy was sturdy and well-formed, a hint of dark curls shading his pink scalp. He fed eagerly, eyes closed in rapturous concentration, snuffling with satisfaction. A vision of the poor Illanun lad with his scarlet coat flashed before him, his young life abruptly ended in someone else's war. Such were the inequities of life; one man leaves too soon, while another is rewarded far beyond his desserts.

When he finally found his voice, as he stroked the downy cheek of his new-born son, Francis whispered. 'It is a good name. My adoptive grandfather's as well as mine own. But the lad must have a second name to distinguish him from his father. I shall call him Lanoon, my little pirate, in remembrance of the fierce Illanun and the many men, warriors all, who will not live to see sons of their own.'

Martinha smiled. 'My little pirate! I fear he may yet live up to his name, for he is already a demanding fellow. Francis Lanoon Light, our little pirate. Welcome to this world. You arrive at the best of times when we look forward to peace.'

'Should God spare us,' added Lady Thong Di, rosary beads in her hands as she prayed for the health of her daughter and new grandchild.

'Indeed, dear Ibu,' Francis replied. 'Today is a good day but we still face many challenges ahead. Yet we have earned the right to enjoy this moment. A glass of something restorative for us all is in order now, don't you think?'

[illegible] pleaded.

[illegible]

When he finally found his voice as he surveyed the [illegible] [illegible] [illegible] [illegible] [illegible] their own.

Meanwhile [illegible] [illegible] the end of times when [illegible]

She [illegible]

Indeed [illegible]

PART FOUR

Between Two Worlds

(1791-1792)

20

Comings and Goings

Prince of Wales Island. Summer 1791

Peace restored; normality returned to Prince of Wales Island within weeks. If Light had feared conflict deleterious for migration and trade, he was happily mistaken. Ships flocked back bringing goods and people in even greater numbers than before, including several visitors of note. Was Calcutta's perspective shifting in the island's favour?

A Company survey ship, the *Carron*, on an expedition to map the east coast of India from Bengal to the Coromandel, ran into fierce monsoon storms that drove the vessel off course, severely damaged. The Andaman Islands lay closest, yet Captain Simpson nevertheless recommended putting into Prince of Wales Island for repairs. Captain Popham, leader of the expedition, agreed. In late May, the *Carron* finally limped into harbour with its exhausted crew.

Home Riggs Popham – who bridled every time his name was mispronounced – ('It's "Hume" not "Home", sir!') was neither archetypal naval officer nor bureaucratic Company official. No sooner had he settled into Government House, he would stride unbidden into Light's private office at any hour, bombarding the superintendent with volleys of questions about the island. Had such an interrogation emanated from any other Calcutta visitor,

Light would have been suspicious. Yet from the start, Popham's curiosity obviously stemmed from his exceptionally inquisitive mind. He was an obsessive, the sort of fellow so engaged in his own thoughts that he was blind to social niceties.

Yet for all Popham's idiosyncrasies, Light grew fond of him. Popham was an original, true to himself and given to complete candour, often to own disadvantage. The superintendent's forbearance was rewarded when, one evening over dinner, Popham made an interesting proposal. Or rather, told Light in no uncertain terms what he intended to do while he was stranded there.

'I cannot bear inactivity, sir,' Popham had remarked. 'Some gentlemen are happy lying in the shade, their days filled with idle pursuits and their nights in drinking and debauchery. While no means disapproving of either, I require mental stimulation quite as much as corporal. Thus, it is my intention, to engage in mapping the island. The Company has commissioned me on a survey; I see no reason not to use my singular abilities for both our benefits during my enforced stay.'

The survey was an outstanding notion. Light gave his blessing, and throughout the month of June Popham sailed the channels surrounding the island, producing detailed and informative charts, discovering a new safe channel, and delivering an excellent map of George Town itself.

Home Popham was a man of an engaging appearance, known for fastidious grooming. His dress was at all times immaculate, his wiry hair well-powdered. But for his overlong nose and fleshy lips, he might even have been called handsome. But his most alluring quality was his passion and curiosity for knowledge. People love to talk about themselves – and Popham loved to listen.

The scholarly naval officer had one weakness, however, that particularly amused Light for its resonance with his own shadier past. Popham had a taste for ambitious 'investment'. The acquisition of money obsessed him quite as much as knowledge. Some of his schemes were scarcely legal, for Popham had no licence from the Company to trade, nor any intention of declaring his interests. In fact, he regarded it as a mark of pride that he had carried contraband right under the noses of the authorities. Inevitably he even attempted to interest Light in one of his more dubious proposals.

Light did not mince his words. 'I cannot approve practices that are illegal. I'm a senior officer of the Company! Please go no further.' But privately he tipped off Scott to Popham's plans, then turned a blind eye to their subsequent collusions. Suffice it to say, by the time Popham sailed off to resume his survey back in India, Light had made an important ally, even friend. And gained some very useful charts.

***

The month of June brought an entire clan whose arrival was intricately connected to Light's personal covert dealings. His pepper plantations had been made possible by Kapitan Khoh's relationship with an Acehnese nobleman, Sayyid Hussain Aidid, whose influence in the trade was substantial. A wealthy merchant in his own right, he had recently been forced out of Achin by rivals, turning his sights instead on the enticing free trade port of Pinang where he had such useful connections. As soon as the peace was declared, he sent envoys seeking permission to settle, with the intention of bringing his company of family, retainers and servants. It was a significant migration in keeping with Light's plan that his emporium was not only for the Company, but for the entire trading networks of the east. He welcomed them with open arms.

No sooner had the family arrived, they settled on a large area of land south of Malay town gifted by the superintendent, soon called Acheen Street. Other migrants from Achin soon flocked to the settlement which speedily established itself as the centre of the Sumatra spice trade. Aidid then began construction on a huge warehouse with jetty, inviting Light to view the construction. After a tour, he entertained the superintendent to a sumptuous lunch in a specially constructed tented pavilion on site.

Seated on a silk divan, Sayyid Hussain Aidid was the very image of an Islamic noble. His manner was gracious, his bearing haughty. He placed himself on equal terms with Superintendent Light and expected special privileges in respect of his high status.

'I am most grateful for the reception you have extended to my family,' he began. 'As I'm sure you understand, my position is quite singular compared to my fellow Muslims. Therefore, it is appropriate I am accorded authority over my people, who must adhere to Islamic law under my supervision alone. Furthermore, as I bring an abundance of trade to the island, I expect sole rights over all my imports and exports, even those pertaining to British monopolies, such as tin and opium, should the goods derive from my personal sources.'

It was an astonishingly highhanded statement of intent. Sayyid Hussain Aidid desired his own kingdom within the British settlement, free from any constraints. Light heard him out, an amiable expression on his face, his instincts on high alert. This man was of great importance – to offend him would be unwise. Yet there was no way he would allow any such indulgence, no more than he would tolerate special licence for European merchants, not even James Scott.

'An interesting request, sir,' Light replied with equanimity. 'Pray give me time to consider it further if you will. I may be the authority on the island, but my position is vice-regal. I must consult Bengal before any such exceptions may be granted. The ultimate decision lies with the governor-general. If it were in my remit, I would have no hesitation. Unfortunately, as a mere servant of the Crown, I must seek permission of my masters, sir.'

The Company had often provided Light with a useful excuse for inaction and prevarication over the years. A lifetime of side-stepping unreasonable demands from local potentates had taught Light well. The matter was never raised again between the two men, although the meeting established a mutual respect that thrived in the months and years ahead. Such was the way of conducting business in the Indies.

***

The arrival in August of two unaccompanied ladies of gentle birth heralded a new type of traveller, British wives on their way to join their husbands in the East. Pinang Island was now considered a safe and secure landing for such gentlewomen. Mrs Elizabeth Beale, a young bride on her way to Macau, and her winsome companion Miss Anna Marie Davis were on the adventure of a lifetime.

The Beales had met in Bath the previous summer; a whirlwind courtship had ensued. Daniel Beale was on a short period of leave from China, where he was one of the most successful young traders of his day, already possessing a fortune in opium, tea, cotton and silk. Once Daniel and Elizabeth had met, they took little time in forming an 'understanding'. Thus, scarcely three weeks from their first introduction, they were married at St Giles' in London. At the age of nine and twenty, Elizabeth did not have time to waste.

Miss Davis was her less fortunate second cousin whose own father had passed away with only bad investments to his name. As it was unthinkable that the new Mrs Beale should travel to Macau unchaperoned, so Anna Marie had seen her opportunity. Even a girl without means might hook herself a decent fellow in the East.

Two days earlier, on as glorious an early morn as one could wish to behold, the East Indiaman *General Coote* under Captain James Baldwin had finally laid anchor in the sunny waters of the island. After a tedious four months at sea to Madras, several weeks on land to recuperate, and then a relative hop, skip and jump to Prince of Wales Island, it was a welcome sight indeed. At last, free from the worry of shipwreck, pirates and hostile natives, under a clear blue sky surrounded by such bounties of verdant nature, Elizabeth and Anna Marie basked in pleasure, twirling their parasols in delight as they stepped onto solid ground.

Miss Davis was looking forward to rekindling an old acquaintanceship. From Madras she had despatched a mail to the office of Superintendent Light, notifying a certain Miss Lydia Hardwick of her imminent arrival. To her delight, the self-same lady was waiting on the jetty.

'My dear Lydia!' Anna Marie gasped. 'How positively wonderful to see you! I can hardly believe our good luck to find you here.' The two women embraced fondly.

Lydia drew back, admonishing her friend playfully. 'You must now address me as Mrs Gray, my sweet friend. It has been my great good fortune to win the heart of the handsome Lieutenant James Gray of the Bengal Marines. Please allow me to introduce him.'

James Gray stepped forward and bowed. There was no denying he was a fine figure of a man; they made a handsome couple. Lydia simpered as they made their introductions, her desire to flaunt her 'catch' impossible to hide.

'Dear Elizabeth, what a delight!' Lydia continued in her effusive fashion. 'Or rather Mrs Beale as I must call you now. We're so starved of genteel ladies on the island that to have two at once is an unlooked-for abundance! Why, all the gentlemen will be cock-a-hoop, fighting each other to be your escorts! Isn't that so, dear James? There will be no question of your sleeping aboard whilst you're in town. We have a charming cottage nearby. I have prepared a room and a whole list of engagements for your entertainment. Come, the carriage awaits –'

***

Lydia Gray had long awaited such an opportunity when she might parade her new status to her peers. Not that Elizabeth Beale considered herself such. Lydia was a woman of uncertain origins who had joined the 'fishing fleet' to Bengal to find a husband amongst the men of the Honourable Company. As far as Mrs Beale was concerned, she was Anna Marie's friend – never hers. Elizabeth generally looked down her dainty nose when in the presence of little upstarts with no income.

'She's prettier than I remember,' Elizabeth observed critically as they freshened up in their chamber with its charming sea view. A local girl was busying herself unpacking their trunks. 'Better attired these days, I will admit. Although I had thought her younger –' Elizabeth added with more than a hint of malice.

'Lydia was always well favoured, although she has "filled out" somewhat since last we met. As to her age, I believe she is still only eight-and-twenty. What a beautiful dress! How surprising to see such fashions in these remote parts. Lydia always did have expensive tastes, but little money to sustain them,' Anna Marie added ruefully.

Elizabeth shrugged. 'A lieutenant's pay is nothing to shout about. Unless he is involved in his own trade on the side, of course. I believe many of these Company men are quite without scruples.'

'Mrs Beale! Lieutenant Gray is a gentleman. And our generous host!'

Elizabeth rolled her eyes. 'You're too gullible, Anna. You think the best of everyone. Whereas I always think the worst until proven otherwise,' she smirked. 'However, if Lydia Gray and her pretty lieutenant wish to roll out the red carpet on our behalf, who are we to complain? I, for one, will take full advantage – and still retain my opinion that she is nothing but a silly flirt with ideas above her station.' With that, the subject was closed.

A few days later the three ladies were lingering over breakfast, nursing the adverse effects of a late night at cards where they had imbibed too freely of a fine ruby port. It had been a heady evening, due not only to the wine; the gentlemen who had made up their table had been most entertaining. There was much to reminisce about over morning tea, especially the matter of one Captain James Hamilton who had appeared most taken with Miss Davis. He had been by her side during all their recent social events.

An unexpected caller disturbed their frivolity. Although decently attired, the ladies had not yet completed their toilette. Yet the guest was of such importance it was impossible to refuse him admittance. Superintendent Light himself had called in person! Begging his forbearance while they dashed off to find mob caps and shawls, the governor was ushered by a servant into the parlour, where he was served tea. Francis Light amused himself by examining the book titles – mostly lurid romances – and the cherubic ceramic figurine collection. There was no doubt this was Mrs Gray's domain.

A whole shelf was devoted to her collection of musical scores, a carefully bound array of precious manuscripts: Hadyn, Vivaldi, and that new young fellow Mozart to name but a few. She must have carried them lovingly with her across the world, probably the most valuable possession she had once owned. They were a poignant testimony to Mrs Gray's social ambitions. Light imagined that she would love nothing better than to hold regular recital evenings at Government House to display her musical accomplishments to the meek and captive audience of visiting captains. Fortunately, Light smiled to himself, there was not yet a pianoforte on the island. They should be grateful for that singular blessing. Then he immediately chided himself for his unkind thoughts. The girl had forged a life for herself far from the conventions of the world in which she had been born. He of all people should show more consideration for her perseverance and her dreams. Imagine, a young woman who delighted in music and was never able to hear the airs she loved again!

'My apologies, Superintendent Light!' Mrs Gray swept into the tiny parlour, her two guests trotting behind.

'The apologies are all mine, dear ladies,' Light replied, jumping to his feet, replacing the scores carefully. 'It is most unseemly of me to call so early. I'm afraid I've been so long in the East I have forgotten all my manners,' he added with a courteous bow.

'Nonsense, sir!' answered Mrs Gray. 'In India, breakfast is open house for callers. It is we who are shameful slugabeds. In our defence, I must declare that yesterday we spent an evening with my dear husband, Mr Scott, and James Hamilton of the *Dutton*. It ended very late.' Lydia fluttered her eyelashes in her coy fashion. She believed gentlemen found it charming. Light thought it smacked of coquetry.

'Say no more, my dear Mrs Gray. No doubt they kept you gaming until the wee hours quite against your will. I recommend a raw egg for your heads this morning,' he replied with a twinkle in his eyes. 'I shall not keep you long. It is my habit to walk the beach of a morning before I am tied to my desk for the rest of the day, so I took the opportunity to call personally with an invitation for tomorrow, by which time I hope you are all well recovered.

'You've already entertained us most graciously at Government House, sir!' Mrs Beale replied. 'We do not wish to occupy more of your valuable time!'

Light gave them a benign smile. Despite having reached middle age, he still enjoyed paying court to ladies. 'To tell the truth, dear ladies, there is nothing I would rather do than escape my duties and spend a day at leisure in your genial company. The pleasure is all mine, I assure you. This time I plan a somewhat different entertainment. What say you to a picnic at my garden house on the Suffolk estate?'

'A picnic? What fun!' Mrs Gray clapped her hands.

'*Quelle divertissement*!' Mrs Beale added, while Miss Davis wriggled with glee.

'An early start is in order, so be ready tomorrow at dawn for the adventure to begin. We must make the most of the day – it isn't often we have the pleasure of entertaining English ladies. I fear Mrs Gray lives a very solitary existence these days amongst us rough fellows!'

The three women waved goodbye to Superintendent Light who set off up the beach back to Government House. Life in the East was certainly living up to their wildest expectations.

'What a fine gentleman!' observed Mrs Gray. 'It's a great pity he did not marry when he was a young man as I dare say he would have made a good husband. How unfortunate he became embroiled with his Malay woman. One cannot fault his loyalty, however. Most men would have cast aside a native mistress in favour of a decent woman once they made their way in the world.' The other women agreed. Too many good men had been distracted by the charms of the dusky maidens of the Indies – but who could blame them? The poor fellows had spent years alone far from home. In future English women would make sure that gentlemen did not have to look elsewhere for wives.

***

In the cool of the early morning a merry party set out by chaise from the Grays' residence, the ladies escorted by the gentlemen they laughingly nicknamed 'the three Jamies' – Gray, Hamilton and Baldwin. The Grays travelled in the first carriage, James Hamilton with Miss Davis in the second, leaving Mrs Beale and the reticent Captain Baldwin as awkward companions in the third.

It was the best time of day in the tropics: warmth without humidity, bright sun without the burning heat of noon, air fresh and fragrant. The journey was a pleasant – if somewhat bumpy – ride, necessitating James Hamilton to lend his arm in support to Anna Marie lest she be discomforted, and Elizabeth Beale and Captain Baldwin to take great pains to prevent an accidental touch.

The outside world soon disappeared as they took the track out of town. A roof of trees encircled them, dappling the sunlight in green shadow. It was cooler in the shade although a soft wetness permeated the air, for the forest canopy prevented the sun from full penetration. It was far from quiet, however. As well as the rattle and jangle of the carriages, strange sounds emanated from amidst the trees: shrieks, calls, scuttling noises, and the occasional crash. Anna Marie tightened her grip on Baldwin's arm; Elizabeth Beale struggled not to do the same to her companion.

'Do not worry, ladies,' Lieutenant Gray announced. 'The forest is alive with life, but we are not in any danger. One soon becomes accustomed to such sounds. It is but a short way.'

True to his word, within a few minutes the trees gave way to a wide clearing where they came upon a rudimentary bridge busy with activity, Superintendent Light at the helm. Like an army on the move, a huge throng of servants was patiently filing across the stream, laden with goods: tables, chairs, couches and beds, boxes of utensils and glassware, crates of food, table coverings and curtains. Livestock was herded in the rear. It was the preparations for their little 'picnic'.

'Good morning, everyone! You're the first to arrive. The others are on their way. Let me lead you to my little garden house where refreshments are waiting,' announced Francis Light with a flourish.

The final part of the journey was on foot. Despite the well-trodden path, the rough terrain (now splattered here and there with dung) played havoc with the delicate satin of the ladies' shoes, requiring them to hop from tussock to tussock. The thought of what might lurk in the undergrowth gave them much consternation. But it was not far, and soon they found themselves in farmland, although it did not yield any crops that they could recognise. Anna Marie enquired of the gentlemen what manner of produce was being grown, eager as ever to give them the opportunity to show off their knowledge to the ladies. It was the first rule of courtship: let a man talk.

'Spices in the main,' explained Lieutenant Gray. 'Of course, there are the usual vegetable crops, but the plan for this estate is to grow the spices that are the lifeblood of the eastern trade. No longer will we buy from the Dutch or the foreigners. Light plans to steal the trade from under their noses and make Penang the central emporium for pepper, nutmeg, and the rest. These are newly planted. It will take some years before full potential is realised.'

Although the ladies feigned polite interest in the ingenuity of the superintendent, by then they were more interested in a cool drink and a shady chair. The heat was rising as the morning advanced; their chintz gowns were wilting in the humidity. With great relief they finally arrived at their destination, a large meadow at the centre of which stood a Malay pavilion raised on stilts. A cultivated cottage garden had been laid out, a charming anomaly aside the wild, untamed nature of the encircling forest. In this extraordinary retreat, breakfast was being prepared.

The cottage was tolerable enough, if rather native in design. The roof was thatched, the house itself of wood. Inside, a lofty space had been divided into three sections by hastily erected curtains of sail cloth. The servants were busily setting out furniture, for the house was usually left empty, such was the rapid decay typical of the jungle environment. If they left it furnished, everything would be mouldy or devoured by insects on their return, or so the superintendent informed them.

The guests left the servants to their tasks and took refuge outside on sofas placed under an awning where the ladies were served tea. The gentlemen strolled about chatting. There were ten for breakfast, the ladies outnumbered three to one. Mrs Gray pronounced it the perfect social ratio, particularly for Miss Davis. Anna Marie blushed but did not argue. Although fond of Captain Hamilton, she had no intention of giving her heart away just yet. Perhaps she might do better than a mere East Indiaman captain if she bided her time? There were other gentlemen present whose acquaintance she had not yet made.

'It would appear that the business of the fort and administration has been abandoned for the day,' observed Mrs Beale. 'Mr Light has invited all the senior men, I think?'

Lydia Gray nodded her assent. 'Quite a worthy gathering to be sure. It indicates the respect in which the superintendent holds you.'

Elizabeth shrugged. 'Perhaps,' replied the shrewd Mrs Beale. 'But I rather think Mr Light is eager to make a good impression. After all, my husband is an important China merchant.'

'You are most discerning, Mrs Beale. The island's reputation suffered much in the recent conflict with the heathens. It is very important that Prince of Wales Island shows its best face to visitors. But I assure you both, this is no charade. The island is an exceptionally benign place – both in climate and society.'

'Undoubtedly, dear Lydia,' broke in Anna Marie. 'May I inquire who the two young gentlemen are?' First things first, she thought to herself.

'The young tousle-haired fellow with the pleasant face is Mr Thomas Pigou of Calcutta. But he is spoken for. He has an understanding with the daughter of a prominent Bengal businessman, together with a Javanese mistress, Ady Bonsu, here on the island. They have children, I believe.'

The two ladies fluttered their fans to hide their blushing amusement while Mrs Gray continued knowledgeably. 'The young man with the superintendent hails from a family of great note. He is Thomas Baring, eldest son of Mr Francis Baring of Baring Brothers, a senior Company Director. The Barings are financiers with fingers in every mercantile pie across the world. Young Thomas has been sent to Calcutta to learn the trade at first hand. His visit to our island suggests that there is interest in its prospects, even amongst the most eminent of investors. As you may imagine, the superintendent is courting him assiduously.'

Anna Marie glanced over at Thomas Baring, apprising him thoroughly. 'He is so very young, though,' she reflected thoughtfully.

The other two chuckled. 'Far too young for you, my dear,' Elizabeth Beale commented meanly. 'He is a mere boy, not yet twenty. And when he does come of age to wed, it will not be to the likes of you. His father will make sure of an heiress, if not a Duchess!'

Anna Marie's eyes returned to Captain Hamilton, remarkably handsome in his white jacket and black stock, auburn curls glinting in the sunlight. James Hamilton had the look of the buccaneer about him despite his gentle nature, the very image of the daredevil Baron Trench from the popular novel she so admired, but without the scurrilous behaviour.

Across the room, Superintendent Light was deep in conversation with Thomas Baring, for whom this gathering was intended if the truth be told. Since the young man had graced Government House with his presence on a short visit, there had been numerous formal banquets and receptions. Today Light wished to show the young man a different aspect of the island.

'Your plan to gain a monopoly of the spice trade is inspired, sir.' Thomas Baring was impressed. 'My father has a maxim that a successful man plays the long game. He will be most taken with your venture. I dare say that one day this island may be known as much for its agriculture as its port!'

The boy was still inexperienced, but with enough of his father's business acumen to appreciate its potential. 'You are perceptive, sir. Most are greedy for short term advantage.' Light was a past master at charm.

Thomas blushed. 'My father is a strict taskmaster. He has no patience with sons who live off their father's endeavour. I fully intend to make my own way in his company.' Light suppressed a smile. How many young men stood to inherit a company as prosperous as Barings?

'He is most wise. I would expect no less of a man of his vision. Your father may also be interested to learn that we shall soon be trading in the products of our own mines. Tin has been discovered, a promising load!'

Thomas looked about with obvious admiration. 'This is a beautiful place, a veritable Garden of Eden. To have such native forest on the edges of the settlement, such glorious verdant mountains towering above and the far-off vistas of the sea, is a precious jewel indeed. I'm afraid Calcutta is so sprawling and crowded and nature so distant a prospect that we need pleasure gardens to remind us of the flora and fauna of Bengal!'

Light smiled. 'Everywhere begins as wilderness, sir. Calcutta was once a tiger-infested marsh. I have many plans for Prince of Wales Island, not all mercantile. On this estate of mine, named Suffolk in memory of my home county, there shall one day be a great house with deer park. Yet I wish for Pinang to keep its pristine nature and bounteous charms. It would be an injustice to destroy it.'

***

After a hearty breakfast, the party visited the spice gardens at closer hand. As the day neared the meridian, however, the fierce heat and humidity drove them all indoors to seek shade. The superintendent had thoughtfully laid out the two small inner 'rooms' for the use of the ladies to rest and refresh, supplied with couches and cool water in terracotta jars for bathing. The gentlemen napped on cots in the dining room. For the next few hours, the little garden house was silent, other than the sonorous snoring of its occupants.

By the mid-afternoon, refreshed, bathed and ready for dinner, the jollities were resumed. Tables held a lavish spread accompanied by fine wines and sparkling conversation. The visitors complimented the food, remarking that it was far better than the tables of Madras and quite equal to Calcutta. After dinner, due to the location and the size of the company, the ladies did not withdraw. Instead, the men passed around hookahs.

'Come, dear Miss Anna,' said James Hamilton. 'Pray take a turn!' Encouraged by the rest, Miss Davis tentatively tested it, only to find herself spluttering and coughing, tears streaming down her cheeks. Her attentive companion insisted she take the fresh air to recover.

'The pipe has made me quite nauseous,' she exclaimed. 'Fresh air would be ideal!' As they slipped out of the door, their companions exchanged grins. No one was in any doubt of their real intentions.

When the picnic finally broke up, the day's amusements were still not at an end. Lieutenant Mylne was hosting a ball in their honour. In a defile worthy of an imperial triumph, the party, servants and accoutrements were carried back to George Town, a night of dancing and carousing still ahead.

Francis Light politely declined the invitation. The day, although fruitful, had worn him out. Yet with Mr Baring, a host of merchant captains and the wife of a prosperous merchant of Macau, the festivities had been worth the trouble and cost incurred. Prince of Wales Island was proclaiming itself to the world as an emporium of great significance, the very centre of high society in the Indies.

21

Thoughts of Home

Government House, Prince of Wales Island. January 1792

Only the month before, his spirits had been high. The discovery of sizeable tin deposits and a rare native species of nutmeg together with the thriving spice plantations offered a future as a centre of production as well as trade. Martinha had been delivered safely of a healthy baby son. In every quarter by which such things are measured, Prince of Wales Island was entering a golden era. It was only a matter of time before Bengal gave its blessing to raise its status to Company establishment.

With this in mind, Light resubmitted proposals for an independent judiciary, a reconstruction for Fort Cornwallis, and plans for an Anglican cathedral, assured that the tide was in their favour. The population now surpassed 10,000 souls, significant for a settlement only six years old. A larger administration and greater investment would enable the superintendent to delegate many responsibilities and enjoy the fruits of his endeavours.

As the new year dawned, even more good news arrived. Events in India and Europe paved the way for greater security in the region from which Prince of Wales Island could only benefit. The intelligence came straight from the horse's mouth, so to speak, brought by a military officer newly arrived from Calcutta.

Lieutenant Norman Macalister was a replacement for William

Mylne, whose sudden death had deprived them of a promising soldier not yet thirty years of age. Macalister was an ambitious young officer whom Light expected to rise quickly, the type of man of action the settlement needed. He was a handsome fellow, whose finely chiselled features gave the impression of nobility, although he had been born on the Isle of Skye, one of fourteen children. With no family connections, Macalister was intent on making the most of the gifts he had been given.

The lieutenant was a forthright fellow especially where his entitlements were concerned. Not long after he first assumed his office as commissary of stores, he asked to for an audience with the superintendent.

'Good day, sir,' he began briskly. 'It's good of you to see me at short notice.'

'My pleasure, lieutenant. Please take a seat. I've been meaning to welcome you personally. I trust you've settled in well?' Light opened in a friendly manner to set the young man at ease. Macalister took a seat, smoothing down his impeccable uniform. He would not have looked amiss at a Council meeting in Calcutta.

'Indeed, sir. My quarters are quite sufficient for my needs at present. Yet I find myself somewhat discommoded by certain obstacles. To be master of all military equipment is an onerous responsibility. I'm sure you agree that the fort must be fully equipped, and the disposition of goods carefully controlled. My position is vital to the day-to-day running of the fort. Is that not so, sir?'

It was not the most diplomatic of openers for an officer to his superior. Light sighed internally. Young men, these days! Surely, he was not expected to oversee every minor grievance. The lieutenant had been on the island five minutes and was already laying down his terms of office. Yet, as he had asked the young man how he fared, he chose to reply with the courtesy Macalister had lacked.

'I would agree, sir. An army does indeed march on its stomach, so they say. In what way exactly do you find yourself discommoded?'

Macalister launched into what was obviously a prepared speech. 'In the present circumstances, it is difficult to render the service to which I am honour-bound. My staff is negligible, nothing but a wet-behind-the-ears corporal and a few untrustworthy sepoys, whom I suspect of feathering their own nests by pilferage. I cannot watch them every hour of the day, nor am I able to dismiss them – I am shorthanded enough as it is. Furthermore, I must draw your attention to the matter of my emolument. It is far less than I expected and insufficient for my needs. I pray you will assist in correcting these issues so that I might execute my office in the manner it deserves.'

An orderly poured out cups of tea, affording Light time to take a sip and consider his reply. Was Macalister guilty of insubordination or naivety? He chose to give the young man the benefit of the doubt.

'You share similar problems with mine own, lieutenant. Or may I address you as Norman?' A curt nod gave assent, deftly reaffirming Light's seniority. 'Since its foundation, our administration has constantly lacked two essentials: men and money. Every member of my staff – including myself – is insufficiently rewarded for his efforts. We labour long hours for low pay, each doing the work of several. I understand your predicament. Permit me to write to Bengal on the matter of your salary. As to the paucity of reliable men, I will ask Captain Glass if he can spare a few reliable fellows.'

Macalister was mollified. 'My thanks, Superintendent Light. Your reputation for fairness prompted my visit today and you have proven equal to it. I hope I did not cause offence. It was never my intent. I hold you in the highest regard, sir.'

Light smiled. 'Nor did I receive it as criticism. For all its blessings, Prince of Wales Island is a continual challenge. What news do you bring, Norman? We're always months behind out here in the back of beyond.' First-hand accounts of current happenings were eagerly seized upon. Light imagined that Macalister was the sort of fellow who kept himself well informed.

The lieutenant brightened up. 'The news from Europe is dominated by the French. Their kingdom is in ruins. The revolutionary dogs have proclaimed themselves a Republic and are holding the royal family prisoner in the Tuileries. Austria and Prussia, in respect of the queen being the sister of the emperor, have already all but declared war. It is only a matter of time until every kingdom in Europe follows suit. The very lives of the royal family of France are at stake!'

The full extent of the deterioration between the French people and its monarchy was a shock to Light. This was a turn of events significant even for the Indies. A king sneezes in Europe and the other side of the world catches a cold.

'A travesty!' Light exclaimed. 'Yet it plays right into our hands. The Dutch will have to mind their manners now the French have quite taken themselves out of the reckoning, both here and in India. It's an ill wind, sir, that blows nobody good. Not that I take any pleasure in the fate of King Louis and his family. It is a monstrous act,' Light added in case his elation appeared too indelicate.

Macalister, however, was more sanguine, but then he was a Scotsman. 'A lesson to all absolute monarchs to watch their step, I'll warrant. The Council is delighted to have the French off their backs at last. But there is more good news. That devil Tipu Sultan is now on the run. Without French assistance, the Tiger of Mysore is reduced to a mere meddlesome kitten. He will soon be declawed for good.'

'Capital!' Light exclaimed. 'It will increase the China trade ten-fold now that our rivals are reduced. This calls for a toast, despite the early hour. What say you to a wee dram, sir?' Macalister revealed his Gaelic soul in the gleam of pleasure that lit his pale blue eyes.

'Many thanks, sir. It's been far too long since I imbibed a glass of the water of life!'

Glasses were raised. 'James Scott assures me this is a particularly fine blend. He ensures we are well supplied here on the island where Scots men abound. *Slàinte mhath,* Lieutenant Macalister! Here's to our future prosperity and your contributions to it!

***

Although good tidings of the British victory at Seringapatam confirmed the end of hostilities with Mysore, the news was accompanied by an announcement that dashed Light's hopes. Hot on the heels of Tipu Sultan's surrender, came word of the appointment of Major Alexander Kyd as Superintendent of Port Cornwallis on Greater Andaman Island, the new British establishment in the Indies. The choice had finally been made by the governor-general with the backing of his brother, Commander William Cornwallis, who now declared himself in favour of a naval base closer to home. Prince of Wales Island was thus permanently relegated to the rank of trading emporium. It was a devastating blow made even worse by the knowledge that he had been superseded by men he regarded friends. Could Kyd and Cornwallis not at least have forewarned him?

The decision changed everything. There would be no further investment. The fort would not be rebuilt. An independent judiciary was no longer possible. The island administration would be required to struggle on underfunded, undermanned and undersupplied. Light's spirits plummeted to a depth of disillusionment he had rarely experienced. Never a man to dwell on failure, picking himself up from misfortune time and time again, he had always trusted that he would find a way through to reach his goal.

Yet here he was, a man in his fifties, facing the truth: his achievement had proved hollow. Fate had had the last laugh after all.

For some years now Francis Light had pondered the question of his future. His role as superintendent had ground him down, his constitution weakened by regular bouts of fever. Only ambition had sustained him. The recent betrayal was the last straw, the Company spurning his vibrant port for a chain of desert islands. No longer did he possess the inner strength to climb back up the mountain, nor did the towering peak hold anything worth striving for.

He had but two options: to spend his remaining days as a Company minion or retire back home a would-be nabob in the old tradition. Only one was realistic. He must ensure his children's future. There was nothing on the island for his girls; they would either remain in Calcutta or return to England with their future husbands. As for his sons, an English education was requisite. Even should they wish to establish careers in the East, without a good school and a military commission, the stain of their mixed race would prejudice their chances. They must be regarded as British gentlemen through and through. That necessitated an English upbringing.

His own mother Mary had also been much upon his mind of late. By his reckoning, she was over seventy now. Imagine her joy to be reunited at last with her long-lost son and family! The more he thought on that dream of home, the more he realised it was what he desired above all else. Yet, what brought him peace would cause his wife sorrow. How could he ask Martinha to leave the Indies for ever? What of her mother? Could he himself tolerate to lose Soliman, Scott and all the other friends and acquaintances he had known and loved these many years?

In the end, it would be the children who decided it. He had no wish to send them away to experience the loneliness he had known himself. The dream of a return to Suffolk, his boys in school nearby, his daughters married to local gentlemen, and a long and uneventful old age tending his manor house, grew more alluring every day. He had made his name in the world, even if it had not made him happier. The past years had broken him, although he would never admit it to another soul. Nor was it only a matter of his health and vigour. His fortune had been squandered in the process. It was time to acknowledge that his day was done – and to retire gracefully.

***

His first hurdle was Martinha. Before he did aught else, she must be party to his intentions. One evening after dinner, he asked her to walk with him on the beach. As they set out along the sand, the sun was a deep orange blush, day's end nigh. A breeze stirred over the water, ruffling his hair and the skirts of her sarong. Grey clouds frothed over the mountains of the distant mainland. There would be rain before too long.

As they walked hand-in-hand, Francis revealed what had been on his mind of late. After a tentative opener, he relaxed and honestly revealed his wishes. Martinha's response was wholly unexpected. He had expected tears, or at the very least some opposition. Forsaking the Straits for his cold northern land would demand great sacrifices of her. Yet she took the matter in her stride, even expressing approval for his decision.

'I do not know how I shall fare in England or if your people will accept me, but that is not significant. If our children remain near for the rest of my life, then there is no other choice. Sending the girls to India has been a great trial. The notion of the boys going to England alone and never seeing them for years is more than I can bear. I dread the day when William must leave. That we might shortly follow him is more than I dared hope! Francis, you have done far more than your duty here on Pinang, yet your reward has been abandonment. This island has cost you much;

to continue this workload will ruin your health and fortune. It is time for us to leave. I am wholly in agreement.'

They had reached the boulders at the far limit of the strand that separated them from the rest of the bay now that the tide was in. Seated on a flat-topped rock, they looked out to sea, Francis idly skimming pebbles, Martinha watching tiny crabs scurrying for their holes. There was a peace in the moment now the decision had been taken.

At last, Martinha ventured: 'My only concern is mother. I cannot ask her to sail with us, although I cannot bear to leave her behind. Would she be content to stay on Pinang with Felipe? There's no question of returning to Ujung Salang. Siam is a troubled place, and her sisters are both aging; they will soon be gone. She knows few people there now. Mother has done so much for us. We cannot abandon her!' Thong Di was yet another mother who had placed her child's needs above her own. Light's list of debts grew longer every day.

'If she agrees to travel with us, she would be at the heart of our family in England as she has always been here. My mother would love her! I feel sure they would make unconventional but firm friends. The choice, however, is not ours to make. And if I know your wise mother, she will already have contemplated this turn of affairs. We must trust in her sound judgment.'

It was enough for him that they were of one mind. Together they would find a way equitable to all.

'Leaving Soliman will be very hard,' Martinha murmured. Francis sat back down, wrapping his arms around her as they watched the sun go down, its flames doused beneath the shimmering purple waters of the horizon.

'Soliman has his own family now. As the years have passed, he and I have grown ever apart from each other. Perhaps I should be grateful for that.'

'He still loves you, and you him. Soliman is wiser than his years. He always was. He saw this day coming long before you ever did.' Martinha was right. The boy had always had an uncanny instinct that his place would never be amongst the British, even if his affection for Francis remained undimmed.

Their decision was momentous. On that cool evening before the breaking of another tropical storm, they both came to an understanding that one day this beautiful island would be nothing but a distant memory, their paradise whose serpent never could be tamed.

***

The following evening, Francis and Martinha planned to broach the subject with Lady Thong Di. Circumstances, however, intervened. When Lady Thong Di entered the parlour, she clutched a letter from her elder sister, Lady Chan. Her pale face and watery eyes alerted them to its contents even before she read it out.

My dear sister

It is with great sadness that I send news of the passing of our beloved sister Thao Srisoonthorn Mook, who left this world as quietly as she lived. Her health, as you know, has been poor of late, although she never complained. Our dear sister died in her sleep. There was little suffering. The traditional rites have been conducted. Sister Mook

was a great lady, wise and gentle, who did naught but good in this world. As you know, her daughter is one of the favoured wives of King Rama himself, an honour bestowed in recognition of our action against the Burmese. Lady Mook was overjoyed to hear that a royal son had recently been born; our line now continues as part of the Chakri Dynasty. Few remain now of those we once knew. The world is changing. I feel the shadows drawing in more and more each day. Her loss has made a deep mark upon me. Please visit me soon. Who knows when our time will be done?
Your sister, Chan

'I must go to her, Francis. Her health is also failing, and her spirits are low. Lady Mook was her rock and now she is gone. I fear Chan has little left to live for.' Thong Di spoke with resolution. 'And it is too long since I was home.'

Home. No matter how far away or how many years pass, its place in one's heart remains.

'Lindesay leaves for Mergui in a few days. I shall instruct him to take you there on his way. I'll send gifts. Lady Chan is proud, but her fortunes are much reduced.' Light insisted graciously.

Lady Thong Di sighed deeply as she rose to leave. 'It shall be a pilgrimage as we Christians say. I shall say my farewells to my family, my people, and my homeland. This is my last duty to the past.'

Martinha reached out to catch her arm. 'Do not leave yet, Ibu. What of your own sorrow? You have lost a sister, too. Let us comfort you. Francis, a glass of brandy.'

Thong Di sat down, patting her daughter's hand fondly. 'I lost my sisters long ago in truth. We grew apart and then I went away, never to return. Of course, I am sad. I think of when we were children, girls, then young married women and mothers. Those days are so far away now. Of course, my sister's death brings me great pain. But as one grows old, loss becomes part of life. It is a burden we must accept, the price we pay for being alive. I prefer to cherish what remains. I am blessed in my family! This is where I belong now.'

Both Francis and Martinha paused, aware this was the moment to broach their plans, but reluctant to add to her current woes. The astute lady looked from one to the other, reading their discomfort. 'You wish to tell me something? I can see it on your faces.'

'What if we should one day return to Francis' home in England. Would you accompany us?' Martinha's spoke so softly that her voice was little but a whisper.

Thong Di brushed the tear from her daughter's cheek, the light of understanding dawning in her eyes. 'Oh, sayang! My dear, dear daughter. I have always known that one day you would leave me. Do not distress yourself. From the day you married Francis Light, it was always bound to happen, if he was spared. We've been blessed with many years together, not guaranteed to many. I shall give the matter thought while I am away, but I don't think that I shall sail across the seas with you. My place is on this island with Felipe and his family. I cannot leave my son, for he has much need of me. Someone must stay here to take his corner against those crafty Khohs! And what of all those others who rely on me, like Janeke and her little girl, and all my churchwork? I shall never be alone, even if I shall miss you deeply. To stay here in Pinang with my son will likely be my future. Yours is elsewhere, as it should be. Do not worry on my account.'

Light watched as his wife and daughter embraced amidst tears of joy and sorrow. They were remarkable ladies from a line of women of exceptional character and wisdom. It would be his welcome duty to ensure that they wanted for nothing for the rest of their lives.

***

Prince of Wales Island
30 January 1792

My dear George,
Belated compliments of the season to you and your fine family. We are well, our little 'pirate' Francis Lanoon now established as the ruler of the House, at only nine months old. That such a little Fellow could wield such power, merely on account of his Cherubic Cheeks and Baby Curls! Now that I am older and appreciate the Benefits the Good Lord has given me at last, I have become a most indulgent Father.

As well as my Good Wishes for the year to come, I write with a Proposition. You have always been my most loyal friend, the consequence of which is that I burden you with inconveniences. The time has now come to retire to Suffolk as soon as I may decently extricate myself from the convoluted tentacles of my office. I have been fortunate enough to acquire sufficient wealth to purchase an Estate in the county of my childhood to live out my days surrounded by family and old friends. You mentioned in your last mail of a Property near your estate, Goldsbery Farm? Would you consent to be my agent in its purchase? I am no Nabob, to be sure, but our needs are humble: a manor house with tenanted farmland will suffice.

In the meantime, I shall put right my affairs with my Bankers in Calcutta and London so that when the time comes, all monies may be directed to you to act on my behalf. I trust implicitly in your judgment.

There is one further boon, an even greater responsibility. I can think of no better man suited. My son William is approaching six years old. I wish to send him back to School. Will you consent to be his Patron? Perhaps you could enrol him in the same school that your own sons attended? Your knowledge of these matters is far better than mine. All I know is Woodbridge school. I must confess it would be comforting to know William was housed within those hallowed walls, even if Reverend Ray no longer presides over his boys as he once did. All monies will be provided, including the extra costs you might incur for his upkeep, especially during school holidays.

This imposition will leave me even further in your debt, dear George. I trust the day will come when I may return the many favours owing. Please inform my mother of my intentions. It will ease her burdens to know that we will all be reunited as a family in the not-too-distant future.

Your undeserving but grateful friend,

F. Light

***

The snow lay deep on the ground beneath a lowering grey sky. George Doughty stood at his study window looking out on the frozen world, contemplating the letter he was about to write. He could put it off no longer. Captain Wall was sailing for China on the 15th inst; he would call on the morrow to collect mail for the East. Despite the months that would pass before it reached Francis, the news would wound him deeply. Kindly George already felt grief on his friend's behalf.

With a deep sigh, he settled at his mahogany desk and picked up his quill. Dipping into the brass inkpot, George scraped precisely at the underside of the tip to remove the excess fluid, then applied himself to his task. He prided himself on his exquisite penmanship. The least he could do was create an epistle worthy of the gravity it contained.

Martlesham Hall
5th February 1792

My dear friend Francis
It is with deep sorrow that I write this Letter for I know the great distress it will bring. Would that I might spare this Pain, but Duty and Friendship require this unhappy

service. Your Mother's health began to fail in the final months of the waning year. In December, she caught a chill – the weather was bitter cold – and was subsequently unable to cast it off. We brought her to Martlesham for Christmastide, but she was frail, unlike her hearty self. Despite the ministrations of several fine doctors, including our old school friend James Lynn of Woodbridge, your beloved mother Mary Light passed from this Life to her reward in Heaven on the twenty-third day of the New Year. Her interment took place in Melton the following week. She received the burial service she deserved, attended by a large group of mourners, Testament to the Respect and Affection in which she was held. Her plot lies in a quiet, shady corner of the graveyard where daffodils and lilies will bloom in profusion in the springtime. Your mother always loved her flowers, did she not?

Mary Light was the best of women, loved by all who knew her. We treasure her memory and will tend her monument until you return. In her final days, she spoke of you often. You made her proud indeed.

Deepest condolences from your friend George, Ann and family. Our sympathies and prayers are yours today, and in the future when this Sad Letter finally reaches your distant shores,

Always your devoted friend,
George Doughty

***

Six months after it had been written on a wintry afternoon in Suffolk, the letter from George Doughty, a literal ship in the night crossing his own, landed on the desk of Superintendent Light at Government House on a steamy hot afternoon. Captain Wall handed over the mail bag, then the two men strolled over to the family home for a few glasses of wine. Wall could not linger, however, for his time in port was short. He would be back around Christmastide on his return from China. Then he would be honoured to escort young William safely back to Suffolk. Only after the captain had departed did Light remember his mail was still at Government House. It would keep until the morning, he decided, unknowingly allowing himself one last night of peace.

The next day left him numb with shock, insensitive to feeling. His mother was gone. When Sir William had died, Light had howled with rage, but the death of his mother brought him to a very different place. He could not cry. The cruel ache of grief became a physical pain akin to the severing of a limb. Francis had last seen Mary Light almost thirty years before. They had been apart much longer than they had been together. Yet the inexplicable bond between a mother and her child was still strong. Mary may not have born him, but in the warmth of her bosom his earliest memories had been made. He still recalled her singular smell, a yeasty tang of bread dough, honest sweat and lavender oil. For hours he sat in silent contemplation of the woman whose sacrifices had allowed him the freedom to be the man he had become. She had never made demands upon him. How heedless he had been in his disregard!

All the while when he had been dreaming of his return, his poor mother had been cold in her grave. When he had written letters to

George about the purchase of a property, there had already been no chance for her to meet his family, nor for him to care for her in the twilight of her days. That he might be too late for that final reunion had never even crossed his mind, as thoughtless as ever to any needs but his own. It had been his unfathomable good fortune in life to be surrounded by the benevolence of those who loved him, a quality he had not extended to them. He was a selfish man.

The loss of Mary Light only stiffened Light's resolve to return home. Life was short. He would wait no longer. As soon as William was dispatched, he would resign his superintendency and make the arrangements for their journey home. The family would travel via Calcutta to collect their daughters, and together they would begin their new life. Kneeling at Mary's grave surrounded by his wife and children to pay homage to her life was the only way that he might now honour his mother's sacrifices.

22
Sea Change

The Duke of Buccleugh, Indian Ocean. February 1793

William Light stood on tiptoe gazing out over an endless sea under a cloud-scattered firmament, his face a study in bewilderment. The little boy was six years old – almost seven, as he reminded everyone – so not at all a baby. Yet in the depths of his despair, it was all he could do not to weep like baby Frannie. The *Buccleugh* was a busy vessel, crew members falling over each other, yet the little boy felt entirely alone, adrift amidst an empty ocean. Never in his life had he been separated from those he loved, not even for a moment. Now every wave pulled him further from all that was familiar. One day, many months hence, he would find himself on the other side of the world. It was beyond his childish comprehension.

Night times were the worst. William had a small cabin to himself, little more than a store cupboard, but better than most aboard were afforded. He had never slept alone in his life. His *amah* had always slept on a pallet by his bed, climbing in with him if he was disturbed by nightmares. The absence of any living soul terrified him. In his bunk, the ship lurching and creaking about him, the dark closed in, bringing its horrors. The intense black, deeper than any night he had experienced in their beach front home under the stars, conjured up all manner of imaginings.

What if he were to drown at sea, his parents believing him safe in Suffolk all along? What if they never arrived to join him? Mayhap the children in his new school would refuse to befriend him? Would Mr Doughty be a harsh guardian? What did snow feel like? If those worries were not enough to disturb the little boy, also came the night terrors: sea monsters and witches, ghosts and spirits, all lurking in the bowels of the vessel, waiting to take his soul. Fed on a diet of scary tales by servants at home, his imagination was primed to run riot. At such times, William's only comfort was a faded scrap of his mother's old sarong, slipped into his pocket whilst saying her last farewells. Her familiar scent still clung to the soft, worn fabric, its feel reminiscent of the soft touch of her gentle hands. William rubbed his cheek against the cloth for reassurance and then, rocked by the waves, her sweet voice in his memory, he would finally drift off.

Several months before, when his parents had first informed him that he would be sent away to school in England, William had initially rejoiced. His three older sisters were already in Calcutta at school. Now it was his turn to leave childhood behind and have his own adventure. The notion of going back to England, that magical land from where all great things originated – or so it seemed to him – set him even above his sisters. As the eldest son, he was to receive an education so that he could become a gentleman and do great things to enhance the family name.

While his grandmother and his mother had wept at the thought of being separated, he had been embarrassed at their fretting, wishing they would stop stroking his hair and kissing his cheeks. There had been times he had lain in bed dreaming of departure, hardly able to wait the many weeks, crossing off each day as it passed. At the jetty on the day itself, even his father had been visibly moved, awkward in his formality, tell-tale tears shining in his eyes. William had attributed that mostly to his father's state of health. Throughout late November and early December, he had been ill again, suffering from the fevers that gripped him every year. Sometimes Father had been barely lucid, rambling nonsense about people he had known in Suffolk and how he had felt when he first went to sea. Perhaps he was still not fully recovered, and his weakened state had rendered him mawkish.

When that final day arrived and William stood ready in his new clothes, his trunk packed and loaded, reality dawned, for which he was entirely unprepared. The family escorted him to the jetty and handed him to Captain Wall, who chucked his chin and told him what a fine lad he was, a born sailor like his father, while little Frannie cried. His mother and his grandmother were there, as well as Janeke and Anneke, Felipe and Lien, and all the other members of the household. It was as if the entire island had turned out to say farewell, the better to remind him of what he was about to lose. There had not been a dry eye as his father swung him up and planted a kiss upon his forehead. 'Be a good boy always, William. Make us proud, as I know you will. Mr Doughty is a fine fellow who will treat you with kindness. The same for Captain Wall. They will be your parents now until we join you in Suffolk. Please God it will not be long until we are reunited as a family again!'

In a reedy voice, suddenly close to tears himself, William had whispered in his father's ear. 'How long?' For some indefinite time, he would be alone, surrounded by strangers who, even if well-meaning, were alien to him.

Francis hugged him close. 'I cannot say, dear boy, but it will be as soon as we can arrange it. The time may seem long to a little boy, but it will pass. In the meantime, your life will be full of adventures, new friends, exciting challenges. Days will quickly turn to weeks and the months will pass.'

'Months?' William repeated, unsure exactly how long a month was. It was thirty days, that much he knew, but he wasn't sure he could imagine the length of thirty days. It was an eternity – and his father had said 'months'.

'Don't be sad, my sweet little man,' his father replied, a break in his own voice. 'The journey will be very long – five or six months. At least a year may pass before we see you again. Chin up, Willie! Think only of the day when we are all together, your sisters too. How merry that shall be!'

That was when the tears finally came. William had lowered his head to his father's shoulder and sobbed silently, clinging on as if he refused ever to let go. Thomas Wall stepped in, prising the little boy away, and hoisting him in hefty arms. 'Come on, lad, dry those tears. You're a young man now, on your way in the world. Show your best face to your parents.'

'Write, Willie!' Francis shouted as they made for the launch. 'Captain Wall will dispatch letters as soon as he is able. Draw pictures of all you see!'

As William watched his world disappear beneath the horizon as the ship ploughed ever westwards, he thought of home. What was happening now? Did his mother still cry? Had little Frannie walked yet? Was Nenek sad that he was no longer there to make her laugh?

'There you are, William! I've been searching the ship for you!'

It was Thomas Wall, his cheery smile looming up before William's pinched face. 'What say you to a trip to my cabin where we might compose a note to your parents? I can help you with the letters and you can draw some of your fine sketches. We never know when a passing ship appears to carry it back to the Straits! I want to have it ready to send.'

William rose to his feet hesitantly accepting the proffered hand readily enough. He liked Thomas Wall. The captain was a kindly man with sons of his own back in Suffolk, boys he barely saw from year to year. Captain Wall understood what it was like to be apart from those he cared about. William was grateful for the offer of help, for he had been worrying the issue of how to write a letter.

As they made their way towards the captain's quarters, they came across Lieutenant and Mrs Gray on their morning walk. William did not much like Mrs Gray, who was intolerant of children. She gave the impression that their very presence was an annoyance, despite having once been a schoolteacher herself.

'Good morning, captain! What an excellent day! We seem to be making good time,' Lieutenant Gray exclaimed, ruffling up William's curls. 'How are you, young fellow?'

'Well, sir,' William answered politely, trying his best to be 'good' in the presence of adults, as his parents had instructed.

'Good man,' James Gray replied. The lieutenant was not adept with children, although friendly enough.

'I hope William isn't wasting your time, captain,' Lydia Gray observed snippily. 'You should be over this nonsense by now, child. Why, boys not much older than you are sent to sea with the Navy and are expected to do the duties of an officer, never mind lollygagging around the deck holding the captain's hand like a little baby!'

James Gray suppressed a wince. It was harsh of her, yet he agreed with the general sentiment. A child should learn to toughen up. Poor Lydia had such high expectations of children! It was a misfortune that they had not yet been blessed. She would make an excellent mother. The presence of little William was a constant reminder of their disappointment.

Thomas Wall could not hide his disapproval, quick to defend the boy. 'The lad has been a little trooper, ma'am. I am merely taking him to my cabin where we will compose a letter to his parents.'

Lydia tutted. 'A big boy like you should be able to write home on your own. Do you think the captain has nothing else to do other than pander to your needs? Are you slow with your letters, William? You must work harder. Fie, sir, leave him with me. I will ensure he is well instructed. It would seem his own mother has not ensured that he is literate, but then it is unsurprising. I doubt she is able to read ...'

'My mother *can* read, Mrs Gray. And she writes a beautiful hand. In many languages, as well as English.' William flared up at what he took – quite correctly – to be a criticism of his beloved mother. He was generally a reserved boy but possessed a fiery streak if he perceived injustice. And as most boys, he was particularly sensitive about his mother, especially at this time.

'Then you must work harder so that you might do the same,' Lydia retorted, not to be outdone by a child. 'Come to my cabin later and I shall begin your instruction.'

William pulled a face, about to voice his refusal in what

would surely be defiance. Captain Wall stepped in before the boy thoroughly blotted his copybook. He did not want William further distressed when his homesickness was still so raw.

'It's no hardship, Mrs Gray. I enjoy spending time with young William for I greatly miss my sons. He's excellent company. Please do not trouble yourself, for he is a fine scholar and requires little assistance. Come, boy. Let's go below. Lieutenant Gray, Mrs Gray – enjoy your walk ...' Wall bundled William down the companionway, muttering: 'Don't worry, lad, I'll keep Mrs Airs-and-Graces at a distance. That's all you need, lessons from her of a morning. Enough to make a boy jump over the side ...'

William giggled as the captain tapped his nose for secrecy. 'Keep this between me and you, lad. I don't want to get on the wrong side of the Grays. We'll be stuck on this boat with them for months, so we must keep cordial relations. But don't worry. I won't let her spoil your voyage with hours of schooling. You'll get plenty enough of that when you're back in England. Now, what shall we tell your father? Perhaps we should mention that school of porpoises we observed the other day? That would make a fine sketch for your mother, too ...'

***

The presence of the Grays on the *Duke of Buccleugh* was a last-minute occurrence which had seemed to Light and Martinha an act of God. Anxious as they were how William would fare on the long voyage surrounded by strangers, it seemed fortuitous that two familiar faces would join the passengers. William knew them both well enough and, although Lydia was hardly the ideal chaperone, she was an experienced governess. Furthermore, James Gray was a decent officer and keen to win Light's favour, so even Martinha felt reassured to know that they would be aboard with him.

To be granted permission for an extended trip home was a rare occurrence for an officer of Gray's lowly rank. A few months in Madras or Calcutta was deemed sufficient unless a commission was resigned. In the normal run of things, Lieutenant Gray would not have been accorded the privilege.

It was not lost on Francis Light that Gray had taken advantage of the superintendent's state of mind to secure this privilege, no doubt prompted by his calculating wife. Lieutenant Gray had approached him with his unusual request when his own judgment had been impaired by a combination of concern for the boy and the aftermath of his recent illness that left him muddled and incoherent at times, easily open to manipulation.

'I trust you are much recovered from your recent ill health, sir,' James Gray had begun when he visited him during his convalescence.

'Better, but not fully on my feet yet. This damn ague has me in its grip. It gets worse each time. Try not to age, Gray. Everything is ten times more troublesome!' Light grunted in reply, attempting humour despite his obvious discomfort.

'I shall not keep you long, sir. I know you need your rest. There is a boon I must ask of you, one that might be of personal value. A *quid pro quo*, as it were?'

Light eyed him up. His head was muzzy, but his acuity undimmed. What was Gray going on about? 'To the point, sir? What exactly can you do for me, and I for you?'

Gray attempted a smile that was more of a grimace. 'I seek

permission to return to England for a short spell. My financial affairs are currently deranged due largely to my absence. The matter of a legacy from an elderly unmarried uncle who passed away a few years ago. More rapacious members of my family desire to take the will to the courts to prise away my inheritance.'

It was an odd story, probably more imaginative fabrication than genuine explanation. Gray doubtless lived beyond his means (who did not on their inadequate Company allowances?) while Lydia Gray made demonstrably expensive demands on his pocket. Whatever he meant by 'settle his deranged affairs', Light suspected that the rapacious member of the family was most likely Gray himself, desperate to winkle out some family money to keep himself afloat.

'I believe you are about to send dear William home with Wall on the *Buccleugh*? It occurred to me that you might desire a female companion to assist. If Lydia and I were to escort him, we could act *in loco parentis,* as it were. It would be a salve to your worries to know that he was with friends known to him who would treat him as if he were their own.'

It was tempting. Lydia Gray had once been governess to his daughters; she had known William since he was a baby. But the request was highly unorthodox. 'We're short-handed as it is, Gray. Who will take your duties for what might be a year or two?'

'We expect a few new officers soon. And Macalister is keen to prove himself. It would be a good chance for him to gain experience.' Gray had obviously given the matter much thought.

'You realise that the decision is not mine, Gray?' Light retorted. 'You're a Company officer. Any change to your orders must be approved by Calcutta.'

'If you supported my request, recommending my leave on compassionate grounds, it is unlikely the Council would reject it,' Gray argued.

Light considered the many years of service Gray had given. He was the last remaining officer of the original party who had raised the flag on Prince of Wales almost seven years earlier; in fact Gray had been the very first to set foot on the island. In those years, his service record had been unblemished. It was a long time to be stationed in one place without a break. Before that, Gray had distinguished himself in the Americas. He deserved some reward for his years of duty.

'We can hardly spare you, but the administration recognises your long service. I will speak for you, although I cannot be assured of success. You must write yourself, resigning your commission temporarily, and I will second your request. There is always a place for you here, James. I will do my best to safeguard it on your behalf.'

'My gratitude, as always, sir.' James' response was genuine. He admired the superintendent greatly; his thanks were truly meant.

Light smiled. 'You'll be doing us a great personal favour. It will set our minds at rest to know that William has the pair of you watching over him on the voyage home. I'm sure young Willie will be delighted to know you'll be on board to entertain him!'

***

William was not. In fact, avoiding the attentions of the Grays became his *modus vivendi*, giving the boy a purpose and distracting from his other concerns. One of William's favourite hideouts was in the waist below the forecastle where the crew gathered when off duty. The boy often hung around, striking up friendships with the younger men, several only a few years older than he. Billy Barnes the cooper also had his workroom there, alongside the smith, Frederick Ainsdale. William began to 'help' them out when he could, ever fascinated by how things were made. The men grew fond of the inquisitive little boy. Life was tedious at sea for weeks on end, especially overnight when the cumbersome vessel hardly moved at all.

Another of William's pastimes was drawing. His father had supplied him with a polished wooden box furnished with paper, chalk, pencils and paints. It was his most precious possession, far more than a little boy would normally own. Although he might still struggle with his writing, William spent hours on deck recording shipboard life. He already exhibited a talent for art and enjoyed not only sketching the boat but also the people who inhabited it. By the time he reached England, he had a wonderfully rich child's-eye view of the long voyage, which he intended to make into a book to send to his parents from Suffolk.

Thus, as the days passed, the little boy found ways to amuse himself, wandering the huge vessel from stem to stern, nosing out its secret places. His mother would never have allowed such freedom. It was some compensation for missing her. The *Duke of Buccleugh* was an enormous space to a young child, a far bigger ship than any he had sailed before, an endless playground. One day William intended to follow in his father's footsteps and join the Royal Navy. He intended to be well prepared for his future service by learning everything that could be learned about a ship of this size.

On a blustery morning, two months after they had left Pinang, Captain Wall summoned William to the upper deck. 'Is your letter ready? The topman has sighted a few of our ships on the outward route. We're diverting to exchange mail and news. Give your letter to me so that I may package it. I shall include my own note to assure your parents of your wellbeing and excellent conduct.'

William nodded. 'I shall bring it to your cabin at once. How amusing that they shall be reading it even before I get to England! Thank you, Captain Wall, for all you have done for me. I am quite settled now and look forward to the rest of the journey.'

'Good lad, but remember we are still a very long way from home, and the times ahead may be hard. It's a curious thing that the closer we get to home waters, the more brutal the conditions. But you have the right spirit, lad. Just like your father when he went to sea as a boy, I'm sure.'

'Did my father go to sea a very long time ago?' William enquired. He had never even known his father as a ship's captain let alone the life he must once have had. In fact, he found it improbable that his father had ever been young at all.

'A very long time ago. Must have been around the '50s, I reckon. He worked up the ladder the hard way, you know? Started right at the bottom, not even a midshipman. You should be proud how he's raised your family through his long and illustrious career.'

'I am very proud of him. He's the best father in the whole world!' replied William with gusto. 'May I ask, sir, how long ago is 'the 50s'. Was Father just a little boy like me then?'

Wall chuckled. 'Not so long ago to me, son, for I was born

in '51, but many lifetimes to a boy of seven years' old. It's '93 now. Can you calculate? How many years since, say ... 1753, do you reckon?' He had no idea at what age a child was expected to master basic arithmetic but saw a chance to instruct the lad.

William frowned, looking to his fingers in vain for answers, before giving up. 'More than ten?' he guessed wildly, but not entirely incorrect.

'Indeed, many more than ten. More like forty years ago. Older than you are now, but still a young fellow. I hope you'll work hard at your calculations when you go to school. A naval officer must master arithmetic to sail a ship. Modern navigation is very scientific, don't you know?'

William was most impressed at what he deemed a grown-up conversation. 'Thank you most heartily for your advice, sir. It is my greatest wish to follow my father into the navy. I promise to work hard at my studies so that I may be a good officer one day.

'Excellent! I'm sure you'll be as fine an officer as your father. 'Now keep your eyes peeled and watch as the ships come together. It's always an excitement to meet others in the middle of this endless ocean. The men will be on pins for news of home! Fetch your letter, then take your position up here to get a bird's-eye view. After that, it will be nigh on eight more weeks until St Helena, unless we make enough time to call into Cape Town for some fresh food!'

And so, the dreary days passed with very few moments to relieve them, other than the frightening storms through which the bulky vessel ploughed and the too-infrequent landings on the way. It was August, before William Light first set foot on English soil. He was an older and wiser boy than the little child who had boarded all those months ago. His life had been forever changed, although it was to be several years before he was to understand the full extent.

23

Council of War

Government House, Prince of Wales Island. 25th March 1793

It was a solemn gathering that assembled in the meeting room of Government House one Monday morning in late March. Although no agenda had been circulated, it was clear to all that this was a council of war. Ever since the French rebels had arrested their royal family, it was inevitable that Britain would join the alliance against the new government. To wait for news from Europe might mean the French were upon them before confirmation arrived. The time to prepare was now.

Twelve men sat around the large teak table, with Light and Thomas Pigou at opposite ends. A cross-section of the European residents from the military, the mercantile and the seagoing fraternities made up the complement: Glass, Macalister and the recently arrived Lt. Robin Duff; James Scott, John Cochrane and William Nason; and Captains William Lindesay and Collingwood Roddam. Dr James Hutton was also in attendance, for should hostilities break out, who would be more important than he? Light had directed Nathaniel Bacon to record the discussion, perched at an escritoire. Then he directed the men to loosen their collars and make themselves comfortable. They were in for a long haul.

No one remarked on the lack of representation from other

residents of the island for it was regarded as unacceptable for Christian gentlemen to discuss matters of politics with the natives. Privately, however, Francis Light disagreed. Defence of the island would require all its inhabitants. He intended to hold similar assemblies with the other community leaders. But that was for another day.

'We have many issues to address, gentlemen. Let's commence without further ado. News from Europe is disturbing. I do not need to remind you we may already be at war with France. We must be primed and ready, for this will have momentous consequences for the Straits.'

'Damn Frenchies! The world's gone mad!' exclaimed Cochrane, a burly Scottish merchant from Calcutta who had invested heavily in the new settlement, especially in foodstuffs, with a monopoly on the island's flourmills and bakeries.

'Indubitably, sir. Captain Lindesay? May I trouble you to report on what you recently learnt concerning French activity?' Light turned to the reticent Lindesay, who cleared his throat nervously. He felt ill-suited to the formalities of council meetings.

'I have just returned from Jaffna where I spoke with a Portuguese captain, a jovial fellow by the name of Borba, who had recently put into Île de France after a storm had caused some damage ...'

'His entire life story is not necessary, Lindesay,' broke in Cochrane impatiently. 'Get to the details, man!'

William Lindesay glanced helplessly at the superintendent, who motioned with a friendly nod for him to resume. 'He had observed the French were fitting out a number of privateers, speedy little vessels, with cannons and gunnery aplenty. Borba was curious, so he asked around. He learned these French corsairs had been recruited to head for the Straits to cause maximum damage to British shipping. They are to make lightning raids on our East Indiamen, plunder whatever they can – and run. The booty will supply the French warships that are to follow.'

There was a sharp intake of breath around the table. No one had expected the situation to deteriorate quite so fast. French preparations were well advanced.

'I've written to Calcutta with this intelligence, of course. We hope it will be sufficient to alert them to the urgency of the situation. There's no time to lose. We must be ready!' Light asserted vehemently.

Cochrane saw it differently. 'Damned if I intend to linger out here to see my fortune lost to French pirates. It's my plan to sell up and return to England directly, before the sea lanes turn into battlegrounds. I suggest you do the same. This island's finished. Cornwallis favours the Andamans; the new French threat is the last nail in the coffin.' He thumped a hammy fist on the table.

Light gave him the cold eye. 'One would imagine that a merchant who has made a substantial fortune supplying British fleets, both here and the Americas, would regard it as his duty at such a time to support the cause. Maintaining food supplies will be crucial.'

Cochrane's jowly face shook with temper. 'I hope, sir, you're not accusing me of dereliction of duty! I've served this nation, man and boy! It's high time for me to return to Scotland to enjoy the fruits of my labour. We merchants are not the architects of political events. Yet we are the ones expected to bear the cost.'

The meeting was only moments old and already sinking into

its own brand of hostilities. Thomas Pigou stepped in. There were no troubled waters through which the mild-mannered Pigou was unable to navigate. 'Dear Mr Cochrane, I'm sure the superintendent meant no such thing! Your company will still be supplying our needs from Calcutta. Your brother Basil acts there in your stead, I believe? However, your expert advice is necessary as we plan for all eventualities. Pray feel free to share any thoughts as the meeting progresses. For once you have left the island, we shall suffer the loss of your expertise immensely!'

Cochrane's simmering annoyance subsided in grunts and harrumphs, although Light's expression was still stony. The rest stared down at the table before them in embarrassment, each willing the others to speak. It was young Norman Macalister who stepped into the breach.

'If I may raise the military issue? Preparedness against attack should begin with an examination of the present state of our fortifications, without which we will be entirely vulnerable.'

This suggestion gave Light the opportunity to climb down from his high horse. 'I agree, Lieutenant. There's no question the fort is a shambles. We must make plans for its reconstruction as a matter of priority. Captain Glass?'

John Glass was slumped into his seat, not at all the usual brisk and efficient commander. His colour was high, but his cheeks seemed shrunken, bruised rings hollowing his eyes. 'Excuse me, gentlemen. I am somewhat inconvenienced today. Perhaps something I ate ...'

'Are you ill, Glass?' Light asked. 'Why did you not say so? Go home and rest, man. We can manage here without you.'

Glass shook his head – and winced. Even that small movement

caused discomfort. 'I can manage, sir. It's nothing,' Glass gamely replied.

Dr Hutton intervened. 'Man, you can barely hold yourself up straight! Come with me and I'll examine you outside. If you'll excuse us, gentlemen? I won't be more than a few minutes.' Without allowing Glass the time to argue, Hutton elbowed him from his seat.

'Macalister? May I trouble you to stand in for me?' Glass muttered weakly.

Once the door had closed, Macalister took the floor. 'I recommend we undertake an immediate survey of the fort, assessing areas that require rebuilding, strengthening or replacement. Once we have ascertained our full requirements, only then will we be fully able to estimate the cost.'

There was general agreement. 'The Council will respond better to a properly drawn up survey if we are to convince the Company auditors to release the funds. Everyone will be making demands at this time, so we must ensure ours is prompt and well prepared,' Pigou observed.

'In the absence of Gray, I suggest you take the lead on this, Macalister,' Light decided. The young man could hardly contain his pleasure. 'Choose a few officers to assist and we'll work on this together. I also have in mind to extend our defences. We've plenty of high ground so we must make full use of it, both as lookout posts and evacuation centres should the Tanjong fall.'

'Are you suggesting George Town and the Fort might be at risk?' William Nason gasped in horror. John Cochrane barely contained a smirk as if the suggestion only proved his point.

Light sighed. 'Nason, this is a meeting to plan for every

possibility. Of course, we believe the fort, our ships, cannonry and coastal defences will be sufficient! But what kind of leader does not have an alternative plan? I for one, do not wish our women, children, the old and infirm to be along the sea front should French ships fire directly on us! I'm fortunate to have a retreat on Strawberry Hill. Most of our residents do not,' he added firmly.

'We defeated Queddah without any aid!' Nason countered lamely.

'Do you imagine the French East Indies fleet may be compared with the hotchpotch army of Queddah and its allies? If the French send their navy to the Straits, we will be the target, of that there is no doubt. This is the single most dangerous moment in the life of Pinang since its inception. We must not be found wanting should the moment come!'

Faces were grim as reality dawned.

'We'll have allies in the Dutch this time, surely?' James Scott broke in. 'Much as I can't abide the Hollanders, they've ships and men aplenty. And without their meddling in the Straits, we shall have an easier time of it in general, for the Bugis are much quietened these days.'

'Indeed,' Light agreed. 'But Malacca is a spent force. I suspect they'll simply withdraw most to Sumatra and Batavia. And how cooperative they will be is hard to say. They might not actively work against us, but I cannot see them extending the hand of friendship either. We compete for the same trade, and should the French blockade the area, we may be competing in ever-diminishing sea lanes.'

Silence fell on the men as they contemplated the implications.

Captain Collingwood Roddam spoke up. 'You're welcome to make use of the ground I've acquired across the river above Batu Lanchang. It's still largely uncleared, but I've built a little stilt house there. With some coolie labour, we could make a rudimentary stockade. There's ample level ground and an excellent view over the southern waters.'

His generous offer was not entirely altruistic. Roddam, now largely retired due to failing eyesight, planned to settle on the island as a nutmeg planter. A solitary man, he had it in his mind to live away from the teeming insanitary streets of George Town, believing that the miasmas of the settlement caused the ill health that was so prevalent. For weeks he had been bothering the administration to provide workers to clear his land, already known as Roddam Hill, but Light had so far refused. As an independent merchant and settler, Roddam was expected to pay men himself to do the work. This offer was clearly an attempt to circumvent that decision. Yet, Light could not argue with his proposal. His hill was an ideal location.

'Macalister, look into Captain Roddam's generous suggestion,' Light replied with more diplomacy than he had earlier addressed Cochrane. 'Let's include the hill in the survey. I suggest we also look at Stoney Hill north of the Tanjong for a similar lookout. Nathaniel, are you noting all this?' Bacon's hand scratched at speed across the parchment as he nodded his assent.

'Let's set a date for completion of our survey six weeks from today. As soon as we're sure of what is needed, we must set to work immediately. I do not intend to wait for Calcutta's approval. I also expect the community to be as generous as possible.'

No one demurred, although his suggestion would be

unpopular. No doubt the larger part would be funded as usual from his own pocket until Calcutta made a decision.

At that moment, Dr Hutton quietly returned to his seat. 'I've taken the liberty of sending Captain Glass home. He has a fever and the fierce body aches. I suspect breakbone fever. There've been several cases of late. We must take care, all of us.'

'Poor Glass. I hope his lady wife does not fall ill. Their child is due,' Light observed. It was a sobering thought that, no matter how dangerous the political climate, the Indies was alive with even deadlier threats already in their midst.

'If I may interrupt?' continued Hutton. 'Whilst military arrangements are of the greatest importance, I must address our medical needs. The infirmary at the fort is in a poor state of repair as you will discover in the survey. It is at present unable to admit many who require assistance, even army persons. Some are left to wallow on their cots in the barracks for want of a bed in the hospital. My belief is that we not only need to extend the infirmary, but we need a civilian hospital as well. Our present numbers surely warrant a decent place to cure our sick – with more migrants joining every day!'

'The matter has been on my mind for some time, James,' Light answered. 'I have already applied to Calcutta for funds. We have also beseeched them repeatedly for doctors and orderlies, but they believe we must see to the civilian population ourselves. With war on the horizon increasing the future demands on medical staff, we can no longer ignore this need. I have demarked a plot of ground at the western edge of my property on the Well Estate for such an establishment. It lies just across Pinang Road by the beach.'

James Hutton nodded his approval. 'An excellent site at

some distance from the noxious air of the settlement. I would like to propose that we train some of our own assistants to service a small clinic there as soon as possible. Marlbro would be an excellent choice as senior attendant. I would visit regularly when my duties at the fort were complete.'

'The black fellow?' Cochrane broke in. 'Is he up to it? I'm not sure most decent people would want to be pawed in their private areas by the likes of him!'

Hutton's face set in disgust. 'Mr Marlbro is an experienced nurse and orderly. He has been a fine assistant to me at the fort. I have never heard any patient complain about his attendance when they have been *in extremis*!' he retorted.

Cochrane shrugged. 'Well, the burial ground is only up the road.' He seemed pleased by his own wit. No one else at the table shared his opinion.

'Dr Hutton? Come and see me tomorrow and we shall work on the arrangements. Mr Pigou, your contribution?'

Thomas Pigou shuffled a few papers and began his update. The meeting continued on with general business, until it gradually wound down to a close. It had been a heavy morning. Superintendent Light announced a lunch was waiting in the dining room to a heartfelt round of applause. As the men filed out, Light called Scott to wait behind. 'I have a task for you ...'

Scott rolled his eyes. 'One you could not mention around the table?'

Light cuffed him lightly on the arm. 'Stop trouble-causing, Jamie! Nothing underhand, I assure you. I need you to draw up an estimation of the entire holdings of the British subjects on the island. When I write to Calcutta with my financial demands, I want them to know exactly what might be lost to them if this island falls to the French.'

With a pursing of his lips, James Scott gave the request some thought. 'And as governor you cannot get a minion for such an undertaking?'

Light chuckled as they walked up the stairs together. 'I require the real sum, not the underestimated values in our inadequate records. Only you know the true wealth of this island. I'll warrant your ledgers could give me the sum down to the last farthing!'

Scott winked, rubbing his hands gleefully. 'I hope there's a decent wine with lunch, Francis, my boy. I expect to be well soused in return for this confidential information.'

'Including your holdings, Jamie!'

'You expect too much of a man, sir,' he retorted. 'But I shall give you what you need so long as the sources remain mine alone. Your word, sir?'

'You need to ask? Francis grinned. They shook hands, laughing like the carefree boys of years before, as if the intervening years had never happened.

24
Paradise Lost

Strawberry Hill, Pinang. September 1793

The view from the hill was incomparable on any day, but on that glorious September morning it was akin to paradise. The air was fragrant, a gentle breeze stirring the fronds and blooms, just enough to relieve the heat. Frothing clouds ambled lazily in a bright blue sky. Far below, the Straits stretched into eternity. Tiny specks, motes on deep green waters, were the only visible signs of the busy trade lanes; from his vantage, they wove an elegant dance, billowing sails and white wakes streaming.

Francis Light breathed deeply. From where he stood, it was possible – just for a moment – to imagine none of his problems existed. Only the comforting sounds of his family breaking fast, and the servants busy at their work to trouble his peace. Martinha had insisted they spend the hot dry season on the hill to escape the disease that was rife in town. He could work just as easily there as in Government House, but in more genial surroundings. As usual, she had been right. Last night he had slept better than in months, the shutters open wide and the night air streaming in. No bothersome mosquitoes had disturbed his rest.

Yet his burdens still hammered relentlessly at the door of his conscious mind, threatening once again to swamp him. Since the news of the declaration of war had finally reached the island, there had been little but one alarm after another. Each ship brought further worrying intelligence to add to the sad news at home. It had been a terrible season.

The tragic loss of John Glass had hit Light hard. The two had not been close friends for Glass was not a man given to confidences. Yet they had high regard for each other, even if they had disagreed on many things. When mutual respect is strong, opposing views can be voiced without bitterness; such partnerships are fruitful. Glass had always been his unfailing support, an honest man who never abused his authority nor tried to undermine his own. Since his marriage, Light had seen a different side of the man; Sarippa had drawn from this taciturn soldier a softer, more amiable side. How John had longed to meet his little child! It broke Light's heart that poor Glass had died before he ever had the chance.

It had happened so quickly. One day Glass had taken ill and within a few days he was gone. That the life of a man of such resilience and strength could be snuffed out as easily as a candleflame had shocked them all. Even more unfathomable had been the survival of Sarippa, who had also succumbed to the contagion. Yet she had shaken off the fever in a few days, despite her wild and pitiful grief. Her body refused to fail her when she had such an important task to perform. Two weeks later, Sarippa had given birth to their daughter, Asha Maria, the 'Hope of Mary' in her language. Standing by his grave at the burial, a feeling of desolation had washed over Light, such as he had rarely experienced. Unexpected death was so common in the Indies that it had become a matter of course. Yet, the loss of Glass was a step too far. Death's cold hand had tapped on his own shoulder that day, reminding him his own days were numbered.

There had been practical consequences. In a few months, Light had lost both Lt Gray and Captain Glass, his mainstays since '86, a serious blow with war on the horizon. Young Macalister was proving ready for responsibility and had been promoted to captain of artillery. George Raban, another stalwart from the early days gamely stepped in as acting commander. Unfortunately, Calcutta had other ideas and the resultant mess had been badly handled.

A new commanding officer, Captain Robert Hamilton, had arrived in June, along with his assistant, Lt. John Gerard. The Council had ignored Raban's temporary appointment, a flagrant insult to a good officer who had served seven years in the settlement on low pay and scant reward for his good service. It marked the disrespect in which the superintendent was held that his opinion had not been considered. Raban subsequently became morose, no longer the industrious soldier of before. Who could blame him?

If Hamilton had proved himself a man of more sensitivity, he might have won Raban over in time, for George was not by nature intractable. Yet the captain proved the opposite. Robert Hamilton was provocative in Light's opinion, riddled with insecurities and prejudices. He humiliated those below him and took issue with those above. Hamilton was the very worst manner of officer to be in charge of the diverse community of the island, for he disdained the native peoples, and was as likely to abuse them as his men. It was not long before Light could hardly speak to his commanding officer without the two men crossing swords. If not for the delicate interventions of Pigou and Macalister, they might have come to blows by now. All this, with a war in the offing.

A flurry of activity accompanied by frantic shouting disturbed his reveries. A troop of monkeys was swarming over the veranda, helping themselves to the leavings of breakfast. The servants chased them off, accompanied by little Francis who was attempting to snatch back a banana. A monkey bared its teeth as he approached, but still the little child came forward.

'Frannie! Stop! He will bite! Stop, I say!' Light raced towards the child. The presence of an adult man was enough to drive the monkey away; it hared up a nearby tree to enjoy the booty from the distant perch. Francis grabbed the giggling child and hugged him tight in relief. Martinha herself dashed across the grass, her face aghast.

'Naughty boy!' she shouted. '*Bahaya! Monyet ada gigi!*'

'*Monyet ambil pisang saya!*' the little boy explained, undaunted. The monkey had taken his banana. He was not scared of its teeth.

Light handed little Francis to his mother, ruffling his dark hair. Francis Lanoon was a beautiful child, a little monkey himself, who caused more trouble than all the others put together. Perhaps the household spoiled him, especially now his siblings were away at school, but Light suspected that it was the child's own nature. There was a fearlessness about him; he acted first then thought later. Nothing dented his curiosity. Martinha constantly worried about him. Recently he had gone to pick up a snake in the grass; by some miracle he had not been bitten. They could not hope for such luck next time.

'We should never have named him for a pirate,' Light grinned ruefully.

'It is not a joke, Francis.' Martinha was not amused by his

levity. 'One day he'll go too far. We watch him every moment, but he disappears in the blink of an eye.'

'*Ma'af, 'bu*! Sorry, Mama, I love you,' the little boy whined, wrapping his chubby arms about her neck. It was hard to resist his charms. That was the heart of the problem. 'You're like your father,' Martinha muttered against his cheek. 'You think a winsome smile can get away with anything!'

They walked back to the house whilst the maids cleared up the mess. Another pot of tea was brought; they shared a few cups, whilst Frannie played at their feet, distracted by his toys.

'Do you think William will be in Suffolk yet?' Martinha asked wistfully. It had been almost eight months, but they had sailed first to Portsmouth and then Deptford, so it would take a while longer before Wall was able to make the final leg of the journey home.

'I should think so. By all accounts they made good time. We've had three mails already. St Helena was reached in April. I'll bet he's tucked up safe and warm in bed as we speak.'

From her waistband, Martinha retrieved William's last letter, read so many times that she knew every word and misspelling by heart. She smoothed out the pages fondly, as if stroking his cheek. 'I miss him so, Francis. Look at his drawings! He's so clever with a pencil. But he is changing. Even through his words and pictures I can see he is becoming a different boy,' she observed sadly.

'The world will have its effect on him, sayang. Children grow up quickly when forced upon their own resources. Sad as it is to lose our little boy, we must be glad for him. It is necessary for him to be durable to deal with life's vagaries.'

Martinha nodded, sniffing back her tears. 'I cannot help but wonder when we shall see William and the girls again now that this war is upon us. It is impossible to think of sea journeys. Were we wrong to send him when we did?' she asked.

Light stared up at the near cloudless sky, deep in thought. 'I think not. The four children are safe. That must be our comfort. Yet, you are right. Our plans to return home now seem naïve in the extreme. Until this crisis is resolved, my duty is to remain here and protect the settlement. Do you wish to take Francis and your mother to Calcutta? At least then I would know you were safe all together until we see this through.'

His wife's response was immediate and definitive. 'My duty is by your side. We will endure this as we have endured so much together. One day soon, even should it be a few years' hence, we will be reunited. Of this, I am sure.'

Whether more wish than belief, Francis chose to agree. When his spirits plummeted to the depths, she always gathered him up. What would his life have been without her?

A noise in the trees alerted them to the approach of a visitor. Moments later, a red-faced Macalister accompanied by sepoys, all done in by their exertions, loped towards the house. Martinha scooped up Frannie and took him inside, so that the child did not disturb official business.

'Hot work this morning, Norman?' Light called out. 'Come sit down. Martinha will arrange a cool drink for you and the lads.'

Captain Macalister was the bearer of a message from Pigou based on reports that had come in during the past few hours. He handed over the note without explanation, but his grim face said enough.

Sir,
Since last night we have received numerous reports that French Ships, one a frigate previously sighted off Achin, have attacked several British vessels. The damage is not yet ascertained but it is feared they were seized. The current whereabouts of this fleet are unknown.
Your servant, Pigou

'The sources are trustworthy?' Light asked.

'One of Khoh's captains and the nakhoda of Sayyid Aidid's vessel. Not to mention every manjack in port, who claim to have seen it for themselves.'

The superintendent groaned softly. 'The mood in the settlement?'

Macalister shrugged. 'Gossip, and the usual alarmist rhetoric. But there's a fatalism, too. There is nowhere for anyone to go. We must all watch and wait,' he added.

'We must prepare, Captain. Any news from Calcutta, perchance? Some message of support or – God be praised – a promise of soldiers and some money?'

There had been none. The survey of the fort had been dispatched four months past. It was as thorough and comprehensive as even the most punctilious of accountants might demand. There had been only silence in response.

'Goddammit! What are they about? I ask for a mere 60,000 Spanish dollars to defend a settlement worth nigh on one and half million in British investments alone! How did these fools ever make a penny in trade?'

Macalister winced at the comment so flagrantly directed at

his masters, but it reflected his own feelings. 'At least we can take heart that the work on the fort is well advanced, thanks to the Chinese contractors supplied by Mr Khoh. The defensive line from the new hospital to Sia Boey on this side of the Prangin is almost complete. As are the lookout posts on Roddam Hill and Stoney Point.' He ticked off each achievement on his fingers. 'We're prepared, sir. Or as well prepared as we can be.'

'We need more men. Do they not understand that we have only eighteen artillerymen fit for duty and but a small body of native *golandazes* to assist? How in God's name does Calcutta expect us to defend against an all-out French attack with a paltry bunch of soldiers? Light blurted out, an angry vein bulging in his forehead. His frustration was understandable; the responsibility on his shoulders was formidable.

'The new gaol is finished, sir. Brick built and secure. Ready for French prisoners,' Macalister's attempt at levity fell on stony ground.

'The defensive line needs to extend beyond the edge of town across the Prangin. What of the Chinese villagers across the river? They need protecting too. As do their crops. Agriculture is of the highest priority. If we are blockaded it will not matter how many bales of silk one owns but if there is enough rice and vegetables to keep us from starving!'

'We will make it a priority, sir. The people are assisting. Kapitan Khoh has been most helpful in providing extra labour, as have the Malay leaders.'

'They have as much to lose as we if this goes awry,' Light replied. 'Anything else?'

The young captain seemed reluctant but added: 'Captain

Hamilton has written a letter of complaint to Calcutta. His orders said we were not to proceed with the new gaol. It was thought sufficient to hold prisoners on ships in the lanes or put them to hard labour in the fields. He says it is further evidence of misuse of Company funds ...'

Light jumped from his seat, pacing on the wooden boards of the veranda to contain his anger. 'And whose damned funds have paid for everything so far? Am I to be called to task for spending my *own* money? The man's a rank idiot. At a time when solidarity is the least one would expect, he tells tales behind my back. And where, pray, does he want us to put this chain gang at night when their work in the fields is done? Would any sane soldier not prefer a stone-built lockup?'

'I thought you should know, sir.' Macalister mumbled. Light pierced him with a stare. 'I'm sure you did, Macalister. Tale-telling works both ways, eh?' The young man's pale skin flushed with embarrassment. Light knew he had been unfair. It was times like these that made a young officer's career. What of it if he wished to stir the ants' nest? Hamilton was behaving abominably; his antagonism was a threat to all. Macalister was ten times the officer and man.

'My apologies, Norman. That was uncalled for. I'm afraid I gave vent to my wrath on you. It is wholly undeserved.'

'I understand, sir. It's easier to rage at those before you when your hands are tied against those who really do you wrong.' It was a generous response that said much about the character of the captain.

'You're a fine man, Norman. More astute than I ever was. I'm still a sea captain at heart. These civil servants bedevil me. It is the bane of the Company that men of little experience sit around tables far away and decide the fate of thousands!'

Macalister smiled ruefully. 'It was ever thus, sir. We do the best we can. And your best so far has proved better than most. Take heart from that, sir. We will prevail.'

Light patted him fondly on the shoulder. 'We *must* prevail. The alternative cannot be countenanced.'

'If that's all, sir, I will take the men back down. Or do you have letters?' Macalister replaced his hat and retied his neckcloth ready to brave the fierce sun.

The superintendent stayed him. 'Rest awhile. I'll send for food for you and your men. I want to pen a few missives. One for Calcutta is especially urgent and needs to make the evening tide. They must be informed about the raids on British shipping. Please God, that will get them moving at last!

***

Despite its urgency, the letter sat for several weeks on the wrong desk before finally reaching its destination. Only then, did the Company act. Troops were dispatched immediately, four companies of sepoys and 40 British artillerymen with a detachment of *golandaz* auxiliaries to assist them.

Under the command of a battle-hardened officer, Captain Thomas Polhill, and accompanied by a large cargo of ammunition, at last the assistance arrived. There was also a response to the survey of the fort from the military auditor-general. The gist of it was that, without the assessment of military engineers, such sums of money could not be allocated. A suitable engineer would be dispatched in good time.

Polhill was a man of energy and enthusiasm who had barely stepped on shore before he was at work, pouring over the survey and entirely in agreement. He sent back an immediate request, on the same ship on which he had arrived, that monies be supplied urgently. The barracks were woefully inadequate for the needs of his men. From the start, Light knew that this commander was a man with whom he could work. He was cheese to Hamilton's chalk.

Robert Hamilton himself took umbrage, leaving for Calcutta on the ship along with Polhill's letter, suffering from some ill-defined illness for which he required convalescence. Scott claimed there was nothing wrong with him but sour grapes. Yet there was little doubt that he would spend his leave stirring up opposition to the superintendent. Light was unconcerned; Hamilton's departure was the best news he'd heard in a long time. Let the objectionable fellow do his worst, he said.

In the meantime, Polhill assumed overall command. Within days, a new optimism was felt by all. The destructive atmosphere that had poisoned the administration for months had been immediately alleviated by the removal of just one man.

PART FIVE

Testament

(1793-1794)

25

Conflict of Interest

Pinang Roads, Prince of Wales Island. Late December 1793

As the sun sank below the horizon illuminating a nacreous sky, the *Aisyah* lay bobbing at anchor, loaded with rice and tin. Two crewmen had remained on board to watch their precious cargo while the rest had gone home. In the morning, port authorities would board to inspect their goods. The system made commerce safer for all.

Several other larger vessels were moored close by; the lanes were crowded at this time of year when Christians celebrated their prophet's birthday. Many China-bound ships had put into Pinang for the festival. The sounds of their carousing could be heard across the evening waters.

Somewhere close by, as they settled down for the night wrapped up in their sarongs, several male voices were singing raucously, probably a rowboat full of drunks on their way back to their ship, their pockets empty. The lapping of the oars grew more distinct, the singing giving way to gruff speech. The proximity of this craft began to cause alarm. The two men rose to assess the situation, their instincts on high alert.

'Oi!' a voice called out from below. 'Give a fellow a hand, will ya?'

Peering over the side, they saw a small boat with three men

aboard. One was scrambling up the side, precariously clinging to the rope ladder.

'*Pergi! Jangan naik!*' said the first Malay, an old hand by the name of Mus, brandishing his keris in warning.

'None of your heathen gibberish now,' replied the sailor. 'It's Christmastide, good will to all men. We just want to say hello all friendly-like.' He continued to haul himself towards the rail, a companion in his wake, while the third steadied the rowboat.

'GO! *Ga weg*!' shouted Mus, his knowledge of English all used up, so resorting to his limited Dutch. His friend Naz waved a pole aggressively at the approaching Englishmen. 'GO! *Jangan naik*!' he warned.

By then the scrawny English man, more nimble than one might expect, had leapt onto the deck. The sailor snarled at them, baring his jagged black teeth. Mus and Naz took an instinctive step backwards, as if confronted by a wild animal.

'Now what have we 'ere, lads?' he jeered. 'Two little brown fellows and a whole boatload of nice things. Too good to waste, eh?'

The two Malays, acting as one, darted forward to catch the ruffian by surprise. In his conceit he had not expected retaliation. Ramming him against the side, they grabbed him as he lost his balance, then tossed him far over the side. He fell into deep water, arms and legs flapping, roaring wildly, to surface a distance from his boat. It was not their concern whether he could swim. Before the next Englishman could react, Naz jabbed the pole full in his belly as he also climbed over the rail screaming curses at them for the fate of his friend. That fellow fell straight down, landing with loud thump onto the craft, which rocked so violently that both men were thrown into the water.

From their vantage, Mus and Naz mightily enjoyed the antics of the three as they struggled to right their craft and climb back in. The second man seemed injured, for he moaned, clutching at his back. Without the aid of the other two, he may well have drowned. Once on their boat, the three shouted all manner of profanities and threats, which meant nothing to the Malays, although they could well imagine their meaning. As the rowboat drew away heading towards its own ship, the *Nancy*, the lascars mocked them in retreat. It had been an amusing incident, a common danger in any port, not tolerated on Pinang. All traders were protected from looting and intimidation under severe penalties.

Deciding that their position in the lanes was vulnerable and not wishing for retaliation from the shipmates of their assailants, the two Malays decided to bring their ship into the jetty where they would be safe from harm for the night under the protection of the authorities. That was an end to it as far as they were concerned. The law was on their side. Illegal boarding was a crime.

***

When Superintendent Light reached the kampong, accompanied by Hutton, Marlbro and a few soldiers, he was met with unbridled hostility, unlike anything he had ever witnessed from the Malay community. Young men swarmed from all sides, brandishing weapons with such menace that his guard instinctively raised their guns.

Light shouted for them to cease, then repeated the words in Malay. His soldiers reluctantly responded, but the Malays remained obdurate. 'You're not welcome, Superintendent,' he was told. 'Go back to your fort and be grateful we do not kill you!'

At that critical moment, the crowd parted to allow Nakhoda Kecil to approach. He greeted Light with a hand on his heart, but his expression was hostile. 'How do you dare to come here after what your men did to my boys,' he spat out. 'Flogged like animals!'

Light's face was ashen. He made no attempt to defend himself, merely rubbing the back of his hand across his eyes as if to wash away tears. When he spoke, his voice trembled. 'I did not know. I swear I did not know!' he blurted out. 'You must believe me when I say this foul deed was not my work. Surely you know I could never countenance harm to Soliman! I know the men are innocent!'

Nakhoda Kecil could not set aside his anger. 'Not your work? What kind of leader are you? This was done by *your* soldiers, ordered by *your* commander at *your* fort. Do you allow your men to act without sanction?' the older man challenged. 'Leave this place. We want no more to do with you and your kind!'

Marlbro stepped forward, holding up his hands. 'Please, Tuan, I beg you. We come in friendship. At least allow us to tend their wounds. It is the least we can do.'

'We can tend to our own people,' the Nakhoda countered, waving his hand dismissively. 'Leave us alone.'

For long moments the standoff continued until Francis Light regained his wits. 'Tuan, please hear me out. We understand your anger. We share it with you. Whatever errors have been made that is for another day. For now, your men need our doctors. Will you add the deaths of these innocent Malays to the evil that has already been done, merely out of stubborn anger?' Light pleaded in respectful tones. 'I referred the case lest anyone accuse me of showing favouritism to Soliman. There was no doubt in my mind, your men had committed no offence. Their ship was illegally boarded; it was their right to act.'

'Then why do they lie with their backs cut to ribbons while villains go free?' Nakhoda Kecil demanded.

Light considered his response carefully. 'Because there are men who delight in tormenting those they think beneath them. Lies were told and lies were believed. The punishment was carried out immediately without recourse to me. By the time I was informed, the act was done. Tuan, I do not seek your forgiveness for I bear responsibility for the actions of those under my command – but I beg you, let me help these men in any way I can to make some small amends.' Even as he spoke, his words seemed trite.

His initial anger somewhat placated, the Malay leader now seemed more sad than bitter. 'I know you're a decent man, sir. But everything goes from bad to worse. When Captain Glass was alive, this would not have happened. These new men have no respect. What will you do to punish them?'

It was the question Light most feared, for he had no answer. He could only offer toothless platitudes. 'In truth, there is nothing I can do. Once I passed the matter to the military, it was out of my hands. They are independent of my administration.'

'But my men are not soldiers! They are free men defending their property!' the nakhoda exclaimed.

'This is a British settlement, Tuan. Captain Hamilton used the powers granted to him by Calcutta, from where even my authority derives. My hands are tied.'

'Then all is lost, Superintendent Light. We are little more than slaves.'

Yet Nakhoda Kecil motioned for them to enter the kampong, ordering the villagers to allow them passage. 'Leave your soldiers outside. We do not want them on our soil. You have no need of guards. I guarantee your safety. But this business will have consequences. Trust is lost, sir.'

Soliman lay on a raised pallet in the main room of his neat and tidy atap house. Aisyah, his wife, and female relatives were attending him, cleaning his wounds, and applying salve. In the background an imam recited prayers. The women backed away when he entered with Dr Hutton, their stony faces expressing their disdain. Light asked politely if he might tend to Soliman; Aisyah nodded to the others to leave but remained at a watchful distance.

Kneeling by the cot, Light stroked Soliman's hair, whispering: 'Sol, lad. Can you hear me?' Soliman lay on his front, his face buried in the bolster. He did not appear to be conscious. At the sound of Light's familiar voice, however, he moaned and tried to raise his head.

'Francis … I am sorry …'

'Sorry? For what? It is I who beg forgiveness. Don't talk just now. Let Hutton tend your injuries.'

The doctor pulled over a low stool asking Light to hold a candle to better see the damage. It was extensive. Across Soliman's bronzed back lay scores of deep slashes, the flesh peeled back in jagged tears, impossible to sew. James Hutton sighed. 'I can put in a few stitches here and there, but the rest will have to heal as it may. Soliman, you'll bear wicked scars, I am afraid.'

'*Saya akan mati*?' Soliman gasped. Would he die?

Hutton laughed softly. 'Not if I have anything to say about it. These wounds are cruel, but they are not fatal, so long as we keep them clean. Mr Marlbro will remain here in the kampong, with your permission, and tend to the three of you until you're well. He is with Mus and Naz now.'

The news calmed Soliman. He lay his head on the bolster and endured the attentions, despite the obvious discomfort. At one point, however, when Hutton was cleaning the gashes, Soliman raised his head, sniffing. 'Brandy? In my kampong?' he asked, but there was amusement in his voice.

'Put your head back down. What you can't see, cannot offend,' Hutton grinned. 'And those other poor buggers have never smelt it anyway, so what would they know?'

Soliman managed a smile. 'I wouldn't be so sure. There are not many sailors who haven't imbibed alcohol, I'll warrant.'

For the first time, Light spoke. 'At least it's French brandy not Jamaica rum, Sol. Nothing but the best. You're welcome to a swig if it helps ease the pain.'

Soliman shook his head, moaning softly. 'You can pour it on my skin, but not down my throat. I will not go that far. I am a good Muslim now!'

Hutton sat back to survey his work. 'You'll heal better if the wound's left open for now. But it must be kept clean. No one is to touch it apart from Marlbro or me until it scabs over. Don't let your wife and her ladies mess about with bandages until you're ready to move about. And I insist on opium for the first few nights.'

Light rested his hand gently upon Soliman's. 'And then

we shall talk, Sol. Later, when you feel better. I would know everything that transpired. I cannot act against Hamilton, but I'm finished with him now. Here's my promise to you: I'll destroy the bastard if it's the last thing I do, my word on it!'

***

It was some days before Soliman was sufficiently recovered for Light to broach the matter, days in which Light's brooding anger finally erupted. It resulted in a fiery argument between him and Hamilton, which became the talk of the town. Nothing was achieved, but it gave Light a release of emotion and demonstrated to the settlers the extent of the superintendent's support for the local people. How Light kept himself from raining blows upon his adversary, was a miracle to those who knew his temper when roused. Only the notion that Hamilton was not worth the trouble, kept him from beating him to the same pulp that he had left on Soliman's back.

When he finally ejected Hamilton – whose temper matched the superintendent's, spouting profanities as he was firmly elbowed out – it was the last time the two men ever spoke. Light ordered Lt Gerard, his adjutant, to stand as go-between in future. He refused ever to be in the same room as the man; and never referred to him again by name.

On his next visit, Soliman was propped up on cushions, his back well bandaged, surrounded by his children. At Light's approach, he attempted to rise.

'Rest yourself back down, man!' Light perched beside him. The children crowded round, curious but shy. They knew the distinguished visitor but were always bashful in his presence.

'Say hello to your *datuk*!' Soliman encouraged them. They complied then ran away to peek from a safer distance. It was hard to accept this old white man was their grandfather. 'I wish my little Francis was so well behaved. He is impossible. Quite the most mischievous child I've ever known. I'd lost count of your brood, Sol, I'm ashamed to say. I counted four. And Aisyah has been blessed again. Why, Sol, you've caught up with me!'

'God is Good,' Soliman replied with a proud smile. 'Children are the heart of any home.'

'Indeed, Sol. Which is exactly why I'm here today. We must talk. Since I saw you last, I have near come to blows with the bastard captain who did this to you. I believe you were caught in the midst of his poisonous grievance towards me. Furthermore, the man holds distasteful opinions on your race and religion. He has no place holding authority on such an island as Pinang.'

'His views are not unusual for your people, Francis. It is you that differ from the rest.' Soliman replied sadly. 'My feelings for the British have changed over the years. Now, I despise them.'

Light rubbed at his forehead wearily. 'I feel like Canute,' he murmured helplessly.

'Who?' Soliman asked. 'I do not know this Canute.'

There was a flicker of his old sense of humour. 'Canute was an ancient English king who thought he might hold back the waves. Take no notice of my foolishness! I'm an old man these days.'

'Stop feeling sorry for yourself,' Soliman grinned.

'Tell me what happened, Sol. Tell me everything of that day, for all I have heard is their fabrications.'

The only reason Soliman had attended the fort for the enquiry had been in his capacity as the captain of the ship. He had wished to attest to the good character of his sailors and confirm that he had charged them with protecting the ship's cargo overnight, which is what they believed they had done. As he spoke fluent English, he could act as a translator. His men would be incapable of giving their story both through language difficulties and their nervousness in such a place. Yet, almost as soon as the charges were read out, matters turned sour. Hamilton did not intend to hold an inquiry but a sentencing.

Mustapha and Nazrul were charged with attempted manslaughter on British sailors who had come aboard to sell rum, for which they subsequently refused to pay. A quarrel had broken out and the Malays had produced weapons, throwing the men overboard after beating them severely.

'Two men against three sailors?' Light exclaimed.

Soliman shrugged. 'The men were not able to defend themselves because they were drunk. Or so they said. I stood up to object, and the next thing I knew, I was also on trial beside them. I was deemed complicit because I had not controlled my men. Hamilton refused us any defence. We were guilty as charged. He insisted that an Englishman might have died. We were lucky we didn't hang for it, but his powers did not extend to capital punishment. Then we were taken out and flogged. Thirty lashes each.' Soliman shivered at the memory, despite the muggy warmth of the day.

Light closed his eyes to shrug away the image. 'I was a short distance away at my desk. If I had but known –'

'Enough.' Soliman held up his hand. 'It is done. It cannot be changed. Hamilton and men like him want to spread discord.

They desire us to run amok and give them cause to shoot us down. This ends here. In future, we must be vigilant and give them no cause against us.'

'Your good sense is commendable, Sol. I would not have your charity in the circumstances. Today I came with something important to say to you that has been on my mind for some time.' Light stopped, struggling to proceed. Soliman watched with concern. 'Hear me out before you speak, if you will, lad. A number of things have occurred of late that lead me to believe my time here is nigh done. I plan to take my family home to England. As you know, William is already there. Sol, I'm of an age when my powers are waning. This responsibility has ground me down. If I leave, I will not return, do you understand?'

Soliman nodded his head gravely, measuring his answer carefully. 'I've always known this day would finally come, Francis. Our lives have taken different paths since the early days so long ago. I will never forget you or what you have done for me, wherever you are in the world.' Tears shone in Soliman's deep brown eyes; he had always worn his emotions lightly, much as his father.

'You will always be that little boy who slept in my cabin with his kitten! Even if you are a man with children of your own. Soliman, one day sons will leave, daughters too. That is life. But that is not all I wish to say. There are many here who would do you harm. It is known you are my son. They do not like it. To them, you are a Malay above his station. They fear your example might persuade other Malays that they have a right to trade side by side with their "betters". When I am gone, it could be even worse for you and your family.'

Soliman did not argue. It had been on his mind as well. This was not the first time that his very existence had been viewed as a threat by British men. 'What to do?' he asked helplessly, even though the answer hung plainly in the space between them.

'I will sign the *Speedwell* over to you. It is all I can spare now that my fortunes have taken such a turn. These years have not been easy on my pocket. Everything I have left is for the education of my children and to ensure Martinha is protected when I'm gone. But the *Speedwell* is for you. It was once our home; there is no one I would rather leave it to. Take it and your perahus and leave this place, Soliman. Many ports in the Straits will welcome you, for your reputation is respected everywhere. I suggest Queddah, for the sultan needs experienced merchants and thinks highly of you. From there, you can ply your trade throughout the region. And in a few years, when the memories of me have faded, you may return to Pinang waters. Soon no one will be left to remember what we once meant to each other.'

The two men sat in silence while the words died away. The noisy village receded into the distance, with nothing between them but the truth spoken. Words were inadequate. A lifetime shared; the world they once knew gone. It was to be their last farewell. They would not meet again.

Soliman pulled himself up as Francis rose. Instinctively they embraced.

'Father,' Soliman gasped, tears now freely flowing. '*Bapakku* ...'

'My son. God speed ...'

26

Bitter Fruits

The Burial Ground, Prince of Wales Island. 25th May 1794

It was the third burial he had attended for Scott's family alone in the space of six weeks. Just past dawn, the early morning cool and overcast after heavy rain, Francis Light joined the sad procession of mourners heading to the grave. The burial ground was a forlorn place at any time. Today it was more woebegone than ever.

The gathering was small. The death of a seven-year-old child was hardly remarkable on Prince of Wales Island. Of late a contagion had been visited upon the settlement; few families had been spared. Light had sent his household up to Strawberry Hill to keep them safe. Poor little Francis Scott had succumbed only a few weeks after the death of his mother. Anna Julhy had died in childbirth and the little new-born mite had followed a few days later, briefly clinging on to life only after the tender ministrations of Janeke Rozells, who had fed the baby from her own breasts.

Scott had been so devastated that he had retreated to his rooms and all but drunk himself to oblivion. The depths of his friend's feeling had surprised Light considering the careless disregard Scott had shown towards women throughout his life. It seems Anna Julhy had broken down his barriers. His friend was utterly bereft. Worse was to come. Poor Scott had only just begun to drag himself back from grief when his little Francis had been taken.

Light's mood was bleak as he stood shoulder-to-shoulder with Scott who sobbed unashamedly throughout the brief committal. Of course, he himself mourned the little boy, but in truth, Light had barely known him. At least a dozen children ran around Scott's house at any time. Even their father had on occasion confused their names and ages. Yet there was a personal edge to these losses that Light could not shake: it might be he standing by the graves of Martinha or his own little Frannie. Only the grace of God had spared them. Francis Scott had been of similar age to his William; the two boys had been friends. If anything were to happen to William far away in Suffolk, he would not know for many months. Who was to say his eldest son was not already in a lonely graveyard somewhere at the other side of the world?

Such dark thoughts possessed his soul as he paid his last respects, bitterly in keeping with the constant stream of recent bad tidings. Death, tragedy and disappointment plagued him on all sides. One by one everything he had known and worked for and all those who had been by his side, were fading away. The graveyard was a testament to that; he only had to turn to the headstones of so many men who had given their lives in the island's service: Murray, Mylne and dear John Glass, to mention just a few.

When the gravediggers began the final brutal act of tossing heavy clumps of earth over the small coffin, Light embraced Scott, offering to accompany him home. He was gruffly rebuffed. Scott wanted to be alone. Not even an old friend could heal his broken heart. Light watched him go, shoulders sagging and feet dragging, the image of a man forsaken. Nodding to other mourners as they filed off home, he was relieved that no one engaged him in conversation. What was there to say? Doubtless everyone felt the same as he, wretched with fear such a thing might happen to them.

As Light made his way back towards the settlement, rain drizzled down, the skies not yet empty of their burden. His sense of isolation deepened. He was a man alone amidst a sea of sorrows and burdens. Who now was left for him to confide in? Only Martinha, but she was on the Hill and had her own crosses to bear. He had no wish to pile worries on her own sadness.

Her brother Felipe had recently left for Jangsylan along with his wife and children, taking Lady Thong Di with him. It had been decided as the best choice for her now that the Lights planned to return to England. With war looming and insecurity surrounding trade in the Straits, Khoh Lay Huan was setting up an office on the Siamese island, an insurance against a future bad outcome for Pinang.

Kapitan Khoh had strong links in Siam where he had begun his merchant empire years before. He was an intimate of several local governors. Felipe Rozells was Siamese by birth and a member of the influential Chan dynasty whose name still held some influence on the island. He was also the brother-in-law of the British governor of Pinang. Felipe's credentials were impeccable. Not only that, but Siam was crying out for foreign investment since many merchants had given it a wide berth. The wily Khoh saw profit to be made.

And so, Francis and Martinha had said farewell to Lady Thong Di and Felipe, the two great rocks upon which Martinha – and Light himself – had depended. Another precious link to the past had been severed.

Back at his office, Light attempted to shrug off his gloom, calling for a pot of tea and settling down to correspondence. He might as well lose himself in papers as dwell to no purpose on what fate had bestowed. If he had hoped to distract his mind from cares, however, he had been sadly mistaken. His first letter was a private correspondence from his banker in Calcutta, William Fairlie. The news was devastating.

My dear Francis
Times continue to be fraught with nothing but War and Loss. At least I am able to send Happy Tidings of your three daughters to ease your Concerns. They are thriving, prettier by the day, and growing into charming young ladies. I had the pleasure to make their acquaintance again at the Ogilvys. Your eldest, Sarah, now lodges with them as companion to Margaret, as I'm sure you know. She was drawing much attention from several of the young officers present, particularly a young lieutenant from Dumbarton, James Welsh, a fine fellow with an impressive record. She could do much worse. Mrs Ogilvy will keep an eye out that all the niceties are observed and so on, but a word in your ear – young Sarah likes Welsh. He's not yet twenty and marked out for promotion, an intelligent lad with a good bearing. If you need me to act 'in loco parentis', I would be delighted to assist.

And now for the ill tidings. There has been a marked decline in trade. Caution abounds as the cost of War increases. Attacks on shipping have taken their toll, adding to the economic gloom. It saddens me to be the bearer of bad news, but this has had a deleterious effect on our Investments. Your Deposits, once almost twenty thousand pounds, have now fallen by more than half. We must all cut our future expenditure according to the cloth. Nor can we hope for any Change for the better in the years ahead. This War will last a long time. The Consequences will be devastating.

As your good friend of many years (almost twenty-five years, God be praised!) I assure you that I will make it my personal business to ensure your daughters are sheltered from any limitations in your finances. If necessary, I will bring them into my home and use my influence to introduce them to Society where they might make suitable marriages. Have no fear on that count, Francis.

I suspect this information will affect your return to Suffolk. This is not the time for retirement, my old friend. Make the most of your office. Shed some of those principles and take every opportunity to re-build your fortune. A man with your experience of trade knows how to exploit the current state of affairs. Guns and Opium, Rice and Salt. I trust you will take my well-meant advice.

Wishing you all the best in these uncertain times
William Fairlie

His investments halved? It was scarcely possible on top of the losses he had suffered on the island. He was all but ruined. It would take everything he had merely to educate William and Francis, never mind buy a country estate. Light sank his head into his hands. If it was not bad enough, to hear speak of his girls being paraded on the marriage market was unconscionable. Yet, what else could they do now? There was nothing for them on Pinang – and a return to England was increasingly unlikely. Better that they settle down with men able to provide for them in a way that he could not. His sense of failure was immense. All those years with only fleeting visits, his daughters had grown up far away in a world which about to claim them forever. There would be little chance of seeing them again for an indefinite period, by which time even little Mary would be a woman. It was a pain that cut deep into his heart.

Just then, a visitor was announced: Commodore Rainier with his report. Light thrust down his profound shock, pain piled upon sorrow, as he had learned to do so many times. Setting his face to a benign expression, he prepared to receive the commodore. If anyone could help lighten his burdens, it would be this hardy sailor in whom Light had great hopes.

Peter Rainier, new commander-in-chief of the East Indies station, successor to Admiral Cornwallis, had been in the Straits for the past few weeks. His arrival had been the one positive note in this season of misadventures. The Company had finally responded to the danger that French marauders presented and had sent their senior naval commander with a few vessels led by his 74-gun flagship HMS *Suffolk*. That name alone had cheered Light, an uncanny presentiment of home.

Rainier was a distinctive figure, particularly known for his eyeglasses. He was myopic, never seen without his Martin's Margins, round tortoiseshell frames enclosing lenses that improved his vision and shielded his eyes from sunlight. Behind his back, men fondly called him 'Tortoise' – but never to his face. The captain was a kindly fellow who treated all men, even native lascars, with fairness. His benign regime had paid off for he was one of the most successful commanders in the Navy, already renowned for taking enemy prizes.

The bluff Rainier strode into Light's office with an air of command. He was a man of average height, who appeared smaller due to the rotundity of his large belly straining at the buttons of his waistcoat. His head was coiffed in a short grey wig that accentuated his heavy jowls and double chins. Rainier's face was red and shiny, his features prominent and his mouth sensuous. Here was a man who loved life. Yet, it was difficult not to focus solely on the spectacles that enlarged his eyes and rendered the impression of permanent surprise.

'Good day, Superintendent. My thanks for seeing me at short notice!' Rainier began, accepting a glass of port and settling his bulk down on a chair.

'My pleasure, Captain. How goes it?' Light was more than ready for the disturbance from the amiable Rainier. A servant set down a plate of fresh fruit and refilled their glasses.

'All good, my friend. We hit a storm yesterday and took some minor damage, so I headed back to port for repairs. It was timely enough, to be fair, for we've been out several weeks; the men are tired, and the food was becoming tiresomely bland. I also believe you're overdue a report. Matters home and abroad are changing rapidly.'

It was an informative meeting, providing better news than he had received for many a day. Rainier had been back and forth between the Andamans and the Straits, driving off the French privateers threatening the region. Once they had faced real warships, the French ships had soon retreated back to Île-de-France, their proverbial tails between their legs. It was now his intention to send two frigates, *Centurion* and *Diomède* (recently seized from the French themselves), to blockade the waters off Mauritius to deter future raids. All-in-all it had been an excellent outcome. In a few short weeks, the Straits had been rendered comparatively safe. Unless the French dispatched an entire armada, unlikely given their current situation in Europe, it might be enough to stave off attack for the time being.

One of the more interesting snippets of intelligence Rainier shared concerned the situation in the Andamans. It seemed the new, much vaunted British base was already in dire straits.

'They sent settlers who signed up for an initial period of three years – which is not the same as settling, as I'm sure you know. That was a mistake, for most had left by '93. The conditions are appalling: natives hostile, disease rife and food contaminated – the families were dying like flies. The locals refused to cooperate and no *orang laut* could be persuaded to settle. The only recourse was to ship out convict labour from India, which has proved its death knell; law and order has broken down, white convicts abuse the Indian prisoners, theft and corruption abound, visiting sailors run riot. Nor is the island self-sustaining. Everything is shipped in, so the colony has become a massive drain on resources, with nothing yet to show for it. Even the admirable Major Kyd has proved out of his depth.'

Light listened with a sense of bitter satisfaction yet held his tongue. It would not do to publicly rejoice in the failure, even if he privately thought it just desserts. Everyone who knew the area had predicted such a fate. But the Council believed it knew better than experienced Indies men. Served them damned well right.

'Your forbearance does you credit, Light,' Rainier observed. 'If any man has the right to take satisfaction in this outcome, it is you. Why Cornwallis put his faith in those disease-ridden islands is a mystery to all who sail these waters. With a thriving settlement already in the Straits? It was madness. Privately Kyd said as much to me himself. He always favoured Prince of Wales Island.'

Light could not help but let out a groan of frustration. 'Yet he was eager enough to take up the challenge when offered!'

Rainier chuckled. 'What is a man to do? Kyd has his own career to think of. But this ought to be in your favour, superintendent. The new acting governor-general, Sir John Shore, is an old Calcutta hand, the usual mealy-mouthed administrator. He'll be quite happy not to rock the boat and could easily be persuaded to shift operations to your island. Anything for a quiet life, if you ask me. Shore will be much more amenable than that old stiffrump Cornwallis ever was. Strike now and get him on your side, Light.'

'I have tried, sir, but the results are not promising. In his recent letter, Shore has not only forbidden me from any expenditure on defences other than repair but has dismissed my claim for monies already spent by referring my claim to London ...'

'London? The best of luck with that, my friend.' Rainier broke in, reaching over to sample a piece of green fruit. 'Good lord, what's this? So bitter!' he pulled out a handkerchief and spat out the pieces, swigging port to wash away the taste.

'*Buah kedondong*. I do not recall its English name. An

acquired taste, I'm afraid. Please, try the guava instead. Most refreshing!' Light placed a small helping on Rainier's plate with a small fork. He approved and tucked into the rest with gusto.

Light resumed where they had broken off. 'I despair of the situation. My personal fortune has been poured into this island! Shore is less stubborn but just as intractable in his timidity.'

Rainier shook his head in disbelief. 'You are the very opposite of most Company officers, for whom such an establishment would serve only to fill their private coffers. That's the damned problem with our "*Honourable*" Company. It is run by merchants and accountants for whom spending is anathema – and profit is all. The fact that men fight and die to make their trade possible seems quite lost upon them. War costs money, like it or not!' he fumed.

'I would be careful voicing such opinions abroad, Rainier,' Light cautioned.

His companion blew out his cheeks; he did not care for what others thought. 'This is not Calcutta, Light. And I know a decent man of good sense when I see him. Be assured that you have my support. My reports will reflect the high regard in which I hold this establishment and your own good self, for what my opinion is worth. Such is life in the Royal Navy. There are those who court favour and are awarded accolades, while others do the real work and live in obscurity. I'm sure you learned that lesson from your own naval days!'

'Indeed,' Light agreed. 'Nor is it only the Navy. It's a wonder how the British have ever succeeded at anything with their practice of promoting posturing fools over experienced men. Yet, as you say, those same men do the work and save the bacon of the rest every time.'

Shortly afterwards, Rainier took his leave, inviting Light aboard for dinner the following evening when they might spend some convivial time improving their acquaintanceship. They both recognised a potential ally, despite the different worlds in which they dwelt. Light felt an unfamiliar sense of camaraderie, something which had been in short supply of late. The imminent downfall of Major Alexander Kyd also brought a much-needed smile to his face. Whether unworthy of him or not, there was satisfaction in witnessing the falling of the once-mighty major. Any crumb of hope was gratefully received these days.

***

Later that evening, in the quiet of his private apartments at Government House, Light downed a bottle of wine, which did little to improve his state of mind. Striding over to his writing desk, he snatched a sheet of paper and dipped his pen into the pot, drinking down the last dregs of his glass before he commenced writing.

Dear George, friend of my boyhood,
I trust all is well with you back in Suffolk and my dear son William is thriving. Please God, he does not cause you and gentle Ann any undue Trouble! We are eternally in your Debt for your Service in acting as his Patron. My health has improved since last year when William left and I sent a somewhat Rambling note with Captain Wall. My wits had not quite returned to me from my bout of fever. Thank God I have them back. Yet, I have the presentiment

that my Time is running out; mayhap we may not meet again, even though it is my dearest wish. But we must accept our Fate, for what else is there for us to do?

As you know, I promised a further sum of money, three thousand pounds at least in lieu of a deposit on Goldsbery Farm. It appears now that time and tide have sunk that particular Ship of Fancy; the current state of my Finances now renders this impossible. My man Fairlie in Calcutta has written with ill tidings of a decline in my Expectations. The business of superintending is not a profitable one, I fear, especially when a man's outgoing more than doubles his deposits. It is a recipe for disaster. Were it not for the loyal Support of my old Partner and most Respected merchant, James Scott, my situation would be even worse than it is. I have been more fortunate in my friendships than I have ever been in the Management of my own affairs, sad to say.

My intention was to remit a large sum for the purchase and refurbishment of the Manor, and in truth I believed myself nearing that goal. Now my luck has sadly changed – or my Hopes have exceeded my Abilities to realise them. I will be fortunate indeed if my whole Estate manages to reach Twelve Thousand at its current value, sufficient only for a modest Farm and the education of my sons. As long as enough remains for my boys to have the best start in Life, it must now be sufficient. I hereby appoint you my Executor in England and William Fairlie in India. James Scott will supervise my holdings on the island, together with Martinha.

It strikes me – would that I had considered this earlier in my life! – that I have never yet heard of any Pioneer who died a rich man. Such men must be Satisfied with the renown of their name. It is those who follow who benefit from their Endeavours and make Fortunes. If this is the last time I should write, know that your Kindness and good Heart has sustained me; your Friendship will be one of the last things I contemplate. We are forever in your Debt. Enjoy the remainder of your Peaceful Days as a Farmer – it is a Thousand Times more Rewarding than Governing, my Friend!

Adieu, Ten Thousand good wishes to your wife and children. Remember me to James Lynn and all the other Woodbridge boys.

Yours affectionately and truly,

Francis Light

Light set down his pen, and exhaled a long, slow breath. He had made his farewells in the event his days were numbered, a presentiment he was unable to shake off these days. His visit to the burial ground had only increased his foreboding. Perhaps it would not be long before the red earth of this island held him forever in its embrace.

27

Sisyphus and the Rock

Prince of Wales Island. September 1794

Although she missed the tranquil peace of her cottage on the hill, it was a relief to return to the family home. Separated from Francis, Martinha had lived in constant fear that he might fall ill himself. There was contagion in the settlement, and he was more vulnerable than most. After his last near fatal fever, Hutton had warned him to take all possible precautions against infection. Yet he continued to be careless of his health, burning the candles at both ends with work or drinking late into the night, mixing with all manner of settlers in their hovels. He believed it his duty to be visible, allowing ordinary folk to approach him with their problems – for how else would he understand their needs?

Her presence changed little. Francis still regularly spent the nights at Government House, particularly when he had guests to entertain. Of late there had been several: Rainier – a seasoned drinker – and Alexander Kyd, recently arrived from his Andaman establishment. Once, Martinha had been fond of Major Kyd; his wife was a dear friend. But she could not forgive the advantage he had taken of her husband by manipulated Cornwallis to invest in the Andaman settlement to the detriment of Pinang. Nothing would convince her otherwise. She had spent long enough in Calcutta to know that no one could be trusted. Backstabbing was a way of life.

Alexander Kyd now had the gall to return to the island on the pretext of re-examining its position after the abject failure of Port Cornwallis. The brazen cheek of the man! Was this another ploy? Francis suspected Kyd was setting his sights on Pinang for his next appointment. Now her husband's days and nights were plagued by a new concern: would Calcutta replace him with a younger, more favoured man? She could not blame him for burning the midnight oil in their company. Francis had to play the game more shrewdly than ever these days.

There was more. In August a letter from the governor-general suggested a rare sign of progress: Light's many requests for a judiciary were to be addressed at last. But not as he desired. Instead of an independent court, they were sending a Trojan horse (as Francis called it) to weaken his authority from within. Two senior officers, loyal Company men, were to assist the administration, particularly in legal matters. In future there would be a council of four, effectively crippling the superintendent and sidestepping faithful Thomas Pigou. But to what end?

'They mean to force me into retirement, then swamp the island with their blinkered bureaucrats,' Francis said.

'Why would they do such a thing with war still threatening? No one knows this region as you do!' Martinha exclaimed.

'That is the point, my dear. They believe me too involved with the local people. It places my loyalties in question. If they abandon the Andamans and turn to our island, it must be on their terms. I am viewed as a contrarian who does not hold to their British values. I give too much attention to the natives.'

Martinha was aghast. 'It is they who built this island!'

Light laughed bitterly. 'They're nothing but grist to the mill, Martinha. The Company builds their establishments on the toil of others but reaps the rewards for itself. I am not a perfect man by any means, for I have lied and manipulated with the best of them. But I have never done harm to those who have supported me. I have been a true friend regardless of the colour of a man's skin or his language and religion. Sharp practice is one thing, but enslaving those who do not share your culture is a wicked business.'

His impassioned speech shocked Martinha profoundly. She had little illusion about the petty prejudices of the British, but the vision Francis described was abhorrent. 'What can be done to stop this travesty?' she gasped.

He sighed deeply. 'I have two choices. I can fight them tooth and nail or we can give up and return home. In truth, I have little stomach left for the fight. I'm weary to the bone, Martinha. Like Sisyphus, I have pushed a boulder up a hill for years, only for it to tumble back each time. There comes a time for a man to accept his race is run and hand over to younger men, despite the inevitable consequences.'

Martinha stroked his face fondly. 'Then we go back to England as we planned. Francis, you have done enough! I am alone here now with Mother and Felipe gone, Soliman too. It is time we gathered our children together for what remains of our lives and make a new life in England.'

He caught her hands in his, kissing her fingertips fondly. 'I know what that would cost you, yet it is indeed time to make the break. I fear there is no longer anything for us here. But it is not so simple, sayang. This war has depleted my reserves. I can no longer afford to resign ...'

Her forehead wrinkled in confusion. 'What do you mean? I thought we had sufficient to sustain a moderate life in England.'

'Oh, my dear girl!' he cried. I wished to spare you this! Yet I fear I can no longer keep you in the dark. We have barely sufficient means to educate the boys as it stands. The Company owes me a substantial sum and my investments have taken a heavy fall. This damned war! Perhaps in time we shall recover but at this moment the prospect is bleak. As pitiful as it is, my salary is all we have, other than the pepper and my trading concerns. It is not enough. We must stay a while longer.'

Martinha absorbed the enormity of his admission. 'Then so be it, Francis. We must accept what God gives. Perhaps we should go to Thalang instead and join Felipe? We still have friends and family there. You could dabble in trade and make an honest living.'

It was something to which he had already given consideration. 'I've already discussed with Scott the possibility of running the office there. But Martinha, I am governor of a British establishment! How can my fortunes sink so low at this stage of my life? It is unthinkable to return to the country trade! What of our children's futures? What chance would the girls have if it were known how far their father had fallen! I have made my mind. My bed is laid, and I must lie upon it, even should it be my catafalque.'

He was obdurate. His pride would not let him accept this final blow. Francis Light would remain in charge of the island, whatever the cost. From her vantage on the veranda of her home, Martinha looked out on the deep blue sea and the endless sky above – and prayed. 'Keep him safe, Lord,' she whispered. 'Give him strength for the battles ahead.'

'Ibu!' little Frannie clambered upon her knee, holding her face in his tiny hands, full of concern. 'Don't cry, Mama! Why are you sad?'

She kissed her little boy, the only child now left to her. Her world was scattered to the winds. What chance now they would be reunited again?

***

Later that week, Martinha paid a rare visit to James Scott under the pretext of bringing Frannie to play with the younger Scott children: Jamie, Robert, Caroline and Harriet. She was accompanied by Janeke and her daughter. Stealing herself for an interview with the unpredictable Mr Scott, she knocked at the door of his study, unsure what she would find. Of late, Scott had been a remote figure, conducting his businesses entirely from home in isolation from society.

To her surprise, she found him busy at work – sober – and unexpectedly pleased to see her. His clothes were clean and tidy, and he was freshly shaven. It seemed he had turned a corner.

'My dear lass, what a pleasure! Please take a seat while I call for a pot of tea.'

They settled down by the open window in a shady spot with a pleasant outlook onto the garden with its ornamental fishpond.

'I'm delighted to find you well, Mr Scott,' Martinha began hesitantly, not wishing to revisit his sadness by recalling recent tragedies.

Scott was a forthright man, no stranger to blunt speech. 'No need to gild the lily, Nona. 'Tis true I was in a dark place for many months, but have found myself at last, thanks largely to the tender ministrations of Mee Ngah. Are you aware we have resumed our former relationship? Some say it is too soon, but they can insinuate all they like. She was once my wife in Queddah so it is no scandal. Anna would be glad we've both found comfort in each other.'

Martinha had heard the rumours, but she did not blame them. The children needed a mother, Scott a wife. If Anna Julhy had accepted Mee Ngah, so should they; it was nobody's business but their own. 'Anna was a great lady, the kindest and most generous woman I have ever known,' Martinha replied. 'Nothing demonstrates those qualities quite as much as her generosity to Mee Ngah and her girls,' she added.

He acknowledged her acceptance with a cursory nod, changing the subject deftly. 'What brings you here this fine morning, Mrs Light?'

Martinha hesitated, unsure if it was unseemly to broach her concerns behind Francis' back. His friend pre-empted her. 'Is it out of concern for Francis? I've seen little of him of late but have heard things. Be assured that anything you say in confidence shall remain between us.' He placed an avuncular hand upon hers. 'We both want what's best for him, my dear.'

Martinha gave him a sad smile. She had always found James Scott intimidating yet in that moment, she saw another side of the irascible Scotsman. He had a kindly heart for those he loved.

'Francis is obsessed with plots against him. He fears the Company plans to replace him. I don't doubt there is reason to suspect mischief, but the whole affair is injurious to his health.

He's not as strong as he once was. These recurring fevers have taken a mighty toll, yet he still works like a man half his age. I fear he will break under the strain!' Her voice began to falter.

Scott was unsurprised. 'It is as you say. Hutton constantly warns him to take some ease. He does not sleep enough, nor does he spare himself from visiting the ordinary folk despite all manner of pestilence in town. Your fears are warranted, my dear. I'm afraid I've neglected my old friend of late when he needs me most,' he admitted ruefully.

'It is not your fault. You have your own burdens. But I would be grateful for your assistance now. Dr Hutton's too. May I ask you something else, Mr Scott?'

'Of course, you may. But call me James. We've known each other too long for such formality,' he replied gently.

'Mr James,' Martinha began, not quite in the way he had intended. 'Do you believe the Company wishes to appoint a new superintendent?'

Scott paused, giving the matter some consideration. 'I cannae stand the lot of them but in this regard, I think Francis has it wrong. They may not entirely agree with him, but I believe the tide is changing. They now view the island in a more favourable light. It is a double-edged sword, however. While Francis governed virtually alone, he had complete control. Yet if the Company accepts Pinang as an establishment in its own image, such independence becomes impossible. Now they will flood the island with their own people and hold the reins from Calcutta. Francis will be retained as superintendent but must adjust to the new reality. There will be many controls on his authority – and his singular vision for this island will be ignored.'

Martinha listened carefully. Even with his fluent Malay, she struggled with his accent; when he spoke in English, it seemed another language from the one Francis used. Yet she gleaned the essence of his words.

'The wishes and needs of the peoples of this island will be disregarded. Is that what you mean?'

'Not entirely, but where they cross the boundaries set by the British establishment, most assuredly they will. This island will become British territory. British law will be imposed. Justice, trade, land holding, taxes, even religion – will be in the hands of the Company. Francis must accept this or be broken on the wheel of his recalcitrance.'

'Do you trust Major Kyd?' she asked bluntly. 'And Captain Rainier? Or these other administrators, Philip Manington and John Beanland?'

Scott pulled a face. 'I wouldnae put them all in the same box, to be fair. Rainier's a decent chap, a navy man with a reputation for fair play. Kyd's a fellow on his way up, I'll allow, but he doesn't play the double-cross. When I first laid eyes on him, I didn't trust his fancy ways, but the fellow has grown on me. You cannae blame him for the Andaman business. Would Francis have been cared if any rival felt short-changed when he was appointed superintendent here?'

She had not considered that. Francis had not always played straight himself. 'Why is Kyd here if not to spy upon us?' Martinha queried.

'Oh, I'm sure he hopes to glean as much inside intelligence as he can. And there's no doubt he may see himself a future candidate for superintendent. Yet he is impressed by what Francis has achieved. The danger does not come from that quarter, in my opinion.'

'But there is danger?' Martinha astutely observed.

Her question made him chuckle. 'You're no fool, dear lady. The two Company men on their way, while not a direct threat, point to the future. Manington is currently stationed in that flea pit, Bencoolen. He'll have his sights on Pinang for himself, I have no doubts. I know nothing of this Beanland, but I dare say he'll be another of those small-minded fellows they churn out by the dozen in Bengal. Once these fellows have their feet in the door, everything will change. Each tiny decision will be referred to the Council, and nothing achieved year in, year out. Francis does not deal well with inaction. It is not his nature.'

'What's your suggestion?' Martinha asked bluntly. 'Should we encourage him to step down?'

Scott shook his head. 'He can't afford to, my dear. Much as I would like him to join me like the old days, there's no stepping down for a man like him. It is more than pride. This is his life's work. He must see it through, at least until this French business is resolved. In a few years, he'll return to England, where no doubt he'll receive a knighthood for his services. In the meantime, we must make him see the writing on the wall. I hate to say it, for the Company is detestable to me, but Francis must accept the limitations imposed upon him.'

Martina sighed deeply. 'I fear it will be the death of him.'

'We all must die one day, my dear. None of us is immortal. A man must be allowed his own fate. Such is the serendipity of life.'

It was not the outcome Martinha had desired, but at least James Scott was on her side to help ease her husband's burdens.

He promised to approach those likely to support him: Hutton, Pigou, Macalister, Bacon and a few others. They would also keep an eye on Francis' drinking. It was an amusing turn of affairs for a sot such as he. A little temperance would benefit Scott himself as well.

28
Full Circle

The Ogilvy Residence, Calcutta. September 1794

Sarah Light read through the letters before carefully tying them with ribbon, placing all four into a leather wallet. Her precious mail was to be delivered into the safekeeping of William Lindesay. Her heart was already pounding, imagining the various ways in which this correspondence might be received: delight, bemusement, concern or – God forbid – downright anger.

She glanced across at Lieutenant James Welsh, who was observing her with a studious expression.

'How does it read?' he said, furrowing his brow. 'Did I express myself well? I had no idea what to say. This is the first time I have ever composed such a missive.'

'I should hope so, too! I had not thought that there might be other ladies about town to whose fathers you had written for their hands! Or did they all reject you, my poor dear?' Sarah teased.

James gave a weak grin. 'Do not jest, Sarah. What if your father puts his foot down? He has never met me. I should not blame any man for refusing such a suit!'

Sarah crossed the room to throw her arms about his shoulders. He was a tall man even for the lissom Miss Light. 'Let us cross that bridge when we come to it, James! For now, we must hope these letters of commendation will impress him. It isn't just my father, you know? My mother will insist on her approval, too. Did you know their marriage was arranged? Such matters are usual in the Straits. They ought to be sympathetic.'

'Perhaps,' James muttered as he played with her dark locks, winding a curl about his finger, and then letting it fall. 'Whatever happens, I shall pursue my suit to the bitter end. I will not lose you, lovely Sarah. There's not a girl in Calcutta or the whole of India could hold a candle to you!'

She threw back her head laughing in delight. 'I do adore you, Jamie! In all the world, I never imagined a young man I could love so much. Never doubt it. We shall marry – with my parents' blessing – or I shall have no other. Rest assured my parents will be happy for us. Once they become accustomed to the news!'

Calcutta 15th September 1794
Dear Sir
It was not my intent to approach you by letter. I planned to visit Prince of Wales Island in person to present my suit. But circumstances have made this impossible as I shall explain. Permit me first, however, to introduce myself and lay my case as humbly and sincerely as I may.

My name is James Gascoigne Welsh, born 1775 in Kirkintilloch, Dumbarton, ten miles from the city of Glasgow. My father John is a gentleman farmer of some standing in the community. As an only child, I am heir to his estate which, although not substantial, is a decent living for any family. Having enlisted in the Madras Army in 1790 as Ensign, I progressed through the ranks to Lieutenant of the 24th Native Infantry, which commission

I gained in '92 at the age of seventeen. In '93 I fought at Pondicherry under Lord Cornwallis where I was wounded, injuries which have kept me from my duties for many months. Whilst convalescing in Calcutta, I had the pleasure of meeting your daughter Sarah at the house of Mr John Ogilvy, with whom you are acquainted.

Since then, I have had the honour of escorting Miss Light on numerous occasions, always in the company of the Ogilvys so no hint of impropriety taints our Friendship. It has long been Sarah's hope that during the forthcoming Christmas season, the Light family might spend the festive period in Calcutta where we might be formally introduced. Failing that, we planned to travel to Prince of Wales Island in December. Recently, however, I have received a new commission: Lieutenant Commander of the Ninth Infantry at Mandurah in Maharashtra. This posting is far from Bengal and has forced us to advance our plans. It is our wish to marry in Calcutta before my departure to guarantee Sarah my pension and inheritance in the unhappy event of my demise during the coming hostilities. In my absence Sarah will reside in Bombay with the other officers' wives.

Which brings me to the Crux of this letter. If I were able, I would bend my knee before you, Superintendent Light and dear Mrs Light humbly beseeching that you look favourably on my request. Light may be her surname, but Sarah is also the light of my life; I have cause to believe she regards me in the same 'light'. Pardon my clumsy attempt at punning. Clever language has never been my skill. Nevertheless, I promise to love and cherish Sarah as my wife for the rest of our lives and welcome most heartily any children the Good Lord might see fit to grant.

A humble lieutenant does not have much to commend him when compared to a man such as yourself whose name has won great renown. But I appeal to you, once a mere lieutenant yourself, that I too cherish hopes of rising in my chosen profession. Should you allow me the great honour of the hand of your eldest daughter, it will be with the assurance that I will make it my life's work to keep her in comfort and ease – and to forge a career worthy of your illustrious name.

I promise also to take the Misses Lucy Ann and Mary under my wing. As they blossom into young women, they too will need protection in Bengal society. Trust that I would be as an elder brother to them in all things. With your permission granted, we wish to hold a marriage ceremony in Calcutta on the 28th December inst. since I must sail to Bombay in early January. It is our fervent desire that the whole family (with the exception of dear William, far away in Suffolk) might reunite for this joyous occasion.

I enclose several Letters of Recommendation from those whose opinion you respect, namely Mr William Fairlie, Mr John Ogilvy, and Mrs Eliza Kyd whom I am reliably informed is a close acquaintance of Mrs Light. It is my hope that their Good Opinion might reassure your Concerns.

Humbly yours,
James Gascoigne Welsh, Lt.

***

Martinha was gathering wild heliconia when she spied Francis, watching her from a distance across the garden. She had the odd notion that he had been there for some time. Her smile lit up, delighted he was home so early in the day. But her joy soon faded when she observed his countenance. Francis looked haggard, his whole demeanour one of disquiet. He clutched a bundle of letters in his hand. Dropping her basket, she ran towards him, suddenly alarmed.

'Whatever is the matter, Francis? Have you received ill news?'

Francis brusquely cut off her words. 'Can a man not arrive home early without his wife raising concern?' His tone was hard to read; did he speak in jest or anger?

'Are you quite well? You look drawn in the face.'

'My head aches like the very devil. This damned heat! I feel so stifled I can hardly breathe,' Francis replied curtly, brushing past her for the large terracotta jar by the steps to the house. He poured a ladle of cool water over his head, groaning in relief.

Martinha looked up at the sky. 'A storm's coming in. The pressure in the air will dissipate once the rains come,' she told him.

At first Francis did not reply, merely glancing out to sea where dark swirling clouds were forming, already roiling malevolently towards the island. Ascending the stairs, he slumped down heavily in a cane chair, pulling off his neckerchief to dab his face and neck. 'Come, sit. We need to talk,' he demanded curtly.

Her heart beat fast as she took a seat across from him. 'One of the children? Please, Francis, tell me straight out! I cannot bear the suspense!' she begged.

He shook his head. 'No, not that, thank God. No news of ill health or worse. Calm yourself.' He held out a letter. 'I received this bundle today from Lindesay. They were sent by Sarah. Read this one first.'

Martinha scanned the letter, relief washing over her. It was but a marriage proposal! 'Oh, Francis – he wishes to marry Sarah! I wondered if it would come to this after Fairlie's letter. What are we to do? We know nothing of this young man! Is it not too soon?'

Her husband was less accommodating. 'I suppose his reasoning is genuine enough. In the circumstances, he offers her protection in the most appropriate fashion. You realise this new commission is dangerous? Yet he wishes her to inherit his pension and estate if the worst happened. It is the behaviour of a man of principle. Now read the other letters. They are commendations of his character from those we trust. James Welsh has the makings of a fine officer and has distinguished himself already for one so young. Fairlie writes that he was mentioned in dispatches by Cornwallis himself after Pondicherry.'

Martinha continued reading. By all accounts James Welsh was a perfect husband for a young woman – and he clearly loved Sarah very much, as she did him. It was hard to disapprove of such an ideal pairing, even if they had not met the boy.

'Then why has this brought you so low, my love? Surely his suit has merit?' she inquired.

Francis clawed at his forehead in despair. 'This damned headache! I cannot think straight. It pounds like a hammer in my brain,' he moaned. 'You ask why? Because I haven't seen any of my daughters in years. The last time that we met, Sarah was but a young girl! And now she wishes to marry? She only turns sixteen this very month! She is too young to be wed!

'I was the same age when we married,' Martinha reminded him.

'But I waited several years before we lived as man and wife!' was his tetchy reply.

'That was your choice, Francis, not mine. And you were a man of twice my age, whom I did not know. James Welsh is only nineteen himself and a close friend already. They are young and in love, Francis! He has prospects and is well commended by all. What else is there to say?' Martinha argued.

'What else? We say – then wait a few years! Good Lord, they've not even been betrothed and yet they speak of marriage!' he fumed.

It was the futile protestation of a father on realising that his precious daughter was now cleaving to another man. Francis spoke of propriety, when it was unwillingness to face that life was rolling on its inevitable course, taking his children one by one.

'We always knew this day would come, Francis. Even you say there is nothing for the girls here. The longer they remain in Calcutta, the more likely they will find husbands there,' she reminded him gently.

'How can you be so accepting? Do you feel no concern at all? We planned to return to England where the girls might marry local fellows and we would grow old surrounded by our grandchildren!' he exclaimed. 'We shall never see them if she remains in India!'

Martinha sighed. 'And how soon might that day come? Each year that passes the girls mature. We cannot always control our destiny, my dear. Children grow up and may choose to leave. Francis, you cannot rule your home as you rule this island! Why, you yourself left your poor mother and never saw her again! How can you prevent your own child from achieving her dreams in life?'

'Dreams? She's nothing but a lovestruck girl! How can she make up her mind at fifteen years of age?'

This brought a wry smile to his wife's face. 'Where were you at fifteen years of age? At least she has a choice. Most girls are bartered by their parents to men much older than themselves. As was I. I don't remember anyone asking my opinion when you agreed to marry me. We are very lucky, Francis. We found love. How many others do? Do you wish to deprive her of that gift with a good man?'

Francis closed his eyes wearily. 'Are you not even slightly worried by the prospect of our daughter being wed to a man we do not know?' he repeated helplessly.

Martinha slipped from her seat to kneel at his side, resting her head upon his lap. 'Terrified beyond words, sayang. But we cannot allow our fears to prejudice our children's future happiness. We shall go to Calcutta in November and spend the season there. It's high time you had leave. Pigou and the new men can hold the reins in your absence. If this James Welsh is all he purports to be, then we shall soon find out. Imagine a wedding at Christmastime with most of the family there! Perhaps Mother and Felipe can join us. It will be a fine occasion and by then all your fears will be allayed.'

Francis opened his eyes and drew her into his embrace. 'My dearest wife! What would I do without your wisdom? You are right. The seas are safer now with Rainier and his fleet on patrol. It is time to see our children. Little Frannie does not even know his sisters! And if this young man proves a suitable prospect, then we can at least rest assured that Sarah's future is secure. I must learn to let go, Martinha. Not just of my daughters, but also of the reins of public office. If the Company sends me more officials, then I must make use of them. I cannot be lord and master of this island alone. As times change, I must change with them. The wheel has come full circle.'

As Martinha curled up in his arms, it seemed her prayers were answered. Francis was beginning to find a way through, with the return of his inimitable resolve to make the best of things that had been missing for so long. It was time to embrace the situation as it was and face their destiny together as a family.

***

The rains brought a cooler night, but still his headache raged. Light missed dinner and took to his bed, declining Martinha's suggestion to send for Hutton. He would sleep it off. Well before dawn, she awoke to find him lying in a fierce sweat, the sheets beneath him damp with perspiration. His head burned with fever.

Dr Hutton was there at first light. One look at the superintendent and his consternation grew. 'The fever has returned. It is not good. I've had my concerns about his constitution of late

– another severe bout might be too much for him,' he confided in Martinha.

His words were daggers to her heart. 'But it was just a headache,' she protested. 'Only last night we were making plans to see the girls!' Even as she spoke, her words seemed trite. Her instinct had alerted her the moment she had seen him. How had she failed to act?

Hutton patted her hand. 'Francis is a strong man. He has fought this illness many times. I suggest, while he is able, we should take him up to Strawberry Hill where the cool and wholesome air will aid his recovery. I shall arrange a team of bearers, with Marlbro to attend him night and day. I promise to visit daily. In the meantime, send for Pigou. Inform him that he must run the office in the superintendent's absence. I recommend that you warn him to make light of his condition. No need to cause alarm. If we act quickly, we shall bite this in the bud, my dear.'

Pigou was summoned; he was aghast when he saw Light, raging with fever, his speech incoherent. 'Leave it all to me, Ma'am', he assured Martinha. 'Let's make sure that Kyd and Hamilton are kept in ignorance – one can never be sure whom to trust. I shall tell them that the superintendent has caught a head cold and will be resting at his retreat for the next few days. That should keep them at bay for a while,' he promised. 'I will call regularly for news, dear Mrs Light. You're not alone in this. We'll make sure the superintendent is back on his feet in no time!'

Despite his words of consolation, Pigou gave a lingering glance towards Light stretched out on the bed, tossing and turning in the onset of delirium. The picture was bleak. How many times can a man survive these assaults? Light had been at death's door several times before. Was his struggle with the dreaded marsh fever that had cut short the lives of so many on the island to be his last?

Heavy of heart, Thomas Pigou trudged homewards, arranging his expression to hide his latent fears. The island without Superintendent Light was inconceivable. It could not happen.

29

Into the Woods

Strawberry Hill, Prince of Wales Island. 14th October 1794

Caffree bearers conveyed the superintendent to his cottage on the heights. They bore him reverentially. Where once they had faced a life of degradation, this man had given them a future. Slaves they still might be, but without Light's intervention they would not have survived. In their wake rode Hutton and Marlbro with an orderly leading a donkey laden with medical supplies. Nothing would be spared to cure the governor.

Martinha was not with them. She had first made a detour to the chapel of the Assumption to light a candle and say the Rosary before the statue of Mary. Little was left for her now but to pray. When the last bead was completed, she rested her forehead on the altar rail of the Lady Chapel, lost in private contemplation.

A comforting hand tapped her lightly on her shoulder. 'My dear lady, forgive me disturbing your meditations. Is there anything I can do?' It was Father Michael.

Martinha struggled to her feet, helped by the priest, wiping the back of her hand across her cheeks to dry her tears. 'Francis is very sick, Father. It is unknown if he will survive this time. I know not where to turn in my despair!'

Father Michael crossed himself. 'You chose the best place. God's will be done, my dear. We must leave our loved ones in His hands. Rest assured he shall be in my prayers both day and night. The superintendent is a strong man. He has pulled through many times. With Mary's grace, he will do so again.'

Martinha nodded, unable to frame an answer. If she opened the floodgates on her fears, the torrent might never stop. 'Thank you, Father. Please pray for us.'

As she turned to go, she remembered Pigou's advice. 'Father, I beg you do not speak of this. Do not alarm the people. For now, it is better they do not know. Time enough for that if ...' her voice broke as she struggled to voice the unthinkable.

Father Michael placed his left hand on her head, blessing her with his right. 'I will keep my silence, child. The less people know, the less they panic. Come, let us say together Mary's special prayer. She will hold you both in her tender care. He began to intone the familiar words of the *Memorare* as Martinha finally found her voice.

***

On the days that followed, little could be done but wait. Hours ticked by as the household held its breath, precious time racing through the hourglass, as they paddled against a great force and yet remained forever in the same place. Even the children were subdued, playing quietly, often fretful, sensing the weight of anxiety that had settled on them all. Outside in the garden, the sun still shone, the birds still sang, the monkeys scampered in and out in search of food – but life as they all knew it had come to a halt.

James Hutton made his daily visit, each time fearing the worst.

Francis Light was gravely ill but clinging on, lost in his delirium. Faithful Marlbro stood sentinel in the sickroom, spooning drips of water through dry lips. Martinha was rarely far away, spending hours by her husband's pillow, constantly wringing out wet cloths to place upon his burning brow. And all the while, Francis raved on in his wild incoherent ramblings. Who knew where he was and what he saw?

'How is he faring, doctor?' Martinha asked of Hutton when he had finished his examination. 'He is still withstanding. That must be a good sign?'

Hutton's expression did not speak of optimism. 'Dear Mrs Light, it is very hard to tell. I've known patients come back from death's door itself while others fade away in hours. Francis has come through this illness many times, but each bout has left his constitution weaker. It is the nature of these swamp fevers. He is older now, not the man he once was. Your husband is still gravely ill, and we can do little now but watch and pray.'

Martinha let out a whimper. 'There must be something we can do! Can we bleed him?' she begged.

Hutton shook his head. 'The poor man needs every ounce of blood. He is beyond the reach of modern medicine. We must pray for a miracle, I'm afraid. The superintendent has been beset with worry and frustration for many years. I fear his spirit may be broken ...'

'Never!' Martinha cried. 'Why, only a few days ago, he was full of plans for our future! His spirit is unshakeable. We must not give up hope! I shall hear no more talk like that!' She returned pale-faced to her vigil, hands trembling with both fury and fear, channelling her emotions into her repetitive ministrations. Hutton glanced across at Marlbro whose eyes reflected similar concern. It was up to Francis now – and the Good Lord.

'Talk to him, ma'am.' Hutton suggested. 'He may seem far away, but he can hear, especially the voices of those he loves. Talk constantly. Sometimes the sound of a loved one can bring a soul back from the very gates of Heaven.'

'What should I say?' she gasped.

'Anything. Talk of the old days. The children. The plans that you have made for the future. Bring little Francis in and let him babble on. Who knows what might pierce through his darkness?'

Martinha had a new task now. She would guide her beloved husband back from the grave. There was much to say, a lifetime of memories to recall.

***

He was in the schoolroom, surrounded by friends, confused because he knew some were now dead, and yet they laughed and played with the carelessness of childhood. A door opened and Sir William strode in, hale and hearty. 'I thought you gone!' he gasped. His guardian merely laughed, his deep-bellied voice booming in his ears.

A moment later he was on board ship. The weather was wild and stormy, a grey forbidding sea scattered with mountains of glacial ice. 'I can swim to that iceberg!' he heard himself say. 'It is no distance at all. I wish to feel its icy cold!' He dived into the roiling waters – and surfaced in a sea of hideous serpents, writhing and yawing.

Then a forest, fiercely hot and steamy. His clothes were sodden yet his lips were parched. He tried to capture moisture dripping from the branches but not a single drop reached his mouth, no matter how he tried. From somewhere a voice: 'Here, Francis. Drink. It is water!' A spring appeared before him, running down jagged rocks. He threw himself headlong into the flow, regardless of the cuts that wrecked his body. The liquid was the sweetest he had ever drunk.

A garden of flowers, wild thickets of profusion. Roses, lilies, daffodils and daisies; lilacs, lavender, marigolds and hollyhocks, tangled with hanging orchids and brilliant-plumed heliconia. He thrashed his way, bruising and crushing the beautiful blooms such was his urgency to find the place beyond, imperative to reach before too late. Why would it be too late? Then he saw her, bent over a basket of roses, trimming the stalks. 'Mother! I am home. I promised I would return one day!' He ran towards her although his limbs were heavy, and the tendrils of the flora dragged him down.

She raised her head and smiled as if it was yesterday. 'What's the matter, lad? Whyever are you crying? In trouble at school again?'

In her arms at last, the safest place in all the world, he inhaled her sweet smell. She stroked his head, whispering softly, words he could not catch. Raising his head, he sought her longed-for face. It was Martinha. 'Francis! Can you hear me? Open your eyes, my love. Wake up. We are all here. Little Francis wishes to play with his father!'

She was gone. He was in a clearing framed by trees before a house he did not recognise but he knew to be his own. Climbing the wooden stairs, he burst into the room. It was empty save for a baby sleeping soundly in a cradle, long lashes feathering downy cheeks. His daughter, he knew that much. Which one, though? He couldn't remember ... what were their names again? Mary? He was sure that was one of them. Or was that his mother? No, perhaps it was Marianne? Who was Marianne? He could not quite recall. A beautiful young woman entered. 'Do I know you?' 'My name is Marianne ...'

A voice calling from outside. 'Scott? Is that you?' He flung open the door to the deck of an old ship, surrounded by a native crew. A fierce Bugis pirate was leaning against the side, carving a piece of wood. Someone shook his arm. 'Francees! It is I, Soliman. Hari is so funny. Look what he does!' A striped cat licked his face. 'Soliman, where are you?' But he was gone ...

His eyes flickered open. 'Soliman?' he murmured.

'It's me, Papa! Frannie! Wake up! Talk proper words. I don't like it.' His little son was sitting on the bed, wet kisses on his cheek. He tried to raise his hand in reassurance, but it was a dead weight.

'Fran ...' He muttered, already sinking back to sleep.

'Come on, man,' a voice urged. 'Stay with us now, Francis.' A Scot. But which one? There were so many of them. 'It's I, Jamie. Come back to us, Francis. I cannae bear to see you in this state!'

Of course, James Scott. 'Jamie ... I am so very tired. Let me sleep.'

'He's weak as a babe – give him sustenance. Marlbro, pass the bowl of broth. Martinha, break bread and soak each piece. Feed him one by one ... not so large to choke him. He can barely swallow. Even soup will revive him.'

Martinha was near him – but he could not find her. Yet

he could inhale her scent. Something trickling down his throat causing him to gag, but he forced himself to swallow. He struggled with a few more morsels.

'Enough for now. His stomach will not tolerate too much. Give him tiny portions every half an hour or so. Now let him sleep awhile. His fever has abated somewhat. Francis is not out of the woods by a long way, but this is a good sign. Take the child away now and let Francis sleep ...'

Woods. A summer day. A river close by. He was home again. On his way to Theberton. To see George and William ...

***

The room was in darkness when he returned to himself. He moved his head, and there was Martinha, perched awkwardly on a stool, her head slumped on the coverlet fast asleep. His fingers inched towards her; it was enough to wake her. 'Francis!' She shot up with a cry.

His lips and throat were so parched it was impossible to answer. Instead, he moaned. Martinha gently raised his head to help him sip a cup of water. It was an effort, but he managed to take enough to moisten his throat. 'How long?' he grunted.

'Many days. We've been out of our minds, Francis! But you're awake now. Everything will be all right.' Tears coursed down her cheeks as she grasped his hand, kissing the palm.

'So dark. Is it night?'

She shook her head. 'We hung heavy drapes to shield your eyes.'

'I want to see the day,' he murmured.

Martinha called out; in an instant, Marlbro was there, drawing the curtains to throw back the shutters. Daylight flooded in, bringing fresh air drenched in orange blossom to wash away the stench of sickness.

'I thought never again to see the light,' he muttered.

A corner had been turned. The fever had broken, his eyes were clear and, although weak as a kitten and pale as a ghost, he was finally lucid. The household rejoiced, dread lifting from them all. For the remainder of the day, the superintendent drifted in and out of sleep, but when he was awake, he ate a little and was able to talk. He was on the road to recovery.

In the early evening, Francis asked Hutton and Martinha to send for Thomas Pigou.

'I'm sure Pigou longs to see you, but no business just yet, sir,' Hutton insisted. 'There's nothing to be concerned about. Everything is under control. Why, Mr Manington and Mr Beanland have arrived, so Pigou has plenty of help! Time enough to meet him when you're up and about.'

Francis grunted in annoyance. 'Not about the office. My will. I need to add codicils. It is not finished … I must make amendments …'

'Your will?' Martinha was surprised. 'It can wait now you're recovered. Please, Francis, do not concern yourself –'

'If not now, then when?' his voice was raised, his manner agitated. 'I am sick. A man must be ready! It is negligent not to arrange one's affairs! Send for Pigou tomorrow morning. First thing! And Bacon – we shall need a witness.'

Light's reasoning could not be faulted, yet his manner was

disturbing. Even now he feared his time was running out.

It occurred to Martinha that her husband had been speaking only in English since regaining consciousness even talking to her, where they usually conversed in Malay. Even in his wild ravings, he had only used his native tongue. It seemed significant, somehow.

'Don't fret yourself, Superintendent,' replied Hutton, intent on reassuring him. 'I'll inform Pigou and Bacon to be here early in the morning.'

'Tell them to bring my will,' Light insisted.

'Of course. Your will. Rest assured it will be done.'

***

Later that evening when Light had sent an exhausted Martinha to her own bed, he found himself wakeful, tossing on the pillow with a deepening sense of unease. There was so much left undone. He had slept too long. He must not waste a moment. His urge for action was strong.

Marlbro entered on bare feet that made little sound. He set down a bowl of water scattered with petals, leaves and spices, ready to bathe the superintendent and change his linens.

'Marlbro?' Light asked.

'Yes, sir. May I get you something?' Marlbro spoke decent English, one of the many skills he had absorbed on the island. The attendant was an invisible presence in any room, saying little and always in the background, but his impact was undeniable.

'I find I have the need to talk. Do you mind listening to my rambles?'

'Of course, sir. May I wash you while we talk?' Marlbro

replied, his duty never forgotten.

Light smiled wryly. 'I must stink like a dog. Excuse my filthy linens.'

The gentle orderly answered with a rare grin of his own. 'I've seen much worse, I can assure you, sir.'

'I suppose you have. You know, Marlbro, I know so little of you. All these years you have stood by Hutton's side, dealing with disease, injury, birth and death, and the health our inhabitants, yet you remain an enigma. Perhaps it is I who am at fault. If I have ignored you, it was never my intention. I have always felt respect and gratitude for your service. Hutton believes you to be as skilled as any doctor. Your contributions to this island have been immense.'

Marlbro carried on his task, removing stained clothing, and sponging down Light's body, placing a towel to guard his modesty. He worked deftly and with great tenderness. 'You've never shown me anything but kindness, sir. You're a very busy man beset with great problems. I don't expect a man such as you to find time to stop and talk to me. It is enough that I can serve you.'

'Pish posh! I'm just a man like any other. Tell me, *Doctor* Marlbro, of your own life? Are you married? Do you have a family?'

At that Marlbro's face softened. 'I am married. With three children. Once I was in a desperate place with no hope. I prayed for death. Then I came to this island and my life changed. Do not worry about me, sir. I am a fortunate man.'

For some while, Light fell silent, thinking on his words. 'Is your wife one of the Caffree women?'

Marlbro shook his head. 'No. She is a free woman of India.

She lost her first husband to the fever. Later she brought her child to the hospital; I nursed him back to health. We've been married now these three years and have two babies of our own. My children are free.' His face lit with an expression hard to describe. Light thought he finally understood the meaning of 'beatified'.

'Tomorrow, Mr Pigou comes to deal with matters concerning my will. I cannot free my Caffree slaves because they are property of the Company, although I will ensure compassionate terms for their disposition in the event of my demise. If it were possible, I would free you all in my bequest. I hope you understand,' Light explained.

'No matter, sir. You've done enough for us,' Marlbro replied whilst re-dressing the superintendent in fresh linens, clearing away the soiled. About to leave, Francis stretched a hand to stop him.

'I've not yet finished, Marlbro. While I may not have the means to grant freedom, I can instruct Mr Bacon to strike your name from the list. The Company will never know. You might have died for all they care. From this day forward, you are a free man.'

Marlbro stopped dead, his eyes widening in disbelief. 'Is that possible?' he exclaimed, more animated than Light had ever seen him.

The superintendent shrugged. 'Who knows? When have I ever cared about the possible? My life has been a series of improbable events. Yet here I am. And here you are. We owe our thanks to Fate, my good man. For naught in this world happens without her hand. She led us here through all our trials to this very moment.

Let us both grasp the chance: I to deliver justice to a man of wisdom and science, and you to allow an old rogue to gain some grace at last.'

30
Not Even Angels

The Light Cottage, Strawberry Hill, Pinang. 19th October 1794

Following a morning revising his last will and testament, Francis Light slept soundly through the heat of the day, worn out from his efforts, but easier in his mind. By late afternoon, Martinha woke him with a tray of food, a steaming bowl of rice porridge flavoured with ginger and thick with pounded fish. He was ready for nourishing food.

Half-awake, he smiled dreamily as she plumped the bolster and arranged pillows to help him upright. 'It smells good,' he observed as she stirred the gruel to cool it.

'You're hungry at last. That means you're getting better.'

He gave no reply but accepted a spoonful like an obedient child. As she fed him, Francis remained pensive, whilst Martinha chattered on about nothing of great importance. She wished to keep his mind away from the worries that had recently plagued him.

As if he had not heard a single word, he suddenly interrupted: 'Martinha, I need to talk to Scott. And Khoh. Send a boy down to ask them to visit in the morning.' The obsessive mood was back.

'Francis!' she chided. 'Stop fretting over your affairs! Wait a few days until you're stronger. Today has taken its toll. There'll be time enough for all that in the weeks ahead.'

He grabbed her wrist, splashing food onto the counterpane. 'Who knows how much time a man has left? Please, I beg you, send a boy to summon them at once!'

His tone was now more pleading than commanding. Martinha took a closer look. There was an odd shift to his eyes. His cheeks were flush although his face was pale. She placed her palm on his forehead; it was hot. 'You're feverish again, Francis. Let me call Marlbro.'

'It's nothing! Hutton said my fever would go up and down at different times of day. Perhaps the hot food has caused it,' he snapped back. 'Stay awhile longer. Marlbro can wait. There are things I must discuss with you. Before it is too late.' There it was again, the sense of time running out.

'Too late? Oh, whatever do you mean, dear Francis! Ban these morbid thoughts from your mind. Think only of getting well. We have so much to look forward to! If you're back on your feet, we shall go to Calcutta for Sarah's wedding. If not, we shall hold the celebrations here. Then, when you are fully recovered, we shall return to England with the other girls and be reunited with William again. So much to look forward to!'

Francis slumped back on the pillow, staring up at the ceiling. 'Have you ever considered that we spend most of our lives planning for tomorrow? Yet what if today is all we have? Who knows when the time is nigh? This illness has taken hold of me, Martinha. It warns me not to waste a moment. I *must* set my affairs in order!' His eyes were wild with desperation.

Martinha perched beside him taking both his hands to reassure him. 'I understand, sayang. This has been a shock. I know you're scared. I promise I will send for Scott and the Kapitan. Tell me everything on your mind, dear Francis, so I may ease your fears,' she consoled.

He took time to compose himself while Martinha placed a cool cloth on his burning forehead. 'The will has been signed and witnessed. I have tried to think of everything and everyone. I have done my best. Martinha, if I could have but a few more years, I believe our fortunes might improve ...'

'You'll live a long time yet, Francis! See how you've rallied!'

'Listen to me!' he commanded sternly, dismissing all her blandishments. 'In the event of my passing, there are things that you must know. You are heir to my entire estate, such as it is. I entrust it in your care on behalf of our children. Apart from small gifts to friends and family, freedom for the Battas, and moderate bequests to the servants, the entire bulk of my fortune passes to you. Scott will be my local executor and Fairlie in Calcutta shall oversee my deposits there. George Doughty has sufficient funds for William's upkeep in the interim.'

'Then everything is well done,' she said. 'There's nothing left to worry about!'

'Martinha, I have not been entirely honest. We have great debts. For years Scott has been advancing me money, dependent on future profits. But this war has affected trade. Not only do I owe him a goodly sum but, if my shares decline, how will I repay the debt? What will you live on? I have the pepper plantations, which Khoh administers. The lands are mine, but the investment in the crops is his. And I have also borrowed heavily from him in recent times. He paid off the contractor Pak Lian who refused to complete the work on the fort because I was unable to pay him. Thus, I signed over future pepper profits until the debt is paid. We are paupers, Martinha.'

It was a shocking revelation. Not that she cared for the decline in their fortunes; it was his peace of mind that bothered her. 'You've carried all these worries on your shoulders, along with the trials of your office? Oh, my love, how have you borne this alone? Do not worry. Once you are better, we will solve this together. In time, your debts will be settled. When the Company repays what they owe, our fortunes will repair. And if we should only have enough left for a simple cottage back in England, it will be enough for me!' she declared.

Francis shook his head in frustration. 'We cannot rely on hope, Martinha! We must plan for the worst! If anything happens to me beforehand, ask Scott to sell the land. You will still own the properties, including Government House, for which the Company must pay rent. Khoh will not call in his debts and leave you penniless. He is family. That is why I must see both men tomorrow. I need to make this clear to them. Promise me you'll send for them!'

Martinha cleared away the tray and wiped down the stained coverlet, then lay beside him on the bed, cradling him in her arms. 'I promise I will call them. Have no fear. Concentrate on your recovery. In a few weeks' time, this will be a bad dream. Yes, you are right to plan. This dreadful illness has taught us all a lesson that we must now heed,' she reassured him of her understanding to soothe away his fears.

Francis breathed a sigh of relief, even managing a weak smile. 'Didn't the Good Lord say as much ... about being prepared? Something in the Gospels about not knowing when the day will come?'

'–But of that day and hour knoweth no man, no not the angels of heaven, but my Father only,' Martinha answered, a single tear trickling down her cheek. A dark foreboding grasped her heart, impossible to cast aside.

Francis chuckled. 'I'll be damned if I ever get a quote right, even on my deathbed!'

'Do not say that!' Martinha cried. 'You are not dying! I will not let you leave us!'

His arm reached out to close the embrace. 'Take no notice of my nonsense, dear. My sense of humour tends always to the dark side. But whatever is to come, know this. I am forever yours, Martinha. Although I would never claim to be a good man, I have loved you as best I can. Our children are my world; for them I would do anything. Remember that. Oh, but I am weary now. More weary than you know. It has been a good life all in all, yet good things must pass in the end ...'

They lay awhile in silence, holding each other, two hearts beating as one. Martinha no longer tried to protest against his brooding. She bore too many dark thoughts of her own. Suddenly he spoke. 'Is it still light outside? I would see the sky and forest once more ...'

She ran to the window. It was a little before sunset, the sky bright but tinged with the palette of evening. She threw back the shutters so that he might look outside, up at the glorious sky, the towering trees and the distant sparkle of the sea.

'Why, it might almost be Suffolk on a summer's eve! I could be lying on the banks of the Deben looking at the cloudless sky with the river rolling to the sea ...' he muttered. 'Did I ever tell you what a summer evening is like? The air is hot and heavy, scented with blossom. It is a curious thing at that time of year for daylight lasts late into the night. The days are long and mellow. It is wondrous to behold ...'

***

In the early hours of the following morning, Francis Light suffered a seizure from which he never regained consciousness. His body, weakened by the ravages of fever, could no longer bear the strain. His heart had failed him. Hutton and Marlbro struggled to revive him, but nothing could be done.

Martinha held on to his hand until she was gently pried away so that the body could be prepared. Word circulated fast; runners were immediately dispatched to inform those closest to the family. Pigou, Macalister, Fr Rectenwald and others rushed up in the dark of night, along the steep and treacherous path. Even Kapitan Khoh insisted on being carried up the hill. It was the early morning of the twentieth day of October 1794, three days from the superintendent's fifty-fourth birthday.

No words could describe the loss to those who loved him – and there were many. When his body was carried down to lie in state in Government House, the route was lined with simple folk cheek-by-jowl with men of wealth and influence. Rites were performed in temples, mosques and chapels alike. And when his body was laid to rest in the simple unadorned plot at the burial ground on the edge of his own land, amongst so many men who had been part of the story of the island alongside him, there was scarce space for all those who came to mourn.

Amidst it all, Martinha clung to little Francis. She was burying her husband alone without her family, for there had not even been time to summon Felipe and her mother. In a sea of people, she was alone. It would be forever thus. Now she must be the protector of them all, as Francis had been for so many years while she had lived her perfect life of tranquillity and ease. The voices of the mourners receded; she did not hear even the whimpers of her little son. 'Do not worry, my love! Rest easy now. Your work is done. I shall take care of them as you have cared for me. This is my promise.'

Epilogue

St Andrew's Melton, Suffolk. 11th July 1795

The portly gentleman held open the lychgate with a cane he carried more for style than necessity. A young boy, in blue cotton jacket and white breeches, a velvet cap upon his dark curls, traipsed ahead, nervously looking about. Taking the child by the hand, the man led him towards the small medieval church. It was a fiercely hot day, mid-morning in the midst of summer.

The church, a narrow belfry resting on a squat base, was bare of all adornment, more akin to a castle keep in its design. Once upon a time its lancet windows must have been decorated with saints in vivid glass, but that was long ago. Only the simplicity of this edifice had saved it from the ravages of monarchs in more recent times. Its rectangular plainness, however, was offset by the glorious profusion of the church grounds. Even the serried rows of grave stones did not detract from the harmonious surroundings, despite the sad tales their inscriptions told. Those buried here were fortunate in their resting place, beneath the shade of ash trees with a carpet of wild flowers to cover their final beds.

A pheasant scurrying around the headstones momentarily disturbed the tranquil peace of the scene, catching the visitors by surprise. The bird startled and then took flight across the fields beyond where cows chewed and sheep grazed. The man and boy paused, breathing in the aromas of new mown hay and summer blossoms, their gloomy spirits uplifted momentarily by the glory of the scene. As if in response, a choir of birds chirruped on the branches while a flock of starlings made its murmuration across the cloudless sky.

Sir George Doughty led William Light along the path between the headstones to the grave they sought, located towards the rear of the building. It stood on a particularly well-chosen plot, surrounded by a profusion of rose bushes and summer flowers, a tiny garden of its own. 'There she is, dear William. Your grandmother. Mary Light always loved her flowers. Her garden was a joy to behold, as fine as in any grand manor. Your Grandmama was a wonderful lady. She would have been very proud of you, my boy!'

William took a step forward to lay his own bouquet of flowers by her headstone, suddenly remembering to remove his cap. 'Uncle George, what must I do now? Should I say any particular words? Perhaps the Lord's Prayer?' He asked helplessly. It was the first time he had visited a grave.

Sir George returned a reassuring smile. 'She's your grandmother, William! Say whatever you will. Bow your head and talk to her, either out loud or in your mind. Tell her all the things that you would say if she were standing here before her. Speak to her about yourself and your family, and of your poor dear Papa.'

William nodded earnestly, a frown of concentration on his little face. After some thought, he knelt down, placing his hand upon the headstone. 'Dear grandmother, my name is William. I am the eldest boy of your son Francis, come back from the

East to seek my education. I am nine years old. I believe I am a hardworking boy at school although I love drawing the most. My teachers sometimes chide me, for I cannot help myself but illustrate too freely in the margins of my studies,' he commenced gravely. He turned back to his guardian ... 'Is that the sort of thing, sir?'

'You're making a fine job of it, lad. Mrs Light would be tickled to hear you speak so. Just like your father, who was ever a singular character as a boy. She always loved children, especially the little rascals! Carry on. Speak to her of your father.'

William considered his words carefully. 'Grandmama, I have very sad news. Recently a letter arrived from Pinang Island. My dear father has died of the fever. It has quite broken my heart ...' the child let out a heartrending sob, his lips trembling and tears welling up in his liquid brown eyes. Sir George placed a caring hand on his shoulders, passing him a kerchief. 'I'm sorry for crying, sir ...' William sniffled.

'Your tears show the extent of your love. Never be ashamed of them, boy. Take your time, now. When you're ready,' Doughty patted him kindly on the head.

William wiped his eyes and blew his nose. 'It happened last year, so I expect you already know. I imagine news reaches you quicker in heaven than from the Indies.'

Despite the poignancy of the moment, Sir George repressed the urge to chuckle at the innocence of the young boy's words. He was such a sincere little fellow with uncommon notions all his own. How Francis must have loved the boy!

'I cannot say farewell to my father in person for his grave

is far away. It hurts me to think that for months when he was already gone, I was in ignorance. All the while that I was laughing and playing with my school mates like a silly fool here in England, my mother and the others were in grief. I am the man of the family now, yet I am unable to be there for them. I don't even know when I shall ever see my mother or my brother and sisters again. I miss them all so much, Grandmama. Especially now. To think, I shall never again behold my father. It breaks my heart. Nor did I ever meet you, although everyone tells me what a fine lady you were. Grandmother, even if we never met, I still love you as I do my father ...'

A voice suddenly interrupted William's sad farewell. 'But you shall meet them again, lad. One day, you shall all be reunited in that other place where sorrows end.' The boy jumped with surprise, swivelling his head towards the source. It was a young man, the midday sun behind his head, a bright halo obscuring his features. For a split second, William thought it was his father, for something of the outline of the man was oddly familiar. He cried out in surprise.

'My apologies, dear boy! I did not mean to startle you.' The young man stepped out of the glare to reveal himself. 'I could not help but overhear your tender words and I wished to ease your sad burden,' he continued, holding out his hand for William to rise.

Sir George joined them. 'William, this is a fortunate meeting indeed. This gentleman is Dr James Light. It is he who is responsible for tending this fine burial place in which your grandmother rests.'

'Light? Are you my relative, sir?' William gasped.

James Light grinned. 'In a manner of speaking, I suppose I am. Your grandmother adopted me after your father left for India. She wished for another child to ease her loneliness. She raised me as she did your father, so I suppose in a sense I am indeed your uncle!'

The smile that lit up the boy's sallow cheeks was so filled with joy it made both men follow suit. 'Oh sir! I am so very pleased to meet you! I had no idea I had a family here in Suffolk. Why did my father never mention you?'

James shrugged his shoulders sadly. 'I'm afraid he never knew of my existence. Your grandmother could not read or write. But like you, I too am heartily glad to finally make your acquaintance. Your father was a great man. I am brought low by his passing. It had always been my dream to travel to the Indies to meet him. Instead, I have met his son, for which opportunity I am thankful indeed!'

He held out his hand for William to shake, but instead the boy impulsively threw his arms about his waist. 'You remind me so of Papa! I cannot help but embrace you!' he cried. It touched his heart. How pitiful this little child must bear his tragedy all alone.

James lifted the boy up to his height. 'Put your arms about my neck, William, and give me a full hug. For I am as sore in need of it as you!'

There could not have been a more perfect outcome for either man or boy. George Doughty watched on, a benign expression on his face. The 'chance' meeting had been engineered – how satisfying to see it work to plan. It had been Mary's wishes not to inform Francis until she might do so herself, but now they were both gone, his silence seemed absurd. Both William and James deserved the comfort of each other's existence.

'Imagine how happy your father and grandmother must be as they look down from Heaven to witness this reunion!' Sir George exclaimed. It was the first time that young William had smiled since the tragic news had reached them.

'William, would you like to assist me in neatening up the grave? I will fetch some water from the church, then we shall find a vase to hold your bouquet.'

William and James set to work together tending to the flowers. All the while James chattered on about Mary Light and her way with plants. Her grave, marked with blooms, was his tribute to her. Her resting place would not be mournful but would bring pleasure to those who stopped to rest awhile. It would have been what Mary wanted. In this way, she would never be forgotten.

'When I'm gone overseas, perhaps you would come here from time to time on my behalf? It would be of great comfort to me that it was cared for in my absence. Furthermore, it will offer you a place to remember your father until the time you return to your island home.'

William sat back on his heels, crestfallen. 'Are you going away, sir? When we two have only just met?' It seemed the Lord gave with one hand and then took back with the other.

'Sadly, I am indeed. I am enlisting in the Madras army. If I receive a commission as a military surgeon, I shall sail next springtime.'

William's face fell further. 'I wish that I could spend more time with you, Uncle James, so that I might know you better,' was his forlorn reply.

'And so, you shall, my boy,' George Doughty intervened. 'I have invited James to spend the summer at Theberton Hall with us.' He had planned it with his Ann. It seemed the best and only remedy for both James and William that they might find each other, even if Francis Light was lost to them.

The boy who left the churchyard in the company of two gentlemen was a happier child than the one who had arrived. He was not entirely alone in this world. Once his education was done, he would be old enough to sail back to his family. In the meantime, he had Uncle James and Sir George to be his guardians. The untimely loss of his father might be a raw wound that would never fully heal, but the world went on – and so must he. It would be his own tribute to his dear Papa to do the best he could to carry on his name. The light burned as bright in this young boy as it once had in his father.

Behind the Scenes of the Penang Chronicles

At the end of a historical novel, the inevitable question is: how much is true? The more compelling the story, the more chance it takes precedence over known history, an unintended consequence. Whether we like to admit it or not, however, our opinion of many historical characters has been shaped more by fiction than history: take the example of Richard III whose public persona is based mostly on what a certain dramatist had to say about him. To what extent is *Penang Chronicles* historically accurate and where do the novels diverge?

The story of Francis Light is fairly well known although before Penang the details are scant. More information is out there than one might imagine, however, but it requires a deep dive into a myriad subsidiary sources to root it out. The East India Company kept meticulous records of their far-flung officers in Council minutes and correspondences. A vast array of other records survives: personal diaries, journals, letters, portraits, newspapers, legal documents, wills, maritime records, registry lists and so on, creating veritable rabbit holes down which a researcher might lose oneself. It's a laborious but highly addictive business. Yet, even with all these sources, a measure of imagination must fill in the unavoidable blanks.

Almost every character is real other than those in the

background who required naming by virtue of their roles. Of the rest, simply to know that minor characters had their own stories off the page brings authenticity; the world of the novels should be a living and breathing reality. As for the events, they follow the chronological record closely, diverging only where there is lack of clarity in the sources or communication delays confuse the timeline. For inspiration, I also borrowed incidents from the accounts of other similar captains of the day; Light probably shared many of their experiences.

The famous novelist Bernard Cornwell (*Sharpe, The Last Kingdom*) described the process perfectly when he wrote that a historical novel has within it two distinct stories: the large tale, i.e. the historical narrative, and the smaller story that imagines the lives of those who witnessed great events. A historical novel thus has responsibilities both to history and narrative; an author must step lightly between where one ends and the other begins. The blending must be seamless.

Tradition states that Francis Light was the illegitimate son of Squire William Negus of Dallinghoo, Suffolk, and a local woman, Mary Light, a view definitively stated by H.P. Clodd (*Malaya's First British Pioneer 1948*), and repeated in every subsequent biography. Yet, in an earlier work, (*A Short Sketch of the Lives of Francis and William Light: with Extracts from their Journals 1901)*, A. F. Steuart describes the early sources for Light as 'extremely obscure'. He can only say that Light was adopted and educated by William Negus and raised by Mary Light; he makes no claim they are his actual birth parents. It was unlikely any landowner of the day would raise his child born out of wedlock in his own village without scandal. Illegitimate children were rarely openly acknowledged at the time. This latter version became my starting point. The obscurity of Light's origin remains intact, a frustrating mystery both to Francis and the reader.

A swashbuckling tale of the life of Francis Light was never my intention, despite my fondness for Francis and his adventures. In essence, however, Light's role is as a conduit into a remarkable period in the 18th century Malay Peninsula, a time of existential change from which modern South East Asia emerged after a long period of colonial rule. It is as much the story of the peoples of the Straits as Light himself, whether sultans, kings, nobles, traders, servants, labourers, sailors, wives, mistresses, slaves, warriors, pirates or migrants. Too often they have been depicted as mere background players in their own history. *Penang Chronicles* brings them centre stage. The stories of Sultan Muhammed Jiwa, King Tak Sin, Lord Thian, Jamual, Theyan, Raja Haji Fisabilillah, Amdaeng Rat, Kapitan Khoh, Marlbro, Nakhoda Kecil and so many others may be largely imagined but they most certainly did exist. I hope I did them justice.

The most glaring invention, however, lies at the very heart of the trilogy in the enigmatic Martinha Rozells. Historical record tells us very little about this woman with whom Light lived for more than twenty years. Only contradictions remain: she was a Malay princess from Kedah; she was a Eurasian girl from Phuket; she was a Nyonya lady of the Straits. A major problem in research is the scarcity of reliable information about the local players, even those of note, like the sultans. Existing primary sources were predominantly compiled by male British scholars whose concern was to tell their own story, thus the indigenous people of South East Asia are largely lost to us. Women are predictably even less visible.

So, hands up, Martinha Rozells is purely my invention. There is no evidence that she was a niece of Lady Chan of Phuket. Yet I did not merely stick a pin in a page when deciding to 'borrow' her ancestry from an existing noble house. Martinha probably did come from the island. The name Thong Di is mentioned in sources as connected to her family. Lady Chan is known to have had a third unnamed younger sister. The mother of these three sisters, Mahsia, was from a minor branch of Kedah royalty. Francis Light remained a friend of Lady Chan throughout his life. From these random facts, I adopted a heritage which allowed Martinha to join all the dots: a woman of Phuket whose mother was a Nyonya lady and grandmother a Kedah royal.

More importantly, this framework connected Martinha to the wider picture. Such mixed heritages are common amongst the people of the Malay Peninsula whose DNAs today reveal complex ancestries. The modern borders of Thailand and Malaysia were irrelevant in an earlier time; the Malay Peninsula was an interconnected region stretching from modern Myanmar, Indo-China and Thailand to Indonesia. The story of Siam, always so intricately linked to the events of the Straits, is the backbone to this narrative, and situates Martinha at the very centre of the story.

Martinha Rozells has always fascinated me. A woman of influence whose invisible hand can be felt behind many of Light's actions, she is the very embodiment of the diversity of the Straits: Siamese, Malay, Indian, French, Portuguese, and arguably even more. Along with Soliman, she bears witness from a different worldview than the traditional European perception. As a British woman married to a Malaysian myself with three children of mixed heritage, the story of the Light family holds particular significance. My research and writing have given me the opportunity to both understand and interpret my own experiences.

Francis Light might be an adventurer in a quintessentially male world, but many other significant characters are women as well as Martinha. In *Dragon* and *Pearl,* we meet Mary Light, Thong Di, Lady Chan and Lady Mook, as well as the feisty old Tunku Mahsia. The final novel of the series, *Emporium,* introduces a variety of intriguing women of the day: Eliza Kyd, conflicted by her true heritage; Jemdanee, the Bengali socialite; Sarippa, a migrant woman; Diana Hill, the famous Calcutta miniaturist; Anna Marie Davis who visited Penang in 1791 and gave her uniquely narrow British viewpoint on the island and its fledgling society.

We do not know if Martinha had siblings, but a certain Mr. Nilip was indeed Light's secretary. European names are often mispronounced, thus Mr Nilip (implying a European or Eurasian) became Felipe Rozells. In *Emporium*, Felipe, a Eurasian trader, eventually marries a Chinese merchant's daughter, adding another dimension to Light's diverse family, in keeping with what history shows us of the early families of the island, even the Europeans.

Soliman, the foundling boy of the stories, was based on a real person, although we know almost nothing else about him. In 1821, an elderly Malay sea captain Juragan Soliman was interviewed by the scholar John Crawfurd, later second Resident of Singapore. He had been trading in the Straits for many years; the captain revealed a deep mistrust for the Dutch but a tolerance towards the British. I first came across him when I was contemplating a

Malay companion for Light. Many old Asia hands had similar confidants who helped them learn the language and understand the local way of life: Enrique of Malacca (Magellan); Munshi Abdullah (Raffles); Ali (Russell Wallace). Juragan Soliman was the right age to have known Light even as far back as 1765. As the novels grew, so Soliman's role grew exponentially until he became an eyewitness to the upheavals in the Malay way of life caused by the tumultuous events of the time. Through him I also examined the issue of conflicted identity in those of mixed heritage or raised away from their birth cultures. Even Light struggles with this problem, in his case caused originally by his illegitimacy and later by divided loyalties.

For at least two thousand years before Light, the Straits had been a cosmopolitan trading world. As a result, the coastal cultures were uniquely diverse and culturally integrated. Despite the inevitable stresses and strains of this clash of traditions, religions and languages, the inhabitants had steered their way to an uneasy symbiosis based on the mutual benefits of commerce. The eighteenth century – a time of political and social upheaval all over the world– brought a new set of challenges. As pressures mounted, regional politics inadvertently contributed to the ease with which colonial rule crept in. Against their adversaries (e.g. Siam, the Bugis), Malay sultans sought alliances with outsiders, particularly the British, whom they deemed merchant traders not empire builders. How ironic that the greatest threat ultimately came from the so-called friend!

I must conclude this note with a heartfelt thanks to the many people who have enabled my books to make the journey from my imagination to the printed page. The list is much longer but the limits of space require me to be brief. I have not forgotten all the rest, the many other friends and family members who have played their part but are not named below. I continue to be overwhelmed by the generosity and encouragement extended to me by so many. My thanks in particular, however, must go to:

Monsoon Books: Philip Tatham. Without you, none of this is even possible!
Pansing Distribution: Leslie Lim. Many thanks to you and your team for getting books on shelves and into festivals.
Marcus Langdon (historian and author) for your friendship and support, particularly with my E&O launch in Penang.
Maganjeet Kaur for your mapping skills – and friendship.
Wong Chun Wai of The Star Newspaper Group for your unfailing support.
Dennis de Witt (historian) for your encouragement.
Museum Volunteers Malaysia: Afidah Rahman, Karen Loh, Hani Abdullah, Mariana Isa.
Malaysian Culture Group: Ay Ling Liem, Marianne Khor, Nisha Dobberstein, Michelle Pease, Vicki Fennessy.
Badan Warisan: Lim Wei-Ling and Vanessa Loong.
Woodbridge Library: Tim Cornford and Lisa Railton.
Woodbridge School: Samantha James.
Adelaide: Sarah Roberts, Jan Thornton.

And as ever, to my beautiful family, always my inspiration and proudest achievement.

Rose Gan, Kuala Lumpur (*roseganauthor.com*)

Dragon

(Penang Chronicles, Vol. I)

The forgotten years of Francis Light –
before Martinha and Penang

The 18th-century Straits of Malacca is in crisis, beleaguered by the Dutch, the Bugis, and the clash between Siam and Burma. Enter Francis Light, devious manipulator of the status quo. From humble origins in Suffolk, Light struggles against the social prejudices of his day. As a naval officer and country ship captain he travels from the Americas to India, Sumatra, the Straits and Siam, enduring shipwreck, sea battles, pirate raids and tropical disease. But Light's most difficult challenge is his ultimate dream: a British establishment in the Indies on behalf of the East India Company. *Dragon* charts the colourful adventures of Francis Light in the decades before the settlement of Penang, the first Company possession on the Malay Peninsula.

Pearl

(Penang Chronicles, Vol. II)

Francis Light, the enigmatic Martinha, and the island of Penang

The eponymous pearl, Martinha Rozells, embodies the rich and diverse heritage of the Straits in the 18th century. Her husband, Captain Light, is the dragon in search of his elusive pearl: a British settlement on the Straits of Malacca. Through their eyes we experience the rich culture of the region and its tumultuous politics. From the courts of Siam and Kedah, to capture by the French and Dutch, from the salons of Calcutta through gun-running in the Straits, *Pearl* takes the reader on an astonishing journey culminating in Captain Light questioning where his allegiances lie if he is to outmanoeuvre the Sultan of Kedah and raise the British flag on Penang.

Legacy

(Penang Chronicles, Vol. IV)

As a new century dawns, Light's family is scattered, its inheritance in jeopardy

Francis Light's family faces an uncertain future. As Penang heads inexorably towards colonial rule, Martinha struggles to claim her rightful inheritance, encountering corruption, prejudice and heartbreak in equal measure. Scattered across the world, her children are forced to negotiate the British establishment alone as best they can with little but their father's name and reputation to sustain them. From Britain to the Peninsular War, from the social pretensions of Bengal to the court of the Pasha of Egypt, from the new city of Adelaide in Australia to Java and Singapore in the company of Raffles, the next generation makes its way, its roots firmly planted in the beautiful island of their home.